Samit Basu is a novelist, freelance journalist, columnist, scriptwriter and blogger based in New Delhi. He has completed the final volume of the GameWorld Trilogy slotted for release in late 2007.

Praise for Samit Basu and *The Simoqin Prophecies*

'*Simoqin* is a romp. It is quite simply the most fun book to see in print this year. In fact this is a book that deserves only a one-word blurb "Enjoy!"'—*The Times of India*

'*The Simoqin Prophecies* is an intelligent, inventive delight. It marks the arrival of a fresh and very original voice.'—*Indian Express*

'Basu draws from a vast source, only to weave it all together with amazing deftness, piecing the fragments together until they fit like a jigsaw puzzle . . . an intriguing tale, full of mystery and suspense, with generous doses of humour.'—*The Telegraph*

'A delightfully understated sense of humour that grows on you as you read on . . . playfulness is the motif of this entertaining novel. Reading it, I couldn't help but think of *Kill Bill*, Quentin Tarantino's vastly referential exercise in homage—a breathless blink-and-you-miss-it amalgamation of all his favourite movie moments.'—*Business Standard*

The Manticore's Secret

Part Two of the GameWorld Trilogy

Samit Basu

PENGUIN BOOKS

An imprint of Penguin Random House

PENGUIN BOOKS

USA | Canada | UK | Ireland | Australia
New Zealand | India | South Africa | China

Penguin Books is part of the Penguin Random House group of companies
whose addresses can be found at global.penguinrandomhouse.com

Published by Penguin Random House India Pvt. Ltd
4th Floor, Capital Tower 1, MG Road,
Gurugram 122 002, Haryana, India

First published by Penguin Books India 2005

Copyright © Samit Basu 2005

All rights reserved

10 9 8 7 6 5 4 3 2

ISBN 9780144000678

Typeset in AGaramond by Eleven Arts, New Delhi

Printed at Repro India Limited

www.penguin.co.in

Prologue

Apart from the occasional croaking of a small and angst-ridden tree frog, the circular clearing in the heart of the Great Forest is silent in the darkness. The tree frog (*Melnkohli flaikatcha*) in question has a lot on his mind. He has spent most of his short life contemplating the historic injustice he has suffered—an old aunt his parents had owed flies to had been allowed to name him, and she had named him Sweetie Croak.

Sweetie's somewhat limited vocabulary prevents him from launching into a moving speech, but from the anguished bulging of his eyes it is clear that his soul is in deep torment. It is all very tragic. But tonight, this clearing in Vrihataranya is about to witness an event of far greater significance than the desolation of Sweetie Croak.

Tonight is the night of the new moon, the third night of Tigermonth. From all over the world, followers of the rakshas Danh-Gem, living in hope of his prophesied return, have assembled in Vanarpuri for a great council. At this very moment, Angda, sister of Bali the vanar-lord, is addressing them. Great gongs are still ringing in the ancient vanar city, but the mighty trees of Vrihataranya have deadened the smallest echoes; not even a whisper filters through to the clearing.

In a small ruined temple outside Vanarpuri, the Brotherhood of Renewal has just assembled. It is a historic meeting; Bjorkun Skuan-lord and Omar the Terrible, Scourge of the Artaxerxian Sands, are meeting the Dark Lord-in-waiting, Danh-Gem's heir, Kirin half-ravian, for the very first time. Their secret deliberations this night are going to shake the very foundations of the world.

But the cloaked conspirators of the Brotherhood do not know what is happening *here*, a few days' march from their temple. Had they known, they would have *been* here. Here, where there is no hum of excitement, no animal night-song, no starlight; here, where there is only darkness.

And Sweetie Croak.

The clearing is no random space in the middle of the jungle; it has been worked upon by hand. There is a small pit in the clearing, hollowed with great skill into a perfectly smooth hemispherical basin, with a raised triangle of earth in the centre. Three large, perfectly spherical globes have been placed in the basin, one at each vertex of the triangle. The globes are made of a metal that is not of this world. It is a ravian metal, irichalcum, commonly known as moongold.

Sweetie Croak croaks soulfully.

Sudden movement. Out of nowhere, a bone-dart suddenly whistles across the clearing and catches him in the vocal sac, causing him to explode in a rude and amusing manner.

As his insides form an interesting pattern on the jungle floor, Sweetie Croak's dying thought is this: If his aunt had been present at his death, she would have renamed him Splatty Croak. Which, all said and done, is a much more respectable name.

He dies, slightly mollified. The silence is now complete.

And then there is a faint sound—heavy boots tramping through the forest, cracking branches underfoot. And a faint buzzing of flies, and the swish of a heavy feline body moving through the undergrowth.

And there is light; bright naphtha lamps, held aloft on sticks, head slowly towards the pit, swaying uncertainly. An intricate pattern of yellow-white light dances on the trees across the basin.

Bearing these lamps are small, squat figures, twelve in number, all except one clad in heavy armour.

Vamans.

They struggle through the undergrowth, which is shoulder-high for them, cursing the forest in harsh voices. Occasionally their leader, Kor Betpo, growls at them to be silent, for there could be vanar sentries abroad, gliding through the treetops like giant birds of prey, and secrecy is essential to the vamans' mission.

In front of the vamans treads an unearthly, grotesque feline form.

Manticore.

From far away he looks like a giant, mangy lion, but he lacks any semblance of majesty or grace. Manticore's mane is thick and shaggy, and his face an obscene parody of a human face, vaguely Avrantic. He lurches through the night, occasionally snarling at the flies that swirl around his drooling mouth, irresistibly drawn to the overpowering stench of dead flesh coming from his three rows of teeth.

3

One row for biting, tearing, ripping: an endless array of long fangs that constantly tear even at his own gums; clotted blood cases his thick Avrantic lips. A second row for chewing: huge molars joined by strings of ragged flesh. The innermost row is for bone-shaping—as he feeds, his inner teeth swirl and grind away at the larger bones, shaping them into darts that he stores in his pendant belly and fires with deadly accuracy out of a muscular sphincter at the end of his hollow tail. The deadly poison that coats these darts comes from his liver. He limps—his left foreleg is scarred and twisted, a reminder of the time he was nearly killed by a human, Hihuspix the neo-Hudlumm of Kol's Silver Phalanx. Apart from the marks on his legs, all Manticore remembers of Hihuspix was that he had been lean, healthy and surprisingly sweet.

Manticore steps out of the trees and stands in front of the pit. The vamans break into frenetic activity; they run around the circle, setting up various complicated scientific instruments—gauges, pendulums, wires, measuring sticks, strange contraptions full of bubbling liquids. The hiss and chatter of steam and clockwork is uncannily loud in the forest as the vamans' machines spring to life.

This is Manticore's hour of glory, his moment of supreme triumph. He has kept the secret, performed the sacred task that was given to him two hundred years ago.

In a strange, broken voice, he sings:

By the sacred circle now
We must fulfill our ancient vow.

A vaman mutters 'Bloody poet' under his breath. Kor waves for silence. He offers Manticore his ceremonial battle-axe.

Servant's blood and vaman steel
Come forth lords to kill and heal.

'Why does the fat cat speak in rhyme?' mutters one vaman to another. 'Can't tell you; I haven't time,' comes the grinning reply, followed by a *clunk* as the questioner's gauntlet crashes into the answerer's helm. Kor barks out a short order, and all mirth is extinguished.

Smiling horribly, Manticore offers Kor a mangy paw. Kor runs the blade of his axe across it. Manticore snarls; the cut is deep. He lays the bleeding paw on the edge of the circle.

A rivulet of dark blood runs down the basin to the raised triangle in the centre. As the machines click and hum, Kor and Manticore watch silently as the sides of the raised triangle are clearly outlined in a pool of Manticore's blood.

The moongold spheres suddenly light up, producing a dazzling silver light. The vamans cry out in surprise and anticipation. Manticore's eyes burn with excitement.

The beacons lit, my blood is taken
I cry out to my lords—awaken!

'Enough,' says Kor suddenly. A vaman swiftly bandages Manticore's paw; another enters the pit and wipes the line of blood heading from the edge towards the centre. Manticore smiles at Kor, a sly and cunning smile.

They wait in silence, casting long radial shadows on the mighty trees around them, watching the glowing moongold spheres and the frothing, lapping blood in the centre of the pit. The blood seems to be disappearing; it is as if the spheres are sucking it in.

A vaman enters the pit, his eyes glued to a glowing sphere. In his hand is a metal rod. He looks up at Kor, who nods. He gingerly touches the sphere with his rod.

There is a loud hissing sound and the vaman is suddenly enveloped in smoke. When the smoke clears, the other vamans wail, because lying in the middle of the pit is a smoking, smouldering corpse in red-hot armour.

Manticore laughs aloud.

Tamper not with ravian magic
Lest your end be brief and tragic.

The spheres are glowing even brighter now; they seem larger in size, and tendrils of pure white light seem to connect them, forming a triangle of crackling, sparkling light, as if three bolts of lightning are being held together by force. Outside the circle, wind sweeps dead leaves into crazy spirals around the clearing.

Two days pass. The vamans and Manticore kill every living thing that comes anywhere near the clearing. But there is no significant disturbance, the vanars do not come; and the vamans know that the rumour of Manticore's approach alone ensures that most creatures will give the clearing a wide berth. This is why they have let Manticore out to feed regularly since he came to them, to the Hidden Ziggurat, a few months ago as the sacred scrolls had said he would, when magic became strong enough for him to reappear, heralding the Second Coming of the guardians of all that is pure.

On the third night, the shining spheres start to quiver. Clouds hide the thin crescent moon.

The vamans gather around the triangle of light and gasp as the spheres slowly rise in the air and start to spin. The triangle starts to rotate as the spheres spin around in a blurring circle.

Blossoming out of nothing, a dome of bright light appears, filling the basin entirely. Manticore shrieks triumphantly.

Secret kept and hope renewed,
My lords approach, stern, steel-sinewed!
Quake and tremble, lowly mortal!
Oath's fulfilled! Behold the portal!

Rham Anpo, the vaman in charge of the scientific paraphernalia, has finished taking readings. 'I have to go back to camp now, could someone else take charge of the instruments?' he whispers. 'I'll explain later—just remembered something.'

Kor nods—he knows Rham is reliable, a brilliant scientist, and this can be dealt with later. Rham runs off in the direction of the vaman camp.

A few minutes later, three shadowy figures appear inside the dome of light.

Kor looks at the only vaman not in armour and says, 'It is time, Rae.' Rae Baipo, a thin, haggard vaman priest, mutters a prayer and runs into the light. And burns.

The others watch him helplessly as he struggles inside the portal, and shake their heads when he falls, screaming. Then they turn their attention to the shadows, which are slowly growing and taking human form.

Three ravians step out of the manticore's portal.

For a few moments they are just indistinct, shining figures of light. Then their shapes become clearer and better defined. Three shapes, two male, one female, naked, perfect. Their eyes radiate power and majesty. The vamans stare in awe, wonderment, and growing lust. They are hypnotized, spellbound; they have neither seen nor imagined such beauty in living form. They kneel, trembling. In a weak voice, his eyes unable to leave the spectacular form of the ravian woman, Kor stutters, 'Welcome back.'

She smiles sweetly at him, and at Manticore. 'Robes, please,' she says in a low, musical voice. The sound of her words *almost* matches the movement of her lips.

The vamans have not brought clothes, but their camp

is nearby. The ravians assimilate this information and smile sweetly, if slightly reproachfully.

Kor makes a brief speech. On behalf of the Rebel Union of Marginal Labour, he welcomes the saviours to this troubled world. He begs them, in accordance with their ancient treaty, to rid the land of the Dark Lord reawakened and teach the vamans the secret art of portal-making. He speaks of other underworlds, of vamans and ravians living in harmony all over the universe. The speech is slightly longer than it would have been if the ravian woman had been either less beautiful or clad.

The younger, taller male ravian steps forward and replies in kind. He speaks of the reunion of the ravians and vamans being just the first step of a journey down a glorious road, a road that would lead to eternal peace and happiness not just for Obiyalis (for that is what the mighty ravians, empire-builders across the stars, name this world) but for the whole universe. He also asks Kor who else knows of the successful opening of the portal; Kor replies, No one. The manticore's secret has been kept perfectly.

Manticore has seen ravians before, of course. He has served them for hundreds of years, but something puzzles him now—during previous entrances, the Pure Ones had always been clad, and had been able to bring anything they needed with them. And they have brought two objects this time too—an amulet dangling seductively around the woman's neck, and a strange black sphere in the older man's hand, which contains what looks like trapped lightning.

Why this spectacularly naked entrance, then?

The answer comes to him in an instant—they are playing a little joke on the vamans. Manticore has never really grasped ravian humour, but he knows it is best to smile conspiratorially in these situations.

The young ravian woman meets his eyes, and smiles back. He is impressed—she has powers he has not seen before. As her eyes flick from the vamans to him, for a moment he can actually taste vaman flesh—a rare delicacy, though more discriminating predators have complained of its toughness.

And when the ravians return from the vaman camp, clad in shining armour and bearing deadly weapons, Manticore has eaten his fill. The ravians stand before him now, their keen eyes piercing the darkness of Vrihataranya, seeing much more than what is visible in the light of the naphtha lamps in their hands.

As he leads the ravians away, a little fat red man appears behind a tree, his eyes tiny points of light. He doesn't know who he is, or where he is or why, but he knows he likes being here.

He stands still for an instant watching the lovely ravians, his button-like, pupil-less, black eyes twinkling comically. Then he scampers off into the endless forest. He is ravenously hungry, and is wondering what to eat. And there's a song in his head, dying to get out, but he doesn't know the words.

Three months later, a new Dark Lord is crowned.

BOOK THREE

BOOK THREE

1

The Civilian's palace, west wing, Turtlemonth 8th, 3 p.m.

Times have participated in enjoyable but potentially illegal and injurious activities: 3. Times have felt distinctly murderous tendencies towards pleasant, innocent person: 2. New combat spells perfected: 7.

Magic 15/20 (there's just so much more of it around, the denominator increased). Attraction for Asvin 85/100 (same reason).

In addition to his numerous other virtues, it turns out Asvin learned a lot more than yoga in his years at the ashram. I mean, I thought *I* was in good shape, but he could be a contortionist in his spare time . . . hmmm.

It's been three weeks or more since I last wrote, but who cares? Birds chirp merrily at me, there's a spring in my step and it's only because I sound like a hippopotamus in heat when I sing that there isn't a merry tra-la on my lips.

Simoqin's Hero (melodramatic sigh, hands clasped on bosom, *My Hero!*) is now at yet another ridiculous social function, meeting important people, simpering modestly. Tall tales are being told right now about how he single-handedly, almost casually, wiped out a horde of rakshases that killed his friends on their asvamedh, and followed that up by also wiping out various international gangs of badly brought up ugly beasts.

Simoqin's Hero is also probably displaying his finely honed combat skills as he deftly deflects the hordes of blubbery society matrons who want him to marry their daughters. All this while simultaneously avoiding excessive swollen-headedness and all other harmful side effects of fame and heroism—the only weakness he's displayed so far is an occasional distressing tendency to grow his hair and raise a moustache. Fortunately, my softly spoken promise to clear any moustache I see with giant fireballs seems to have had some effect.

I'm lounging around on my bed, alone for a change, in my new room in the Civilian's palace—I've finally moved out of Enki. Nice room it is too, except for a grim-looking oil painting of an old man in silvery armour holding a severed werewolf head aloft. Sometimes it feels like the wolf's eyes are watching us.

Tiara was very sad when I left Enki—poor thing, I've really had no time for her lately, and I can't pretend to be interested in her stories about the rather controlling man she's acquired over the last few months. And she doesn't like Asvin at all, which is a problem. She's taught me a valuable lesson—never talk about the man you love to your friends, because they will shuffle their feet at you and suddenly remember dying relatives. She's changed since I left. But then, so have I, changed forever and much more than she has, the little airhead.

Being in the Palace is rather strange—there's this sense of swimming around in a whirlpool of world affairs, which is really exciting, but the constant presence of guards can be both annoying and embarrassing. There was that time when Asvin and I suddenly met in a mirrored corridor and there was no one around, so we thought . . .

Anyway, I should lose the glow and get down to business. Kirin.

Another report came in yesterday, confirming what we'd already heard. He's declared himself Danh-Gem's heir, and will soon be crowned the new Dark Lord of the world. That's right, Kirin, my partner in crime and fellow roller under Frags tables, my former best friend and business associate, the one person I thought I knew, is now the Dark Lord of Imokoi, master of monsters, badshah of the bestiary. He must have been a rakshas all along—or a ravian traitor, Father says, we can't rule that out—and really, if you look at it dispassionately, you can reach only one conclusion.

And that is—I'm an utter fool. Complete. Utter. Fool. Who sat up nights worrying about him. Worrying about the enemy that Asvin and I have been trained to fight. Danh-Gem's son, apparently.

But *is* he the enemy? Can't say. It really is a new Age, and from what Father says, it seems that just after the wave of relief that the Rakshas isn't back came the realization of Kirin's immense economic and military significance. So people have stopped thumping their chests and are now scratching their heads a little. Because the Dark Lord of Imokoi might make a very useful ally, if he's not a raving monster.

Of course, a lot of important people are making loud noises about war crimes and historical grievances but in the end everyone knows it's the money, or even just the smell of it, that counts. Emissaries from many nations have set out already towards Imokoi—junior diplomats, that is, not important enough to be considered a major loss if they get eaten by rakshases.

Also, since Kirin was quite well known and liked in Kol, people here aren't getting stirred up into a panic at all, so there haven't been any serious riots—just a manageable spurt in crime that gives all these new leagues of heroes something to do.

Hero leagues are the new rage in Kol, and their battles with the equally new gangs of very colourful villains are distracting most people from the whole let's-flap-around-like-headless-chickens-because-war-is-coming school of thought. I think the Civilian is behind the whole thing somehow—maybe because it entertains people and she has a very twisted sense of humour. It also buys her some time—she hasn't taken a stand on Kirin as yet, and like the whole world, she's waiting for him to make his move. Some kind of peace treaty has already been signed, I think, but then who cares about peace treaties? Kirin certainly wouldn't, if his attitude towards promises made to supposed best friends is anything to go by.

I don't know how many people have noticed, but Kol has changed since Kirin's ascension. It's not just the excitement and the wild rumours and the strange songs doing the rounds—even physically, things are different. Carpets are flying just that little bit faster with all the extra magic, and making strange humming sounds (like flies on a dung-heap, Kirin would have said). The river's fuller than it should be this time of the year and soldiers keep marching through the city towards the barracks on the south bank of the Asa. The army is very quietly and unobtrusively preparing for a fairly large-scale campaign—but are we being invaded, or will we be the invaders? I try not to know too much about politics—it makes it difficult to support anyone, even the Civilian.

Phoenix guards in their new Goshawk high-altitude vroomsticks are soaring high above the city, scanning the sky for dragons. I saw Marshall Askesis, the Chief Commander of the army, in the palace yesterday. It's funny to think the Civilian won't actually be in charge of the army outside Kol if—when—war breaks out. But then, knowing her, she'll still control everything.

I had a long discussion with Father yesterday about what's going on in Imokoi. Apparently a huge new Dark Tower has been built. Which is very strange—this must have taken years to build, why hadn't anyone noticed it before? After all, every nation uses avian spies, and surely no one would be stupid enough to ignore Imokoi—though Father said birds that fly into Imokoi usually don't come back. Still, the idea that thousands of asurs could work for years to build this giant tower in the middle of a barren wasteland and manage to evade the world's attention is completely ridiculous.

Which means, of course, that it was inevitable. I don't know why people are still surprised by anything. It's almost as if they expect magic *not* to happen.

No word of Gaam either—but I haven't lost hope. His brother doesn't talk to me much, he just comes and visits the Civilian and disappears. They look so alike that I sometimes wonder whether it's just Gaam pretending to be Mod, but why would he want to do that? Come to think of it, I haven't seen Queeen or Steel-Bunz for a while either. Must be off on some secret assignment.

One person I *am* seeing far too much of, on the other hand, is oh-so-pretty Queen Rukmini, who like a typical

Durgan woman has come to get what she wants and is not too happy about the fact that Asvin is mine. So she's floating around the palace in her flimsy saris waving her stupid long hair and flaunting her perfect little navel and being all elegant and stunning whenever Asvin is around. Shameless flirt, that's what she is. And Asvin being Asvin is flirting right back. Those two are so made for each other I feel like beating them with a big stick. Which also applies to those random twinkly-eyed old crones who sprout mysteriously out of the undergrowth when Mr Princey and Ms Queenie pass by arm in arm, and say things like 'Bless yer sweet hearts, dearies! Tis a royal match made in the heavens!' I'm sure Rukmini pays them. Well, she can go and do her lotus-waisted, almond-eyed courtship display with someone else.

I sound like I'm half in love with her myself. Hmm.

In a way it's good she's here and keeping him happy when I'm not (though in fundamentally different ways, I hope) because Asvin is beginning to feel slightly tired of this hero charade. He's got this new theory that he's a throwback to a forgotten age, a society the rest of the world is familiar with but that Kol has left behind. And therefore he's irrelevant and useless and just a pretty face (Ridiculous, I keep telling him, it's not just his face that's pretty). He complains about being controlled, being a puppet. It must be a part of the process of growing up, for him—he's really changed, too, over the last few months. We all have—when I think of what we were like when we started off towards Bolvudis, it's really funny. How on earth can Simoqin's Hero feel irrelevant? But I guess if you've been the centre of attention all your life, your expectations are very high.

The real problem is that we have nothing to do. After all that excitement and high drama up in the Mountains of

Harmony, we've just been lazing around these last few weeks snapping our fingers.

I need to be more careful when I snap my fingers—I almost set the bed on fire. There's just so much magic in the air that spell-casting has become ridiculously simple. I'm really excited—my residual/intrinsic thaumaturgy studies will be so much easier now. And besides the whole passive power-lattice thing, I've been dabbling in some rather violent magical attack spells—funny, considering I'm generally very gentle and misty-eyed nowadays. But then I needed to learn much more about magical attacks, because fireballs, however pleasing and aesthetic, just aren't enough—and I'm pleased to say the illusion defences are coming along nicely. Besides, it's always good to have an outlet, and I think I have a very healthy appetite for violence that needs to be indulged once in a while. If I bottle it up, I'll end up fireballing Rukmini, which is not a good idea.

I just read what I've written so far, and I'm deeply disturbed it's mostly Current Affairs and Worthy Subjects of Interest, with a Touch of Light Romance. This is not *right*. I'm trying hard to be happy, but something's gone. Something's missing. Maybe it's just all a part of leaving University, of moving on— I'd never thought anything would really change, but everything has. I'd thought I was all grown up, that dealing with change was not a problem. I mean, look at everything I've been through this year. Surely I'm adaptable, if nothing else.

But somehow, things aren't *fun* any more. Everything's about Life and Death and War and Responsibility and Power and Great Big Significant Things. Everything's so bloody *serious*. Even Father seems to have completely lost his sense of the absurd. Or maybe I've lost mine—maybe it's something that always happens when you face the world for the first time. You lose that shining quality, that voice that tells you putting a dung-oli under the Chancellor's chair is a *good* idea, an idea that needs to be tested right *now* . . .

Not that I thought this whole be-a-hero-save-the-world job would be that much fun in the first place. But it didn't seem so real before, so grim. It was all one great big game, where you died if you lost, but if you were good and clever you would have a rollicking time, and save lives in the bargain. Now even the good days are filled with politics, and the bad days . . . the bad days are mind-numbingly dull, sitting in the palace, listening to Asvin and the rest go on about duty and honour and all that nonsense. Sometimes I make jokes, but they always fall flat, and then there are embarrassing silences, and everyone looks at me with that awful mixture of annoyance and sympathy . . . oh look, what great big feet Maya has, and how nicely they fit in her great big mouth . . .

No, General Self-pity isn't working either, because I know what's really wrong. You know what, I'll just admit it—I miss Kirin terribly. And I still keep having conversations with him inside my head. Especially now that I'm back in Kol, where every street, every sound, every smell brings back memories of things we did together. Little, funny things, Kirin-and-Maya things.

I act angry when Asvin starts railing about him—sometimes I feel angry too. But I can't help thinking there must be some explanation. I wish I could just talk to him once. No. I don't actually. He'd probably tell me another set of elaborate lies.

I don't know.

I have to go now, and that's good—I've rambled more than enough. Where's Asvin? I want to be kissed like a hungry anaconda.

2

T he Dark Lord sneezed and felt very sheepish, because Dark Lords weren't supposed to catch colds. It was bad enough that he looked most un-rakshas-like, lacking even the primary qualifications for membership (the deep belly-laugh, the instinctive tendency to abduct any maiden in a two-league radius and the moustache small children could get lost in). It would never do, he thought, to sneeze in Izakar. His magical healing powers could weave flesh and bone, but had not yet evolved enough to cure the common cold.

Four days march south from Taklieph, the Asurian capital mine buried in the Mountains of Shadow in west Imokoi, stood Izakar, the new Dark Tower, an architectural masterpiece built for the new Dark Lord on the foundations of Danh-Gem's tower by his kinsmen, the rakshases, and his servants, the asurs.

Every masterpiece of architecture is wrought from the bones of the earth with the sweat, blood and tears of thousands of labourers. While many minds might shepherd the actual process of construction, at the core of any grand architectural structure is *one* driving, obsessed, brilliant, inspired mind, a mind that dreams in squared hypotenuses. And the mind behind Izakar was that of the renowned Ventelot druid Andmartine, master of stone, who had studied Dark Towers down the ages and had distilled and compressed his immense learning into two blindingly brilliant edicts that he had given his chief subordinates.

Edict One: The Dark Tower should be Dark.
Edict Two: The Dark Tower should Tower.

The great thing about simple instructions is that they are usually easier to follow than complex instructions.

Andmartine's greatest creation, Izakar, was the Dark Tower that out-Darked and out-Towered every Dark Tower ever dreamed of, an immeasurably high spike of stern basalt and obsidian that stabbed out of the earth like a spear-thrust. The lofty Mountains of Shadow threw it into stark relief from the west; to the east, it loomed over the landscape, a mind-numbing, dizzying edifice of terror. Grotesque gargoyles sidled sardonically along the battlements, faces frozen in masks of madness. Enormous pazuzus, the eagle-winged scorpion-tailed demons from Elaken, lurked in its turrets or soared menacingly in the air, occasionally finding and casually munching on spying birds, or gliding vertical-winged amidst the massive banners fluttering in the howling wind; the banners of Danh-Gem, black dragon on red, raised again by his heir to strike fear into the heart of the world.

Built around the Dark Tower was a nine-layered city-fortress, imposing obsidian-walled concentric alcazabas, impenetrable and teeming with activity. Great sentry-kravyads, flesh-eating bulls with boar's heads and iron tusks, prowled the outer walls; vanar archers manned the sentry-towers, giant horned rakshases marched the city's winding cobbled streets in ceaseless vigilance. Raucous screams and yells punctuated the ever-present creaking, groaning and grinding of giant smithies, furnaces and factories underneath the outer layers, belching shimmering pillars of smoke and fire from the depths of the earth as they spat out weapons, armour and war-machines for the hordes of the Dark Lord— some of the larger factories were as yet unutilized in terms of actual production, and produced only noise and smoke, but what was a Dark Tower without the ominous death-screams of soulless machines?

The parched, barren plain that lay to the east of the Tower was crawling with asurs. Tens of thousands of danavs were assembled in the huge barracks of Imokoi, ready to march forth on the Dark Lord's command. And not just asurs, several thousand infantry and cavalry and a few cohorts of jinn from Artaxerxia were already encamped there, and the first squadron of vanar heavy infantry from Vanarpuri had just entered the city to present arms to the Dark Lord. South of the barracks were great mines and furnaces, where the first brood of elite pashans was being bred to form a deadly guard of honour for the Dark Lord's personal bodyguard, Spikes, son of Danh-Gem's most faithful servant, Katar lord of pashans. The great city-fortress lived to the heartbeat of thousands of tramping boots; it breathed with the hiss and throb of steam and noxious vapours; it drew sustenance from (and poured a great deal of sewage into) the Abet, the underground river that the vamans called Carotide, which ran from the Mountains of Shadow through the caverns of the vamans down to the Tydlez Sea.

And then there were the tunnels. Following plans laid down by Danh-Gem himself before his death, the crafty asurs built narrow, spiralling parasite tunnels that leeched on to the underground storehouses of the vamans, and it was from these secret tunnels that the asurs stole tools, weapons and the precious metals they used for construction and decoration in the halls of Izakar.

This then was the Dark Tower, Andmartine's monument to Danh-Gem's legacy of terror, a dark palace for a dark prince, a dark capital for a dark world.

And where Andmartine's architecture ended, the labours of the rakshases began. The Tower was a mighty citadel of sorcery as well. The rakshases, embodiments of magic wild and relentless, turned the smooth stone mountain into a capital worthy of their might and majesty.

The skyscraper clan of rakshases, mighty elemental beings, called forth clouds from the Mountains of Shadow to hide the construction of the city from prying eyes. The shadowsnatching rakshasis of the Mountains of Shadow killed every avian spy that dared venture near the Dark Tower, animating their victims' shadows and simultaneously sucking life out of their bodies until they crashed listlessly to earth. And the songscaper clan, earth rakshases, tore out rock and metal from the earth with their songs of power and sculpted large sections of the city from rock with brute force and subtle magic.

But the most powerful rakshases, the rakshases of Vrihataranya, saved their strength for more challenging tasks. These ancient masters of illusion were craftsmen not of stone, but of fear and confusion. They trained the mindless lesser rakshases, the pisacs, to assume a multitude of hideous shapes

24

and make forays into the surrounding lands, ravaging south Ventelot and the northern Free States, filling the night with ghastly sounds, mauling children and small animals, stealing crops and livestock, scrawling obscene messages of despair and hatred in blood on the walls of nearby towns. A cohort of pisacs was even kept for diplomatic duties—harassing the initial convoys of ambassadors as they travelled the wastelands and marshes of Imokoi, filling them with a sense of dread that caused significant damage to their trade-negotiation skills.

The rakshases of Vrihataranya cast vision-distorting illusion-spells into the sky, making the Tower appear even larger than it was, changing the patterns of the stars to make travellers lose all sense of direction, creating horrible visions of nameless beasts silhouetted against the horizon. Sometimes they tampered with the very fabric of the land, distorting perspectives and meddling with scale—for travellers on the road leading to the Tower from the north, a small bush became a sea of nettles, a puddle became an endless swamp, a little pile of rubble became a plain of smoke, ash and dust.

Inside the Tower, the rakshases took the forbidding maze of corridors and giant halls the asurs had wrought and turned it into a nightmare of treacherous stone. They made passages twist and spiral endlessly into nothingness, enchanted stairs and doors to move of their own will, and filled the fortress with an array of magically concealed pits, mazes, chambers and traps. The numerous levels of sprawling dungeons, however, the rakshases left untouched—they could think of nothing to add to the vileness of the asurs' instruments of torture, and there were some monsters lurking in the lower levels of the dungeons that even rakshases didn't want to meddle with—strange beings with tentacles and suckers and claws and teeth that only Dungeon-master Ublyet the asur knew about (and fed, which was why it is advisable *never* to annoy Ublyet in any way).

But the principal purpose of this vast spider-web of deceit and illusion was to conceal two things.

First, Imokoi was actually still a green and beautiful country, and while the asurs enjoyed laying waste to nature's beauty almost as much as humans did, rakshases loved their earth fiercely and would never wilfully harm it. So while war and asurs had left Imokoi irreparably damaged, the rakshases saw no reason to mutilate the land further when they found it perfectly simple (and entertaining) to create the spectre of all-pervasive ugliness and desolation with just a little hand-waving and element-shaping. Besides, by using enchanted twisting roads and distorted skyscapes, the rakshases often managed to make travellers avoid the beautiful parts of the country completely, making them think they were heading north when they were actually trudging dolefully southwards through the most desolate regions of Imokoi. The green-fingered rakshases of the mountains also contributed to the illusion-web. They grew Stray Sods in their rock-gardens—little enchanted, portable clumps of grassy earth that acted as portals, transporting travellers who stepped on them from one Sod to another—and scattered them in occult patterns on the plains of Imokoi. Someone who stepped into a Stray Sod and out of another could wander around in confusion for days, not recognizing any landmarks, unable to find any sense of direction whatsoever. The only way to cast off the spell was to wear your clothes inside out, which was obviously not the first thing that would occur to people marooned in the wild lands of Imokoi, where trying to keep the locals from turning your skin inside out was always a more pressing concern.

The second fact Izakar concealed was this—something was missing from this superb Dark Tower.

The Dark Lord.

Kirin, heir of Danh-Gem the mighty, had chosen not to live in Izakar. He lived a day's march away in a secret palace, built for him by the songscaper rakshases, on the banks of a clear, sparkling lake by a beautiful hidden valley in the foothills of the Mountains of Shadow.

The motives behind this were simple and sound. Rich, powerful people tend to live in quiet, beautiful places. Also, they like to live in a degree of luxurious solitude, away from the bustling masses, and the masses didn't get any more bustling than they were around Izakar. Besides, the Dark Tower was where the Dark Lord worked—and his miraculous chariot took him to work in just a few hours. There was no need to actually *live* in that rather depressing and potentially lethal environment.

Kirin's palace was all he could ever have dreamed of, from its stately gardens and avenues of trees to its overflowing kitchens and garrulous kekeko-birds. It was secure, too— the valley was closed in on all sides by lofty hills ceaselessly watched by sleepless stone guardians, and the only way in was through a tunnel bristling with pashan guards. Besides, another rakshas illusion veiled the entire valley in a magical mist, making it look like a cloud-capped, tree-clad hill from above.

While Kirin found both Izakar and his palace extremely impressive, he could sense that the rakshases had been disappointed by the fact that he'd not gasped or cried aloud in amazement. He couldn't help it; he'd just seen too much—

27

after living in Kol, it was difficult to be awestruck by buildings. This was something the rakshases, returning to the world after two centuries, simply could not comprehend. However, he had been impressed by Danh-Gem's beautifully crafted Iron Throne, which the asurs had preserved and now placed in the Tower. They'd even kept Danh-Gem's old slippers by the throne for centuries, awaiting his return. Kirin, who had no intention of stepping into his father's slippers, merely thought that they must have been useful, through the long dark years, for killing cockroaches in the throne room.

At this moment, the Dark Lord was deep in thought, standing by a fountain in a hexagonal courtyard and watching a flimango tree trying to balance itself on one fruit. There was no one else in sight except his friend Spikes, the sole ugly ingredient in the perfect beauty of the courtyard, seated on a marble stool contemplatively eating a rare butterfly.

Kirin had just eaten a magnificent seven-course Avrantic lunch and was feeling bloated and vaguely sleepy, but he knew the rakshas Aciram, his father's cousin, would soon be arriving to escort him to Izakar. He would have to spend the whole evening squabbling with and sneezing at some Skuan envoys, besides sorting out blood feuds and other interesting asur pastimes. So sleep was not on the cards just yet. Which was a good thing, because with sleep came dreams, and Kirin didn't want to dream the dreams he had been dreaming lately, those mind-altering visions that made staying awake seem like a rest . . .

He shook his head, trying to dislodge the residue of last night's dreams from his mind.

'Spikes,' he said.

'Yes?' said Spikes.

'Let me ask you something.'

'Right.'

'How long have I been Dark Lord?'

'Three weeks or so.'

'And what have I achieved in these three weeks?'

Spikes thought for a while. 'Nothing,' he said.

'Ah. Nothing. That's what I thought. Have I managed to slow down preparations for the war?'

'No.'

'Have I managed to persuade people in other countries that I do not mean to eat their children?'

'No.'

'Have I managed to let Maya know I'm not a monster?'

'No.'

'Do I have any idea as to how I'm going to achieve any of these things?'

'Probably not.'

'In short, nothing.'

'Yes.'

'I'm glad you see it that way too. For a moment, I was afraid I was being unduly pessimistic.'

'You weren't.'

'Thank you, Spikes. You're always a great help.'

'Yes.'

'But the good thing is, no matter how bad I get, I won't be the worst Dark Lord in history.'

'Why is that?'

Kirin grinned. 'I've been reading asur histories,' he said. 'And long ago, before the days of the Ventelot Empire, the world was briefly shaken by a Dark Lord known as the Great and Terrible Zorgani, who had a Dark Tower somewhere north of the Mountains of Shadow, an army of asurs and

29

pashans and everything. Zorgani's great army once threatened
to overrun the whole of the north and the west. But the twist
was, Zorgani didn't exist. He was just a big red balloon in the
shape of an eye which the asurs had stuck on top of the Tower
to scare people. And so the asurs would invade countries,
pretending the Great and Terrible Zorgani was behind
everything, and using the sheer terror his name invoked to
destroy enemy morale. Zorgani was this great shadowy enemy
who no one saw, who could take any form he chose. Added
to the mystery and everything.'

'Smart. And what happened to this Zorgani?'

'Well, the kings of the west, with typical spinelessness,
ordered a khudran to sneak into the Dark Tower and assassinate
Zorgani. The khudran found out the secret and simply untied
the ropes of the balloon eye. Once it had floated away, the
asurs gave up—without the deception, their armies didn't
have much. The Great and Terrible Zorgani floated around
the world for some months before landing in Skuanmark,
where he was cut up and used for sails for their ships.'

'Yes. You're a better Dark Lord than him. Only just,
though,' said Spikes.

'Kind of you. And with that encouraging example in
mind, I should get going—more ambassadors are on their
way and I have to meet them. Painful, as always.'

'Well, you could let the rakshases meet them.'

'No. My father apparently allowed his ministers to
shapeshift and pretend to be him while he was away with
my mother. But I don't want to do that. He didn't care how
many deaths they ordered, but I do—they're all mad. We
might have invaded the Free States yesterday if I hadn't come
back from the toilet earlier than Nasud had expected.'

'He was only joking. They wouldn't dare.'

'Still,' said Kirin, pulling the flimango out from under the tree with his mind and starting to peel the luscious pink fruit in mid-air, 'I wish I was more interested in politics. Bjorkun and Omar can go on about it for hours. I just wasn't brought up to it. I don't know the rules.'

'What would have been useful,' said Spikes, 'is if *you* could shapeshift. Maybe you can, and you just haven't pulled the right muscles.'

'I can't. I don't know how. I've looked into the mirror and willed my face to change many times, for a number of reasons, but nothing happens. It's really something you need to start when you're very young.'

'Maybe you need to be all rakshas to do it.'

'Maybe. Speaking of which, it was quite a shock when I realized they knew I was half ravian.'

'But they do not know who your mother is, do they?'

'Aciram knows. The rest think it was some random ravian woman my father forced himself upon, and I think that's something they quite approve of. Half of them don't know who their parents are anyway. But Aciram's knowledge makes him a threat.'

'Hardly. He wants to use you, not replace you. They will not unite under him. Besides, he is your kinsman.'

'True. In any case, I don't think rakshases take naturally to politics—they're too wild and solitary to understand collective action, and too strong and fearless to realize why people stab one another in the back. They follow human war strategies, and only do better because they're naturally stronger and more dominant than humans. But they will be slow to betrayal, especially if humans are their fellow conspirators. For them, helping humans overthrow me would be like plotting world domination with cattle.'

'So you don't see yourself as human any more.'

'*Well, I'm not, am I,*' said Kirin without opening his mouth.

'Yes, you are different now. You're certainly more full of yourself than you used to be before.'

'Respect, Spikes. I'm the Dark Lord, remember?'

'And I am your most loyal servant.'

'Don't say that, even in fun.'

'It doesn't matter. Let me ask you something instead. Why did you say no when they asked you if you wanted a harem?'

'Possibly because I don't *want* a harem?'

'Why not?'

'I don't want to talk about this.'

'I know. But you should forget Maya. A harem would help.'

'No, it wouldn't. And I don't want to talk about this.' He sneezed defensively.

'You talk about it all the time in your sleep.'

'Well, talk to me when I'm asleep then.'

'Not that you need a harem of humans, the way the rakshasis have been trying to seduce you.'

'Yes,' Kirin grinned. 'They're not very subtle, are they?'

'I don't see why they should need to be. It's interesting, the way they change shapes to find out what you like. I don't see what your problem is, you should just play along. I like rakshases for being direct. When they want something, they take it. When they're hungry, they eat. And when they want love . . .'

'The clever ones are twisted enough, Spikes. Don't mistake directness for simplicity.'

'You are wise, Dark Lord.'

'Stop it. But isn't it funny how rakshasis are generally not that ugly? So much for history books. But to be fair, they would need to change to monstrous form in battle, which is where most humans met them. And they look nice when they dress up for dinner, but it's difficult for humans to write about that, since they'd usually *be* the dinner in question. Perspective, and all that.'

'Should I tell them you have changed your mind about the harem, then?'

'Can we stop discussing my love life, Spikes? There are other things on hand that are more important. Here, I'm not eating this.' He tossed the uneaten flimango at Spikes, who caught it with a claw.

Kirin sighed deeply. 'While we stand here, talking about seductive rakshasis,' he said, 'there are armies preparing to slaughter millions in my name. They want to give me a world, and I have no idea what to do with it. And there is so much that needs to be done. There are so many suffering people—humans, asurs, vanars—I could help them, Spikes, but I have no idea how. I know I have the power to change things, but how do I prevent those under me from using my powers to ruin the world?'

'Have some fruit,' offered Spikes, chewing contemplatively. 'It's very good.'

Kirin glowered at him in silence.

'You know I don't have the answers to your questions,' said Spikes after a while. 'And I'm not good at long speeches either, but you obviously need one now. I think you should just calm down and see what you can do. Getting melodramatic is not going to help anyone. You're well on your way towards madness anyway. There is a saying among pashans—a headless chicken may move fast, but it's only good for eating.'

'Nice.'

'So stop worrying. You're more powerful than anyone else here. Maybe you're also cleverer than anyone else here. But spluttering and raving is only going to make things worse. You will never be able to make things perfect. And you've just started out on your new job—don't expect to change everything at once. If it means anything to you, I think you are doing very well.'

'Thank you.'

'Not very well, perhaps, because you haven't achieved anything, but you haven't made a terrible mess of things either.'

'Thank you.'

'What you need to do is relax. And get yourself a harem.'

Kirin laughed, and then suddenly raised a warning hand. His eyes blurred. 'Someone's coming,' he said. Spikes casually flicked out his claws.

There was a shimmer in the air, and suddenly Aciram materialized inside the courtyard.

'I apologize for intruding, Kirin,' he growled. 'But by the bones of Adnus my father, it is so good to feel the mountain-roots under my feet that I cannot help using the magic sometimes as it surges through me. You may feel it's childish, but you would have done the same in my place.'

'I feel only jealousy at this moment,' replied Kirin. 'I can't teleport at all.'

'Only short distances, kinsman. But it's a useful power.'

'Have you come to take us to the Tower?'

Aciram nodded. 'The Skuans are here, besides a puffy nobab from Potolpur—good eating, should discussions prove fruitless—and a few asur chieftains. There is some important news as well. The werewolves are on their way and should reach Izakar to swear their allegiance soon.'

'How do you get along with the werewolves? I have never met one.'

'Dead dogs grow brains, kinsman. We learned a lot from them during the War. Before our paths crossed, we thought fighting in groups, working together for a common cause was something only cattle, two-footed or four, did. Tigers of the world, we were obsessed with ourselves and with our territories in forests and mountains; we marked them magically and guarded them with our lives even against our brethren when necessary. The Pack taught us that it was possible to stay strong when united, that even rakshases needed to work together sometimes. This was a lesson we learned with great difficulty, but it was a lesson learned just in time—we rakshases were so powerful before that no threat was strong enough to make us huddle together and whisper to one another of allegiance and help. But when the ravians, who are joined together in their minds almost as much as bees or ants, descended from the skies to threaten our world we had to unite, and the Pack showed us how. It bodes well that they are beside us again, as we prepare for the next onslaught.'

'The next ravian onslaught?'

'Yes. And we do not have much time, so let us get to work.'

'You think the ravians will come back?' asked Kirin as he knelt to summon his chariot.

Aciram smiled sadly. 'Think? I have walked this earth for many centuries, Kirin. I have breathed fearless air under the stars before the Hidden Ones came to take away what was ours, before they changed our order, our very world, forever. And I know how the land, the earth that has nourished me and mine through endless winters, trembles at their approach.'

He looked at his huge, gnarled feet, on the edge of a giant circle of rippling earth as the Chariot of Vul rose from the depths to perform its master's bidding.

'I hear the songs of the land, and they are sad songs, Kirin,' he said. 'The ravians are here already. I feel it in my toes.'

3

An impudent morning breeze sneaked across the rooftops and unravelled the loose loincloth of Thog the Barbarian as he stood on one foot, meditating, on the roof of his one-storey house in Eurekus Place. The loincloth flew off gracefully, causing intense consternation in the bosoms of a group of pimpled schoolgirls taking sitar lessons in the house across the street.

The sound of a few thousand E's rolled together into a rock-hard ball hit Thog squarely between the eyes, causing him to open them, realize instantly what had happened, and chase his errant loincloth across the roof, to whoops and cheers from more than one building.

As he reclaimed his modesty and assumed a defensively conservative lotus position, Thog reflected that the spiritual realms had never really been meant for him. Still, a Barbarian had to try.

Not that Thog was really a barbarian; he'd lived in cities all his life and was far more culturally evolved than most of his colleagues in the Guild of Superb Heroes. For that matter, his name wasn't even Thog, it was Arathognan.

When the Guild had been assigning hero identities, he'd wanted to be cast as a complex, brooding, possibly accursed wanderer type, but his fellow heroes, happily sozzled on Triog's best vodka, had looked at his massive muscles and rugged, weather-beaten face and chanted 'Barbarian warlord!' Someone had also pinched him under the table—he wasn't sure who.

But this forced mantle of barbarism wasn't the main reason why Arathognan searched for solace in spiritualism. The real reason was his mad aunt Ugtha, who lived with him and was the bane of his life. Her rhinoceros-skinned imperviousness to other people's need for privacy (and, a few years ago, Thog's ex-wife's desire to beat her into a pulp) had not diminished even slightly as he grew from a thin, dreamy-eyed, love-struck youth to a rugged, dreamy-eyed, divorced man.

His spiritual guide, a lapsed Anchin monk he'd met at Frags, had once told him, 'To achieve self-enlightenment, one simply exerts oneself with all one's might towards the state in which no thoughts arise.' A state of being which, Arathognan had realized, Aunt Ugtha achieved every day with no apparent effort, and therefore a state that he constantly strove to reach as well, to deal with her relentless nagging and whining.

'Arathognan!' Aunt Ugtha's shrill, piercing cry rent the morning calm. 'Are you blind or just plain stupid? Can't you see your bloody beacon's up again?'

Thog opened his eyes quickly. The beacon! He'd missed it completely. The maniacal crone had her moments.

There it was, the magical blue griffin symbol, hovering over the football stadium, no, over the Wrestling Association of Kol Arena, which meant that a registered hero had decided that there was trouble happening there that was worth everyone's time. In the early days, when the Hex Men had just invented the beacon flares and started distributing them to the other heroes, the beacon would hover above Frags every time there was a problem, and all the heroes would gather there first and be told what the problem was. But soon it was seen that most of them hung around for a drink, and then another drink, until everyone had forgotten what the problem was in the first place.

Finally, one day after The Bulk had used the beacon to summon the other heroes to his birthday party, the leader of the Guild of Superb Heroes, Reinforced Iron Man, had decided that the beacon should be set to hover over the scene of the crime, where heroes could find things out for themselves.

Thog ran downstairs, oiled himself quickly to make his muscles stand out even more and got dressed. He pulled on the fine silken thong, the coarse camel-hair loincloth, the spiked leather straps. He strapped on the battle-axe, the tiger-claws, the wickedly curved kris on the belt around his waist. He tied back his long, prematurely greying hair, reapplied the fake scar to his left cheekbone and sprinkled on his favourite perfume. League Rule 2:3 stated you had to look exactly like your wooden action figure—the scar, for example, he'd had to wear since the first Thog the Barbarian toy (Plain Rugged Adventurer of the Rugged Plains: Free Replica Battle-Axel) had been scratched accidentally by the toy-maker.

Aunt Ugtha, talking at two hundred words a minute, rolled out his carpet—a vroomstick would have been cheaper, but impractical, given Thog's costume—and tried in vain, yet again, to persuade him to take a lunch-box and a water-bottle with him.

Minutes later, Thog was in mid-air, his carpet speeding towards the wrestling arena.

In the beginning, there had been just GOSH, the Guild of Superb Heroes, a motley collection of heroes who'd teamed up in the Fragrant Underbelly to fight crime. Then the black-clad young spellbinders called the Hex Men had changed everything, as spellbinders tended to do, by actually ridding the city of some notorious villains. When it was known that Kirin, the boy who used to make the Stuff, was the new Dark Lord—this was about three weeks ago or thereabouts—the Civilian had finally acknowledged Kol's heroes' genuine contribution to keeping the city peaceful (and entertained). She had declared that hero organizations were to be officially recognized, publicly encouraged and rewarded according to performance.

There had been an explosion in the number of hero associations in days, with a bizarre array of new masked crime-fighters crawling self-consciously out of the woodwork, adding to the general mayhem in the city by fighting both crime and one another. To organize things, the Civilian had formed a competitive association of the city's defenders, called the Champions League. Clashes between Champions League heroes and bands of organized criminals (who operated under the sinister umbrella of the Unabashedly Non-heroic, Illegal and Criminal Endeavours Federation) were fast becoming the stuff of local legend and serial soap-box operas.

Thog jumped off his carpet, rolled it up outside the WAK Arena beside a sign that proclaimed in glittering letters:

'TONIGHT'S SPECIAL—MIGHTY MASK-A-RAID!!!'
He nodded briefly at one of his favourite fellow heroes,
Mr Seik, the slightly insane eight-foot-tall behemoth berserker,
who'd just trundled along as well, accompanied by a hero
in a green mask and an 'I (heart) Kol' vest whose name Thog
didn't know.

'Door's unlocked,' growled Mr Seik. 'Must remain calm,
must remain calm. Nothing to worry about.'

'Entrances graded for this one are?' asked the green-
masked one. They looked at him dubiously. He shrugged.

'Why take chances?' asked Thog.

They ran up to the door and high-kicked it simultaneously
at different heights, causing it to splinter and crash in a
satisfyingly spectacular manner. Unsheathing their weapons,
they ran into the building together, pausing for a moment
to appreciate the exquisite figure of an innocent-looking
young woman who was standing quietly by the fallen door,
looking scared. She reached out and touched Thog's arm
briefly as he ran by her.

There was a moment of still, intense eye contact, and
Thog's vision blurred briefly. He was tempted to linger, but
duty called.

As the heroes raced down mirrored corridors towards
the main arena, Thog saw his reflection and stopped. His
reflection was wearing an amulet—he reached to his neck
and yes, there it was—an amulet that he didn't remember
putting on in the morning. On the other hand, something
told him he had always worn it, that it had belonged to
him forever, so why on earth would it look unfamiliar now?
He shook his head and ran on into the main arena.

What had happened at the arena was this:

The next match on the schedule on that day's wrestling extravaganza was a Mighty Mask-a-raid. A number of wrestlers in disguise were supposed to enter the ring and pound one another to a fine jelly, and in the end the last man standing would remove his mask and reveal his identity to his rapturous fans, who'd been told weeks in advance by the not-so-subtle ring announcers who would win but had managed to steadfastly ignore this.

So when four jakyinis, dancing zombies from the islands south of Elaken, entered the arena, no one in the audience was perturbed—they'd never seen jakyinis before, so they'd thought these surprisingly thin contestants' disguises were rather strange—expressionless, pointed white faces framed by long, stringy hair, death-white, frayed skin with patches of deep-brown tissue visible beneath and tight shiny trousers didn't exactly make an inspiring picture. But then wrestlers did always take chances where fashion was concerned. The completely peeled nose of one, though, provoked several comments. What had really pleased the fans was the fact that the ground lit up with a pretty if eerie phosphor light wherever their feet touched the ground.

The jakyinis had danced forward in a strange style, simultaneously fluid and jerky, sliding along without seeming to actually walk all the way to the ring, winning much applause from the beer-swigging cognoscenti.

They had then climbed into the ring and proceeded to unleash a liberal dose of what Xi'en masters called The Laying of the Foot on the Donkey.

Crooning melodiously in their soft and shrill voices, they had knocked a few wrestlers many times their size out of the ring to tumultuous applause. Two had then leapt spectacularly off turnbuckles into the audience, grabbed two children and vaulted back into the ring while the other two zombie dancers grabbed an unfortunate wrestler and ripped off his mask, and with it, his head.

At this point, when the ringside announcers were shrilly demanding their revised scripts and most of the punters were explaining kindly to their wailing children that it was all fake, the more brilliant minds in the audience realized that something was amiss.

One of the zombies picked up the announcer's caco-conch-shell mouthpiece and asked the audience, in a soft high-pitched voice, to hand over their children or watch them be eaten. The two who'd picked up the children dangled them threateningly over the ropes.

That was when the Man of Reinforced Iron, who'd dropped into the Arena to see how the youngsters were doing in his absence, had run outside and sent up the flare.

When Thog and his companions reached the ring, Reinforced Iron Man was somewhat busy being swung around by the ankles by a jakyini. As he went flying into the audience, Thog vaulted into the ring and, as an introductory gesture, cut one of the undead dancers in half across the waist with his battle-axe. 'Come on, Seik!' he cried.

Seik did not reply.

Thog looked back over his shoulder and cursed. 'Got scared, did you?' he asked bitterly.

'Sorry, Thog,' quavered Dr Heina, the tiny, mild-mannered, balding dentist Mr Seik transformed into whenever he was angry or upset, 'I tried. Good luck.'

The hero in the green mask whose name Thog was destined never to know somersaulted whooping into the ring and got a fist right through his heart for his pains. 'I die!' he cried, and did.

Which meant that the ring now contained the following:

Item: Barbarian. Description: Heroic. Nos.: One.

Item: Corpse. Description: Twitching. Nos.: Two.

Item: Jakyini. Description: Murderous, dancing. Nos.: Three.

Item: Bisected-jakyini torso. Description: Crawling jerkily across ring. Nos.: One.

Item: Leg of said bisected jakyini. Description: Crab-stepping across said ring. Nos.: Two (one pair).

Item: Child. Description: Extremely ungrateful, has decided through some convoluted juvenile logical process that all blame for ongoing childhood trauma is to be attached to said heroic barbarian. Nos: Two.

Fortunately, Thog's experience of a lifetime of adventures and of Aunt Ugtha's nagging had left him capable of calm in the most trying circumstances. Perhaps more fortunately, the lapsed Anchin monk had taught Thog more than meditation—he'd also taught him how to chop people up.

First, he stooped, picked up the charging children and tossed them outside to Dr Heina. Then he assumed his Barbarian Battle-stance, his action-figure pose (League Rules 4:41: All fights have to start with stipulated hero pose, except in extenuating circumstances such as underwater or mid-air combat) and sighed wearily as he faced the undead dancers, battle-axe at the perfect angle.

The musicians in the pit next to the ring struck up a stirring beat, and the audience settled down to watch the action.

I'm too old for this, thought Thog, as the jakyinis leapt at him.

For the next minute, Thog was a whirlwind of muscular arms, kicking legs, swooshing steel and occasionally, to the delight of the women in the first two rows, flashing silk.

More Champions League heroes rushed in through the door, eager to win points for their teams and glory for themselves. But they were too late—Thog had fairly won first attack rights as per League regulations (2:12) and was chopping up the zombies with vim and vigour, taking bone-crushing blows in his stride. He ducked and weaved in efficient silence, emitting barbaric yawps whenever he remembered to stay in character. When the exclusive first-attack time decided by the League elapsed, other heroes vaulted into the ring, but Thog had matters well in hand.

The heroes stood in the ring and applauded as Thog severed the head of the last jakyini and surveyed his handiwork—a pile of groping, severed limbs twitching about and spewing smelly fluids, and four balefully glaring severed heads.

There were sacred traditions to be followed when combat took place in the WAK Arena, so Thog grabbed a head and pinned it to the mat (while it rolled its eyes and tried to bite him) and Mr Seik, grinning, counted to three. Then Thog climbed a turnbuckle and, severed head in hand, raised his arms in a victory gesture, driving the audience wild with joy.

Because of the generally low intelligence quotient of everyone in the Arena, no one paused to consider a few details. First, while it was known that jakyinis loved children and used them either as familiars or sacrificial offerings to their undead god, they had never been known to make a public spectacle of this sort before, normally preferring to lure children out of village huts with their dancing and singing and pick them off in quiet places. Second, jakyinis were normally unable to survive for long when far from their native islands, let alone work as a team, unless they had the guidance and support of an extremely powerful will.

Also, in the raging applause, no one noticed a man somewhere in the fried-potato-digesting belly of the audience turn to his wife and whisper 'That hero looks just like the old king, doesn't he?'

It might not have been a terribly clever thing to say—especially considering the fact that the whisperer had never seen a portrait of the old king—but it was significant. Because whispers, like rabbits, breed very, very fast.

4

O nce upon a time, Lady Temat, Chief Civilian of Kol, had been capable of love. She had been a beautiful innocent, an idealist, a young girl with stars in her eyes and a marked weakness for flowers, chocolates and simple, handsome young men.

Sadly, for people who are saddened by the Death of Romance, and conveniently for her, those times had passed. The most influential human in the world still had soft corners in her heart—you had to, if you were human and not an accountant—but when she looked back at the men she had loved over the years, some now great and powerful, leaders of nations, she wondered how she could have been so stupid.

She still had a weakness for simple, handsome young men, but that was completely different—it was all about exercise now. And it was only because she had a razor-sharp mind and paid remarkable attention to detail that she even remembered their names afterwards.

Sometimes, though, they did things that made them linger

on in her mind—like the actor who had eleven fingers and knew how to use them, the football player who thought he had the hands of a god, and the brilliant young scientist who'd suddenly jumped out of the bathtub they were sharing one hot, sultry afternoon and run out into the street naked, yelling about the principles of water displacement.

She never let her lovers into the palace at night, of course; that would have been like placing a large mat with ASSASSINATE ME written on it in huge letters by her bed. And only the ones who held her attention for more than a month even got to know who the mysterious, glamorous older woman who'd walked into their lives and taken over their minds really was in the first place. After that, they were sometimes allowed to stroll around in her palace with guards and sniggering palace officials following them at a discreet distance.

Captain Rupaisa, chief of the Red Phoenix guards and one of the Civilian's trusted advisers, was very unhappy with the whole situation—all these boys, she told the Civilian repeatedly, were threats to her security. She put herself into grave danger every time she made one of her nocturnal visits to her lovers' houses. And the Civilian, looking at the distorted, foam-flecked face of the young painter who had ceased to be her favourite toy two minutes ago when he had tried to kill her, had to admit that Rupaisa had been right all along.

She'd told her bodyguards, the three young female Silver Phalanx trainees who accompanied her on her amorous nocturnal adventures and sunlighted as a team of crime-fighting heroes called the Sadori Sisterhood, not to kill him. They were presently, therefore, holding him very still, upside down, his limbs splayed at interesting angles. He looked strangely like the distorted figures he'd painted in the murals on his walls—loud colours, strange lines, angles and curves, normal spatial rules discarded in favour of a more imaginative attitude towards perspectives, he'd said between kisses. A whole new form of art, as yet unnamed. And now it would have to wait for years before someone else discovered it.

The Civilian stood up, adjusting her robe.

'Who paid you to kill me?' she asked him.

His expression changed to one of complete confusion. The Civilian was suddenly stricken with guilt—he was so young, so talented, and he could have had a nice life . . . if he'd never met her, if he'd been just a little less beautiful . . .

The Really Pretty Sister twisted his arm. 'Answer the question,' she snarled.

'What happened?' he asked.

'We want to know why you tried to kill the nice lady, darling,' said the Sweet and Quirky Sister.

'I tried to kill her? No! Who are you? What's going on?' His eyes were wide, shocked—he looked at Temat beseechingly and flinched as the coldness of her gaze hit him like a sock full of cold nails.

The Violent and Brooding Sister kicked him where it hurt. 'Who sent you?' she yelled.

The painter started to cry.

The conversation carried on along these lines for a few minutes.

Then flying carpets drew up outside the painter's tiny apartment and Rupaisa and Mantric the spellbinder rushed in, accompanied by more guards.

'Tell me,' said Mantric to the Civilian.

'He suddenly went berserk and tried to strangle me,' she replied.

'But why did you send for *me*?' asked Mantric, his bald head glowing in the soft orange oil-and-jellyfish mood lighting.

The Civilian looked at him sharply, noting the slight hostility in his voice. 'I fear that something is very wrong,' she said. 'He was so docile and gentle. I usually know when people are acting. He wasn't.'

'People often make mistakes in these situations.'

'I don't, Mantric. I have a feeling there's magic involved. Could you check?'

The Sisterhood flipped the painter up. Mantric examined his terrified eyes, felt his pulse, and then held his trembling hand for a while.

'I really don't understand,' gasped the terrified painter. 'Who is she? She's an old model, right?'

Mantric snapped his fingers and put him to sleep before turning to the Civilian. 'Something's definitely happened here, but it's not the kind of magic ordinary sorcerers can perform,' he said. 'Tell me exactly what happened before he attacked you.'

The guards withdrew discreetly, leaving Lady Temat with Mantric and Rupaisa.

'We were talking to each other, and suddenly he went mad,' said Temat. 'And what was that about ordinary sorcerers?'

'His mind has been altered ever so slightly. By someone really good—I don't think he has any memory of what happened. What were you talking about when he went mad?'

'He said he wanted to spend the rest of his life painting me, that he would make me an immortal symbol of new art, and I told him not to fall in love, because I would leave him soon. He suddenly started foaming at the mouth.'

'It's either some potent drug—and the heavens know what artists use—or his mind has been commanded to react to a particular phrase or word, some word his enchanter was expecting you to use.'

The Civilian thought for a while. 'Under the circumstances, I expect the word might have been love. I've been . . . meeting him for a few weeks now, but I can safely say tonight was the first time that word came up. That must be it, because I really don't think he was an assassin. He's had plenty of chances to kill me before, in any case.'

'In which case, this wasn't a serious assassination attempt,' said Rupaisa. 'I mean, this reedy specimen could probably not have overpowered you in any case. This was a warning from someone. Rakshases?'

'A rakshas would have eaten him, changed shape, taken his place, and eaten me. They don't really believe in warnings,' said the Civilian. 'This was the perfect opportunity. In fact, that's what confuses me—even if some human ruler had been behind this, I would have been dead by now—this was not a very professional assassination attempt.'

'Unless it was carried out by someone or something that seriously underestimates humans,' said Mantric.

'What are you going to do with the boy?' asked Rupaisa.

'Take him to the palace and persuade him to tell you everything he knows, and about everyone he's met since he first met me. There's no need to be gentle.' Again, a pang of guilt. There's nothing to feel guilty about, the Civilian reprimanded herself sternly, more weakness now will just not do.

'I'll see to it,' said Rupaisa, her face a bland mask. She left with the guards and the painter.

The Civilian walked around the apartment for a while,

staring at the brightly coloured, twisted figures on the walls. Eyes, noses, mouths scattered over twisted faces, frozen forever in lust, joy and war. She shuddered.

'I usually know who's trying to kill me,' she said quietly. 'I really hate not knowing.'

'It can't be that many people,' said Mantric. 'The usual suspects wouldn't kill you now—even if they want to stop you from stopping the war, they need you to protect them when war breaks out.'

Temat sighed. 'I'm tired, Mantric,' she said. 'I've never felt this old before.'

He sat down on the wooden floor, his face impassive, not meeting her eyes. 'You need to be more careful,' he said. 'A lot of lives will be lost if you get yourself killed. The people need you.'

'The people would be far more comfortable if they had a ruler who worked to preserve the way things are, Mantric.'

'I don't understand.'

'You wouldn't. The people don't like me, Mantric. Sometimes, at times like this, it matters to me. I have carried them too far into the future, and all they want is the good old days—of innocence, ignorance, disease and danger that I have worked ceaselessly to change. The people couldn't care less if I were killed.' Her voice broke and she stopped, embarrassed at her own display of emotion. You're losing your grip, she thought.

'But we both know you have no intention of getting killed just yet.'

'Not just yet,' and she smiled suddenly as she paced the room. Mantric was a fool in some ways—most ways, in fact, but he knew just what to say sometimes.

52

He watched her in silence as she stopped and looked for a while at the canvases stacked carelessly in a corner.

'This doesn't make sense, Mantric,' she said finally. 'I should be dead.'

'Consider yourself let off with a warning,' said Mantric.

'Who from?'

'Someone who believes you should drastically re-examine the way you conduct your love life? No, your parents are dead and there are easier ways of warning you—this must have been more than a warning. It boils down to this— whoever's behind this is someone capable of meddling skilfully and subtly with minds, and someone who hasn't done much research on your abilities or your security systems. In other words, someone who doesn't think of you as a serious problem.'

'I find it extremely insulting that there's anyone in this world who doesn't think of me as a serious problem,' said the Civilian.

Mantric frowned. 'I didn't say they had to be from this world,' he said slowly.

They both knew the word, but they didn't say it.

Ravian.

5

Kirin's dreams were full of dragons.

He never remembered putting the Gauntlet of Tatsu on before going to sleep, but somehow it was always there, burning red, on his right arm in the morning. And most days he would wake up in the morning shivering and trembling in places where he definitely hadn't gone to sleep, huddled up in a corner or curled up in a foetal ball on some cold stone floor. And every morning, standing over him, keeping him from harm, would be Spikes—whose face, while not the first thing anyone could want to see in the morning, was reassuring in its immense strength and extreme ugliness. At least, thought Kirin, when you saw Spikes's face you knew you weren't dreaming any more, because you would have woken up if you were.

He had barely closed his eyes when sleep smothered him again, and it wasn't long before he felt the now-familiar sensation of being lifted up from his bed and sucked smoothly into a diamond-studded sky.

Fly with us, master, whispered the dragon-voice that dwelt on the borders of the uncharted territories of his mind. *Let us show you what power and freedom really mean.*

And suddenly, joyously, he was soaring again on dream-wings into the skies, where the dragons surfed the rippling currents of air-magic, waiting for him, and soon he was seeing with a young green dragon's eyes, experiencing the exquisite pleasure of dipping and gliding with cold winds over the mountains as the moonlight kissed him gently. He felt his eyes change, knew somewhere in his mind that far, far away, where his body lay in restless slumber in his palace, his pupils had turned into vertical black slits in bright red eyes. He watched his shadow streaking over the hills as he beat his great green wings in an ancient slow drum-beat paying tribute to the stars. And then he raised his great fanged head and filled the sky with primal fire. He was Dragon, he was Dragon-master, lord of the world, iron claw and eternal fire, and the very firmament sang his praises. He raced eastwards to meet the sunrise, and space and time lost meaning—he was pure spirit, an elemental being, a thunderbolt of pure power unhindered by temporal bonds.

And suddenly he took shape again, in curls and claws and sleek sinuousness, and now he was different, a great Xi'en dragon hovering over the lofty peaks of the Mountains of Harmony, warming his heart in the morning sunshine. No longer just a raw force, he was now whole, dual, united— he was heat and cold, fire and water, summer and monsoon, strife and harmony. The mountains bowed to him as he crawled his way through massive, dense white clouds, turning and watching in satisfaction as they followed in his wake, giving up their cotton-puffed slumber, racing behind him as dark, threatening tornadoes, slithering like giant snakes over the plains, tracing his flight-path in loops, knots and spirals over the rice-fields of west Xi'en. It would rain in Xi'en that day—loud, thunderous, crashing rain, where every raindrop sang as it landed. And the peasants would honour him as they toiled in their fields—it had been a long time since the land had last seen dragon rain.

His thoughts turned to the north, where cold blue magic arced through the cracking air, where thin ice was sometimes the only barrier between magic and matter. And there he was, in a roar of wind and fire—the patchwork quilt of Xi'en paddy-fields was torn, forgotten in the brutally magnificent shadow-mazes of the fjords of Skuanmark. His northern-dragon skin, now red and leathery, was dappled crimson and maroon, scarlet and vermilion in the moonlight as shadows raced over his skin, painting him softly as he flew madly in complete silence through rugged snow-covered valleys, translucent black wings spread out, riding the fierce North Wind, letting it cover every scale on his gigantic body with its icy caresses.

Be one with us, master, said the dragon in his mind, suddenly urgent, anxious, pleading. *This is but a taste of the joy we can bring you. Surrender the Gauntlet, Lord, free us from the chains of human oppression. In tribute, in exchange for our freedom, we will give you the sky. We will be one with you, and together we will rise above the petty and vicious world we are bound to now. Together we shall discover a realm where true freedom will be ours. Be one with us. Surrender the Gauntlet.*

No, replied Kirin, dragging his mind away, reminding himself that dragons were the greatest predators in the world, and that these wild seductive voices were probably doing whatever they could to fight the power he exerted over them. He lost his concentration and with it his hold on the dragon's mind, and suddenly he was cast off, thrown down like a stone through the black, biting air, and then he was alone, on a barren, snow-covered mountain-slope, in human shape again, and his dragon-flight seemed like a dream within his dream.

But he still bore the Gauntlet, he still ruled them—he cast his mind up into the sky, felt the strength of the Gauntlet radiating, pulsating as it searched the thin air, and he was airborne again in the body of another magnificent Skuan sky-drake.

We bow to your strength, master, said the dragon. *We cannot, we will not fight your power. We submit to you, and we urge you—if you will not free us, at least unleash us. Call us, let us come to you, let us show the world what dragon-fury is. We will lay a world in ashes at your feet, if you so desire. Call us to you, and take the world—it is yours.*

But Kirin was not interested in a world in ashes at that point—he was speeding over the Skuan forests, oblivious to everything except the beauty of dragon-flight. He swept down, over the trees, in a great arc, and spotted a cluster of speeding black dots in the forests of the tundra. To his delight, he found that if he looked hard enough, he could see them in incredible detail. He slowed down his flight and dipped a little to get a better look.

The black dots were a small party of werewolves, running southwards in the glistening moonlight through the sparse black forest. Kirin was lost in admiration as he watched the grace of their sleek, grey bodies and the effortless ease with which they loped over the hard ground, ignoring the endless leagues before and behind them in proud disdain of mortal fatigue.

He looked closer as they converged on a rocky outcrop that jutted out over the edge of a cliff, where a single human shape was seated, cross-legged, as if in meditation. The hunt of the Pack, thought Kirin, flying even lower, his ferocious north-dragon body inexorably drawn towards the stench of potential bloodshed, his ravian nerves already anticipating the first wolf-leap for the jugular, the sight of spurting blood staining the grey, moonlit rocks . . .

But as the werewolves reached the outcrop, the seated figure jumped up and whirled around in one smooth motion and Kirin beheld a giant bearded man in a wolfskin loincloth holding out his hands in what looked like a welcoming gesture. And the werewolves were changing to human form as they drew near him—many, Kirin saw, had their heads bowed in salute to the bearded one. He's their leader, thought Kirin, observing him more closely, noticing now the piercing blue eyes underneath the long, shaggy, grey hair, the giant muscles knotted across his arms.

And suddenly they were aware of him—the leader pointed one great arm and they all beheld him, the giant reptilian winged beast hovering in the sky, silhouetted against the giant moon, watching them in silence. And at a signal from their leader, they turned their faces or muzzles towards him and howled in unison, saluting the great predator of the skies. Then the leader leaped off the cliff-edge, changing to wolf-form in mid-leap, and the others followed him in a mad slide down the cliff-face.

Kirin switched dragon-minds again—it was getting more difficult now—and this time he was perched on a cliff near Taklieph, and in a great fire-lit pit far below he could see thousands of asurs celebrating in the early hours of the morning. Were they celebrating the war he was supposed to lead them into, he wondered. Their bodies, possessed by the beats of hundreds of drums, were locked in the motions of some frenzied, ancient asur tribal dance. Even from his perch high above, Kirin could feel the throbbing excitement in the giant, glowing pit, could almost taste the heat, sweat and passion of the underground revelry, could almost hear asur instruments weaving pulsating webs of melody around the giant drums pulsing a defiant rhythm to the drowsy eardrums of the rest of the world. He saw many couples, male and female asur lovers, standing still amidst the heaving dancers, or dancing locked in violent embrace to a different beat, completely ignoring the pushing, shoving bodies surrounding them in the fierce strength of their desire. And then Kirin, perched alone on the cliff-top, felt the sharp bite of the loneliness of power.

He sensed his sleep growing lighter as morning approached in Imokoi, but he still wanted more—he turned his mind southwards and briefly visited the body of a huracan, a spike-tailed giant black dragon of the southwestern volcanic isles, who breathed volcanic lava and whose very presence caused earthquakes. As the huracan, he flew over the deep, blue seas of the south above live whirlpools, sea serpents shimmering in silent pursuit of schools of fish and ships of buccaneers speeding their way raggedly eastwards in the dark.

Completely exhausted but insatiable, he twisted his head and flew for a while in the intense heat of the Artaxerxian desert, the beating of his wings creating beautiful patterns in the swirling sand, disturbing giant marids lurking under dunes in deep corners of the desert no human eyes had ever seen. And then he looked down, and suddenly he was a wurmdrake inside a vaman tunnel, crawling and sliding on his belly on a silvery-white vaman road towards something he sensed he wanted very desperately. But he was too tired to think about all that now—his mind was fading, he was slowly slipping away from this quagmire of interlinked visions and into the sweet restfulness of awakening. The dragons were bidding him farewell, hissing *We wait, master, for your call. We are ready* . . . filling him with a fierce desire to let go, to summon them and command them, his Gauntlet blazing with a savage fire that would burn the world as he rode the dragons in the eye of a storm of destruction, flattening civilizations, making those feeble insignificant humans scurry and crawl like ants at his slightest whim, dazzling Maya with such a display of raw, pure, uncontrolled power that she would forget all else and run to him, embrace him with a passion as savage, as untamed as that of those asur dancers in their drum-induced trance . . .

'You all right?' asked Spikes as Kirin sat up with a jolt, eyes staring into nothingness.

'No,' said Kirin. 'I'm going mad, I think.'

'Right. Good morning.'

Kirin looked at his arms and legs, secured with heavy manacles to massive iron weights in the corners of his room. 'What's all this?' he asked, his mind searching inside the locks on the manacles for the right lever to push. He was still shaking, feeling like he'd run for days in the desert and that his lungs were about to burst. And he was incredibly thirsty—breathing fire in your dreams probably did that to you, he thought.

'You were floating around in mid-air and shaking,' said Spikes as Kirin clicked the locks open and got out of bed. 'I thought you would have started wandering around again, and I felt like a little sleep last night. Didn't want you hurting yourself wandering around, lots of sharp corners. This palace wasn't built with children in mind. So.'

'Kind of you.'

'You're welcome.'

'Beautiful morning, isn't it?' and Kirin slumped back, desperate to steal a few moments of sleep.

'Get up. You're late for work.'

So Kirin rose, grumbling, and started putting on his sinister Dark Lord robes, trying in vain to blink away the dragons behind his eyelids.

* * *

And elsewhere . . .

You have? *Show it to Me at once!*

Yes, that is the one. Well done, *Sambo! You found it, how delightful. Just in time, too. Why am I so excited? This world is important.*

Why? Because this is where the next Game will be played . . . and bad things would have happened to Me if it were missing when the Players arrived. I was worried.

Look. Is it not beautiful? Those mountains, that big dark forest. Even that funny splotch over there, which is a towering city . . . and this whole spread, oceans and rivers and plains and deserts and things. Delightful. Delectable. But above all, look at the lighting, Sambo. Fabulous, isn't it? Thank you.

Now shut all your eyes except one—any one—and look closely at one spot on this world. Any spot, Sambo. Don't be silly.

Ha ha. Yes. You looked funny, jumping like that. And when They get here, the Players will jump too, each and every one of Them.

It startled Me too, the first time I realized I could see the pieces in such minute detail if I just bothered to really look . . .

things changed then, Sambo . . . I changed. For some reason, I started . . . caring.

I digress.

This is a new Game, Sambo. We do not need the flat board and those silly figurines for the important pieces any more. This world—this whole world will be the board this time. The map is the terrain. The representation is reality. This Game will be real. The pieces will be alive, Sambo. Alive. And the Players will have to look at details, Sambo. Things are always different if you really look at the details.

Yes, I know, I know. They will be surprised. They might even be angry—but, Sambo, consider the possibilities. Once They play this Game, there is no going back to the old one. Everything changes.

They don't like change, Sambo. The powerful rarely like change. But change is good. And change is needed here. There's so much I need to show Them, so much They need to understand . . . so much We could all learn . . .

I wonder how many of Them have been playing with this world while I was otherwise occupied. Quite a few, I suspect. But then, why should gods play fair?

Let Me look at it again.

Oh, Me.

There are creatures here I have not made, Sambo. So many of them, and quite interesting too . . . look. There are creatures on this world that do not belong—that do not know they are changing the board by just being on it. Anything could be happening down there. They're actually making their own choices, playing their own games, living their own lives. Wonderful.

They are growing, Sambo. This is what happens when

You mix them up and leave them alone. Better than the most confusing thing I could have dreamed up.

Now, listen carefully. No mistakes. The host's duties are sacred. Everything must be perfect; Our guests will not be easy to please. And I want Them to like this Game. I need Them to like it.

Pay attention. First—since this world is important now, Sambo, We shall have to give it a name. Something that will stay in Their heads. Something that tells Them how useful and important this world is, how right it is for playing the Game . . .

Something, you know, catchy.

GameWorld?

What sort of name is that? No, no . . . call it something nice and curly. You know . . . imaginative. Lyrical. GameWorld . . . too obvious.

But then, who said obvious was bad?

Yes, on second thoughts, call it GameWorld. It sounds official, and more importantly, it's easy to remember. It's simple.

Something about this Game should be simple.

Imagine, Sambo, just imagine, what if They like this Game? What if this world, this little lost-and-found maybe-round world with the funny standing sea, changed Us even as We changed it? What if all Our Games change? It could all start here . . .

Yes, yes. GameWorld. Good name, Sambo.

It's better than My idea, which was to name it after Myself. But I'm not very good with names. Worlds, yes. Names, no. At least I remember your name, Sambo.

What?

The Manticore's Secret

Your name isn't Sambo?

What is your name?

Nagual? What sort of name is that? It's too curly to remember. I will call you Sambo, Sambo. I like Sambo.

It's catchy.

Don't grumble. I know, I know, I should try harder. Never could remember names, I'm afraid. I'll be forgetting My own name next.

Sambo?

My name is Zivran, isn't it?

Of course it is. I was worried for a moment.

6

He was one of the three members of the super-elite martial-arts cult referred to in hushed whispers by members of merely elite martial arts cults as the Extremely Secret Society of the Puissant Purposes and Painted Toenails—and since one of the two other members of this cult was a hundred and twelve years old and only ate mouldy turtle-shells and the other had vowed to spend the next five years working on his Dissatisfied Pelican technique in a lonely cave high in the Mountains of Harmony, he was effectively the most dangerous fighter in the world. He was immune to most poisons, even the deadly venom secreted by his pet blowfish, Go-Fugu. He could kill with any weapon, from a multi-pronged kusarigama to a flat-bowled wooden spoon. He knew the secrets of the dim mak assassins of south Xi'en, who could kill with a single touch and whose unit for time measurement was the *ak*, the time it took between the delivery of a spine-cracking jab and the death of the brain. He was a master of all the five animal styles the warrior-monks of Xi'en taught, and all the secret methods they didn't teach—the element-based combat styles, the five-unrelated-monkeys-in-a-jail-cell style, the aggressive-schoolgirl-with-a-fan-and-a-hairpin style, and even the devastating-sidewise-lurching-attacks-best-practised-when-drunk style. In a world without magic he would be the most dangerous killer alive—and in this world, he was definitely the most lethal mortal. But he was no brute killing machine—he was also an acclaimed master of, among other things, massage (Avrantic, Xi'en and Skuan), cooking, calligraphy, flower arrangement and interpretive dance on weekends. He was beyond pain or fear; only small things moved him now—the sound of blue tea falling into a Long dynasty porcelain cup, the satisfied hiss of a silk-cleaned samurai sword sliding into its sheath.

He was three and a half feet tall.

In up-market Kol, the assassin feared all over the world as the mysterious Silver Dagger was better known as Amloki, the Civilian's lively, friendly and very efficient khudran page. Many of the Civilian's enemies, recognizing his immense value to her, had kidnapped him to make the Civilian accede to their demands. He had always proved remarkably easy to kidnap. It was only afterwards that he got a little difficult to deal with, especially from the point of view of those kidnappers who liked staying alive.

Amloki was currently in the Chief Civilian's palace, enthusiastically engaged in hugging Mantric's daughter, the brilliant young spellbinder Maya, whom he hadn't seen for the last three weeks. He'd been out on duty, running errands, meeting friends, killing important people.

Asvin and Captain Rupaisa, also present at this affectionate reunion, watched them indulgently and suspiciously, respectively. When Rupaisa noticed the Dagger's hands inching slowly towards the pleasure points on Maya's back, she cleared her throat loudly, causing Amloki to break the clinch.

'Where have you been, my friend?' asked Asvin.

'I went home for a holiday,' said Amloki. 'I just returned this evening, in fact, just in time to catch up with all the gossip. And I've heard all the latest about the Dagger!'

Amloki was the Dagger's principal outlet for vanity, one of his many besetting sins.

Asvin and Maya looked at each other and smiled indulgently—the little khudran's hero worship of the mighty and mysterious Dagger was at once touching and endearing.

'Why can't we know who the Dagger really is even now?' Maya asked Rupaisa.

'As I told you the last fifteen times you asked me, it's not in my hands,' said Rupaisa. 'When you are ready to know, he will tell you himself. Now follow me.'

As she led them through the broad, pillared corridors of the palace, Amloki trotted along beside Maya and looked up at her, his big, confiding eyes brimming over with enthusiasm. 'They say the Dagger made a spectacular entry into the palace in secret last night, making a complete fool of the palace guards and many Red Phoenix guards who were on patrol,' he said. 'He avoided all the new traps, escaped all watchful eyes and surprised Captain Rupaisa with a kiss out of nowhere—is that true, Captain, begging your pardon?'

'Who on earth said that?' asked Rupaisa, her eyes flashing.

'I have my sources,' said the khudran defiantly. 'I also know that because of the Red Phoenix guards' terrible performance, the Civilian has asked the Dagger to place some Silver Phalanx members in the palace under the Captain's command. How is it working with the Silver Phalanx, Captain?'

'You should learn to keep a hold on your tongue, Amloki,' snapped Rupaisa. 'I will not have you compromising Lady Temat's security with your idle chatter. And if you must know, the Silver Phalanx is a collection of overbearing, overrated, self-important fops.'

Amloki looked wounded.

'Where are we going now?' asked Asvin, to fill the awkward pause that followed.

'To the south wing, where the Civilian and Mantric are waiting for us. Chancellor Ombwiri wants to show us something. And she said nothing about bringing you, Amloki.'

'How was your holiday, Amloki? Are you going to stay in the palace for a while now?' asked Maya, feeling sorry for the crestfallen little khudran.

'No,' he said, looking sadder still. 'The Civilian is lending me to the Commander, Marshall Askesis, because I know more about the city and its administration than most of the ministers in charge—I am to be by his side at all times and help him decide exactly how the army is to run itself alongside the city administration during the war, if there is one. The Civilian and her ministers are too busy to advise him on the everyday details, and I was the only other person with the necessary expertise. It's a noble duty, but I have heard the Commander is a harsh man, and I will miss all of you.'

'And you'll be reporting to the Civilian about what the army is doing?' asked Maya with a conspiratorial smile.

'No,' he replied innocently. 'The Commander asked me the same thing when I met him earlier today—he said I couldn't do that if I were working for him. I don't really understand——they're both working to protect Kol, but they don't seem to trust each other much.'

'Amloki,' snapped Rupaisa. 'Don't talk too much about politics, a subject you are too simple to understand. You aren't even supposed to be here.'

'I'm sorry, Captain. It's just that I gave up a career as a Muwi-vision star to be *here*, not anywhere else. The Civilian needs me. I cannot understand why she would send me away.'

'We're here,' and Rupaisa knocked thrice on an intricately carved door.

They entered an Alocactus-lit hall full of priceless Psomedean marble statues of the heroes of old, recovered from the ruins of the ancient Psomedean Empire. Amidst the intricately carved, flowing marble figures, many of them tragically defaced and broken by time and soldiers, stood the Civilian, Mantric and Chancellor Ombwiri of Enki. Maya noticed a big black butterfly sitting on Ombwiri's shoulder.

'The reason I wanted to see you, Asvin,' said Ombwiri, 'is that, yet again, our world is under threat.'

There was the usual grim silence that follows this sort of announcement.

When is the world not under threat, thought the Dagger wearily. Now that would be news. He hated being around when these philosophical discourses were taking place, being much more of a Give-me-a-list-and-I'll-have-their-corpses-in-by-sunrise kind of person. He caught sight of his reflection in a mirror and thought, You handsome dog, you.

'Under threat from the rakshas Danh-Gem's son?' asked Simoqin's Hero, hand on sword-hilt.

'No,' said Ombwiri. 'Rakshases may threaten kingdoms, but they have been a part of this world as long as humans

69

can remember. Their reawakening does not trouble our world. But the world *is* troubled, watchful, throbbing with fear. Something is about to happen, something or someone that must be stopped. And if we cannot stop it, our world, saturated as it is with magic, will take its own steps to defend itself—but in taking these measures to protect itself, the powers the earth unleashes might forget to protect us. Therein lies the danger.'

'How did you learn this?' asked Maya.

'Well, we're all aware of the existence of the Global Self-defence Theory, but reports from the spirit world have actually confirmed it now. The centaur shamans told me,' Ombwiri replied. 'The shaman-foals, standing in sunlit streams reading the ripples, heard the whispers of their ancestors. They said strange beasts walk the woods, beasts never seen before, foul creatures that have sprung out of nightmares into the flesh. They prowl the land, confused and angry, unaware of their role in this world's helixes of life. We do not know if all these beasts are from our world. The spirits say that at least some are guardians the world has produced to defend it against some hideous new threat. What this threat is, I do not know.

'And there is more, they said. Something twists the very earth we stand on. Some hideous force tugs at the roots of the trees. The mountains groan as something cracks them from within. What the centaurs have observed is the geophysical phenomenon we know as the Cartographer's Dilemma, but it seems to have accelerated considerably in recent months.'

The Cartographer's Dilemma was well known. Owing to random meteorological influences, largely caused by the Vertical Sea and the concentrated flows of magical energy permeating every part of the world, the world was reshaping itself constantly, making the drawing of maps that stayed valid over a long period of time almost impossible.

The consequences of this were often devastating—shifting tides, volcanic eruptions and earthquakes had recently claimed thousands of lives in Elaken and Xi'en, and whispered rumours of collapsed vaman tunnels, of entire vaman cities disappearing into giant cracks in the heaving earth sometimes crawled up to the surface. Politically, this made drawing clear borders between countries impossible as well. Potolpur, for example, had annexed a large part of Olivya by doing nothing (a Potolpuri specialty)—the hills that marked the border had moved drastically westwards over a few years.

This also explained, to some extent, the completely random climate and vegetation distribution patterns in the world—it was possible to travel from ice-wastes to sand-wastes in just a few days. In many parts of the world, the seasons came and went in random order too, making agriculture largely a matter of luck. The dual threat of floods and famines was forever on farmers' minds. And magic and other mysterious forces were constantly tearing at the very fabric of the elements, reshaping, isolating, merging, distorting. This was a world where grandfathers, when they told their grandchildren (while dandling them on their knee or in other social situations not involving knees) that the mountains were higher when they (the grandparents) were young, were often telling the truth.

'And magic tangles the web even more,' continued Ombwiri. 'The weather grows increasingly magical, and sensitive to sentient moods, all the more so where large numbers of people huddle together and experience similar emotions—as they do in Kol. From now on, if the people are afraid, expect storms. In times as dark as these, every person's aura, augmented by residual aerial magic and the Heart of Magic, churns up the mixture a little further. I fear we are on the brink of collapse.'

As if to illustrate the truth of his words, a bolt of lightning split the sky above Kol, and an ominous roll of thunder roamed growling through the palace. Everyone smiled in spite of themselves.

'What should I do?' asked Asvin.

'Your duties as a hero do not extend as far as slaying threatening geological and meteorological patterns, Asvin,' smiled Ombwiri. 'But however unexciting these may be, it is on forces such as these that things like agriculture and the economy as a whole largely depend, and if these systems collapse, so does our state. Which make these new problems potentially disastrous. And given the state our world is in, it is quite possible that the key to this is in the slaying of some terrible monster, as yet unknown——a task for Simoqin's Hero, in fact. But I called you here not merely to tell you about the problem——I bring you a powerful gift, that might even become a powerful weapon at need.'

He nodded at the butterfly sitting on his shoulder. 'A gift from the centaur shamans to the Hero of Simoqin, a secret they have never shared before. This is a Kaos butterfly.'

'A who?' asked Maya, speaking for all present.

'Kaos butterflies can, with a single precisely timed flap of their wings, set into motion chains of forces that determine the weather in regions they choose to influence.'

The others looked closely at it and noticed for the first time the thin, swirling grey lines flowing on its black wings. They looked like storm clouds.

Since butterflies don't inherit property and thus don't attach much importance to family trees, the butterfly in the Civilian's palace didn't know that it was a distant relation of the Kaos butterfly that one of Danh-Gem's pashan soldiers, a perennially hungry bedrocker named Khudito, had swallowed whole one lazy afternoon, thus making the condition of his stomach the determining factor for the weather in a particular part of Imokoi during the darkest years of the Age of Terror. When guests were coming and Danh-Gem needed scary, forbidding storms and howling winds, Khudito used to be put on a lobster-only diet.

'One would presume the increase in magic levels causes these butterflies to breed faster, thus making weather control even more complex,' said Ombwiri, looking at the butterfly affectionately as it suddenly flapped its wings, causing a cool breeze two days later in its favourite part of the Centaur Forests. 'But the good thing is, the shamans feel that the Hero should have a butterfly of his own, who will be with him and keep the weather favourable around him. I know it doesn't seem that important, but you would be surprised how crucial it could be to your survival.'

'I can control the weather with this?' asked Asvin, wonderstruck.

'To be honest, I do not know. The shamans are adept at manipulating animals' emotions, but these butterflies are very sensitive and can somehow guess what weather you desire. The mechanics are frankly beyond even my comprehension. Besides, the Kaos butterflies, however powerful, are just an example—merely one of the thousands of factors affecting the weather. Now strong magical forces are at work—and in this maelstrom of conflicting influences,

I do not know how much difference one butterfly can make. But on a very local scale, I'm sure it can help you greatly if it chooses to.'

'Specially as vaman potions are no longer accessible to you,' Mantric pointed out as the butterfly fluttered over to Asvin's shoulder, causing a sudden gust of wind that blew a bandit off a cliff-top in Ventelot four months later.

'May I ask a question?' asked Rupaisa. 'Why are we talking about butterflies and vague fears? What do we know about this unknown person or power that threatens us, and what steps can we take against it?'

'I think the real question is even simpler,' said Mantric. 'Have the ravians returned?'

The weather obliged with a dramatic thunder-roll, but it was the directness of the question that caused everyone to flinch.

'Everything seems to point that way,' said the Civilian. 'Strange rumours, mysterious signs and portents, guardian monsters . . . The thing is, our mysterious guests could be beings from a completely different world, completely unrelated to ravians. But given the year, the Simoqin Prophecies and the fact of Kirin's ascension, I suspect that the ravians are back, and are at least partly responsible for the turmoil the world is facing.'

'Besides, all this happened last time they were on this world as well, though to a lesser degree,' said Mantric. 'There were some monsters that attacked them ceaselessly, and definitely contributed to their leaving. There's also a legend that speaks of a ravian hero, Zibeb, and how he single-handedly reversed an earthquake that would have destroyed Asroye. The ravians did not leave just to save the world from spiralling magic levels—they left because they were under threat themselves, from a world that was in danger of collapsing under the weight of their power combined with its own explosive magic, and saw them as the cause of its pain.'

'And if they are back,' said the Civilian, 'it must mean they were extremely fond of this world.'

'Kirin,' said Mantric. 'He is the key to all of this. And we know nothing about him.'

'But why are the ravians a threat?' asked Asvin, perplexed. 'The ravians were heroes, champions of all that is noble and true! And you taught me it was always difficult for societies to accept outsiders—which is why there would always be some amount of conflict when new races arrived, be it in a city or a world. But surely we all agree that eventually the ravians will make this world a better place, and rid us of the terror of the rakshases, the dragons, and all these other hideous monsters! After all, they are our natural allies, and their coming is as the sounding of trumpets of triumph, and the death-knell of our vile enemies!'

The Civilian smiled at his impassioned face. 'It isn't that simple, Asvin,' she said. 'Two centuries have passed. The world has changed.'

'It should change back then!' he retorted. 'What sort of world is this, where we make peace treaties with rakshases and worry about the glorious arrival of the ravians?'

Angry roll of thunder. The weather was listening, and Asvin was exceptionally well-endowed (aura-wise).

'There is a lot you don't know, Asvin,' said the Civilian gently. 'A lot happened two centuries ago that no one remembers, that was never recorded. The coming of ravians is about more than history, about more than immigration and its problems. I was the one who let asurs into Kol—do not speak to me of integrating aliens into societies! The problem is that the ravians are so much more powerful than us. And all power is threatening. Do you think I do not see Imokoi as a threat?'

'I've accepted there is no absolute Good or Evil,' said Asvin. 'But when you reach out in friendship to monsters, and devise plots against heroes—I beg your pardon, but I think you are wrong.'

'Let me share something with you, Asvin,' said the Civilian. 'Something I learned quite recently myself. The real reason for the Departure was not, as we supposed, ravian nobility in trying to rescue our world—really, who would do that?—or even, as Mantric suggested, that they escaped a world that was hostile to them, where their presence was disturbing the very fabric of the world itself—that might be true, but it wasn't the most important cause.'

'And what was the most important cause, he asked, agog,' said Mantric.

'The real reason for the ravians leaving was that the vamans were on the verge of finding out the exact location of Asroye, and they were afraid the vamans would attack their hidden city and uncover all their secrets.'

Temat looked calmly at the stunned faces of the rest of the assembly. 'The vamans did not tell me this, of course—I had to find out using very ignoble methods. But I will be judged another day. Tonight, all I ask of you is this—and this is something I have learnt to do myself, the hard way—keep your eyes open and your minds guarded. Something hidden and powerful walks the land.'

The weather seemed to have missed the Civilian's last pronouncement, so the Kaos butterfly flicked an antenna to compensate. Three cracks of thunder converged in the sky, rumbling ominously above the Civilian's palace.

7

Avery confused crow sat on one of the tallest spires of Enki University, half-heartedly watching a white sunrise over the river Asa. He was no ordinary crow—in Commander Kraken's elite force of crows, the Cromandos, Captain Forty-Six 'Abacus' had long been regarded as one who counted—at least literally, if not politically.

Abacus was the crow who spied on the nefarious goings-on of the spellbinders of Enki, and the mathematical knowledge he'd accidentally acquired (by conduction through the ancient building's bricks and tiles) had not only enabled him to devise the numeric rank-based coding system the entire air force used, but had also shown him (statistically) that advancement in the ranks of the Cromandos was not a good idea for those who liked counting their body parts and finding them all present and intact.

Abacus's life was reasonably easy—normally, his chief complaint was that the students who fed him, occasionally threw him magic dye-dipped scraps that turned him yellow or pink. But recently he'd noticed particularly nefarious goings-on that intrigued him not only as a spy, but as a mathematician as well.

Through the window of the Ancient Rites and Rituals department's lecture theatre, fifteen suitably ancient statues could be seen. These statues had been gifted to the University by the famous Olivyan explorer Kristo Nalegamo, who'd discovered more than a hundred of them on the tiny Isle of Omphalos, a mysterious island where the chief occupations of the tribals appeared to be getting eaten by sharks and fashioning large, primitive statues of flat-faced, open-mouthed, coral-eyed fat women out of red volcanic rock. Fifteen of the Omphalettes, as they were called, had been gifted by Nalegamo to the University the year his son had been admitted there.

Abacus could not have cared less about the rituals the spellbinders conducted using these mystic stone figures; what bothered him was something that just didn't add up. On some mornings, he would flap his wings and croak in consternation because without warning, there would suddenly be *sixteen* statues—and someone as well versed as he in the modern theories of Logic and Dynamics considered this mystery, this imbalance in the equation, a personal insult. Because espionage demanded discretion, he could not fly up to the window and try to enter and investigate—but even from a distance, he would sometimes notice that on the days when there were sixteen statues, one of them would occasionally move its mouth as if talking to itself, and even blink sometimes. This whole set of logically inconsistent data caused Abacus sleepless nights, and it was with a depressed and beady eye that he ignored the slanting rays of the morning sun and looked through the window at the sixteenth statue, the source of all his confusion.

And it was perhaps fortunate that Abacus could not hear the conversation the statue was having with itself, and that the statue had no idea it was being watched by the cunning Cromando—because Red the shapeshifter, who liked sitting still among the ancient Omphalettes and thinking with her mouth hanging open, could, when the occasion called for it, hurl an extremely accurate fireball. And it has been (statistically) shown that dead crows, while rarely confused, are always dead.

Soma: Calm down.

Tamasha: *You* calm down. This is serious, and we must act fast. Listen to me, Red. Don't wait for him to attack the Civilian—he'll do it tonight, I'm sure. Don't complicate matters by going to the Council. Find him, fight him, *kill* him. Now. That's what I say.

Soma: That's what you *always* say, Tamasha—hunt them down, kill them, blood, gore, ooh, aah. Remember the rules. Red, you must go to the palace and inform the Council immediately. He's obviously made up his mind and is on the move—what he did to that poor girl Tiara proves that. He might even attack the Civilian during the day, so the Council needs to be told quickly—besides, there's the other matter, which directly concerns the throne. If we run around the city today looking for him, while he's in the palace killing the Civilian, it will be your fault.

Tamasha: That's what *you* always say, Soma—do nothing, tell the Council. We all know what the Council will do. The Council will do what it always does—debate for hours and decide in the end that intervention would be a risk—that intervention could mean exposure. And so the Council will decide to do nothing.

Soma: The Council will decide what's *best*. We have to be discreet, and we cannot run amok like you evidently want to. That's how the Council has stayed secret all these centuries, Red.

Tamasha: But more people will die while we sit around in the palace, waiting for the ravian to attack! Are you willing to bear that responsibility? Did you not see what he did to Tiara?

Soma: She's alive. I'm sure they'll cure her.

Tamasha: Don't be silly. That's not what I call alive. Did you see her eyes? He's destroyed her mind completely. He couldn't unlock the doors, so he just broke them when he didn't need her any more. *We* couldn't heal her, so the spellbinders don't even stand a chance. And Tiara was no weakling. This ravian must be really powerful, if he could do that to her, Red. He means to go after Maya, I know he does. And Maya's important, Red, even if Tiara wasn't. You *know* that.

Soma: It doesn't matter. We can't save everyone. In an ideal world, Red could have used her powers to make everything perfect. In this one, we obey the rules. Remember the Oath. We cannot strike first. We serve and protect the throne of Kol, not Lady Temat and her associates.

Tamasha: So we should sit around and do nothing while he kills Maya?

Soma: We don't *know* he wants to kill her.

Tamasha: We *do* know he spent these months seducing Tiara just to find out everything she knew about Maya and Kirin. He's a ravian, and Kirin's the son of Danh-Gem and Isara, so it's not likely he wants to buy Kirin chocolate. Kirin isn't here. Maya is. We have to protect her. We've followed her for *years*, Red. That forms a bond whether you like it or not. We owe her something.

Soma: We can't protect her. We risk discovery. It would endanger the Council. How many times do we have to have this argument before you finally understand that Red has to follow the rules?

Tamasha: Come on. You know rules. There's always scope for creative interpretation.

Soma: No. Not the Rainbow Council's rules. All aggressive action requires unanimous agreement. Red could be expelled. We cannot throw away the work the Seven have done over the last few Ages based on a snap judgment—especially one coming from *you*, Tamasha. And you've worked hard, Red, to get in the Council. And you've taken enough risks already—you've broken rules before and haven't been found out yet. You can't do it again. They'll get you.

Tamasha: If she hadn't broken the rules, Soma, we wouldn't have existed. We'd just be voices in her head.

'May I point out,' said Red wearily, rolling her white coral Omphalette eyes, 'that technically, you *are* actually voices in my head?'

Soma: No, dear. You named us. We're *people* inside your head now.

Tamasha: Yes. Though you could always get rid of us by attaining the supreme spiritual state you shapeshifters have been working towards all these centuries.

Soma and Tamasha (boisterous laughter): Ha ha, hee hee, etc.

Tamasha (still giggling): The point is, good things happen when Red breaks the rules.

Soma: Good for us. But not for her. Or for the Council. We're dangerous, Tamasha. We make Red a threat to the rest of the Seven. No—with the kind of powers she has, she's a threat to the whole world. Because of us, she's dangerously out of control, and a shapeshifter out of control is the same thing, essentially, as a rakshas.

Tamasha: Rubbish! Besides, you're a bloody hypocrite. You *love* it when Red breaks the rules.

Soma: What?

Tamasha (annoyingly singsong): Right. Soma is such a good girl. Soma hasn't had a string of affairs over the last few months. Soma didn't kiss a vroomer last evening. Soma doesn't even know what a vroomstick is . . .

Soma: Be quiet. That's different.

Tamasha: How, pray? The oath of eternal celibacy is one of the most important Rainbow Council rules. And you break it even more than I do.

Soma: Council members can't have identities. They can't have names. But *we* have names. We have individual needs. And we aren't members of the Council. So the rules don't apply to us.

Tamasha: Really? Then let's leave Red out of this completely. How about I go after the ravian, and you go tell the Council?

Soma: I'm just saying what the best course of action is for Red. I'm not as selfish as you.

Tamasha: You're twice as selfish as me, you little two-faced half-wit. And ten times as man-crazy, too.

Soma: Be quiet.

Tamasha: *You* be quiet.

Soma: You're mad.

Tamasha: You're boring.

Soma: Delinquent.
Tamasha: Cow.

'Will the two of you please shut up and let me think?' asked Red. 'You're driving me insane.'

Soma: But you *are* insane, Red.
Tamasha: And it's all right. We love you anyway.

Names, thought Red bitterly, that's where she'd gone wrong, that's where it had all started. How could she have been so stupid?

Everyone, from asurs to gods, knew that names were dangerous things—that there was a whole branch of magic devoted to gaining power over objects and people by learning their true names was a fairly big clue, to say the least. And though most people didn't know it, this worked both ways—sometimes names *themselves* could exert power over their subjects, by defining them, giving them identities and egos, which is why it was safest not to name anything you didn't want to identify, from feelings to monsters under your bed. But on a girlish whim, Red had gone and named the arguing voices in her head (that she was drunk was no excuse—that was *another* sacred Rainbow Council rule she had broken) and cursed herself with immortal indecisiveness, and *two* powerful, wilful and permanently quarrelling egos.

It wasn't even as if they were each other's mirror images, permanently locked in argument—they were just two different people. For example, they both liked coffee, but Tamasha liked it sweeter. On the subject of men, though, they were united—both agreed enthusiastically that having as many as possible as often as possible was the only way to go. It helped, of course, that Red could change shapes . . . her romantic life had become incredibly complicated, and somehow empty at the same time. She sometimes felt as if she were outside her own body, watching Soma and Tamasha with their lovers, who never touched *her*.

And there was no solution—they wouldn't go away, and she couldn't even tell the other shapeshifters about it, because the consequences would have been dire—names, egos and favourite faces were strictly forbidden amongst the Seven. Not without reason—it was no coincidence that nearly every powerful shapeshifter who had taken a name had turned insane and tried to take over the world. Although the shapeshifters tried to ignore it, their ancestors had been rakshases—and it was dreadfully, deliciously easy to walk back down that ancient road to chaos. Taking a name was the first step. Taking two was . . . well, silly.

I couldn't even go mad and take over the world properly, thought Red bitterly, I'd just plunge the world into permanent civil war, and lead both sides.

Soma was annoying, but she was all right. She was like a little sharp-tongued, flirtatious conscience. But Tamasha . . . Tamasha was a problem. Tamasha argued. Tamasha rebelled. Tamasha tempted. And sometimes Red listened.

She wondered whether rebellion was in her blood. Her father, Icelosis, had been Red before her—he had been amongst the mightiest of the Seven during the Age of Terror, but he had been disgraced and expelled from the Rainbow Council. Through no fault of his—he'd been seen by humans during a transformation and had had to admit he was a shapeshifter. He'd spent the rest of his life atoning for that one error, but sometimes Red thought he'd had a good life—he'd taken a name and a wife, had a daughter, and though he'd died during the last battle of the Great War, he lived forever in the annals of history as one of the Seven Heroes—as the leader of the elite warrior alliance he'd formed, in mockery and imitation of the Rainbow Council. All the other shapeshifters in Kol thought the Council had been too harsh in expelling him—and it was widely rumoured that Red had been chosen to be part of the Rainbow Council (ahead of other, older shapeshifters) to placate that ancient guilt. On the other hand, Red was so powerful that to have her running around unsupervised, taking a name and settling down in one form would have been very dangerous.

Because Red was very young, barely an adolescent compared to the rest of the Seven, she'd been on library duty ever since she joined—readjusting altered histories, keeping the Council up-to-date with modern magical techniques, writing spells and crucial information in artificially aged books the spellbinders were allowed to 'find' just when they needed to. They'd thought that would keep her out of trouble. It usually did, except that spending years in the library led to reading, and when people like Red read a lot, it usually led to trouble anyway. It was after reading a particularly strong-minded treatise on the Female Principle in Ancient Magic one evening that Red had gone to the Fragrant Underbelly, gotten wildly drunk and named the trouble-makers inside her head. And things had gone downhill from there, though she'd stuck to her duties faithfully.

The last few years had brought new challenges—confusing the spellbinders when they had been on the verge of reading Danh-Gem's Untranslatable books, aiding the search for Simoqin's Hero, letting little Amloki steal books on secret, ancient martial arts, helping Mantric find the information about the mirrors of the Seven Heroes that led him to Bolvudis in the first place, leading Mantric to Jaadur's diary, leading the Civilian's divers to Jaadur's mirror. But Red had done her job well as the hidden guardian of Enki's secrets, though she had almost broken the Council rules and intervened when vanar-lord Bali had abducted Maya.

Soma: Hello? You're not listening, Red.

'What?' asked Red.

Soma: What I said was, you're forgetting the most important thing in your distraction and Tamasha's ravings. The papers you found on Tiara. You have to show them to the Council. They change everything, don't they?

Tamasha: You can look at papers later. You'll lose the ravian's trail unless you go after him now.

'No,' said Red slowly, shaking her rocky head. 'Soma's right. And I'm a fool for even sitting here and thinking. The papers can't wait. I have to go now, I've wasted enough time already.'

Tamasha: Why?

'Because they're marriage documents. Royal marriage documents.'

Tamasha: Whose?

'The last King of Kol's. With some Hudlumm chieftain's daughter. Two centuries ago, in secret.'

Tamasha: What are you saying?

'What I'm saying,' snapped Red, 'is that we've just been handed a challenge by this ravian. And shut up, will you? This is important.'

Tamasha (pauses, but is irrepressible): Fake documents, probably. Don't bother with them.

'I don't understand,' said Red after a while. 'Ravians don't need to forge documents. What they used to do was manipulate public memory, put opinions and oral recollections into historians' heads, which is why history books always speak fondly of the ravians—at least until I get to them. Magically forging documents to attain our goals is what *we* do. The papers she has—they are genuine, there's no forger in this world who could fool *me*.

'Which means that what they say is actually true, and this ravian plot was hatched before the Departure. More than two hundred years ago, the King of Kol *did* have a secret marriage, presided over by the ravians. He *did* have a child, two in fact, brought up in secret by the ravians then, now lost. There are also conveniently mentioned heirlooms over which the marriage vows were sworn, complete with authentic drawings. And these can't be the only copies of these documents—he just put them here to mock the spellbinders, to issue a challenge. They weren't in the library before—they must have been hidden away somewhere else. I'm sure the Civilian will discover another copy soon. He broke Tiara's mind so that she could not describe him, so that the most powerful magicians in Kol would find news of their doom in the hands of one of their own.'

Tamasha: You've lost me there.

'Do you know what this means? This means that the ravians plan to produce an heir to the throne of Kol out of their hats, bearing these heirlooms, and make the people of the city declare him king. Which is also why they made that poor painter attack the Civilian the other night—killing her will only help their cause, while they make people believe in some poor fool they use as a puppet. It's not just Kirin they mean to destroy—they want Kol as well. Nothing's changed.'

Soma: Can they really make the people of Kol think whatever they want? I thought ravian mind control didn't work in Kol, because of the spellbinders and the shapeshifters and the Heart of Magic?

'It's not as simple as that. Yes, they can't control minds directly when powerful magic-users from this world are around, but they can catch their victims and take over their minds slowly, over a period of time—make small alterations that produce dramatic results when they need to. It's difficult, but a ravian powerful enough to do what this one did to Tiara would be able to do it. Besides, they wouldn't need to do it to a lot of people—they would just start rumours, create artificial romantic memories of the good old days. And they have terrible powers, Soma.'

Soma: Which means all of this directly involves the throne of Kol. And the Council.

'Yes. Which is why I cannot go after the ravian myself, Tamasha. I have to go back and let the Council know.'

Her mind finally made up, Red transformed into a first-year Potolpuri student named Peyaj she particularly loved impersonating (people leave brilliant students alone, because they're nearly always crazy), walked to the window, turned Abacus the crow into a worm with a lazy flick of her fingers and then left the room swiftly.

Within seconds she was out on the street. She ducked into an alley, transformed into a random middle-aged woman who'd just entered a nearby building, emerged, hailed a fast taxi-carpet and set off for the palace.

Tamasha: You should have named us earlier, now we have to catch up on so much.

Soma: You would have known more if you'd kept your ears open.

Tamasha: I suppose you think you know everything.

Soma: Well, I know a lot more than you.

Tamasha: Tell me, then. Have the ravians and the shapeshifters always been in conflict?

Soma: No. They liked the ravians at first, especially Simoqin, though they were always wary, obviously. The wave of sheer awe and amazement that the coming of the ravians created in Kol was useful for the Council. They created all manner of powerful magical objects—the seven mirror-portals, the Heart of Magic—and publicly gave Simoqin credit, and everyone just swallowed what they were told.

Tamasha: Then?

Soma: Well, the ravian king summoned Simoqin back to Asroye pretty quickly after that, I can tell you, because they had no idea what was going on. Then, of course, when the ravians stole the Heart of Magic back from Enki and tried to infiltrate the royal palace and the vaman cities, the Council decided they were a direct threat to the throne.

Tamasha: The ravians took the Heart of Magic?

Soma: Where have you been? Do you never listen? Yes, they unlocked the golden mesh with the spikes and stole the ruby. Of course, they didn't know—hardly anyone knows—that the ruby was just for show, it's in the grid that surrounds it that the magic lies—it's forged in underworld fires, tempered with the blood of krakens, inlaid with powerful magic field stabilization spells and so on. Anyway, the ravians went home and tried in vain to work out why the ruby was so special, and the shapeshifters just climbed the spire and put another ruby in the grid. No one outside the Council even knew. But the Council made sure the spellbinders of Enki never trusted the ravians after that.

Tamasha: So what happens now? Now that the throne is directly involved the Council will have to do something.

Soma: I don't know. They won't let the ravians anywhere near the throne. But if the papers are genuine, and there is a legitimate heir to the throne, then we have what people less ignorant than you call a conflict of interests.

Tamasha: Don't tell me any more, I can't take it. This is too complicated.

Soma: It's not. The problem is that you're stupid.

Tamasha: You're boring.

Soma: Ignoramus.

Tamasha: Cow.

'Shut it,' said Red, looking around her, at the airways of Kol dotted with flying carpets swarming like angry bees about a hive under threat.

Peace, she thought. I'm going to miss it.

'Save your breath, ladies,' she said. 'Get some rest while you can. The ravians have made their move. It's going to be a long day.'

8

Elsewhere . . .

Zivran Game-maker, god of accidental inventions, youngest son of the bountiful food goddess Nessisitii, touches his chin and looks mildly surprised as he feels his flowing beard. Did I not, he asks himself, shave?

His new seven-headed attendant spirit (just call me Sambo, it is easier that way) flutters around excitedly, bowing repeatedly at the four gods who have just appeared in Zivran's fragrant garden, earlier than expected. But then, Sambo reminds himself, the gods are never early; it is always the right time when they arrive.

The gods walk among myriad worlds, of many shapes and hues, floating suspended in Zivran's strange and wonderful garden. Some of the worlds are complete, some still merely clouds of dust and fire and ideas, worlds in waiting. Scattered around in dark corners lie dead, decayed shells of ice and debris. Ghost worlds.

Sambo has already taken care of the guests' steeds; he has taken them to a nearby Bahan Park, where they now rest happily.

He brings the gods the customary offerings; incense, divine elixirs, fruits of virtue. The gods accept these with grace and smile at Zivran as he wanders distractedly through his garden, fascinated by the interplay of light and shadows on the spinning worlds that float by him. They follow him as he meanders gently to the GameWorld, which now floats in the centre of a vast jet-black courtyard paved with stars.

'The Players will be here soon, Zivran,' says Petah-Petyi, goddess of chance, smiling charmingly. 'And yet We see no Game-board. We knew You would not be ready. And as the four of Us cannot take part in this Game, We have come to help You prepare.'

The Goddess of Chance is never a part of the Games—no one plays against her, she always wins. Sambo gazes at her in awe as she stands shimmering regally by the GameWorld, a coin in one hand, a pair of million-sided dice in the other, probability distributions and fractal curves zigzagging across her glowing multi-coloured robe.

'Thank You, thank You, old friend,' says Zivran, smiling distractedly at her. 'Are the three of You going to be the referees?'

'Yess,' hisses the Sinister King Reptile God Tsa-Ur, the snake heads above his smooth, scaly muscular torso nodding in unison. Tsa-Ur the Magnificent, Devourer of Worlds, Hood of Destiny, Wielder of the Divine Poison, has been banned for three Games for Unbecoming Conduct—he had bitten the Sacred Ibis during a points dispute in the last Game. 'Zsivran, iss it too much to exspect a place to ssit?'

'I apologize profusely, O Fang of the Apocalypse,' says Sambo hurriedly. 'The fault is mine—my master had told me to set the Table.'

'Yes,' improvises Zivran, looking gratefully at Sambo. 'Sambo, the Table, if you please.'

'Quickly,' snaps Tsa-Ur, all his heads looking menacingly at the trembling Sambo, 'before I turn you into a heap of ashhess.'

'We are here to help, Tsa-Ur, My scaly star,' reprimands Stochastos the Trickster, with his charming lopsided grin. 'Not to tread on poor Zivran's feet.' Stochastos is the other god who is never allowed to play Games; the chaos-lord is such a cunning cheat that many other gods refuse to even sit near him while a Game is in progress. It is seen, though, that goddesses who play the Game are never averse to sitting near Stochastos, and admiring his many imperfections.

It is said that the key to physical attractiveness lies in symmetry. This is said by people who have not seen Stochastos.

The little maroon bundle Stochastos is cradling in two of his arms emits a little gurgle and the mystic sound 'Dadda-oo'. The Infinite Infant, Baby of Destiny, Future Bearer of the Thunderbolt of Universal Doom, is too young to take part in this Game, but so incredibly powerful that the gods are afraid she will destroy worlds with her heaven-splitting crying if left unsupervised. Stochastos, who has displayed a certain knack for tricking the Infinite Infant into silence, has become her chief and most effective, if slightly reluctant, guardian. 'Better give Us somewhere to sit quickly, Sambo, most noble of naguals,' he says with a rather apprehensive grin. 'I think She's a little uncomfortable.'

Sambo flies forward and takes a deep breath, trying not to explode with sheer tension. He utters the Word his master has taught him, and heaves a huge sigh of relief as the Table materializes successfully.

Circling the world, shining gently above the foaming crest of the Vertical Sea, invisible to the inhabitants of the GameWorld *but spectacularly beautiful on the divine astral plane, an immeasurably massive white table arcs across Zivran's lawn. Curling tendrils of magic trail from its inner perimeter to the watery ring around the world it encircles.*

Ornate chairs of distilled darkness materialize around the table. Silvery lines curl across the backs of the chairs, tracing the names of the gods who will sit on them.

'*A csircular Table?*' *spits Tsa-Ur, forgetting to sit in his indignation.* '*What nonssensse iss thiss? Where iss the Board?*'

'*This is the Board,*' *breathes Stochastos, fascinated, peering down at the GameWorld.* '*Wonderful idea, Zivran, My bearded beauty.*'

'*But how do We tell which sside the Playerss are on?*'

Zivran clears his throat. '*There are no two fixed sides in this Game. It is . . . complicated.*'

'*Madnesss!*' *Tsa-Ur's heads hiss malevolently at Zivran.*

'*Think of it as a chess game,*' *says Zivran,* '*where all the pieces have their own colours and want to stay alive.*'

'*So We do not have to set the Board after all,*' *says Stochastos. 'All the pieces are already on it, though they do not seem to be set in any combat formation I can recognize. But without duality, Zivran, call it Good-Evil, Dark-Light, Interior-Exterior, Order-Chaos or what you will—without duality, most puissant of play-makers, how do We know who has won?*'

'*There are multiple dualities, but on individual planes. I have not worked out the scoring system as yet,*' *admits Zivran.* '*The Players will play until They know who the winner is. Or as long as the Game interests Them.*'

'*That is fine, Zivran,*' *says Petah-Petyi.* '*We can simply invent another fixed-ending performance-based system like the Good-Evil Game—where We know Good will win the battle eventually, but the Players running Evil may still win the Game if They play better to achieve the same outcome.'*

'And this way, there will be no quarrels about seating,' says Stochastos. *'I like Your Game already, My inventive illuminator.'*

'One chair has no name on it,' says Sambo suddenly.

'Probability,' says Petah-Petyi, nodding. *'A nameless chair— We shall name it the Nameless Chair—gives the Game a frame of reference. The Laws of Chance have spoken, Zivran—your Game meets the requirements. Now tell Us how it is to be played.'*

'But who will sit on this Nameless Chair, my fragrant friend?' asks Stochastos, grinning in evil glee as he foresees hierarchic disputes on a circular table.

'The Game will tell us,' says Zivran, rubbing his hands together as he looks down fondly at the GameWorld.

'In other wordss,' says Tsa-Ur, *'You do not know, Zsivran.'*

'Hush, Tsa-Ur,' says Stochastos. *'Do not spoil the Game just because You cannot play, My regal reptile. Zivran, ignore Him. Tell Us more.'*

Zivran smiles gratefully. *'Well, gods control pieces,'* he says, *'not races, not armies, but significant individual pieces, call them heroes, villains or monsters, that in their turn control armies, races, and wield great powers on this world. The Game will assign pieces to Players—thus.'*

He waves his hands, and in front of each seat three crystals appear: red, blue and green. They spin furiously in intersecting orbits and gradually blend into one another, creating first a blur of mingling colours and then slowly a crystalline image that sharpens to show, in incredible detail, the pieces on the GameWorld. Some of the crystals show rakshases, some ravians, some great sea serpents, some vamans. A few even show humans, great and powerful warriors, sorcerers and politicians.

The crystals in front of the Nameless Chair show a young man, clad in black, a red dragon-hide gauntlet on his right hand, travelling through a wide tunnel in a clay rickshaw drawn by a mighty golem. His eyes are closed; the winds of the underworld rush through his unruly black hair.

'To lounge about in comfort while putting one-eyed monsters in front of heroes just for fun——or to give opposing sides weapons and advice and watch them kill each other——or to push symbols around on a board——or to simply set up outcome paths and cast dice——these are not Games worthy of the gods,' says Zivran. 'This Game is about subtlety, and skill, about delicate control without overt choice minimization. This Game will ensure the survival and happiness of our creations. This Game, my friends, is the future.'

'Thiss Game ssoundss ass entertaining ass watching cowss grazse,' says Tsa-Ur.

'No, my dear Tsa-Ur, this Game will be bloody and violent enough to satisfy even You,' says Zivran. 'By simplifying all our previous Games, we made wars simple, quick, easy to understand. But this war——this war will be like no other war in space or time.'

'In that casse,' says Tsa-Ur, looking slightly mollified, 'I shhall sstay.'

'Has this war already begun?' asks Petah-Petyi. 'But the important pieces don't seem to be fighting.'

'Not yet. The Game will truly start when the war begins, when the Players' achievements can be defined better in terms of victory and defeat,' says Zivran. 'Which brings Me to the task We must now undertake, My friends. We must bring this world to the brink of war, and find out more about this Game and the rules it makes for itself. So that when the Players arrive, We have understood the Game better, and We know what the Happily Ever After equilibrium for this world and this Game is.'

Stochastos grins. 'And We can have some fun playing as well, in private, can We not, My delectable divinities? Knowing that We are setting about the noble task of bringing order into the Game,' he says. 'Order, focus, rules. How nice. How delightful.'

He conjures up a golden cup full of mead and drains it in a gulp. 'To the glorious GameWorld!' he says, still smiling.

Petah-Petyi looks at him sharply and he stares back innocently as he snaps his fingers under the table, distorting the movement of the spinning control crystals ever so slightly.

Stochastos has always been mildly amused by the fact that the other gods always assume he will not cheat if he does not have anything to gain by cheating.

There is one thing they do not realize.

Some cheat to win.

Stochastos cheats to be.

It was always freezing cold in the Hall of the Iron Throne, where the Dark Lord held his audiences. Always, that is, except when it was boiling hot. From the walls behind the parallel rows of tall rune-engraved onyx chairs that flanked either side of the dark enchanted hall, running from the huge, forbidding Iron Throne at one end to the giant cedar-wood doors at the other, air-raiser gargoyles constantly breathed f... or ice (depending on what sort of weather Kirin's guests were more likely to find intimidating).

Kirin sat on the Iron Throne with an expression of complete concentration on his face as an Artaxerxian general droned on about modern military tactics and drew complicated diagrams on a black pillar, which a helpful rakshas redrew in mid-air with suspended blue fire.

This lecture was another of Omar's bright ideas. Kirin had been hoping to stall war plans even further by telling the rakshases at the very last possible minute that their battle strategies were two centuries out of date, but Omar had gone and spoiled that scheme. Not that Kirin could blame him for trying—ever since the rakshases had set up court in the Dark Tower, the human leaders were desperately trying to prove their worth—to guarantee themselves a larger share of the spoils and avoid getting accidentally eaten. It was a difficult time for humans—even Omar, as he sat in the Dark Lord's hall flanked by two dour-looking jinns, knew he was no longer one of the few who would be in the Dark Lord's innermost circle—not, at least, until he succeeded his father, the Sultan, and became the official ruler of mighty Artaxerxia.

The Dark Lord's current chief concern, though, was his extremely numb posterior—he was alternately flexing his right and left cheeks to keep them from getting pins and needles in the cold. And he suspected that a lot of the assembled rakshases and human leaders were doing the same. On Kirin's right, Spikes, unmoved by the cold, watched the fiery attack formations calmly, his yellow-green eyes unwavering, occasionally nodding as the general made a good point.

As the lecture ended (to tumultuous applause, inspired at least partly by relief) attention in the Hall of the Iron Throne turned to the two soothsayers seated on Kirin's left—Duamu, the jackal-headed shabtic demon, and the Lady in the Iron Mask.

'Well, Duamu? Have you had any interesting visions lately?' asked Aciram.

'*Thank you*, Aciram. Well, it's *all* happening here, the crowds are going *wild*, and we've *just* received *updates* from our *panel* of *experts*. They have *confirmed* that seas of blood and savannahs of bone are expected in the east,' said Duamu, who was up-to-date on the latest fashions in mad prophecy delivery even if his actual predictive abilities were non-existent. 'We're not sure about the *exact* number of casualties, but a *tragedy* on this *scale* will be *unprecedented* in *history*. In a while I'll be able to tell you more details about the *lice* and the *maggots* and the *entrails*, right after a *short break*.'

Kirin grinned to himself as he saw terror written on every human face in the hall. Duamu wasn't a bad sort; always willing to talk, and a noted authority on matters like boils and brimstone. The truly mad are always good company, once you get to know them.

'We have *exclusive* reports that *pestilence* and *war* and *famine* will sweep across the world,' continued Duamu after a pregnant pause, 'and we're not *quite* sure what the skies will rain but an *inside source* told us on condition of *anonymity* that we're expecting *fish* this time.' He picked up a skull and thrust it at the Lady in the Iron Mask. 'How does that make you *feel*?'

Without waiting for a response, he looked at Aciram again, his jackal head grinning obscenely. 'Back to *you*, Aciram.'

'Thank you,' said Aciram dryly. He turned to the Lady in the Iron Mask. 'Zolaa? Do you have anything to report?'

'Nothing,' replied Zolaa, the last gorgon, her voice flat and muffled behind the beautiful iron face she wore. 'The gods play with our destinies. The true stars are veiled. My sight fails.' She folded her bronze wings behind her sadly and looked at the floor. Inside her iron mask, the snakes in her hair hissed and squirmed, and then were silent.

Kirin stared at her in fascination, as he always did when he heard her rasping, strangely hypnotic voice. Once again, he felt the sudden mad temptation to throw off Zolaa's mask and turn the entire assembly in the hall to stone.

Danh-Gem had met Zolaa centuries ago, when he had first explored the Mountains of Shadow. He had found her crying alone in a corner of a dark cavern in the roots of the mountains, surrounded by stone statues, desperate for someone to talk to but scared of the light, for light meant either more innocent victims or would-be assassins with mirrors. He heard of the horrors she had faced underground, of vamans in reflecting armour who had hunted her family through underground tunnels from Psomedea to Imokoi, who had heard of the gorgons' prophetic abilities and wanted to enslave them. In that darkness he had befriended her, sent blind asur craftsmen to her aid, and they had fashioned for her a mask of iron that completely covered her head with its death-dealing eyes and its swirling, hissing snake-hair. Yes, blindness was uncomfortable, but it had let Zolaa face the world without turning everyone she met into stone.

The new age, Zolaa had told Kirin when he'd suggested liberating her from her mask, was not a good one for gorgons anyway—the modern obsession with physical beauty meant there were far too many mirrors in the world, and she would have gone mad with anxiety trying not to turn herself into stone.

Danh-Gem, renowned for his perverted sense of humour, had appointed Zolaa his court wit—she had enjoyed making people laugh, and everyone had laughed enthusiastically—when people telling jokes also have the ability to whip off their masks and turn unresponsive listeners into statues, they *always* do well with their audiences, even if the laughter they provoke is tinged with hysteria.

But then some enterprising rakshas had come up with the idea of the Rakshas Laughing Club, where Danh-Gem could hear all the soothing belly-laughs he wanted to, and Zolaa, seeing that Danh-Gem's inner circle was laughing a little more than they wanted to, had magnanimously decided to concentrate on fortune-telling instead. It was very, very rarely that she was able to see the future, but when she did, she was almost always right.

Kirin was largely unconcerned with Zolaa's skills as a prophet. The reason he kept her by his side was that he really liked her, and was trying to match-make between her and Spikes, who was obviously not someone who could be turned into stone.

'Your sight has not failed, Zolaa,' Kirin said warmly. 'And if I had more people around me who were silent on matters they knew nothing about, my task would be much simpler. Is that not so, Spikes?'

Spikes was silent.

The festivities in the hall did not end here; a few more ambassadors from a few more small countries, the names of which Kirin had forgotten, came forward and offered tribute to the Dark Lord on his Dark Throne. As always, the size of the country was inversely proportional to the length of the speeches the ambassadors made.

The Dark Lord on his Dark Throne was hungry, and more than a little annoyed. Beside him, Spikes, looking utterly bored, which is easy to do if your face is essentially incapable of expression, was flicking his claws in and out in a desultory fashion.

After a point, Kirin gave in and unleashed his ultimate boredom-defeating weapon—he thought of Maya. Maya drinking coffee in the morning, bleary-eyed after a night's work in the library and Frags, Maya laughing deep and loud at all the wrong bits in some serious society-changing play, Maya wrestling with him enthusiastically and startlingly effectively as he threatened to read one of her old diaries, Maya snuggling up to him on the Enki terrace on a winter evening as the soft, romantic sound of drunk spellbinders, bellowing like moon-calves as they chased one another through the University's maze-hedges armed with magic paint-balls, floated up through the crisp, chilly air . . . Maya's lips in the moonlight as he set her down and fled towards the Centaur Forests . . .

Spikes cleared his throat loudly. The ambassadors were done, and were looking at the Dark Lord expectantly. Fiery eyes they'd expected—glassy eyes they hadn't.

Kirin jumped forward and smiled suitably imperiously at the ambassadors as they finally left, walking backwards, bowing and scraping.

'Are we done?' he asked Aciram, who was seated on the first seat to his right, watching him very carefully.

'Soon, kinsman, soon. But first—grave news has just arrived. There have been some rakshas deaths in Vrihataranya. Not very powerful rakshases, but powerful enough not to have died as quietly as they did,' said Aciram. 'We do not know the cause, but it seems somewhat related to the matter we spoke of a few days ago. Especially since these deaths occurred in a historically significant area.'

'We will discuss that later,' said Kirin smoothly, not wanting to bring up ravians in public until he had to. 'What else?'

'This is even further proof that they have returned, Kirin . . .'

'Is there anything else, Aciram?'

'Yes, there is. The shadowsnatchers have slain a Wu Sen monk they found crossing the mountains with the objective of assassinating you and regaining the Gauntlet of Tatsu.'

'Just one monk?'

'He was one of those monks of the Societies of Virtuous Stomachs—or some such name. The secret martial arts cults whose mystic warriors can fly, walk on water and trees, and shoot blue beams of light with their hands.'

'Right,' said Kirin. It seemed the only thing to say under the circumstances.

'I have rewarded the shadowsnatchers with gold and livestock.'

'Excellent. How did they kill this monk, incidentally?'

'They attempted to overtake and overpower him, and failed. Three shadowsnatchers felt the bite of his sword before he died. Luckily, the shadowsnatchers have dealt with his kind before. The only way to really overcome these monks is to debate with them; to persuade them that they have dishonoured their monastery in some way, which always makes them commit ritual suicide.'

'Excellent. And will there be more flying monks?'

'Almost certainly. But a full coven of shadowsnatchers has just finished training and been sent to the mountains. And in any case, once the war starts, we will have much more to worry about than one-man armies, even ones that walk on water.'

'You haven't told me about the initial response to my asur education scheme.'

Kirin, undaunted by his utter failure to make the asurs

interested in learning anything in Vrihataranya, had launched an innovative scheme for asur social reform—the Free Education scheme, where asurs imprisoned in the dungeons for various crimes could learn a skill or philosophical concept and earn their freedom by passing an examination.

Aciram cleared his throat and shuffled his feet. 'The scheme has failed, my lord. I have ordered the execution of those responsible.'

Kirin shook his head. 'Cancel the order. I will not tolerate these random executions!'

Aciram cleared his throat even louder and shuffled more vigorously.

'Too late for that, is it?' asked Kirin in a voice of steel.

'It would never have worked,' said Aciram sullenly.

'Not for you, Aciram, perhaps. You probably think I'm mad, trying to break a hierarchy where I'm at the very top. But it needs to be done. You must understand, as a people, the asurs cannot go on like this. And if . . . when, I mean, the war happens, the asurs will get slaughtered in thousands if they remain ignorant, just as they have in every war they've been involved in. But if they are organized properly and taught the value of not rushing around senselessly into the path of powerful enemies, they could be a mighty force.'

Aciram smiled. 'It is noble of you to think in such terms,' he said, 'but there is much you have not considered. Hierarchies exist for very good reasons. The asurs *need* to die in their thousands—otherwise, they would overrun the earth, breeding like maggots, and their own society would have no means of sustaining itself. And it is not as if they *mind* dying, they look forward to it. They live to fight your wars and die gloriously in them—after all, what is a Dark

Lord without fanatical brute soldiers who get butchered by hopelessly outnumbered heroes, thus balancing cosmic equations and appeasing the gods' blood-lust, thereby enabling the Dark Lord's sorcerer elite to then butcher the heroes in turn without enraging the gods?'

'What?'

'And if we are talking about asur society, Kirin, asur society is fine as it is. The asurs believe in progressive reincarnation—the quicker they die in battle, the greater their status in the next birth. Death, you might say, is a means of social climbing for asurs.'

'Stop,' said Kirin coldly. 'First, I don't believe a word of this. And even if it were true, it does not explain why my plan to educate them failed. Surely they can be shown another way of life, and at least be given the choice to adopt it?'

'Your scheme was flawed.'

'How?' The air-raising gargoyles exchanged impressed glances. They'd thought *their* tone was chilly.

'You assumed that asurs *wanted* to be freed from the dungeons, not realizing that they think of imprisonment and torture as a *reward*. You wanted asurs to spend their peaceful holidays *reading*?'

And there was really nothing Kirin could think of to say after that.

He was spared the trouble of thinking, however, because things suddenly got very distracting.

The giant doors crashed open, and Kirin watched as Kirin entered.

'Halt!' cried Aciram. 'Who are you?'

'Kirin,' said the newcomer. He smiled. All over the hall,

rakshases, who had keen noses and could smell trouble long before it occurred, sat up and looked cheerful. Finally, entertainment!

Kirin scanned the ranks of the seated rakshases quickly. But he knew who it would be even before he checked. The one he'd been worried about from the start, the one nearest his age . . .

'Cousin Nasud,' he said. 'I wasn't aware you admired me this much.' It felt odd; he had never had a conversation with his own face before, apart from in mirrors of course. He kept having the feeling that if he changed his expression, Nasud would as well.

Nervous laughter emanated from the rakshases.

'This one is trouble,' whispered Spikes beside Kirin. 'Don't let him come near.'

Nasud stepped forward, his eyes glittering, his Kirin face wreathed in a lopsided smile. He was very drunk, which only made him more dangerous.

'Rejoice, my kinsmen!' yelled Nasud, his voice echoing across the hall. 'The war is begun!'

'What?' Kirin's eyes narrowed.

'The Dark Lord just ordered an invasion of Ventelot,' smiled Nasud. 'I know we don't really want Ventelot—what would we do with it? No one wants to live there, the weather's terrible—but it will be good practice for my mighty troops.'

'I hope you're joking ,' said Kirin. He spoke softly, but everyone in the hall heard him clearly.

Nasud met Kirin's eyes with Kirin's eyes. 'No,' he said simply.

'I will not tolerate such insubordination. I think I remember forbidding you personally to order attacks in my name,' said Kirin.

'But I didn't order anything in just your name, cousin. I ordered the attack in your face.'

'And I forbade that too.'

'Really?' Nasud's teeth flashed white. They looked *just* a little more like fangs than Kirin's did. The muscles rippling in his arms were a lot bigger than any Kirin had ever had. 'In that case, I must have forgotten.'

'How *dare* you?' asked Kirin, stunned. Beside him, Spikes did his famous angry porcupine impersonation.

'How dare I?' asked Nasud, stepping forward, smiling. 'How dare I, cousin?'

Aciram stood up. 'This is just a misunderstanding,' he said reassuringly. 'Kirin, there are always minor incursions happening along the borders—we haven't invaded anything. The people of Ventelot expect raids from asurs and Skuans—it's their most popular sport, after football, and they return raids with great vigour. If anything, the asurs constantly have to defend their own—and since you came back, morale has been so high they're actually winning. Nasud, you are drunk. Sit down and be quiet.'

'This is not the time for silence, this is a time for rejoicing,' smiled Nasud. 'And this is no *raid*. Today, uncle, three thousand danavs march northwards on my command. On the Dark Lord Kirin's command. We will probably lose most of them to these new war-machines we keep hearing about—but then they are asurs. They will die laughing. And I am sure the survivors will give us valuable information for the next campaign.'

It's so much easier to be a tyrant, thought Kirin, if you have a dozen mad rakshases all issuing orders in your name. He wondered how many of Danh-Gem's atrocities his father was actually responsible for. Most, he suspected.

His father had been great and wise, but he hadn't exactly been *nice*.

Aciram spoke again, his voice filled with worry. 'What have you done, Nasud?' he asked.

'I only do what must be done, uncle,' snarled Nasud, beginning to walk faster down the hall.

'Kill him,' whispered Spikes.

No, replied Kirin without moving his lips.

'He means to kill you.'

No.

'This isn't the Underbelly any more, Kirin. Mistakes will be fatal. Kill him!'

'I don't like killing.'

'Who cares what you like?'

Nasud stopped, halfway down the hall.

'What if I said you were an imposter and I were the real Dark Lord?' he asked slowly.

The rakshases sat very still.

Do not do this, said Kirin inside Nasud's head. *Sit down, and we will forget about this.*

'You do not impress me with your cheap ventriloquism and your conjurer's tricks!' yelled Nasud, Kirin's features contorted in a mask of hatred. 'I will not be your puppet, son of Danh-Gem! I reject you and your false wisdom, and challenge you to a duel by the ancient laws!'

Aciram sat down, looking broken.

'What ancient laws?' asked Kirin.

'The kin-strife laws. Rakshases support the winner,' said Aciram briefly.

'Right.'

Nasud drew his sword, a massive sabre, jagged-edged, with a cobra drawn on the blade.

'Shall we have a shapeshifting duel?' he asked. 'But no, the Dark Lord cannot change his shape? I wonder why that is?'

'There's no need to . . .' began Aciram, but Nasud cut him off.

'You have been given respect and honour beyond measure, Kirin, son of Danh-Gem,' said Nasud. 'But your father, who was like a father to me, won his throne through strength, not guile, and not through his bloodline. And it is an insult to his memory to let his mighty army be run by a half-ravian whelp!'

'Enough,' said Kirin.

'I remember the ravian maidens fondly,' said Nasud. 'I myself have carried off quite a few, and fathered quite a few of their children. A lot of brats were spawned by nameless pretty ravians in the woods in the dark in the days of the war, Kirin. You were just one of them. The only one left alive, possibly. But that will change soon.'

'So come here and change it,' said Spikes. The Shadowknife slithered snake-like over Kirin's arm.

'For a month,' snarled Nasud. 'I have held back and taken orders from one I knew as ravian-spawn the days I clapped eyes on his craven face. It is common knowledge that the ravians have returned. They rise in secret, plotting in the shadows of the forest, seeking to topple our towers rebuilt. And we are led by a traitorous half-ravian, who will not send our forces assembled to do battle with his kin! Too long have we stayed our sword-hands. But no longer. Prepare to die!'

He raised his sword, which hissed malevolently at Kirin, and ran full-tilt towards the throne. Kirin stared at his own contorted face, transfixed.

'Get back,' said Spikes. He moved swiftly, trying to get between Kirin and the charging Nasud.

But before he could, Kirin rose, raising his hand, aiming to knock the sword from Nasud's grasp . . .

What happened next amazed everyone in the hall, but Kirin most of all.

With an ear-splitting crack, a bolt of blue lightning streamed from Kirin's outstretched finger and forked across the hall, ultimately obliterating one of the great cedar-wood doors at the other end.

Even as the door's splinters spiralled to the floor, Nasud slowed down, and changed back to his own shape. Kirin's face melted into his own fierce, red-bearded features, his arms swelled up and turned blue.

All eyes in the hall followed Nasud's as he stopped and looked slowly downwards.

At the huge, perfectly circular, sizzling hole in his chest where Kirin's lightning-bolt had passed through him.

He looked up at Kirin, amazed.

'Dark Lord,' he whispered.

And then he tumbled forward, stone dead, at Kirin's feet.

The hall erupted.

Aciram leapt forward. 'Let us end this kin-strife now!' he cried in a great voice. 'If any of you has anything to say about Kirin's lineage, or his claims to the throne of Imokoi and the world, let him speak now or forever hold his peace!'

Immediately, ant-drop silence reigned in the hall. Obviously. No one was *that* mad.

'The rakshases have spoken,' said Aciram (technically untrue, but Kirin let it pass). 'The kin-strife has ended!'

In a clatter that sounded like a dyspeptic wolverine let

loose in a kitchen, the rakshases prostrated themselves on the floor.

'All hail Dark Lord Kirin, son of Danh-Gem!' cried Aciram, raising his sword in salute. And the rakshases roared in reply.

But even as all Izakar echoed to the thunderous sounds of revelry in the great hall, and the drooling pisacs emerged from the corners to drag Nasud's charred body away, Kirin's awestruck gaze remained fixed on his finger.

It was still smoking slightly—he resisted the temptation to blow on it—and his nail had turned black. It looked just a *little* bit like a claw.

The Dark Lord spoke.

'Whoa,' he said.

9

Thog the Barbarian's mild-mannered alter-ego, Arathognan the Civilized, rolled up his carpet at the stand, paid the attendant and plunged into a storm of thrashing arms and haggling voices. The Stupendous Season Sale was on at Keynsmith Bazaar, the biggest and most boisterous market in all of Kol, and Arathognan had arrived ready to do battle—not with nefarious crime-lords, but with a species of monster far deadlier—the Koli fish vendor. Aunt Ugtha wanted fish, and when Aunt Ugtha wanted fish, she got fish, and usually Thog got a headache.

Thog was never really comfortable with the idea of strange women (and men) ogling at his underwear, so the sheer relief of walking around in discreet shirts and trousers as mild-mannered Arathognan was immense. He often wished that his transition from harassed nephew to Superb Hero could be a little more spectacular, could involve more than just taking off his clothes and tying his hair. But he wasn't influential enough in the Superb Hero pecking order to demand his own Secret Identity, one of the proper ones, that came with either an elaborate disguise, or fancy weapons, or a personality change, or at least a separate alter-ego toy. But he knew he would get there, and quite soon—his feats at the WAK, for some reason, were being bandied about all over town, as well as his supposed remarkable resemblance to the last king of Kol, who'd been killed by the rakshas Danh-Gem during the War.

He was well-known enough to get the occasional sharp sideways glance from fellow bazaar-brawlers, but the combination of his diffident demeanour and poor visibility owing to the jostling crowd in the Bazaar ensured that no comments on the lines of 'Haven't I seen you somewhere before?' came his way. He wandered undisturbed amidst the shack-shops and narrow twisting lanes of Keynsmith Bazaar towards his destination, the fish-market known as the Pungent Potolpuri Piscine Paradise.

Keynsmith Bazaar had been a slum before market forces took over. Sprawling, brilliantly located and frequented by both bargain-hunters and the extremely fashionable, it was now the most colourful, noisy and vibrant place in Kol. Thog strolled by alleys selling tourist souvenirs, furniture, books, tools, flowers, clothes, made-in-Xi'en jewellery, pets magical and non-magical, carpets and spices, and 'second-hand goods' from Lost Street, absorbing the incredible chutney of smells, sights, and sounds that made Keynsmith Bazaar every tourist's favourite place to get robbed in. He closed his eyes virtuously and walked past the more disreputable (and most crowded) alleys, where colourful and friendly women of various species called out to him, where makers of some very unusual personal household objects and vendors of mind-altering drugs plied their trade. He did pause, though, for a moment, in a shop where they sold vroomer

113

gear, where he saw an interesting ring with a skull on it. But he discovered that it was meant to be worn through a part of his body he preferred without a hole in it, so he sighed and moved on.

As he came out of the shop, he stopped abruptly and looked up, apparently engrossed in watching the carpets in the sky above Keynsmith market, circling like vultures, dipping and soaring, dragging huge promotional banners and megaphone-toting salesmen, announcing the many delights to be found at the Sale.

And then, abruptly, Thog broke into a run.

He raced through alleys he'd already passed, cannoning into people, stepping on toes, leaving in his wake a steadily swelling wave of angry yells. Through the Gastronomix, the world's greatest food court, past noodles, pastas, pickles and sushi, he sped resolutely, ignoring the seductive aromas that tugged even harder at his primal instincts than the women moments ago. Through the toy-lane he raced, miraculously avoiding stray children and squashable pets. And only when he reached the Piscine Paradise did he slow down. Which was fortunate, given that Four-Ps Alley was covered with a thin layer of scales, not exactly the best surface for athletic sports.

He looked around again, very carefully this time. Yes, he'd lost her.

He wondered, yet again, who she was and why she was stalking him around the city, smiling mysteriously. He'd try to talk to her a few times, but she'd disappeared whenever he got too close.

A lot of the Champions League had stalkers—it went with the costume. Thog had once thought he had one, too, an innocent-looking schoolgirl who'd run after him squealing madly for over a week. He had always run away, but she had hunted him down eventually, and he had discovered it had all been a big misunderstanding—she had just wanted to find out where he bought his silk underwear. But this girl—something about her was different, he'd noticed it even when he'd seen her first, at the WAK. Apart from having the kind of body that made strong-minded men fall on their knees and mew like soulful kittens, she had an incredibly *nice* face—the kind of face you wanted to talk to, that you would always trust and believe.

And there was the matter of the amulet dangling around his neck. Even though he had surprisingly clear memories of always having possessed it, some corner of his mind told him that he had *not* worn it every day, and that the girl was somehow responsible for its sudden appearance around his dominant-male neck. And ever since that day at the WAK, he'd been having very disturbing dreams—of walking on a barren plain towards a huge dark tower with a wheel of fire on his chest, of standing over the giant green corpse of a dragon in melting, sizzling snow, of leading a mighty army into battle against a charging horde of giant rakshases . . .

And he'd been dreaming of the girl. Very pleasant dreams, but not ones he could tell anyone about.

But he did not think he was going mad or anything like that; everyone had strange dreams from time to time. And it wasn't even as if any of the new dreams were stranger than the dreams he'd had before. Why, there was that one involving him and the Sadori Sisters and the talking duck . . .

He felt sudden movement behind him; someone crossing the alley. He turned swiftly, but saw no one—two fat men being attacked by large crabs looked back at him curiously. It was *her*, he thought. She always seems to *know* where I am.

He shook his head, and started haggling with the fishmongers. Haggling in Keynsmith was an art form in itself, and Thog was no artist. But the fishmongers knew him, and did not cheat him too much. Not out of kindness or affection; it was just that once, after selling Thog ridiculously expensive fish, they had met an enraged Aunt Ugtha. Ideally they would have just given Thog his fish, taken his money and moved on to safer targets; but there were traditions to be maintained in the Pungent Potolpuri Piscine Paradise, where you haggled not to gain or lose, but because it had to be done.

As Thog and the fishmongers began their dance of demand and supply, a crippled beggar dragged himself painfully on hands and knees through the mud, scales and thin streams of blood on Four-Ps Alley. People around him looked at him in surprise as he struggled towards Thog; beggars were rare in the touristy parts of Kol thanks to the vigilance of the city guards. They looked away quickly, though—the beggar's twisted, mangled right leg dragging through the mud was not a pretty sight.

'Yeg is blurry image blurry king,' wheezed the beggar at Thog, who jumped in alarm.

'Spare change, king boy?'

'Please go away,' said Thog.

The beggar laughed, pausing to cough horribly. He spat, ignoring the streams of invective flowing from the fishmongers, and dragged himself towards Thog again.

'Fancy yeg. Looks king blurry rich, yeg? Spare?' He flailed his arms wildly, trying to grab Thog's leg, and fell face first in the fish-scales on the street.

'Look, my good man, I'm not a king, and I have no idea

116

where you saw any king's picture in the first place,' said Thog, annoyed. 'Now be about your business.'

'Biz'ness blurry beggin'!' the beggar slurred, lunging towards Thog and gripping his hand.

'Hands off!' Thog leaped back. Someone called out for guards.

Then a huge collective gasp flew through Piscine Alley.

The beggar stood up. His leg straightened. He prodded it tentatively, and looked at Thog again, amazement plastered all over his face.

'You cured me!' he cried.

'I did nothing of the sort.'

'He cured me!' cried the beggar, and everyone in the alley heard. There was a sudden buzz of whispers. 'I can walk, the king cured me! It's a bloody miracle!'

'This is some kind of trick,' said Thog loudly, as passers-by stopped.

'The hands of a king are the hands of a healer and thus may the rightful king be known!' cried the beggar, hopping around on his right leg in delight. Evidently Thog had healed his grammar as well.

And other people shouted in answer.

''Ere, 'e's the splittin' himage of the hole king! Hand 'e 'eals like a king!'

'It's Thog the barbarian, rugged plain adventurer, in disguise!'

First, there was a curious ring of people. Two seconds later, there was a crowd.

'He's gorgeous!'

'The king!'

'How dare you touch me, you disgusting man!'

'Aaaargh! Ow! It wasn't me!'

'If he looks like a king, and he heals like a king, then he must *be* the king!'

The crowd parted, creating a space around Thog so everyone could gawk at him better. He felt a rush of panic, looking into their wonderstruck faces; something was wrong, they were *all* looking at him as if they knew him. Normally, nothing male *and* not bleeding ever held a Kol crowd's attention for more than ten seconds. But this crowd was swaying gently like some sort of obscure religious congregation whose rituals involved holding fish; its members looked like people on the verge of breaking into a huge choreographed dance on the lines of those Bolvudis spectaculars one of Thog's fellow heroes had told him about. They were smiling, their eyes were shining and filled with admiration and love.

'The king has returned!' yelled a female voice somewhere in the crowd, and quite a few Kolis took up the call.

'I am no king!' Thog cried, alarmed. 'There's been a mistake!'

And then he saw *her* in the crowd, she smiled, and he knew that somehow, there was no mistake . . .

'Hail King Thog! The king, the healer!' A sea of bodies closed in on Thog, clutching, patting, poking, feeling; a blind panic overcame him. Pushing and shoving, he raced out of the alley, thrusting aside those in his path with his mighty arms, forgetting completely the fish that had brought him there in the first place, but they were everywhere—they embraced him, jostled him, tore at his clothes.

Though undoubtedly in distress, Thog was no damsel; but then, the hero who arrived dramatically just in time from amidst the fawning horde was no Prince Charming either.

'Need a hand, Thog?' A low, angry growl, people

scattering; Mr Seik appeared out of nowhere, a sack full of tomatoes clasped in one hand. With rhinoceros-like grace, he barged through the throng, giant hands parting people like silken curtains.

'Save me,' said Thog. 'They've all gone mad.'

'No problem.' Seik looked at the crowd and for a moment, he looked scared; a flicker of frailty flashed across his snarling face as his hidden dentist called out to him. But it was Seik's day, not Dr Heina's. Muttering defensively about tranquillity and cosmic harmony, Seik half-dragged, half-carried Thog out of the Bazaar.

The crowed followed them for a while, but as Thog's carpet escaped their grasping hands and soared away and all they were left with was a wild-eyed giant armed with extremely dangerous-looking tomatoes, the spell broke; the crowd dispersed, to the relief of the watching city guards, who'd feared a riot.

To the undiscerning eye, Keynsmith Bazaar seemed to be back to its normal madness within seconds, life-hardened Kolis going about their daily business, buying, selling, arguing, eating. But had anyone looked deeper, they would have noticed that something was still in the air; that people were smiling a lot more than they normally did. And when they went home, they carried the memory of one ruggedly handsome face in their minds, and felt just a little bit safer in their hearts.

Evil was rising. But the King had returned. And they had seen him.

That very evening, the beggar's body was found, floating in the Asa. The asurs who fished the corpse out of the river and cremated it had never seen him before; as far as they were concerned, his right leg must always have been as bent and mangled as it was when they found him. They did notice his eyes, though, which were wild and bulging, and the strange, demented grin on his frozen face.

10

A storm was coming.

Clouds had been gathering purposefully in the sky all day, and though it was now barely evening, the night-lamps were lit outside the Civilian's palace. A strong wind was howling through Kol—people were returning home early, no one wanted to get caught in mid-air when the thunder started.

It was going to be a long night.

A solitary guard marched outside the outermost gate of the Civilian's palace, whistling a tune, watching dust-clouds chase each other around the broad, empty street.

Two hooded, black-cloaked figures walked slowly towards him, hugging their cloaks close to their bodies, hoods flapping against their faces in the wind.

'Yes?' he asked, his confidence stemming from the knowledge that they were being watched by five other guards from a sentry-post behind the gate.

'Could you take us to the Chief Civilian, please?' asked a sweet, girlish voice. Her hood fell off; the guard fell in love with an audible thud. What *a nice* face she had. The kind of face you could take home to your mother. Though she was no girl, he noticed, looking appreciatively. Oh no, this was a *woman*.

He smiled. 'Do you have an appointment?' he asked indulgently. Really, these tourists . . . He wondered if he could keep her talking till he got off duty, then he could *really* show her around town . . .

She waved a hand about in front of his face. 'Take us to your Chief Civilian,' she said again.

Suddenly, he had a novel idea. What if he did take her to see the Civilian? Would she really mind? If she saw this girl, wouldn't she realize how difficult it was to say no to her?

He shook his head. What was he thinking?

'I'm sorry, I can't do that,' he said. 'Here, where are you going?'

This was to the other black-cloaked visitor, a man, who had walked up to the huge, solid iron outer palace gates and was looking at them. A tall and, as the hood whipped back and was swiftly drawn again, very good-looking man. What was the word . . . patrician, that was it, thought the guard. He looked sort of noble. No wonder he got to go out with a girl like that. Lucky.

The man turned and smiled. 'Your gate is open,' he said, in a deep, soothing voice.

Behind the locked gates, huge bars suddenly groaned and moved of their own accord. Bolts sprang open with mighty clangs.

A little window opened in the gate and another guard's face could be seen.

'What's going on?' he said.

'How would *I* know? The noises are from your side.'

'Here, you! Get back from the gates!'

The ravian stepped back, smiling. The last bolt opened with a clash and the gates swung open.

The guards inside came out suspiciously. Two drew their swords.

'What just happened?' asked the Captain of the Gate.

The woman walked up and pointed at him.

'Take us to see your Chief Civilian. *Now,*' she commanded.

The Captain suddenly realized that he really wanted to do that very thing . . .

He shook his head. 'Don't be silly,' he growled. 'Move along, please.'

She looked at him, sadly, and his heart almost broke.

The ravians exchanged glances.

'Strong rakshas magic,' said the man. 'It protects them.'

'What a shame,' said the woman. 'They were such nice boys, too.'

The Captain smiled. She had called him a nice boy. But duty called. 'Back inside, men,' he called. 'Close the gates!'

'No,' said the woman softly, still smiling.

The Captain turned, surprised. The last thing he saw was a black-gloved hand streaking like a striking cobra towards his face.

Captain Rupaisa looked up from her book as the Dagger swung in through the window.

'You're here again?' she asked, exasperated. 'Why are you deliberately disobeying the Civilian's orders?'

The Dagger looked confused. 'But she sent for me.'

'No, she didn't.'

'Yes, she did.'

'No. She didn't.'

'This is ridiculous. I received a message commanding my immediate presence.'

'Not from the Civilian. I would have known.'

'Ask her.'

'You're not supposed to be here. You've been told why. And the Civilian has Phalanx protection as well. Your friend Roshin is with her even as we speak.'

'I did not know that my test of your defences the other night would lead to this,' said the Dagger. 'I am truly sorry.'

'You don't really think about other people very much, do you, Silver Dagger?' asked Rupaisa. 'Thanks to you and your little games, I have lost my position as the Civilian's last line of defence. What sort of bodyguard am I, prowling outside her room like a dog? But despite all your plotting, I am still here in the palace.'

Rupaisa leaned forward and met the khudran's eyes.

'And you're out, Amloki.'

'But why?'

'Just go.'

The Dagger went.

A Red Phoenix guard on his high-altitude Goshawk vroomstick flew over the beautiful green park that lay between the palace and the outer walls, cursing the wind. This was no weather for flying.

He noticed two people walking down the broad tree-paved avenue. They saw him too, and waved cheerily.

Odd, he thought, no guards with them.

He stopped in mid-air and looked at the sentry-post near the gate. One of the guards, sitting on a chair outside the post, raised an arm in greeting.

Lazy ass, thought the Red Phoenix guard. What bad

posture, too. Lucky sod, lying about in a chair all day, neglecting his duties.

He made a mental note to report the outer gate patrol to Captain Rupaisa for negligence, and waved at the visitors, who walked on.

He wondered vaguely whether he should have checked further. But they were almost at the main entrance to the palace, they were walking straight in. The palace guards could deal with them. Dangerous making altitude changes in this weather, anyway.

He flew on.

Somewhere in the labyrinth under the Civilian's palace, six members of the Rainbow Council huddled together in the dim light of a small Alocactus.

'Have the guards been summoned?' asked Yellow.

'Yes. Phalanx, Phoenix, and magic-users. The palace is well guarded,' said Orange.

'How much do the ravians know about us?' asked Red.

'They know we exist, but that is all,' said Yellow. 'We flicker on the edges of their tales, Red. But we know them. But it has been centuries since we last met. They may have powers beyond our knowledge. And they are bolder now, to attack unprovoked like this. Boldness is foolishness— remember, a moment's rashness could undo all the work the Council has done in secret down the years.'

'I've heard that before,' said Red.

The man walked calmly into the palace first. The inner gate captain and two palace guards ran up to him. 'Who are you? We didn't get word from the gate that anyone was coming,' said the captain.

The ravian cast off his cloak. He was clad all in black below it as well—on his belt were two shining daggers, and a scimitar in a scabbard.

'You've got to be . . .' said the captain, his jaw beginning to drop.

The ravian hit him. As his body arced backwards through the air, the ravian threw his daggers into the hearts of the two other guards.

The captain landed on the floor.

The ravian held out his hands and the daggers flew spinning back into his hands. As the captain rose, he threw both of them into his chest.

Four other guards, standing near a staircase, drew their swords. One grabbed a horn and prepared to blow on it.

Before he could, the woman leaped in their midst. For a frozen instant, she seemed suspended in mid-air, cloak swirling around her, a metal spear with a long blade at either end shining in her hand.

Two strokes. Four lives. She landed, cat-like.

From the top of the stairs, a horn rang out. One guard. The woman hurled her spear, which flew with deadly speed towards his heart. Before it could strike him, though, he vanished in a puff of smoke.

The ravians exchanged glances.

'Guardians,' said the man, as the spear came flying back into the woman's hand. He wiped his daggers on the fallen captain.

'To the east wing. Hurry,' she replied, casting off her cloak. A short sword hung by her slender waist.

They heard the sound of running feet. Alarm bells began to ring. The ravians ran up the stairs.

'And thus the war begins,' said Green.

'This is your first experience of active combat, young Red,' said Violet. 'The gods be with you. But remember—as we have told you before—nothing is more important than our secrecy. Do not reveal your abilities when any humans are alive in the room. The Rainbow Council's role in the history of Kol is more important than our lives.'

'I know, I know,' said Red. 'We are the shadows, their ignorance is the core of our strength. And so on.'

'But we have immense faith in you—immense faith, Red. Think of the combat posting as a reward for good work in the library.'

'I do,' said Red.

'I still think she should be given an easier duty tonight,' said Yellow. 'Remember, she is too young to teleport. It is a disadvantage.'

'We will protect her,' said Blue. 'Besides, she will have to learn either way.'

'And it is no small honour, Red, to be recorded in the annals of our secret history as a Counsellor whose first fight was against the ravians,' said Green. 'They are worthy opponents. They are strong, they are fast, they are . . .'

Smoke. Indigo materialized.

'They are here,' he said.

'How many?' asked Green.

'I saw two. Walked in through the front door calmly. There may be others.'

Green rose.

'Then let us dally no longer. For Ages untold, we have protected this palace from rakshases and ravians, from vamans and humans, and tonight, my brothers and sisters, we must do so again.

'Violet, library. There are secrets there they must not discover.' Violet bowed and left.

'Yellow, treasure chambers. The heirlooms may be a target.' Yellow vanished.

'Indigo and I shall stay near the Civilian,' said Green. 'We know the labyrinth best. Besides, these two ravians might just be trying to draw our attention. And as for you three, I can only wish you luck. Remember the Code, and keep to the Plan.' He clasped their hands, hugged them in turn, and then teleported to the Civilian's secret chamber with Indigo.

Blue, Orange and Red stood in silence for a moment.

'Battle colours,' said Blue. He transformed into a gigantic barbarian warrior, battle-axe in hand, strange blue tattoos crawling all over his body.

Orange became an old, tiny Xi'en monk in a saffron robe. His beard was long and his eyebrows were bushy and white.

And Red, after thinking for a few seconds, transformed into a leather-clad, short-skirted Psomedean warrior-woman. Her hair was bright vermilion. Orange and Blue looked appreciatively at her huge metal breastplate, with its spiral pattern of encrusted rubies.

'I-yi-yi-yi,' she said tentatively.

Tamasha: Brilliant.

Soma: Disgusting.

'Interesting pattern,' said Blue after a while, his voice shaking a little.

'Let's move,' said Orange.

Orange and Blue disappeared in a puff of smoke.

'Thanks,' said Red, and began to run.

The Hall of Mirrors was one of the most beautiful rooms in the whole palace. Gleaming gold-framed mirrors covered

either wall, and the beauty of intricate mosaic-work on the
floor was surpassed only by the power of the battle-scenes
painted on the ceiling, which were centuries old yet looked
just as fresh and powerful as they were on the day they were
painted, just after the Great War. On the ceiling, ravian heroes
battled rakshases, the kings of Kol stood over fallen dragons,
Ossus and Amrit and numerous other heroes performed
numerous other heroic feats.

The thirty-strong squad of Red Phoenix guards waited in
the Hall of Mirrors, trying to draw inspiration from the noble
bearing of their reflections in the mirror and the heroes on
the ceiling. Their arms were bristling with weapons, their chests
heaving with anticipation. Behind them were two corridors
that separated the Hall of Mirrors from the Civilian's quarters.

Screams and clashes echoed from the hall outside, which
led to the central section of the palace.

Holding the hall against an army of two seemed easy
enough. But the guards knew that this army had killed its
way right from the main entrance of the palace to the
Civilian's wing within minutes. This was not an encouraging
piece of information.

The doors flew open and the ravians ran in. A moment
of silence.

'You are under arrest,' said one of the Phoenix guards.

The ravians clenched their fists and punched the mirrored
walls.

Cracks cobwebbed through the great mirrors, huge sheets
of plain glass turning to a million splinters in an instant.

'Attack!'

Bows twanged. Swords rang.

And then the ravians raised their hands, and there was a
gale of glass.

Like leaves in a storm, like a horde of angry locusts, the glass shards flew at the guards, slashing, tearing, blinding, and ripping them to shreds. The glass-cloud flew through the room like a tidal wave; guard after guard fell screaming. Behind them came the ravians; stabbing, thrusting, slashing, methodically and efficiently terminating all life in their path, crushing the Red Phoenix guards like insects. They moved like panthers, sometimes running on the floor between the pillars on the walls, sometimes using the walls to jump, soar and somersault in a breathtaking dance of death.

Red, Orange and Blue entered the hall, behind the ravians, disguised as guards. Red gasped, and magic swelled up within her, but Blue grasped her arm.

'Wait till they have killed all the guards,' he said.

'But we can stop this!'

'We cannot risk discovery. Wait.'

'But they're dying!' screamed Red, wanting to hit him.

'They are soldiers. This is a war. Sacrifices we must make. If we save them with magic, we risk exposure.'

'But . . .'

'Be silent.'

They waited, watching the butchery with clenched fists. They did not have to wait long.

The ravian man cut off the last guard's head. The woman emerged from behind a pillar. They took off towards the next hall, glass shards falling about them like snow.

'Now!' said Orange.

A wall of fire sped across the hall towards the ravians. They saw it, stepped behind pillars, and waited until it passed them by.

Then they stepped out, and walked down the hallway

to meet the shapeshifters. Glass flew up and buzzed around them like the deadliest bees in the world.

In warrior-woman shape, rubies shining in front of her, Red felt battle-fever slowly take over. Beside her, the blue-skinned barbarian and the saffron-robed monk poised for battle.

The ravians stopped. 'Just three?' asked the man.

'Three is enough,' replied Orange. Fire raced through his veins and blossomed from his fingers.

The ravians looked at each other. They kissed.

'Good luck,' she whispered to him.

'I won't need it,' he said.

She turned, blew the shapeshifters a kiss and ran, back down the hall, over the fallen bodies towards the Civilian's chambers.

The man looked at the shapeshifters.

'This won't take long,' he said. He held out his hand and broken glass streamed down the hall.

Blue muttered a charm and the glass shards' flight wavered; the next instant a cloud of white feathers fluttered harmlessly towards the ground.

The ravian raised his eyebrows. His sword gleamed in his hand.

The air crackled.

'Come on, then,' he said.

The woman entered another many-pillared, high-ceilinged corridor, with a big closed iron door on the other side. Dark and empty. Storm-howls outside, winds whistling in through open windows. The door slammed shut behind her, and large iron bolts creaked shut. He will be fine, she thought.

There are just three of them. She walked forward into the dark hall.

Danger. She felt movement to her right.

She turned and kicked out, a perfect stabbing high kick, which would have normally knocked her assailant's head off.

But this was no normal assailant.

'Missed me,' said a voice near her waist, as the Silver Dagger's silver dagger tore into her knee. Shouting in pain, she fell to the ground, the Dagger leaped back, his fingers curling for the death-strike.

But she was a ravian, and he was not heavy; she raised her hand, and the Dagger flew through the air and hit a wall.

He spat blood and flipped up on his feet, only to duck again as his dagger grazed his ear and shuddered into the wall. She raised her arm, and his dagger flew back into her hand.

She smiled kindly at him.

'Coward,' he spat.

'Corpse,' she replied.

Outclassed at last, he thought. He looked behind him. Window. Left. Five feet.

She hurled the dagger. He caught it.

'Later,' he said, and jumped out of the window.

Ah, he thought in mid-air, forgot it was the third floor.

He groped around for his grappling hooks in his ever-reliable Necessity belt. Found one. He hooked it on a convenient statue on a convenient outcrop on the palace wall, and landed softly on the ground.

The statue then fell on his head. It broke. The statue, that is, not his head.

Really not my day, thought the Dagger, and passed out.

'Dagger's out. Second hall. Move in, move in.'

Eight Silver Phalanx assassins, dressed in Xi'en ninja black, flew into the corridor on black vroomsticks, circling pillars silent as bats.

Shuriken and poisoned darts streaked towards the ravian.

Some shuddered harmlessly into the floor. The others stopped in mid-air and flew back.

There was a scream, and a thud by a pillar.

She was beside the fallen ninja in a flash, spear-blade stabbing into his throat.

Movement, directly above her.

Her spear-shaft knocked the dart away. Pulling with her mind on the assassin above her, using his weight, she ran up the pillar as his vroomstick flew down. He died before he hit the floor.

The ravian mounted the vroomstick halfway up the pillar and deflected another volley of shuriken.

'Your sticks and stones are useless,' she said.

Six swords hissed through the air as the vroomstick-borne assassins flew towards her.

The Hall of Mirrors was, to put it mildly, a mess. Well, not so much a mess, perhaps, as non-existent. The floor was entirely gone, for a start; the mirrors had gone a while back, and the plaster on the ceiling was still falling in chunks of scantily clad heroic figures to the floor of the second-floor hall below. Some of the pillars were missing as well.

And the ravian, who had proved impossible to hit, was gone.

They'd fought with swords for a while, dancing along the walls, but he had been too quick, even quicker than Orange. He had dodged a deadly array of attack spells and illusions, destroyed the bits of the hall the shapeshifters had missed, and finally leaped spectacularly from pillars to pillar stumps across the missing floor, back to the central section of the palace.

Red had tried to follow him, but Orange had held her back.

Red, Orange and Blue sat on pillar-stumps, wondering whether the whole building was about to collapse.

'Why did he go that way?' asked Red.

'It doesn't matter. We've rested long enough. Come,' said Blue.

'He could have followed the woman, he could have gone towards the Civilian's rooms, but he ran off in the opposite direction. Why?'

Tamasha: May I point out something?

'What?' asked Red wearily.

Tamasha: Maya is in the west wing.

'We should follow him,' said Red immediately.

'No,' said Blue. 'Our duty lies in the opposite direction. In any case, he tries to escape us by seeking another route— he is tired, and the others will finish him. Besides, while we argue here, the other one could be cutting the Civilian's throat.'

He stood up and pulled Orange to his feet.

'I want to follow him,' said Red. 'There are others in the palace who need our protection.'

'Pay attention, Red,' said Blue. 'How many times do we have to explain things to you?

He began to dissolve in smoke.

'Follow us,' he said.

'Right,' said Red, after a few seconds. 'I'm sorry. I won't be any more trouble. Everything is clear to me now.'

'Hurry up.' Orange vanished too.

'Everything,' said Red, 'is clear.'

In the last long corridor leading to the Civilian's private quarters, Mantric and Rupaisa stood with five powerful spellbinders, war-mages from the army who had, like the Dagger, been mysteriously summoned to the palace. They stood listening to the muffled sounds of clashing swords, dying screams and the thud of bodies falling to earth in the hall outside the thick, iron door.

'Ravians,' said Mantric. 'They must be ravians, or rakshases, to be this good, and this arrogant. Two of them, and they storm the palace.'

A scream, and then silence.

'Where is the Civilian?' asked Mantric.

'Somewhere in the labyrinth. Roshin of the Phalanx is with her, and a few others.'

'You should go there. This is no place for you.'

Something powerful struck the door. It shook, but held.

'Defending this corridor is what I do,' said Rupaisa. 'I am Red Phoenix.'

'At least get behind a pillar or something. Whatever comes through that door . . .'

The doors caved in with a mighty crash.

'Stand aside,' said Rupaisa.

She walked to the fallen door, her long, black hair flying in the wind, and drew her sword. 'You are no mere assassin,' she called to the silence outside. 'If you enter the Civilian's chambers, you will be committing an act of war against the state of Kol. Think carefully, for . . .'

'Dive!' yelled Mantric.

She did, which is why the spear that came hurtling out of nowhere towards her heart pierced her shoulder instead. Then it spun horribly out of her and flew back to its owner; Rupaisa crumpled to the ground silently.

'Behind the pillars,' said Mantric to the other spellbinders, who were already behind anything they could find.

They waited for the ravian in the dark hallway.

She limped in slowly, warily, whirling her spear.

'Five-man Blur,' hissed Mantric.

They cast a Blur on him. Invisible, he stepped into the middle of the hall and unleashed a fusillade of green comets at the ravian.

She moved in a blur of her own. Impossibly fast, she dodged, weaved, ducked, swerved, in several positions at the same time, as the comets brushed past her and exploded spectacularly on the walls. The spellbinders watched in awe—she looked, for a second, like a ten-armed Avrantic goddess. They gasped as she bent backwards at an impossible angle; the last three comets flew over her, ripples of magically heated air spiralling outwards in their wake.

A second later, the spellbinders realized they weren't watching Mantric any more, which meant he was visible.

The ravian rolled over, knelt and punched the ground.

A ripple seemed to pass through it, and then, in a straight line from the ravian towards Mantric, the stone slabs on the floor began to fly upwards, torn apart by the ravian force-bolt.

'Pentagram,' said Mantric.

The spellbinders stepped forward, around him, and pointed outwards, crossing their arms. From their hands, streaks of white light stretched out, forming a five-pointed star with a spellbinder at each point and Mantric in the central pentagon. He knelt and put his hands on the ground.

The star glowed brilliantly, and went out. The tiles fell back into place.

The ravian turned back and pointed, and a black

vroomstick from the hall behind her flew into her hands. She hopped on it, and streaked up to the ceiling.

'Oh no,' said Mantric.

The spellbinders looked up.

Then the ceiling fell on their heads.

A monk and a barbarian appeared at the entrance to the corridor.

The ravian flew forward, and the stones from the ceiling rose up in the air, revealing six unconscious spellbinders beneath them. She lifted the stones up further, intending to smash the spellbinders. She let go.

A shower of rose petals fell on the unconscious spellbinders.

She turned her vroomstick around and smiled. 'You again,' she said, her big innocent eyes shining. 'How nice to see you.'

'We killed your friend,' said Orange. 'Prepare to die.'

'You lie! It is beyond your puny tricks to kill him,' she said. 'Or me!'

Orange and Blue weaved magical threads through the air and a shining fiery net shimmered into being between them.

'We smell your fear,' said Blue. 'It is over.'

They cast the net into the air and teleported to the other end of the corridor, barring the door that led to the Civilian's bedroom.

She flew upwards, into the hall on the floor above, and out of a window into the raging thunderstorm. The net reached the wall and vanished.

'It is not over,' sighed Orange.

'To the labyrinth.'

They disappeared.

11

The Civilian's palace, west wing, Turtlemonth 15th, 8 p.m., maybe?

Magic 85/100. Camels I could eat now: 3

Hungry again. And handwriting's really bad, as am on bed on stomach and movements are restricted by man draped on side. Said man is also snoring gently. But these trivial considerations apart, everything is perfect. Alone in my room with Asvin. Limbs aching pleasantly. Dark—only strong light sources are dim bedside Alocactus and huge silly grin plastered on my face that refuses to go away. Even the knight with the werewolf head is not as ugly as he usually is. Werewolf smiling encouragingly. Quiet, stars shining gently through window. Would have put in nightingales or something, but it's too much effort.

All this, well, the lovely atmosphere of calm anyway, is thanks to me—local ambience illusion, about level three, that I've invented all by my very own self. Will have to name it—in my head, I call it the Cocoon-o-Lurve, but I don't see that name working too well in lecture halls. The point is, because of the spell I've cast on this room, no sound or sight can disturb us unless I choose to let it. Elephants in red skirts could be limbo dancing outside the door and we wouldn't even know. It's weak magically, spells can pierce it but hey, I'm not using it in a fight, am I? It has definite violence potential though—but now is not the time to think about all that. Good thing I used it—it was looking like really bad weather when we got back this evening, and the sound of sinister winds howling outside the window is not conducive to romance. And I wanted Asvin all to myself for once, with no distractions. It's been such a long time since we had any time together.

Well, maybe not, considering we spent the whole day together, but you know what I mean. The Cocoon is making me all girly. I sound like Tiara talking about the new one—forgotten his name. They were supposed to meet us at the Bazaar today, but she forgot, the silly thing.

The Hero Sleeps On. Looks completely exhausted. I wonder now, what's he been doing that's so tiring? She asked the question innocently.

I'm happy.

What nice hands Asvin has. I wish he could take that silly armour off, though, it's very distracting. It makes him look like some kind of giant toy—which is nice sometimes, but only sometimes. And I shouldn't be complaining about the armour, it's saved his !ife more than once. If only it could save him from glamorous princesses and heroic duties.

But it's good to escape your heroic duties once in a while, as I'm sure he'll agree after this. He seemed most enthusiastic, anyway.

I wonder when the next dramatic thing will happen to us. It's been a month now we've been sitting around, and all this training has left Asvin hungry for action. Me, I'm quite happy pottering around libraries and occasionally flying down to Frags, but I suppose it takes all sorts to make a world. I mean, all this talk about the world spinning out of control and lands changing is all very well, but there's not much we can do about it on a local scale, is there?

I'm strongly tempted to just stay in this cocoon all night. In a bit, I'll wake Asvin and ask him what he thinks about it.

Wait a minute. The door is shaking, someone must be banging on it. Wonder how long they've been knocking, could have been ages, wouldn't have heard them.

Don't want to open it. Want to stay here like this.

Ah well.

Maya shut her diary with a snap and removed the Cocoon spell. Noise, lots of it, assaulted her ears. She blinked, adjusting, separating sounds. Someone was banging on the door.

Asvin sat up, suddenly wide awake. 'What's that terrible noise?' he asked.

'Storm. Put some clothes on,' she said, following her own advice.

'Who is it?' she called.

'Miss Maya?' It was Shubro, the very discreet Red Phoenix guard who patrolled the corridor outside. 'Are you all right?'

'Yes, how are you?'

'Is Prince Asvin there with you?'

'Technically, no.'

'Good. I've been knocking for a long time now. May I come in?'

'Give me a minute,' she said, watching in amusement as Asvin tried to put his trousers on over his head.

Through the howling wind outside, Maya heard what sounded like a series of huge explosions.

'Is something wrong? What's that noise?' she called.

'The palace is under attack.'

'What?'

'Didn't you hear all the explosions?'

Not likely, thought Maya guiltily, I'm a very good spellbinder.

'Who's attacking the palace?'

'Two unidentified sorcerers are storming the east wing. We're on full alert. Miss Maya, if you could come out, we've been instructed to shift you and the Hero to a more secure location.'

'What's the matter?' asked a fully clad Asvin.

'Invasion,' said Maya. She was about to open the door, but then stopped and looked at her hand.

Whump. Little blue fireball, a girl's best friend. She smiled. She opened the door and blew the fireball out.

Shubro stood outside, with four other Red Phoenix guards, all looking very annoyed. Trying to look nonchalant, Maya and Asvin stepped out into the corridor. All the lamps had blown out long ago in the wind; the only light in the corridor came from Alocacti in two guards' hands. Maya looked down; one guard was running across the enclosed courtyard six floors down, a white dot of light moving in a straight line. There were guards on vroomsticks zooming around in the sky——lit flares, like giant fireflies, leaving vapour-trails behind them.

The guards who'd come with Shubro were carrying vroomsticks. One unrolled a carpet. 'Flying in this weather?' asked Asvin.

'It's the fastest way down, save falling,' said Shubro. 'And we're on patrol duty after we escort you to the labyrinth.'

'So where's the battle? East wing?' asked Maya.

'Yes. They walked in through the main gate and up the stairs, killing everyone they met,' said Shubro. 'We think it's a diversion, and the main attack will come from elsewhere. On the carpet, please. We must hurry.'

'You can leave,' said Asvin as he and Maya sat on the carpet. 'We'll be fine. Besides, we're going to the east wing.'

'Sorry, sir, but you're not. The Civilian is safe, and this is a battle for guards, not heroes. These are the Civilian's direct orders.'

'Very well. Though flying in this weather is insane,' said Maya.

'At least it's not raining,' said Asvin.

An instant later, torrents of rain hammered the city. Asvin was very well-endowed, aura-wise.

'Thanks,' said Maya.

The Kaos butterfly fluttered gently out of her room and sat on Asvin's shoulder, flapping its wings.

The guards swore softly in amazement as suddenly, there was no rain or wind in the courtyard, though the storm thundered on everywhere else.

'Let's go,' said Asvin.

The carpet and the vroomsticks rose, flew out to the middle of the courtyard, and began their descent. Sixth floor, fifth floor . . .

A hissing sound, two groans; the two guards carrying Alocacti fell off their vroomsticks.

'Move!' roared Shubro. They hurtled downwards. A flash of lightning. Maya saw, below them, a black-clad figure standing on the railings of the third-floor balcony. Daggers glittered as they flew down into his hands. She gasped, and launched two fireballs at him as the carpet passed the fourth floor. He jumped off the railing even as they left her.

For an instant, he seemed to hover in mid-air as an empty vroomstick flew towards his outstretched hand. He let go of the daggers, landed on the vroomstick, and snatched the daggers out of the air.

They were level with him now. Maya's fireballs exploded loudly above them, bathing them in a flash of blue light.

They all flew downwards in silence for a second.

Asvin grabbed the corners of the carpet; it stopped with a huge lurch.

The guards and their assailant sped downwards.

Maya sent a fireball crashing behind them into the second-floor balcony. In its light, they saw the black-clad man move closer to the three guards; he raised his arm, and their vroomsticks snapped in half. The guards landed on the ground with sickening thuds; their necks broke.

The carpet sped upwards. Maya lay on the edge and looked down. Another flash of lightning. He was following them, clinging to his vertical vroomstick. Another fireball; he dodged it with ease. Maya looked around in amazement; the fireball hadn't been hers. She looked up. Another fireball. Above her, another figure on a vroomstick, hurtling downwards towards the black-clad man. She felt the heat of the fireball as it sped by her. And missed its target below them.

He raised his arm, and their carpet bucked crazily. They held on somehow, but the carpet slowed down; the next instant, he was beside them.

A dagger flew into Asvin's chest. Maya screamed as Asvin fell off the carpet.

The black-clad man jumped onto the carpet beside her; his vroomstick spiralled off crazily. Before she could even think of anything, he jabbed her in the side of the neck with a long finger.

As the carpet sped upwards, Maya's world blurred, she dimly saw a woman on a vroomstick crossing them in mid-air, hair streaming upwards behind her as she hurtled downwards like a Dragonjuiced stone. Fire fizzled in Maya's fingers, then went out. She looked at her black-clad captor.

Abducted again, she thought. Why *me?*

As her eyes closed and the roar of the thunderstorm faded to silence in her ears, the last thing she saw was his smile.

His very *nice* smile.

It seemed to Asvin, as he watched the ground rising up towards him, that he had all the time in the world, that he was floating, that the wind in his face was some kind of cosmic joke. He plucked the dagger out of his armour and released it, watching it fall beside him.

He wondered if there was any way he could fall on his chest. The wind rushing up against his face seemed almost gentle.

He wondered if there was anything he could have done back there. The decision to stop the carpet had been quite a good one, he thought. One good idea. Not as bad as having none at all.

Even in the dark he could see the broken bodies of the guards below him.

And thus falls the Hero of the Simoqin Prophecies, he thought. Falls. Ha ha.

Goodbye Maya. Hello earth.

He shut his eyes.

Someone grabbed his arm. A sickening jolt; he groaned as his shoulder almost broke. His eyes snapped open. Now someone was beside him in mid-air, then beneath him; the world spun around, ground and sky blurred crazily as they both spun in mid-air for a while and stopped inches above the ground.

Somehow, incredibly, he was on a vroomstick, sitting in the lap of his rescuer. And a very beautiful rescuer she was, too.

'Rukmini?' he gasped.

'Get off me,' she said.

He jumped off lightly and stood on the ground. Everything around him was spinning.

'Well, come on,' she said impatiently. 'Are we going to follow them or not? Get on a vroomstick.' She pointed.

'They're broken.'

'Well, get on behind me, then, and hold tight.'

He sat on her vroomstick and they zoomed upwards; he clasped her close, his shoulder throbbing insanely.

They flew above the palace into the stinging rain and looked around desperately for the carpet.

'We'll never find them!' yelled Asvin.

'They're over there!' she yelled back, and they sped off in pursuit.

As the wind buffeted their bodies, Asvin was suddenly aware that he was pressed up against a very beautiful woman. Her hair smelled sweet; her waist was firm and slender; it helped that they were both completely drenched . . . he'd dreamed of Rukmini sometimes . . . she seemed to lean back into him . . .

What was he doing? They were trying to save Maya! Stricken with guilt, he let go of Rukmini's waist.

And fell off the vroomstick again.

Really, he thought, I'm quite useless.

She turned, raced downwards and caught him again. 'Do you want to catch them or not?' she screamed.

'Where are they? How can you see them??'

'The palace guards are following them; I can see their flares! Look!'

'Let's go. And thank you for saving my life, Rukmini.'

'What?'

'Let's go!'

They raced through the empty air-ways of Kol, through stinging sheets of rain, watching the flares ahead of them fall one by one as the ravian disposed of his pursuers. Finally there were no more flares—they were too far behind the carpet to do anything but follow, just managing to keep their quarry in their sights, flickering through the webbed beams of light shining from the towers around them. They zigzagged crazily through the bridges and towers of the Big Mango behind Maya and her captor, fighting the thunderstorm, lightning splitting the skies above them.

Carpet and vroomstick vanished into the howling night.

12

'**Y**ou know, Spikes,' drawled Kirin, looking at the mug full of bubbling blue liquid in front of him, 'if I drink about two more of these truly excellent—what are they called again?'

'Squidrivers.'

'—these truly excellent Squidrivers, I'll be drunk enough to convince myself I'm back in the Underbelly. And this isn't even the strongest drink he has. He has something called the Magmus, which he said would guarantee insanity for at least a week. Should I try one?'

'No. I wonder what he puts in them,' said Spikes, eyeing Kirin's drink with deep suspicion.

'Now that,' said Kirin, 'I most definitely do *not* want to know.'

He was sitting, hooded and cloaked, in a corner of a large underground tavern called the Pits, in the smoking belly of Izakar. Spikes stood in the shadows behind him, silent and menacing, calmly eyeing the other patrons of the Pits, mostly rakshases trying hard to get roaring drunk and pretend they didn't know perfectly well that the Dark Lord was in their midst.

Kirin surveyed the pounding, jostling, steaming chaos around him and thought that in many ways, the Pits made even Frags look tame. In the flickering red light cast by torches along the walls, rakshasis and Artaxerxian dancers cavorted seductively around sinister-looking totem poles, their spectacular bodies swaying, grinding and thrusting to the music of raucous cheers, howls and the raw, pounding drumbeats of the world-famous all-asur band, the Sluggs. Kirin's table (not too near the band) looked like an overturned rack— the Pits was, until recently, a well-equipped torture chamber. Now various intricate torture devices were put to productive use as furniture—for example, an Iron Maiden stood open by a wall, its death-dealing spikes serving as skewers for a mouth-watering array of kababs. Looking around, Kirin saw various oddly shaped metal blocks, sometimes with attached spikes, bars, chains and wheels, being used as tables, chairs, dance platforms or revolving spits for roasting animals. Asurs with trays that looked suspiciously like detached Chariot-of-Pain wheels scurried around, distributing drinks and food, collecting money, kicks and insults, adding their salty stench to the heady mixture of smells in the air—roasting herbs, spices, strange perfumes and the united odours of strange beings from around the world.

Conducting this orchestra of alcohol-fuelled revelry was the oddest creature Kirin had ever seen—Tentatron the bartender-cook, an amphibious monster from the Tydlez Sea who looked like the love-child of a giant squid and a really messy road accident. Tentatron stood in the centre of the dungeon, surrounded by cases, grills, kegs and ovens, singing a strange sonorous ocean song as his dozens of long tentacles cooked, poured, sliced, collected coins and occasionally arced over the bar in a giant sweep, multitudes of full glasses and mugs attached to the suckers. Wet, squelching noises punctuated the roar of hoarse rakshas voices raised in song, as Tentatron's customers detached their orders from his tentacles and swigged a bewildering variety of strange ocean-themed drinks, sometimes complete with colourful little floating sea animals.

Kirin drained another Squidriver and his head spun. As his eyes blurred and flickering phantoms of firelight began to dance across the room, the throbbing, clashing sounds of the Pits fused into one low, dull hum, and suddenly he was back in the Fragrant Underbelly, suddenly everything seemed to fade and melt and become familiar. The Battered Monsters Support Group swapping hero horror tales and comparing scars in one corner of the Pits transformed into Teetotallers Anonymous; the trembling group of lost exotic-budget-holiday tourists from Ventelot complaining querulously about the filthy, barbaric ways of foreigners looked remarkably like the men named Abhishek; the Psomedean conjoined twins named Mutunus and Tutunus loudly telling a group of giggling rakshasis that they'd thought they'd been invited to an orgy seemed to blend into Houstarr, the World's Worst Lover . . .

And the beautiful woman smiling brightly as she walked across the room towards him, turning heads effortlessly, was Maya . . .

'Hello, Kirin,' said Akimis the rakshasi smokily, slithering on to his lap, pushing his head back and kissing him long and deep.

He detached her politely after a while, his head spinning from the sudden, strong scent of jasmine.

'Should we wander away from this den and find ourselves a quiet place to talk?' she purred.

'No, thank you,' said Kirin. 'I've got a few things to think about.'

She got off his lap and sat on a stool beside him. 'You have much on your mind, Dark Lord,' she said. 'I could ease your worries—with counsel, if nothing else.'

And suddenly Aciram was there too, looking stern and worried. 'Off with you, young Akimis,' he said. 'Do not trouble the Dark Lord as he enjoys a moment's peace.'

'Peace, Aciram?' smiled Kirin. 'Here?'

'You don't have to worry about me, Aciram,' said Akimis. 'We both want Kirin's ear, you and I, but for very different reasons, I suspect.'

'Run along, child,' said Aciram. 'We have weighty matters to discuss.'

'Very well,' she replied, rising and shooting another smouldering look at Kirin. 'We will continue our conversation on matters less weighty some other time, my lord?' Without waiting for a reply, she headed off towards a group of rakshasis dancing in a ring around the Sluggs. The asur musicians were looking more than a little nervous.

'What is this weighty matter, Aciram?' asked Kirin.

'Military strategy, Kirin. Not the best subject to hold a pretty young rakshasi's interest, is it?' said Aciram.

Kirin nodded, wondering why Aciram would choose to discuss the war with him when he knew he was drunk. Under the table, his fingers moved slowly in the series of mudras that Maya had taught him, the instant-sobriety spell that she used to win Dragonjuice-drinking contests.

'Your orders have been carried out, Kirin. The asur army that had set out for Ventelot has been recalled, and Nasud's followers have been found and executed,' said Aciram. 'You laugh. Is it because the news is good, or did I amuse you unintentionally?'

'No, no,' said Kirin. 'I'm just glad to hear my orders are followed once in a while.'

But that was not the reason he was smiling. Whether it was Maya's spell, some brain-improving fish in his Squidriver or just coincidence, the sudden magical clearing of his clogged brain had just given him the first bright idea he'd had in weeks . . .

'What I wanted to tell you,' said Aciram, 'was that while the rakshases have sworn fresh oaths of allegiance to you today, I believe it would be wise to give them a further show of power—military power, ideally—to make them submit completely to your leadership. The world must know the glory of the rakshases reborn.'

'Tell me, Aciram,' said Kirin, 'can the rakshases ever really trust me, since it is common knowledge now that I am half ravian?'

'They do not know the tale of Narak and Isara; I am the only one who does. So they do not realize how powerful you might be among the ravians. And they know that the ravians will not offer you anything that compares with the power and glory you will attain by leading the rakshases into battle. Know this, my lord; when the ravians attack, they will either seek to kill you, to remove you completely as a threat, or to lure you with false promises into betraying the rakshases. But your father's tale has taught you one thing—the ravians cannot be trusted. They will never let anyone of rakshas blood hold a position of power. This the rakshases know, and so we do not see your ravian blood as a threat.'

'In that case, the rakshases will not lose faith in me if I

say that our war plans are flawed, and that the answers lie in peace with Kol and the vamans.'

'The rakshases have spent two hundred years trapped between worlds, between times, and they are hungry. We are the lords of the earth, and the humans must acknowledge it. We care not for land or thrones or wars. What we do care about, Kirin, is pride: pride and honour. We are the greatest of all beings that walk this earth, and the earth must *know* it. We could have broken each and every human empire down the Ages, before the ravians came, but we did not— what mattered to us was that the humans *knew* we could, and they respected and feared us. Yet when the ravians came with their sweet words and false promises, we lost our place and our honour. It is on the ravians we must be avenged. The vamans are the asurs' enemies, not the rakshases'. As for the humans of Kol, they were enemies in the last war, but much has changed since then in that city, and if the Dark Lord says peace, his kinsmen say peace as well. We have spilled more blood than we have shed, and we have never cared for accounts. We care not for humans; they are not adversaries; they are followers, or they are prey. But you must be seen to act promptly and force where the ravians are concerned, for they are the source of our suffering, our humiliation. The ravians must be destroyed.'

'Why did Nasud order an attack on Ventelot, then, if mortals are unimportant?'

'It was not war he wanted. All he wanted to do was challenge you to a duel. And his actions were not entirely without reason. The armies of Ventelot are marching southwards towards us even as the asurs march back home.'

'Are we already at war, then?'

'We are not sure. The heralds of Ventelot came to Izakar a few days ago, but their message did not reach you.'

'Why not?'

'Our sentries at the gates did not recognize their insignia or understand their accents, so they ate them. We have sent messages back to Ventelot, asking them to send their heralds again.'

'This must not happen again.'

'It will not. Everyone involved has been executed.'

'Try and leave some people alive in case we have to defend Imokoi.'

The grizzled rakshas looked confused. 'Are you saying I have failed you, kinsman?'

'No. You have always given me wise counsel, Aciram,' said Kirin. 'And now I want you to listen very carefully to what I have to say.

'What you told me about the ravians having returned— it worries me. Even as we strut around, displaying our towers and our armies for the world to see, they might be lurking in the shadows, plotting our downfall, taking over the minds of our troops. I do not know how much you have learned from old defeats; I have read many books on the subject, and know what we must now do.

'I want you to sit in council with the mortal leaders and tell them to return to their native lands with rakshases, and weed out the ravian spies among their ranks. For if the ravians have returned, it is through the mortals that they will seek to destroy our forces. I will not have my armies controlled by my enemies.'

'But this will mean abandoning our current war plans and disbanding our troops,' said Aciram, looking very confused.

'If our armies are corrupted, our plans will lead us into defeat and despair,' said Kirin. 'But there is hope yet. Send the mortals home, and tell them to take as long as they need—the war can wait awhile, but we must be absolutely sure there are no ravians hidden amongst the humans. The greatest danger always comes from those closest to you, Aciram. Surely you cannot deny the force of my arguments.'

Aciram thought for a while, head bowed. 'You are wise, Dark Lord,' he said. 'Wise beyond even my understanding, and I have walked the earth for many Ages. We had simply not thought of this before—perhaps because we rakshases do not worry overmuch over the mortals who form our rank and file. I will tell the mortals what you say. But I warn you, they will not take it well, for they have short lives, and no patience; even now they fret and fume, seeking to use our power to achieve their petty desires. Two hundred years ago Danh-Gem's fury drove him blind—in his shadow the mortals made merry, and they seek to do so again now. They will be most distressed to see they cannot—that the mind driving the rakshases now is steel-cold, not fiery.'

'Times have changed, Aciram. The world has changed.'

'We know. It is not the world we left, and perhaps peace with the humans of Kol is the answer. Defeat has taught us wisdom, and patience. But know this, Kirin—you do not seek war, but you will not be able to avoid it. For when the ravians fall upon us—and they will—then the rakshases will remember their battle-fury, their ancient grudges, and then there can be no peace on this world. The ravians cannot be forgiven. Blood debts must be repaid in blood.'

'Be that as it may, we must ensure that ravians are not already in our midst. And if they were powerful enough to defeat rakshases and dragons combined before, perhaps we should be looking for new allies.'

'You will make a great military leader when the time comes, Kirin.'

'Thank you. Could you do this quickly, Aciram, before some other mad rakshas sends thousands of asurs off on some errand somewhere and forgets to tell me about it?'

'I will make arrangements at once,' said Aciram, and vanished.

Elsewhere in the Pits, a brawl had broken out. Two rakshases squared up for a duel by transmogrification. One turned into a lion, another into a goat, and then the goat leaned forward and bit off the lion's head. A second later, the winning rakshas was back on his feet, buying drinks for cheering onlookers who had been baying for his blood moments ago, and scavenger pisacs giggled in glee over the fallen body on the floor.

But Kirin was oblivious to the pandemonium around him; he was grinning broadly.

Spikes stepped out of the shadows and sat next to him.

'Did I just push back the war?' asked Kirin.

'Possibly,' said Spikes. 'In any case, this will at least stop you from whining about how little you've achieved.'

'It was a good plan, wasn't it? It just came to me, suddenly.'

'Yes.'

'Now the question is, how long can I hold them back with this?'

'Until you think of something else.'

'And the great thing, of course, is that the ravians might not actually have returned at all. So if we can keep thinking up ways to pretend that they have, we can push the war back indefinitely.'

'I doubt you'll be able to stop the war completely,' said Spikes, 'but this was a good start.'

Kirin.

Kirin looked at Spikes. 'Yes?'

'What?' asked Spikes.

'That wasn't you, was it?' Kirin asked Spikes.

'What wasn't me?'

Me, said the voice in Kirin's head, sounding mildly amused.

Kirin banged his head on the table. 'Thought I was sober,' he said. 'Spikes, I did just push back the war, didn't I?'

'Yes.'

Kirin grasped his head in his hands. 'My head hurts,' he said.

Kirin, listen closely. I am in grave peril, my hiding place is most unsuitable and I do not have much time.

'Spikes,' said Kirin wearily, 'what do I have in my hands?'

'Your head.'

'Is this a head, Spikes, or a public toilet?'

'A head.'

'Well, there's someone messing about inside it.'

Kirin, listen to me, said the voice in Kirin's head. *Listen closely, for the fate of the world is in your hands.*

'Go away,' said Kirin sternly. 'Come and talk to me in person, whoever you are. I've learned the hard way not to trust voices in my head.'

I cannot come to you, though I am agonizingly near. To come closer would be suicide. The rakshases that surround you would slay me.

'Well, go away, then. Spikes, I realize now why you get so annoyed when I talk to you inside your head.'

'Good,' said Spikes.

Do not jest with me! The voice sounded angry now. *I have travelled across worlds to save your life!*

'Kind of you.' Kirin sighed. He shook his head. 'All right then,' he said, 'who are you?'

Ask yourself that.

'You know, you voices in my head—dragons, dreams, rakshases pretending to be my father, whoever else—you all tell me you're in such a hurry, and then you waste my time being pointlessly mysterious. If I'm supposed to recognize you, I don't. So just tell me who you are, or go away.' Kirin raised a finger, and an asur scampered off to get him another drink.

I am a ravian, continued the voice in his head, *and not just any ravian. I am Behrim, friend and brother-in-arms of Narak the Demon-hunter, cousin of his wife, Princess Isara of the royal house of the ravians. And you should remember me well, Kirin, for it was I who taught you how to fight, centuries ago, under the green leaves of Vrihataranya.*

'I suppose this is not Aciram trying to be funny,' said Kirin.

No. I understand that you are in a position where it is perilous to trust, but you have to listen to me.

'Supposing I believe you are who you say you are,' said Kirin. 'What do you want?'

I had been sent here to assassinate the Dark Lord.

'I thought you'd travelled across worlds to save my life.'

Yes.

'Well, take some time, make up your mind, and let me know.'

I do not jest. I came here to assassinate the son of Danh-Gem, the Dark Lord of Imokoi. Or rather, to supervise his assassination. But a while ago I laid eyes on you, Kirin, and I remembered you—how could I forget? I do not know how you came to be where you are, how the son of Narak and Isara tricked his way to the throne of the rakshases, but I do know this—you must come away with me. The fate of this world, and, more importantly, the fate of the ravians hangs on this. Leave this place, and escape with me.

'So that you can assassinate me more easily?' Kirin inquired.

No. So that I can help you become what you were born to become.

'Dead?'

No. Lord of the ravians. Lord of this world. Leader of the glorious republic of the ravians on the world of Obiyalis, saviour of the ravian race from the terrible darkness that threatens it from within and without. This is your destiny, Kirin, and I am the only one who can help you achieve it.

I know this is difficult to understand—I will try to explain quickly, as I realize it is foolish to expect you to obey my instructions based on the scraps that I have given you.

'Kind of you to see that.'

Three of us came to this world, to make it better, to pave the way for the return of the ravians. One sought to aid the return of the rightful king of Kol. One went to Asroye, to prepare the city for its rightful dwellers, and to seek out Kirin, son of Narak and Isara, who was mysteriously left behind in the Great Departure. And I came to darkest Imokoi, to slay the Dark Lord returned. For it is these three tasks that the ravians have returned to perform, these three burning questions whose answers will decide the future of the ravians, and the future of all Obiyalis.

'Of all who?'

Obiyalis. We now call this world Obiyalis.

'Right. Go on,' said Kirin.

I cannot linger here. I risk discovery. Meet me in the woods east of the Tower, tomorrow night, midnight. I must go now.

'No,' said Kirin. 'Tell me now. First, how were you planning to assassinate me?'

I have altered the mind of the bartender over the last few weeks. If you say the word money *anywhere near him, he will rip your head off.*

'Thanks for the tip. Now, listen to me closely.'

Yes.

'I don't believe a word you say. However, there is one question I really want to know the answer to. If you tell me the truth, I will do as you say.'

Ask.

'Is my mother alive? Where is she?'

Your mother, who was also my cousin, is believed to be dead. She did not leave Obiyalis with us. We searched far and wide for her amidst the scavengers on the plains of Imokoi, but could not find her, or rumours of where she might be found.

Kirin took a deep breath. 'Very well,' he said. 'Against my better judgement, I will meet you in the woods tomorrow night. At midnight. And I've forgotten your name.'

Behrim. Kirin, one more thing—

The voice stopped, abruptly. And then there was a scream outside the Pits, in the dark corridors leading to the lower dungeons. A rakshasi screaming.

She was screaming 'I smell RAVIAN!'

One moment, the revels continued unabated in the Pits; the next, the rakshases were running full-tilt at the door, changing into hideous battle-shapes. 'To war!' some cried in terrible voices.

'Akimis!' called Kirin.

'Yes, my lord?' she stood in front of him, hands on hips, fangs glittering in the firelight in a wicked smile. 'Are you not coming? By the light of the moon we shall hunt ravians across the dwimmer-fields of Imokoi. Will you not lead our hunt, son of Danh-Gem?'

'No, but I have a task for you,' said Kirin. 'Catch up with the hunters. Tell them I want this ravian brought to me alive. Alive. Unharmed. Go now.'

'Why?' she said, pouting.

'Just go.'

'I hear and obey,' and she was gone in a puff of smoke.

Kirin looked at Spikes, who looked back at him expressionlessly.

'Now what?' said Kirin.

'You were talking to yourself,' said Spikes. 'Sign of madness.'

Kirin swiftly told Spikes everything Behrim had said. Spikes thought for a while, vertical eyelids blinking in concentration.

'Assuming you are not mad,' he said, 'we still have no idea who is telling the truth.'

'I know,' said Kirin.

'But it means the ravians are back. And everyone seems to want you to rule the world, and you are in grave danger one way or another.'

'I used to be able to sense danger before,' said Kirin. 'Now everyone around me is so dangerous that my head is always buzzing.'

'What you do not want,' said Spikes, 'is an army of Koli spellbinders and vamans and ravians arriving at our doorstep.

Especially now that you, with your usual brilliance, have just ordered your troops to disband.'

'Which means I need to go to Kol, speak to Maya and the Civilian and actually make peace with Kol and the vamans on my own,' said Kirin.

'Yes. But if you leave Izakar someone like Nasud could start a war in your absence.'

'Which is why,' said Kirin, '*you* are going to Kol. As my ambassador.'

They stared at each other in silence for a while.

'How?' asked Spikes.

'Rickshaw,' said Kirin.

'I'm not very diplomatic,' Spikes pointed out.

'Yes, but people listen to you.'

'True. But what if the Civilian kills me on sight?'

'Who's going to kill you?'

'Good point. But will you be all right?'

'I don't know, Spikes,' said Kirin. 'Probably not. But this must be done.'

Elsewhere . . .

'I had written down some rules, on two tablets of stone,' says Zivran Game-maker worriedly. 'I put them down somewhere and lost them. I remember reading them near that bush over there . . . where did they go? I am very bad with small things . . . and names . . .'

The other gods, absorbed in observing the crystals in front of them, look up in concern.

'Sit down, Zivran, and stop fretting so,' says Petah-Petyi

kindly. 'A hunt is in progress. Powerful pieces are involved. Quite fascinating. Come and watch.'

But Zivran is walking around his garden anxiously, muttering to himself, Sambo fluttering about in front of him and removing the various small and trippable-over objects in front of his master's ambling feet.

'World-weaving is an option if They are interested,' Zivran says absent-mindedly, 'You know, where Players control weather, terrain, resources, and the development of the GameWorld, and thus the prosperity of the races who live on it.'

'I thought you said Players control individuals, My benevolent builder,' says Stochastos sharply.

'Yes, but in addition, skilled Players can also change the GameWorld itself, and bring new races on it,' says Zivran. 'There is no fixed way to do this; it is a matter of intuition. But it is a slow way to success, though it involves the most skill. It has few uses in a time of war. Still, I think it might lead to fascinating Games later on, where We could actually cooperate and make species evolve, instead of making them by Ourselves in Our own little gardens . . .'

'A charming conceit, but We shall save it for later, Zivran,' says Petah-Petyi. 'We do not have much time. The Players will be here soon, and We should get this Game running and the war started before They arrive.' She looks at the crystal before her. In it, she sees a pretty, short-haired girl lying unconscious in a room in a small inn.

'Some of the important rules were about perceptions,' says Zivran, still to himself. 'All Player's actions must be such that their pieces can rationalize the consequences of the Player's moves in the pieces' natural environment without considering divine intervention—which means the Players' actions must obey the pieces' laws of nature or logic, or behaviour, or magic. Divine

intervention is only truly divine when it is subtle, imperceptible, when it does not obviously minimize the choices available to the individual, and thus limit the individual's freedom—the illusion of freedom, that is.'

Stochastos nods approvingly. The chaos-lord is pro-choice, though not particularly pro-life.

'Previous Games tested the endurance and abilities of the pieces; but it takes no skill to test the pieces; they are Our creations and by nature less powerful than Us,' says Zivran. 'My Game will test the Players, for in the end it is the Players who win or lose; the pieces' fates are inconsequential, except for the stories one might draw from them.'

Tsa-Ur hisses angrily, as despite being all-knowing, as all gods are, he cannot understand a word of what Zivran is saying.

'You must speak of practical things, Zivran,' says Petah-Petyi. 'We have not time enough for philosophy.'

Zivran looks at her striking face, at the worried wrinkles creasing her perfect brow, and smiles reassuringly. *'Yes, old friend,'* he says, *'let Us speak of practical things.*

'You may not remember, but this GameWorld has been used before—two hundred world-turns before it became what it is now. The Game was different, of course, We used a Board, and all the other tools We have always used—direct intervention, prophecies, visions, physical force, visible presence, natural calamities.

'But for this Game, all control must be through the crystals. The Players will bind the pieces to Their will by concentrating on the crystals before Them. It will take time, but it is surprisingly easy. They will see the pieces responding to Their commands, carrying out Their will—unless Their opponents are shaping events in other directions. The Players may leave messages in the collective subconscious—songs, riddles, cloud patterns, sentient

*weather, that all can see and talented pieces can interpret—
but there can be no direct communication with the pieces, through
dreams or otherwise.*

'*And no prophecies, or any other kind of plot-setting. As We
have seen on numerous occasions, this makes the pieces indolent
and fatalistic, and therefore less entertaining. We know they know
We rule them. We also know they will forget that We rule them,
given time, and assume they are masters of their own futures.
For the Game to be a success, they must believe they are shaping
their own stories, that it is not all predetermined according to
some mysterious Plan.*'

'*But it is not predetermined according to some mysterious
Plan, Zivran,*' says Petah-Petyi, troubled. '*Why do they believe
it is?*'

'*They like to believe someone knows what's going on, the
poor things,*' grins Stochastos.

'*I remember now!*' says Zivran, smiling benevolently.
'*Many other rules, to help avoid confusion, especially on the subject
of intervention.*'

'*A wise move, O prudent protector,*' nods Stochastos.

'*Yes. It is of utmost importance that divine egos are suppressed
during the course of the Game, as We have seen that Our creations,
when left alone, tend to invariably do extremely foolish and
provoking things. Hence, in this Game We will swallow all
perceived insults, whether personal or to Our followers or to Our
temples, no matter how foolishly the pieces behave. Even more
importantly, no matter how attractive the denizens of this world,
We will not have children with them for the duration of this
Game. And no avatars, no oracles, no divine weapons and no
stray curses. There were some more, but I have, unfortunately,
forgotten. Perhaps I will remember in time.*'

Samit Basu

'*You are good, Zivran, My enlightened enforcer,*' says Stochastos, *genuine appreciation shining on his cunning face.* '*Your rules make it difficult even for Me—they would have, that is, had I been playing.*' He avoids Petah-Petyi's stern eye.

'*Of course, there will be cheating; there always is,*' says Zivran blandly. '*Given the complexity of this Game, and that there are no distinct moves, it will be difficult to identify cheats, but it will also be difficult to cheat towards planned, readable outcomes.*'

'*How do We punishh the cheatss?*' asks Tsa-Ur, fangs gleaming.

'*Expel them from the Game, that is all, o sinuous sultan,*' says Stochastos hurriedly. '*More important is the question of identifying cheats in the first place. I would suggest the common rule—the only cheats are those who are caught. All in all, an excellent GameWorld, Zivran—one that really makes Me wish I could play. Even Petah-Petyi could be defeated in a Game like this. The war will really be like no other Game-war We have ever experienced.*'

'*The war should be fascinating indeed,*' says Petah-Petyi, smiling. '*We will be able to see the combat in fabulous detail, thanks to these excellent crystals. And the whole issue of control, of the illusion of choice, will not be a problem during the actual battles, when the Players will be able to do what They will, bound only by physical rules and the limitations of the pieces, because pieces will find it so much easier to believe that their actions have been guided by instinct, or by training received long ago. Yes, Zivran, You have outdone Yourself. Your Game is complicated, but We are gods—why should We need or want simplicity? Well done, old friend.*'

She kisses Zivran, who beams with joy and mutters embarrassedly into his beard.

'Until the Players come, then,' he says, 'let Us play. There is much of the Game We have yet to understand, and more importantly, We have a war to start.'

'I sstill think thiss iss madnesss,' snaps Tsa-Ur. 'Why make thiss pretencse of control when it iss sso much ssimpler to play the old way? And if We are not to play the old way, why can We not forget thesse crysstalss and thiss pointless ssubtlety, why do We not jusst abandon all ssensse and relesse complete chaoss upon thiss world? That might at leasst be pleassant.'

'We do not all share Your passion for destruction, My sly slitherer.'

'Enough talk. My decsission iss thiss,' says Tsa-Ur, standing up, uncoiling his necks and unfurling his hoods.

But the universe is destined never to know what Tsa-Ur's decision is.

For the Infinite Infant chooses this very moment to release a little burp.

And the Baby of Destiny's little burp creates a mighty asteroid, which hurtles towards the GameWorld, threatening to obliterate it within seconds.

One of Tsa-Ur's snake-heads lunges faster than lightning and swallows; the asteroid becomes a cloud of dust and an odd-shaped lump travelling down Tsa-Ur's throat.

Looking at the other gods as they politely applaud his marvellous skills, Tsa-Ur suddenly knows . . . that having seen how unbelievably fast he can strike, the others now know he was behind the mysterious disappearance of the BetterMouse in the last Game . . .

And they know he knows they know . . .

And so on.

And so Tsa-Ur acknowledges the applause, bowing his snake-heads gracefully, and does not voice further objections to the Game.

But he knows in his scaly heart that something is wrong. No one is even playing seriously yet, but Tsa-Ur knows . . . someone is cheating already. As Tsa-Ur's tongues flicker in and out of his mouths like streams of black fire in the air, they can taste the flavour of deception.

T he Chief Civilian stood with Mantric on a wide
      terrace of her white marble palace in Kol, looking
      upwards at the guards on vroomsticks and the
spellbinders on carpets flying furiously above the palace
grounds. The palace echoed with the sounds of hammers,
stone slabs scraped across the ground and raised voices; the
voices of vaman architects hurling instructions at workmen
and workmen hurling invective back at architects.

The Civilian sipped her tea.

'Too many questions, Mantric,' she said. 'And after hours
of discussion, we have no answers.'

'Ravians,' said Mantric. A large bandage was tied around
his head, and one of his arms was in a sling. 'I am quite sure
they were ravians. Not too many people will support me,
but that is because they killed nearly everyone who saw them.'

'I believe you. The ravians, then, are one step ahead of
us, as are our mysterious rescuers from last night—they
outwit us, they mislead us with magic, they are hidden from
our sight and understanding. Despite all the webs I have

woven all over the world over all these years, despite all the spies and all the vaman technology at my disposal, I do not know the answers to even the simplest questions. I feel like some ancient tribal chieftain, trying to understand the shadows beyond the campfire. Who are these new powers walking the earth so arrogantly? What do they want? Who do they work for? Whose allies or enemies are they? How many times will we keep asking ourselves the same questions?'

'And the vamans must be breathing down your neck too,' said Mantric.

'I do not think any vaman has ever been anywhere near my neck,' said the Civilian with a sudden smile.

'And I am of no use to you here—you would have to search very hard before you could find a political adviser as inept as I am. War is upon us, and we do not know who we are fighting or why,' said Mantric. 'We do not know if Kirin is a rakshas or a ravian, and we are even faced with the frightening possibility that the rakshases and ravians are working together to achieve some hidden end. And now Asvin and Maya are gone too. And like all young people in a hurry, they have not bothered to leave messages for their elders.'

'My mind seems to have deserted me when I need it most. I do not even know what goes on inside my own palace, let alone outside. Whoever drove those ravians away is very powerful, Mantric. I knew I was safe from ravian mind control thanks to Ojanus's venom,'—she patted her amphisbaena on a head—'but there is some hidden power in the palace and the city that prevents the ravians from taking over our minds, and compels them to use force. And I must know what it is, because I cannot stand the thought of being watched over, of being manipulated, even by those who wish me well. *I* must be the one pulling strings.'

'You must tell me more of what you know about the vamans, and what they have to do with the ravians,' said Mantric. 'There is so much you are hiding from me.'

But Temat was not looking at him any more; she was watching a black dot in the sky, growing as it headed towards them.

'She's back,' she said. 'We will speak of vamans when we need to, Mantric. And if we are to share all our secrets, perhaps you can tell me why you have not helped the army's war-mages with any of the death-spells they are working on. And if you have the time, perhaps I could also learn what happened to those new magical spying techniques I heard you had invented, with bugs and birds and the gods know what else, which have strangely reached neither the army nor the Silver Phalanx.'

Mantric said nothing. Temat smiled bitterly.

'Whose side are you on, Mantric?' she asked.

'Yours. Whose side are *you* on?'

'Mine. Come; let us cease this childlike bickering. She is here.'

Roshin of the Silver Phalanx jumped lightly off her vroomstick and bowed to them.

'What news of Rupaisa and Amloki?' she asked.

'Amloki is well, though I have had to speak sternly to him about his foolishness in returning to the palace time and time again in direct violation of my orders,' said Temat. 'Rupaisa is alive, but only just. The healers say there is hope, but very little. And now that I have made my report to you, perhaps you will be gracious enough to make yours.'

'Your pardon, my lady. I was concerned.'

'So am I. Now tell me—what news from the gates?'

'Guards attempted to follow both the intruders last

night. Unfortunately, they could not capture them, and anyone who got too close died for their pains. The woman is still in the city. The man who abducted Maya has not been seen since dawn. They were last seen in mid-air in north Kol. Maya was unconscious.'

'I wonder why he took her,' said Mantric. 'Kirin's orders? A trap for Kirin? A trap for Asvin? No, if he had wanted to kill Asvin he would have done it last night. This is something to do with Kirin. Of course, for all you know there might be some other prophecy involving Maya that we don't even know about. We'll just have to wait and see.'

'You seem remarkably composed,' said the Civilian.

'I am a very bad parent,' said Mantric. 'But she has been through a lot, and whoever's abducted her will find he has his hands full. She knows how to take care of herself.'

'And what of Asvin? Where is he?' asked Temat.

'He was last seen at dawn riding northwards on the Kol-Ektara highway. Queen Rukmini of Durg was with him. They were sharing a fine stallion our man at the gate lent them. Two Phalanx members are following them discreetly.'

'Two horses would probably have been more practical, but less romantic. The Hero always manages to find interesting company,' said Mantric with a smile. 'It's good in a way, he has something to do now to justify his existence and his training. With Maya and two Phalanx members he should be all right.'

'Just a moment,' said Temat. 'What do you mean, Queen Rukmini is with him?'

'She was with him, my lady. The reports even described what she was wearing.'

'That's impossible. I just spoke to Queen Rukmini. She's in the palace right now.'

The Civilian finished her tea. 'This is really most interesting,' she said.

'Shapeshifters, you think?' asked Mantric. 'Or rakshases? In the palace? They could be anywhere, actually.'

'That seems to be the only possible explanation,' said Temat. 'So which is the real Rukmini?'

'The one in the palace, I would imagine,' said Mantric. 'Did she say anything unusual?'

'She came to ask me if I was safe, but all she really wanted to know was how Asvin was.'

'That's the real Rukmini, then,' said Mantric. He paced the terrace for a while. 'It was just before the Great War that Icelosis the shapeshifter revealed himself,' he said. 'And he was found in the palace, wasn't he?'

'If there is something like a secret society of shapeshifters in the palace,' said Roshin, 'is there anything we can do about it? They probably know all the passwords and secret ways.'

'We can be watchful, that is all,' said Mantric. 'Perhaps we will notice small things we missed before. The problem is, anyone we talk to could be a shapeshifter, if there is more than one—I see no reason to assume there was only one.'

'*You* could be a shapeshifter, Mantric, or Roshin,' said Temat. 'How could I tell?'

'Well, I'm not,' said Mantric. 'Are you a shapeshifter, Roshin?'

'No,' said Roshin.

'That's all right, then.'

'Have your men warn Asvin that he travels with an imposter,' said Mantric.

'Perhaps it would be better if they did not,' said Temat. 'If the shapeshifter with Asvin meant him harm, she could have killed him already. I suspect she is on his side—and that Maya's abductor is an enemy of hers. Interference might not be a good idea.'

'Didn't think of that.'

'Thinking of things like this is my job, Mantric,' said Temat. 'Besides, if the shapeshifter is skilled, the Phalanx men will have no chance against her. The Phalanx, the Phoenix and the palace guards have all proved completely useless against the powers we now face. Let us speak no more of this in the open. Even the statues might be listening.'

'So we will finally find out whether Simoqin's Hero and my daughter learned anything or not,' said Mantric. 'I wish they were up against easier opposition. That ravian woman was more powerful than any I have even read of, Temat.'

'And she is probably still in Kol,' said Temat.

'Spreading rumours about this hidden king?'

'Yes, the king returned. Another problem, and a growing problem. These rumours are most peculiar. I know where most rumours originate in Kol, Mantric, and I know the people responsible for spreading them. They usually work for me. And these usual suspects have no idea where the rumours about this Arathognan spring from. And the rumours have been spread effectively, by professionals.'

'Or by mind-controllers?'

'Precisely. They have done a thorough job—the marriage documents, people remembering old portraits of the king, snatches of old songs, miracles, mysterious signs and portents. The Dark Lord has risen, and now the people want a king. They needed a hero and I gave them one, Mantric. But now they want a king, and I wonder what I should do.'

Roshin cleared her throat nervously. 'I do not mean to cause offence, my lady,' she said, 'but historically, hasn't it usually been irrelevant what the people want? Why do these rumours bother you? Let them spread! They will distract the people, keep them happy, just like this hero-league circus.'

'The problem is that ravians just might be able to lead the people in organized revolt if matters get out of hand,' said Temat. 'And there is the army to think of as well. I do not want to see Arathognan and Askesis marching together, no matter how noble they look. These are no romantic dreams of ideal kingdoms, Roshin—this is just a well-planned move to remove me, or to make sure the people are not dismayed by my death by assassination. The ravians have hundreds of reasons for wanting a king back in Kol.'

'I wonder why they do not even bother making a pretence of peace,' said Mantric. 'They must know now, after last night, that they have revealed their presence here.'

'Perhaps they continue to underestimate our collective intelligence,' murmured Temat.

'What would the king rule?' asked Roshin. 'The Free States would never surrender their independence. Everything is so different now.'

'Who cares about the Free States? They want Kol,' said Mantric. 'Kol is the centre. To control Kol is to control most of the world, and everyone knows it.'

'What makes it interesting,' said Temat, 'is that this plot was hatched *before* the ravians left two hundred years ago. They must have thought themselves very noble, secretly preserving the royal bloodline, so they could restore the true king to the throne of Kol when they returned to save the world . . . and it appears that Arathognan's claims to kingship are legitimate. I have looked at the documents of marriage, both the copies they found in Enki yesterday and the ones that mysteriously surfaced in the Hero School library this morning. They are genuine.'

'And this Arathognan—he is one of the Champions League heroes?'

'Yes,' said Roshin. 'Thog the Barbarian, they call him. Nice fellow, actually—I've met him a few times. And he now wears an amulet around his neck—the amulet that the documents conveniently say was the only royal heirloom by which the true king could be known. Somehow the rumours speak of this as well—that the true king will wear a precious amulet—though how the rumour-mongers knew of these secret documents is yet another mystery.'

'We waste time, standing around and talking. The war has already begun,' said the Civilian abruptly. 'Roshin, bring me this Arathognan, wherever he is. I desire speech with him. Go at once.'

'Shall we fetch him at any cost?'

'Alive, Roshin. Alive.'

'I will see it done.' Roshin bowed, got on her vroomstick and zoomed off.

'What will you do with this boy?' asked Mantric.

'I am not sure,' she replied. 'But I have a few ideas.'

'I am sure you do. But these are not matters I should dabble in, are they?'

Temat smiled enigmatically. 'When has that ever stopped you, old friend?'

'There is, however, something else. I am not supposed to have observed this,' said Mantric, 'but I am a strange old man, and I have a suspicion that you have an old and trusty secret adviser in the labyrinth. Someone or something very wise.'

Her face was expressionless. 'Yet another thing I will not speak about, Mantric.'

'If you truly know nothing of these shapeshifters,'

continued Mantric, unperturbed, 'and if these shapeshifters are not your all-knowing underground oracle, why do you not go to your adviser and simply ask what is to be done?'

'I never ask what must be done,' she snapped. 'I make my own decisions. But I am not as young and sure of myself as I used to be, Mantric. Sometimes it feels good to be told I am right.'

'It is out of concern for you that I speak. Why do you not go, then, and let him—if it is a him—tell you that you are right? It might ease your burden.'

'I have already tried that and failed,' she said. 'My adviser is asleep, or dead, or has left. And it was not the right time to ask him for advice in any case—that time is many months away.'

'What will you do, then?' asked Mantric.

'What I always do,' she said. 'I will do what is best for me. What is best for the city. What makes sense.'

She smiled again, and touched his arm lightly.

'But before I do all that,' said Lady Temat, Chief Civilian of the great city of Kol, 'I will have some more tea. It is Avrantic tea, Mantric, very strong, very good. Do you want some?'

'Can't stand the stuff,' said Mantric amiably.

14

A white horse carrying a white rider streaked through a black wood. The earth below and the sky above were grey; the trees around them were twisted, clawing, leafless.

A dry wind whistled in Behrim's ears; the hoofbeats of his stolen steed echoed through the lifeless wood, thudding quicker than his hummingbird-winged heart.

His horse's eyes were closed; its heart beat in perfect unison with his. It was running faster than any horse could run, blurring legs powered by bone, muscle and the driving force of its ravian rider's mind. When the ride stopped, when his mind moved away, it would drop dead. Its own mind had died long ago, when Behrim took control. Now it was just an extension of its rider's body; it ran at the speed of his thoughts. They flowed through the black wood smoothly, centaur-like.

Behrim felt no guilt for this murder he had committed; if the horse had been in its own senses, if it had seen with its own eyes the horrors of the rakshas illusions around the

Dark Tower, it would have died of fear long ago and taken its rider with it.

But then ravians never felt guilt; the righteous never need to.

The white rider's eyes were not open on the physical plane of the world as he rode through layer upon layer of rakshas illusion in a ravian trance, urging his horse-legs to leap and swerve when he felt obstacles looming up at him. He let the landscape be shaped in his mind by the jagged edges of danger as they screamed out to him from behind the illusion-veil.

It was dangerous even for a ravian as mighty as Behrim to run this mad blind race, but he felt no fear. He had walked the wilds of Imokoi before, he had pierced rakshas illusions, seen through the mist of demonic dwimmer-craft centuries ago. The younger ravians had powers of telekinesis beyond his, but here in the shadow-world of Imokoi, that meant nothing—his experience counted far more than their raw strength. That was why he was here, in Imokoi; that was why he had been chosen, to be the one to walk into the heart of the Dark Lord's realm and return with the Dark Lord's heart.

Behrim did not know how long he had ridden or how far, it might have been hours or weeks, miles or leagues. But he knew that to stop would mean death. Rakshas-roars rent the air somewhere behind him; if he shut out everything else he could hear the faint throb of giant feet pounding the earth, running tirelessly in his wake. The hunt was far from over.

But the rakshases had fallen behind, thought Behrim exultantly. They would not catch him, he would escape. They had been fooled by their own illusions, fallen in non-existent swamps, hurtled into invisible rocks, stepped into their own enchanted grass-portals and out of the chase. Evil contained the seeds of its own destruction. But the more powerful rakshases, the ones who had *created* the illusions, whose very existence kept the illusions in place, had kept their eyes open and stepped backstage, sidestepping the traps they had set. Sometimes, though, they had needed to pause to pick up their weaker companions; and though they knew the land and their giant steps crossed it with amazing speed, Behrim was faster; his horse outran even the carrion-fowl giving chase in the skies above.

Now the crows had gone, they had sped off northwards, or what had *felt* like northwards.

He had last seen the rakshases from the top of a great hill, seen giant blue man-shapes pushing through the trees in the valley below under a red sun. But he had had to open his eyes for that; and his horse had almost died. How many hours, how many days ago was that? He did not remember. But the rakshas illusions were wearing thin now as he rode farther away from the Tower; he would sometimes open his eyes for a second and be gladdened to see that the worlds of seen and envisaged reality were slowly beginning to overlap; the trees were standing where their shadows said they would.

Behrim smiled grimly as he thought of his impossibly daring escape from the Dark Tower—the chase through the dungeons, the *very* invigorating sword-fight in the stables, the hot breath of leaping sentry-kravyads as they missed his fleeing horse by inches. They would remember him; they had felt his blade. He had been second only to Narak in the last war; and the younger ones would outshine him in this one. But *some* things only he could do. He was a burning brand in the halls of evil, a shining light in the darkness.

Even now, far from the Tower, illusions glimmered in the shadows of his mind, flickering, beckoning, seducing, deceiving. The rakshases were strong; he dared not even steal a glance at the sky, for they had distorted even the stars with their evil spells. To be confused, to be lost, would mean capture and a slow death in the dungeons of Izakar, agonizingly close to his quarry and his hopes.

Failure was out of the question now; not after all he had been through since the rakshases had discovered him. Shutting out mind-numbing visions, through great swamps and whispering forests, over jagged rock-teeth, through fire and hail and fearsome monsters' fangs he had ridden blindly, trusting in his skill and the holy light that guided him through the traps of the sinful. Through the belly of the beast that had mysteriously swallowed the son of his best friends— the son of light whose fall into darkness might spell doom for the ravians. But Behrim knew he would overcome the evil tide somehow—he would save Kirin from the spells of the rakshases and reunite him with his parents' faithful friends. For Kirin alone could save the ravians from the rotting arrogance that even now threatened the heart of their empire.

But before Kirin could be saved, he would have to save himself.

He tightened his grip on the horse's mind, feeling the strong muscles in its hind legs sending dead black twigs flying in his wake. He held on, closer, stronger. When control became unconscious, when he reached a stage of sublime effortless mastery, he opened his eyes.

Grey earth. Black trees. Grey sky with a huge white moon casting white light on him. Swift, colourless peace. The world was his; he was in control. He would make it.

And then he felt an ice-cold stab of danger grip his spine. He cast his eyes into the half-light, and saw nothing but trees streaking past him.

He closed his eyes and looked harder.

In front of him, to his left, to his right. Sitting silently in the shadows. Bright glaring red eyes. Waiting.

They felt his gaze, and sprang to their feet. Sleek grey death-engines of fang and shadow and claw. Wolf-shapes under the moon. A trap.

The Pack had joined the hunt.

A chorus of wolf-howls sliced through the air.

He swerved to the left in sudden panic, feeling the horse's muscles tear and scream in pain, holding tendons and sinews and bones together with sheer strength of will. Slicing time desperately, grasping in the gaps between seconds, between heartbeats, for that extra moment, that slowtime ravian-space where fights were won. He could not slow down; he could not go back. He had no bow, no arrows; in any case, even an archer of his skill would have needed great luck to hit the grey ghosts speeding through the trees.

With an amazing burst of speed, the werewolves closed in.

He would have to go *over* them.

The white horse soared through the air. But the wolves leaped first. In slowtime, Behrim watched them arc through the air, on either side of him, saw their glistening bared fangs, saw drops of wolf saliva glittering in mid-air like diamonds. Crazed hunter's eyes met his. Snarls rumbled like frozen thunder.

He dropped the horse from his mind just as the werewolves crashed into it and somersaulted over them, landing like a cat. He was up in an instant, running wildly, not looking back, not seeing the horse's body ripped in half before it touched the ground.

Red eyes ahead. He drew his sword. Two werewolves leaped at his throat. He ducked, slashed; a shriek of pain. Blood arcing through the air. More wolves charging. Surrounded. Nowhere to run.

The ravian and the werewolves moved smoothly, gracefully in the moonlight, in a silent dance of death that lasted for what seemed like hours. His sword struck like a snake, slicing, cutting, biting. Tooth and claw hissed past him harmlessly. But there were too many of them, and some blows struck home. Behrim knew he was beaten. It was just a matter of time. And time passed swiftly.

Fangs in his wrist. He dropped his sword. Fangs in his thigh. He fell. Fangs in his shoulder. He screamed. A huge grey wolf on his chest. He looked into his eyes and saw death. The wolf howled in victory, and then fangs dipped towards Behrim's throat.

Comets of fire streamed through the sky.

'Alpha Laakon! Wait!'

The wolf's head snapped sideways. He snarled.

Giant bodies crashed through the trees.

'The Dark Lord wants him alive!' A rakshashi towered over the circle of wolves surrounding the fallen ravian. 'I beg your pardon, Great Wolf, but this is a direct order. Please. Alive, unharmed.'

And then muscles melted, and there was a huge bearded man sitting on Behrim's chest.

'Did I hear you issuing an *order* to the *Pack*?' he growled.

'The order was for me,' said the rakshasi. 'For you, Alpha,

it is a request. From a friend. I welcome you to Imokoi, hunter of the north, and thank you for coming to our aid in our time of need. But your prisoner is wanted in the Dark Tower.'

'Already the Dark Lord comes between the Pack and its prey,' snarled Laakon angrily, but he rose.

'I promise, on the Dark Lord's behalf,' said Akimis, 'that after we have questioned him, he shall be given to you. And now, Lord Laakon, it is my great pleasure to offer you an escort to the Dark Tower, where our Lord and kinsman awaits you eagerly.'

Behrim looked around, wondering whether there was the slightest chance of escape. But the circling werewolves never took their eyes off him. They had changed into human shape now; beautiful powerful bodies, male and female, clad in wolfskin loincloths. Low growls still lurked in their throats.

As huge waves of fatigue crashed over Behrim, he sent a silent prayer to the heavens. He was alive; his hopes were alive. And they would take him to Kirin. Kirin had saved him. And now he could save Kirin in return . . .

But Laakon shook his head.

'*Alive* I grant you, as a token of my friendship, as a gift to the Dark Lord and his dark brethren, and to you, noble rakshasi, my sister in the hunt,' said the Alpha werewolf. 'But he has drawn the blood of my brothers, and *unhurt* is too much to ask. Wolf blood must be avenged.'

Shadows changed. Great wolf-shapes closed in on Behrim, their eyes burning. He closed his eyes and waited for the pain.

15

Thog awoke in a bedroom that was not his.

Unlike some of the more sociable heroes in the League, Thog wasn't used to waking up in strange bedrooms. Especially when he hadn't even gone to a party the previous evening. But there was something oddly comfortable about the bed he was in now—he didn't feel scared, or even curious. He looked around slowly. He was in a large, cold room, with ancient-looking stone walls, bare apart from an ornate mirror to his left and several teak shelves to his right, where stacks of dusty old books were carelessly piled. He heard bird-song and splashes outside, and looked towards the foot of the bed. At a woman's profile. She was seated by a large open window, looking outwards at the river, humming softly and contentedly as a purring cat, her fingers drumming on a large polished rosewood desk, where a number of small, mysterious-looking objects of various shapes and sizes were scattered, the largest of which was a cloth-covered sphere about the size of a human head. But scattered objects on a table were completely incapable of holding Thog's attention at the moment. It was *her*.

He stared at her in silence, blinking, waiting for the slower parts of his brain to wake up, feeling far more relaxed than he would have expected under the circumstances. But then the view from where he was was quite spectacular. She was the most attractive woman he'd ever seen. Not beautiful in the manner that, say, the Sadori Sisters were—that blatant, obvious, earthy attractiveness that suddenly seemed so ordinary, so *coarse*. She had, what was the word, an ethereal, other-worldly quality. Yes, but there was something more. What was the word? Yes, *glamour*. She had an *aura*. A sense of mystery, of remoteness. He sat up slowly.

She turned and looked at him, with huge, liquid brown eyes, and he realized he'd got it all wrong. Nothing catlike at all about her—it was strange that he'd thought of that, because he couldn't stand cats. Cats made him uncomfortable. This woman, on the other hand, she put him at his ease. She looked so *nice*, she had the kind of face you *knew* you could trust. Cats? Rubbish. She was as soft and sweet and innocent, like a kitten, at most.

She smiled. He suddenly realized he'd been gaping at her for a while. He looked away, embarrassed.

'Hello, Arathognan,' she said.

Various questions wrestled in Thog's mind. The more important ones shoved the others aside and lined up behind his tonsils.

'Where am I?' won.

'In south Kol,' she said, 'in my house. If you want the address, it is 32B, Cravenstick Street, a pleasant villa on the banks of,'—she gestured outside the window, smiling—'the river Asa.'

'Who are you?'

'My name is Peori.'

'That's an uncommon name.'

'And I am no commoner. But Peori is not an uncommon name for a ravian.'

'A ravian,' he said in wonder.

'A friend.'

'You sit there, as real and solid as the bed beneath me, and tell me you are from another world.'

'I only said I was a ravian, Arathognan,' she said softly. 'And yes, I have come here from another world. But *this* is the world I am from. *This* is the world where I was born. And if you must know, I was born on the bed you are now lying on, in this room, in this house, in this city, in this world. *My* world.'

'Before the War.'

'*During* the War. I was born weeks before it ended— before we went away.'

'You don't look two hundred years old.'

'I am not *old*, Arathognan. Time is unimportant. We ravians age slowly, but you humans *learn* faster. But we can talk about me later. Look around, and you will find more questions.'

He looked at himself. His clothes were different; rich, finely textured. 'These clothes . . .'

'Are yours now.'

'But who . . .'

'I changed them.'

Thog blushed furiously.

'There is no need to feel ashamed,' she said, smiling broadly. 'I liked what I saw.'

Time, thought Thog, for a *really* quick change of subject. 'How long have I been asleep?' he asked.

'I really do not know,' she said. 'It is difficult for us to keep track of time; we do it only when really important. You slept as long as you needed to. Long enough for the lines of weariness on your face to fade.'

Now he was scared. He jumped out of bed, looked at his reflection in the mirror and cried out in wonder.

He didn't look tired any more. He looked at least ten years younger. Some scars were gone entirely. His skin was almost glowing. Even his hair was almost completely black.

'What have you done to me?' he cried, but then she smiled again, and his sudden panic dissolved away instantly.

'There is no sorcery here, Arathognan,' she said. 'You have healed yourself. You have woken up. That is all.'

'This house . . . where, what is going on?'

'I told you. This is my house. 32B Craven . . .'

'No, no, how did I get here? When?'

'I brought you here, on a carpet.'

'Why?'

'To save your life, and to save your kingdom.'

'What?'

'You know this already,' she said. 'I know you know. You are the rightful king of Kol, and I have come to this world to help you regain the throne that has been unlawfully stolen from you.'

Thog shook his head. 'I'm dreaming.'

She smiled.

'Wait,' said Thog. He sat quietly for a few seconds. 'Are you controlling my mind?' he asked her.

'Would you be asking me that if I were?'

'No.'

'Well, then.'

'But what if . . .'

'I am not controlling your mind, Arathognan.'

'Thank you.'

'In fact, I will help you out. The question you now want to ask me is *why* I brought you here in my carpet.'

'Thanks. Why did you . . .'

'To protect you. From the Chief Civilian's men, who are now in your house, being shouted at by your aunt.'

'Poor them. But why . . .'

'They have orders to capture you and take you to the Civilian. Who will then imprison you, or possibly kill you immediately. The Civilian is a sensible woman, and will not waste her time talking to you.'

'But . . .'

'Because you are the rightful king, as I have told you. And therefore a greater threat to her than any Dark Lord in the world.'

'. . .'

'And that is why we are here. For it is my duty, my given task, to protect you, to instruct you, and to restore you to your rightful place.'

'!'

'Sit down and listen to me. Very carefully.'

So much for mentors being mysterious old bearded men, thought Thog. Hells, I'll do whatever she wants, just to be near her.

Thog sat.

And listened, very carefully.

Peori told him the tale of the ravians, and their long friendship with the kingdom of Kol, their most faithful ally during the Age of Terror. She told him of the grandeur and nobility of his ancestors, and the power and glory of Kol of old, stories of great deeds during the War, of battles nobly won, of monsters and evil hordes nobly slain, of apocalypses narrowly and nobly averted.

She told him of the rakshases, and their secret and slow infiltration of the innermost sanctums of power in Kol, and the corruption they spread secretly among the once noble spellbinders, once true friends of the ravians. She told him of the moral decay of Kol, its decline from being a lighthouse on stormy seas to becoming a festering pit of vice, and how this fall stemmed from the passing of the great kings.

Morning slept, then metamorphosed into afternoon and fluttered away as Peori's low, melodious voice filled Thog's ears and heart. He could almost *see* his ancestor, the last King of Kol, a lone light fighting the darkness in the world around him, the darkness that grew and enveloped even his own kingdom. Peori told him about the treason committed by the ministers of his court, who chattered in palace corners, plotting against their great ruler in secret alliance with the merchants and smiths of the underworld, the treacherous, greedy and selfish vamans, and separatist human rebels.

She spoke of the struggles for power in court, and the beginnings of the rift that led, after the War, to the partition of the great kingdom into bickering provinces, now called the Free States, and one beleaguered city-state, Kol as she was today, a queen in rags in a court of corpulent merchants.

And then she spoke of the ravian discovery of these evil plots, and a secret counter-plot to preserve the royal bloodline, to guard the line of kings, to restore the hidden King when the time came.

In the time of the Great War, the King had escaped from his treacherous courtiers for a while; he had secretly married a young Hudlumm chieftain's daughter, a beautiful bride the ravians had chosen for him. He had dwelt with his young bride under the care of the ravians, before embarking on his ill-fated, ill-advised journey to the halls of the vaman Vul. And he had died in that vaman's halls, torn apart by Danh-Gem, and never met the children his wife had borne him.

As he listened to her voice, calm and serene, Thog was transported; he saw as if with his own eyes the whispers in the dark behind the throne, the crumbling of a great kingdom accelerated before his eyes. He saw the slow but ruthless annihilation of all that was green and good in Kol by the crafty vamans and their soulless grinding machines, their pots of gold and their endless streams of molten iron squeezed from the sulphurous bowels of the earth. And at the centre of this web of metal, money and machinery, he saw the Chief Civilians, gold flowing into their hands, darkness flowing out of their mouths.

He saw them conspiring with greasy, bloated usurers, saw them cackling as they tortured the last faithful servants of the kings, tempting and threatening the brilliant but guileless spellbinders, perverting the ancient laws, *buying* magic and knowledge and power most high, tainting the purity of magical wisdom with their grasping, avaricious, withered hands.

He saw them spreading cunningly worded nets of deceit to trap the simple, honest folk of Kol, blinding them with illusions of wealth, prosperity and power while letting evil into the city, letting in the hordes that their fathers had given their lives to keep out. He almost wept as he saw Kol changing, saw the machines of the vamans rise out from the depths of the earth, saw mighty trees being hacked down in their prime and replaced by stinking, smoking factories, thick, slimy industrial ooze in the once-clean Asa, stinking fumes melting the pristine temples of the sleeping gods, mountains of rotting filth full of frolicking asurs smudging the face of the once-beautiful city he had been born to love. All in the name of progress, of technology, of science. He saw a society blinded and confused by a drugged leap into a bleak future, an illusion of material comfort that was nothing more than a conjurer's trick, a diabolical plot to hide Kol's rotting heart.

He saw a great, dying city that needed to be restored, to be returned to its former simplicity. Its former glory. He saw a land that needed a healer. A kingdom that needed a king.

'Are you sure I am the one?' he asked. 'How do you know *I* am the heir?'

'First, your face,' Peori said. 'You look just like the old King. Second, blood will tell, and look at your life now—you work as a hero in your city, dedicating your life to upholding truth, justice and the law, defending the downtrodden, destroying the powers of darkness. Third, your capacity for nobility and self-sacrifice, the burden of great kings down the ages. You have lived all your life with someone who has methodically removed your every happiness, who scorns even your years of faithful care, and yet you do not complain. And finally, you wear the sacred amulet of the Kings of Kol . . . the heirloom upon which the secret marriage vows of the last King were sworn. It has been handed down to you, passed on by generation after generation of hidden kings unaware of its true value, its true meaning. And yet it reached its true destination, travelling sure and swift as an arrow. Perhaps the goodwill of the ravians guided it from afar. I came to your city to search for the heirloom, and my hopes bore fruit—it adorned the neck of a true king. But I would not have needed the amulet to find you, Thog. Your royalty is obvious, it is magnificent, monumental. It cries out to be noticed.'

'But I . . . there must be a flaw somewhere. The city is not

as bleak as the picture you paint of it. And the Chief Civilian
. . . she's the greatest ruler in the world,' he whispered.

'She is a *great* ruler,' said Peori. 'But she is not a *good*
ruler. We respect intelligence and learning, but we know
that they can be used to justify all wrongdoing, to break
honest minds by showing different, overlapping truths, like
broken mirrors in men's souls. But there can *be* only *one*
truth—the rest is shadow-play and puppetry. The people
do not need puppeteers in these dark times. The people
want a *king*. They *need* a king. A king who is the key to a
glorious renewal, a time of romance reborn, of legend and
chivalry remembered, of innocence and peace regained, of
brave men and beautiful women watched over by benevolent
guardians, who seek neither power nor fame, but seek only
to live in their woodland realm content in the happiness
they selflessly spread. A king who will be a conduit for
destiny to run its course—a destiny shaped and directed by
the selfless and wise friends of the kingdom and the whole
world, not by the greedy and lustful beings that surround
the throne of Kol today . . . do you not *see*, Arathognan?
Do you not understand? We will stand by you. We will ask
nothing, except the right to bring light to the shadows so
you can see. We will guide you through the labyrinth of
worldly traps and snares to the gardens of paradise. But before
that, terrible deeds must be done.'

'What must I do?'

'Your kingdom must be cleansed, purged of the evil that
befouls it. You must smite the forces of the dark with the
light within you. You must set the land free.'

'What do I have to do? Do I have to go on a quest?'

'No. You must do something more difficult than any
quest, more hazardous than any journey, any great beast.

You must strike at the very heart of the darkness. And the heart of the darkness is not in faraway Imokoi, it is right here. It is the black heart of Lady Temat.'

'You want me to murder Lady Temat?'

'Yes.'

'I cannot do it.'

'You must.'

'But I don't understand,' said Thog. 'Why can't you just *talk* to the Civilian? Kol and the ravians have always been allies. The Chief Civilians have made their mistakes in the absence of the ravians. Now that you are back, I am sure things can change again. Killing Temat is not the answer, it will lead to anarchy. I do not want a crown washed in blood. Make peace with the Civilian! If it is Kol's welfare you want, do not ask me to plunge it into confusion!'

'No, Arathognan. There will be no anarchy; the people will be one, the people will be yours. If we revealed ourselves to her, she would make peace with us, seeking to learn out weaknesses, and then betray us. Yes, peace with Lady Temat would have been easy. But the ravians do not do what is *easy*—they do what is *right*. She has been corrupted by the vamans, and is too far in their counsel.

'Besides, she is protected by strong dark magic—her mind is closed to the advice and counsel of the ravians. And to tell you the truth, we do not even know if she is human. We fear she is a rakshasi in disguise . . . why else has she not declared war upon the Dark Lord, when even her masters, the vamans, hate the asurs and want to destroy them? There is no other way. As long as she is alive, the vamans will own Kol. She must die.'

'But . . . why do *I* have to kill her?'

Peori sighed. 'Because of the Simoqin Prophecies.'

'What do they have to do with this?'

'Simoqin the ravian made *three* prophecies before he died, Arathognan, not two as you have been told. There was a third prophecy that never reached the ears of the citizens of Kol—a third prophecy that was well known before, that the Chief Civilians have cunningly concealed over the years, a prophecy only you, the true heir to the throne, can fulfil.'

'What was this third prophecy?'

'That when the Dark Lord arose, and the hero who would be his mortal enemy answered his challenge, the true King of Kol would return, and with his own hands he would strike down the Dark Lord's servants who had usurped his throne. This is why you have to kill the Civilian, Arathognan. Because it is your destiny.'

A voice in his head whispered that this was all too convenient, too pat. But Thog looked at Peori's face, heard the conviction in her voice, and felt ashamed of his own baseness, of his unworthiness in doubting someone so infinitely above him. If she were not true of heart, he thought, she could simply have taken over his mind, forced him to carry out her every whim. She did not need to lie. He hung his head in shame.

'Will you take up the challenge, Arathognan? Will you bear a great burden to save the innocent, to save your kingdom? Will you face your destiny? Will you be King?'

She touched his arm, feather-light, and looked very deep into his eyes. 'The ravians want only the welfare of Kol,' she said. 'We do not seek control. We never have. We offer you power, Arathognan, to make a choice. To make the *right* choice. The power to set things right.'

He looked at the *pureness*, the *goodness* of her and his heart almost burst. And at that very moment, a slow fire was kindled within him. Finally, he had purpose. Finally, he knew what his whole life had trained him for. The fire burned brighter and set his heart ablaze.

'I will do as you say,' he said quietly. 'I will be the king you want me to be. But nothing is clear to my sight, and all paths before me seem covered in shadow.'

'Do not fear. You have a friend now,' she said, kissing his brow.

He looked at her face, and it was honest. He looked at her heart, and it was pure.

The fact that it was covered by the most spectacular cleavage he had ever seen helped, too.

The amulet on Arathognan's chest shone like a star. But his eyes shone brighter.

E lsewhere . . .

The gods drift around the GameWorld slowly, pausing now and then to observe crystals that catch their fancy. Already the little people of the GameWorld have begun to fascinate them; already they have their favourites, regardless of the fact that the Game has not even begun, and that even when it does, they will not be playing.

A chase involving four heroes catches their eyes; a ravian hero carrying an unconscious woman on a chariot speeds inexorably northwards, while a human hero and a shapeshifter masquerading as another human ride behind them.

'They will never catch them,' says Petah-Petyi slowly. 'What a shame. I like that girl, I do not want her to die so young.'

'Ssave her then,' says Tsa-Ur. 'The Game hass not even begun, and You are not bound to obey Zsivran's ruless in any casse.'

She shakes her head. 'No, the pieces must fall into place on their own. And We are bound not only to obey Zivran's rules but to enforce them as well, Tsa-Ur. A referee's duties are sacred.'

'It would be quite entertaining, My delicious dice-caster, to just point the pursuers in the right direction, though, and perhaps speed them up a little,' says Stochastos. 'The balance of power there is interesting. I would like to see them face each other in combat.'

'Thiss iss a wasste of Our time,' says Tsa-Ur. 'Let uss jusst sset the piecsess on the battlefield. We know the war iss inevitable in any casse. Why do We ssit here watching them sscurry around like antss?'

'Because it is fascinating to watch them play out their lives,' says Petah-Petyi. 'And it is the only way We can truly understand them.'

Tsa-Ur does not reply, but his expression makes it clear that he does not want to understand anything, and that as far as he is concerned the only point of watching living things scurry around is to calculate how best to trap and eat them.

'For this Game to work,' says Zivran, 'the pieces must be able to write down a history of events afterwards that explains things in such a manner that Our very presence is concealed.'

'So, Zivran, most optimistic of omnipotences, You are assuming the GameWorld will survive the Game?' asks Stochastos, with the slightly sinister smile of one who has surreptitiously caused apocalypses on the last three Games he has watched.

Zivran shrugs.

'That iss no reasson not to intervene, Zsivran,' says Tsa-Ur. 'The piecesess would write a hisstory that explainss thingss away in any casse. They alwayss do that when We meddle. Amazsingly adjusstable thing, the mortal mind. It makess up exsplanationss to fill in all the gapss between the pointss when We move the sstory forward.'

'My fabulous fork-tongue is right,' says Stochastos. 'We will *follow the rules as you have set them, Zivran, but human history is hardly Our concern. They always manage.'*

'Humans,' sighed Petah-Petyi. 'Zivran, I have told You already that I love Your Game World, that I think it is beautiful, that I believe Your Game will outshine any other Game played yet. Yet Your Game brings to My mind a few questions, questions that the simplicity and mindless brutality of the other Games never raised. There are some aspects of Your Game that I do not comprehend.'

Now Zivran looks troubled. 'What are they?' he asks.

'I believe, and have always believed,' she says, looking benevolently at the Game World, 'that the best stories are human stories. The deepest stories, the most moving stories are about the powerless, the struggling, the deprived, the dislocated. For these are the tales of love and loss, of innocence and ambition, that We gods have always loved. I have seen all the crystals, and so many of the important pieces are magical, powerful, more than human. What interest have We, with the powers that We possess, in watching them struggle for power, watching them cast their feeble spells? Why do the stories We create not look for the real stories beneath the flashing lights? Who are these humans? What does life mean to them? Where are their families, their pasts, the little things in life that they must love and cherish and die protecting? The humans on Your Game World seem as twigs floating in the ocean, hopelessly adrift as the currents of power they do not comprehend carry them this way and that. Why? Why all these adventures and weapons and castles and heroes and monsters and displays of magic? Is this why We have inherited the task of creating these worlds, these people, these lives? What does it all mean?'

For the first time since his arrival in Zivran's garden, Tsa-Ur throws Zivran a sympathetic look. Zivran catches the look and passes it on to Stochastos, who passes it back to Tsa-Ur.

Women, *the look says.*

Zivran clears his throat nervously. 'Well, this is a Game,' *he says.*

'But it is not a Game for the pieces down there. It is their lives.'

'We are gods. This is what We do.'

'Why do We do what We do?'

'There are other places where these questions are asked, Petah-Petyi. There are the Artworlds. Perhaps you should seek Your answers there, among the Eternal Seekers.'

'I have been to the Artworlds, Zivran. I have seen colour and beauty in the creations of the divine artists, I have watched Tablus and His musicians shape worlds out of sound, I have even been to Tubriya, I have seen the showers of the primal light-fountain. But I do not understand. We give life, We take it away, but We do not care, We just play. Why did We create these worlds, these realities, if they are mere meaningless illusions?'

'Personally, My probabilitous princess, I think the Artists are all mad,' *says Stochastos.* 'I mean it as a compliment, of course. I go meet Them sometimes, and see what They have been doing. Fascinating. And I never miss the exhibitions, though the only reason I go there is for gossip and free mead.'

'You jest, as is Your wont, Stochastos,' *says Petah-Petyi.* 'But They do great work. Surely even You cannot but marvel at Their creations, that test the limits of life and creation and the universe itself.'

'Their worlds, most charismatic of coin-tossers, are usually uninhabitable,' *says Stochastos.*

'It's the ideas behind these worlds that are important.'

'I seem to remember My perfectionist permutator saying not too long ago that We had no time for philosophy, that We *should consider only the practical questions before the Players get here,' murmurs Stochastos, amused.*

'I see You feel I have wasted Your time,' says Petay-Petyi icily. 'Zivran's GameWorld is a creation of wondrous complexity, which led Me to wonder whether He had any answers. It does not matter.'

'To answer a part of Your question, Petah-Petyi,' says Zivran, still looking troubled, 'I do understand that humans, and human stories, are important. And yes, many of the crystals do show beings that are not human. But the beings that they show are mostly essentially human—there are the usual modifications, improvements if you will, that We make to make the Games more spectacular, more interesting—but the questions that drive these beings are the same ones You want answers to. The crystals do not show the pieces in order of raw power; they show pieces in terms of importance to the Game, in terms of crucial choices, crucial moments. The pieces in the crystals are the ones whose decisions, guided by Us, will shape the future of the Game and the GameWorld, be they dragons or khudrans. These are the pebbles that will start the landslide. Their choices, the Players' choices, will guide love and hate, freedom and bondage, life and death for the world as the Game progresses. I hope You will see this, as I do, as an improvement over other Games, where We bring about landslides by making Our puppets hurl boulders at each other. Perhaps We will learn something from this. Even I do not understand how, and the objective of My Game is not to teach—it is to play. But in My own way, however unsatisfactory, I do seek the same answers as You. The wings and horns and tails and balls of fire are just decoration. Entertainment. The Game has the answers. It is through studying the mandala of the Game that perhaps the rest of Your questions will be answered as well.'

'I am content with that, old friend,' says Petah-Petyi.

'Sstudy, analyssiss, quesstion, ansswer,' snarls Tsa-Ur. 'You will bore the universse into desstruction. Who caress about humanss? I csertainly do not.'

'Humans are the basic unit of the Game, Tsa-Ur. They are the building blocks from which We derive all other significant creatures,' says Zivran.

'And the only reasson thiss iss sso iss becausse You are human-shhaped Yoursself?'

'No. Game-makers have tried many non-human intelligent units, but somehow the most interesting ones were human variants. From rakshases to centaurs, mermaids to werewolves, it is the humans and half-humans who have made the Games what they are.'

'But reptiless work too,' says Tsa-Ur. 'Dragonss, sserpentss, and all thosse half-reptiless with no human partss at all. They are much more interessting than humanss. Reptiless could be the bassic unitss.'

'Make a Game Yourself with reptiles, then, My fearless fangster,' suggests Stochastos.

'I tried to create a Game oncse,' says Tsa-Ur ruefully. 'But I losst patiencse and ate everything. But would it not be posssible to make a Game with reptiless?'

'Yes, it would, I suppose. It is just not done that way,' says Zivran patiently. 'Possibly because You are the first one to have thought of it.'

'Or fish.'

'True.'

'Birdss. Inssectss. Or even new formss of life that You have not even tried, all becausse You want to play with toyss that look like You. It iss unfair.'

'We leave the creation of completely original species to the

201

Artists,' says Zivran. 'When We create Our worlds for the Games, We do not start right at the beginning of evolution, tweaking and pruning molecules here and cells there. It takes too much time. We simply take the works of the ancient masters, the beings They created, as well as interesting creatures from recent Games, and place them on Our worlds, adding Our little footnotes and twists where We think they would be amusing. And then We play.'

'Placse them? But what of evolution, then?' asks Tsa-Ur, his heads twisting in bewilderment. 'Where do they get all thosse big lizsard bones in the ground from? And thosse fosssils? And thosse drawingss on rockss?'

'We make them up and bury them conveniently so they can be discovered over time,' says Zivran smugly. 'The pieces need to believe in and decipher their pasts, to have a sense of belonging in their world, to have a sense of growth as they strive to understand the mysteries of their existence. It gives them something to do. It keeps them from asking the real questions, and simply refusing to play the Game. That is the reason for little clues like dinosaur bones, Tsa-Ur. That is why We draw mysterious patterns on hills and fields, and bury frozen half-apes under continents of ice.'

'All thiss sstill does not answwer My real quesstionss. Why humanss? Why nothing elsse?'

'Let me finish My answer, then. It is partly self-indulgence, I suppose, but not completely so. A lot of it is tradition. In the very first Game, that S/He started out of the first void, the humans were the first ones to write things down and try to understand them, the first ones to even suspect S/He existed. Hence We give them the honour of entertaining us in every World We create. Just as We honour the memory of the first Game-maker by being silent for a while every time S/He is mentioned.'

The gods are silent for a while.

'Which is why We do not speak of Him/Her very often', says Stochastos.

The gods are silent for a while.

'Because whenever We speak of . . .'

'Stop it,' snaps Petah-Petyi. Stochastos bows and grins.

'Sometimes I think the earliest Games were better than the ones We play now,' says Petah-Petyi. 'But the battle-Games are more popular, of course. Most gods love violence. Me, I admire the patience of the evolutionist gardeners, and envy the looks of perfect bliss on Their faces as they watch Their cells grow over millennia, tending them with water and light and love. Yet I do not have the patience for world-building.'

'But if it iss jusst tradition, then why do you alsso put in humanss in their original sstate? Why not make them all more powerful, more magical, more interessting?' asks Tsa-Ur, almost humbly.

'We like to watch them struggling. Humans are survivors, My deadly delight,' grins Stochastos. 'Forget the powerful human-shaped beings, the rakshases and jinns and ravians and the rest. Take away all the power, all the magic, strip them down to flesh and bone, they will still find a way to surprise You. Even though this Game has fewer significant humans in it than Petah-Petyi would like, in the end the humans will be as strong as the rest—or as dead as the rest. Without magic, without brains that are particularly different from the rest, without natural weapons, they have done well in every world they have been placed upon. This is why even Game-makers who are not human-shaped put humans in Their Games.'

'How do they do it?' asks Tsa-Ur. 'What makess humanss better ssurvivorss than reptiless?'

'This is a new side to you, My cruel crawler,' smirks Stochastos.

'I have never seen You curious about anything before. Why this sudden urge for education?'

'It iss thiss world. There is ssomething about it that troubless me. Ansswer My quesstion.'

'What makes humans capable of holding their own in magical worlds? The gods have pondered over this question for aeons. Initially We thought the humans just believed in themselves more, that they had more pride, more nobility and a deeper sense of the world belonging to them than the others.'

'But?'

'We were wrong. The reason for human survival in worlds of power and magic can be summed up in one word.'

'What iss that one word?'

'Denial.'

'What?'

'Denial. They are simply not clever enough to understand when they are beaten.'

As Tsa-Ur nods in comprehension and agreement, Sambo suddenly giggles aloud, and then looks astounded. The giggle was not his, one of the gods at the Table has just used him as a ventriloquist's dummy, concealing their mocking laughter by projection. He looks at them sharply. None of them appear to have heard him laugh, they are busy watching a sleeping hero in a crystal. Sambo feels his stomach suspiciously, trying to remember what he has eaten in the recent past.

Soma: Awake, arise, my sweet delight! Behold, the sun-lord's chariot has passed the crystal gates of Bhor, and the golden stallions' hooves have put the dark to flight, and nightmares are no more!

'There's no need to be sarcastic,' mumbled Red. She hadn't slept. An hour or so earlier, she'd dozed off, sitting with her back to a tree in a shady little wood in what was, as far as she was aware, eastern Potolpur. But she'd been woken in ten minutes by a large and sticky insect making love to her ear.

Tamasha: Just let her be, Soma. You can keep your morning nature beauty crazy talk to yourself.

But the beauty of nature in the morning wasn't giving up that easily. A pretty blue bird flew through fresh air in an elegant arc and perched on a branch above Red. Its breast engorged passionately as it looked at the sun and burst into a beautiful trilling melody.

Tamasha: Damn bird.

Soma: Shush. It sounds lovely. Appreciate nature, Tamasha.

Tamasha: I'd appreciate nature better deep-fried.

The bird heard. A second later, there was a resounding *splat* and Red's chest was covered in splotchy bird droppings.

Red's eyes narrowed. She shot a quick glance at Asvin. Still asleep.

Another second later, the bird took off, screaming indignantly, its tailfeathers smoking.

'I need coffee,' snarled Red.

Tamasha: *We* need coffee. So much for nature. I hate the country. I want to go home.

Soma: We should never have left.

Tamasha: Face it, Red. We're city girls.

City girls indeed, thought Red. She'd always wanted to see the world—all the other Rainbow Council members had, at some point in their long illustrious lives, travelled around the world, gaining experience, understanding different cultures, creatures and climates, and she'd always felt vaguely downtrodden for not having her share of sight-seeing. She'd always wanted to hit the road, see the great outdoors, sing the song of the open sky and so on.

But she was seeing the world now, at close quarters, and frankly, it was overrated. Perhaps under better circumstances her first time outside Kol could have been better—it could have been great fun, no doubt. But getting to know the country through this mad unplanned ravian-chase through the north-eastern Free States was not much fun at all.

It was the little things that you took for granted that were getting to her. And the things you never really thought about until they turned around and stuck their tongues out at you.

Like horses.

She'd never learnt how to ride a horse. She was a civilized city shapeshifter, skilled in the use of carpets, scintillating with vroomsticks thanks to Soma's extra-curricular escapades, and a tireless walker too. But horses filled her with dread. She hated the ones she'd met over the last ten days with all her might—great temperamental snorting beasts. At the city gates, when she'd thought there was an actual chance of catching up with the ravian and Maya within minutes and returning to the palace triumphant without anyone noticing her absence, she'd jumped on Asvin's horse in a flash. It had seemed the right thing to do, considering she had no idea whether pulling the strange rope thing attached to the horse's mouth made it go forwards or backwards or stop. And sharing a horse with Asvin, feeling her new body respond to him, had been pleasant . . .

But after a while they'd realized they were far behind, that they'd embarked upon a chase through the countryside to the gods knew where, and that they were remarkably short of essential supplies. And she'd had to get a horse of her own from one of the towns they'd passed—Rukmini, great warrior-queen, tsarina of stables and so on, would never have stooped to anything as helpless as horse-sharing.

Thankfully, her new physique and reflex-system were innately suited for horse-riding, and once she'd gotten over her initial qualms and relaxed enough to let her body take over she'd been all right.

After the first three days of wild riding through little towns, she'd grown bolder, and started fiddling with the horses' minds and eyes—she'd made them gallop much faster than normal horses would, by filling their eyes with illusions of food she'd dangled in mid-air before them. Of course, she had no idea what horses ate—she'd tentatively tried hay, which had failed, and she had no idea what oats looked like. Finally she had settled for cubes of salt and sugar—which were not only easy to do but were, in some convoluted way, urban revenge. The horses rode on tirelessly towards sweet or salty paradises, depending on the day of the week, and Red grinned to herself as she bounced up and down in a very correct riderly posture.

It was hazardous, though, riding around with someone who evidently thought he had a lot in common with her. Red knew all about nature—she'd read dozens of advanced biology books, knew her classifications, her evolution theories and her natural first aid techniques by heart, but translating theory into practice was difficult. Trees, for example. She wouldn't know a beech from an elm if it came up and pinched her bottom. And Asvin did look a little puzzled sometimes when he pointed out some natural marvel and his precious Rukmini looked in the wrong direction . . . .

She looked fondly at Asvin, curled up in a borrowed blanket in a hollow some distance away, sleeping the sleep of the righteous, untroubled by nightmares or amorous insects.

It wasn't fair, he looked so handsome even with his mouth open. And so peaceful, too. The fact that he'd last seen the love of his life about ten days ago, and that she might easily be dead wasn't bothering him as much as she'd expected. Or maybe that was just his way, doing the strong and silent routine. He certainly talked a lot about other things, though.

Soma: But then he's the kind of person who *knows* that he's going to be successful in everything he does. It's not a matter of *whether* he's going to win—it's *how* he's going to win, and *when*.

Tamasha: Or who's going to do the work for him.

Soma: I mean, look at the way he's calmly accepting the fact that Rukmini, Queen of Durg, has given up everything, including the kingdom she's supposed to run, just to help him save Maya. And Rukmini gets nothing out of it—I mean, she'd be happier in a way if he didn't save Maya, wouldn't she? I'm sure the thought has never entered his brain.

'Easy' said Red. 'He's just a boy.'

Soma: And he'll stay one as long as he's not left alone to do his Heroic work. Go back, Red, go back while you can. The Council might still take you back, it's not too late.

Tamasha: We've talked about this before. It *is* too late. She can't go back now. We have to keep going with him, we have to save Maya.

You cannot leave him now, he would be lost without you, said a voice in Red's head. Besides, he bears great love in his heart for me. He is only trying to save Maya out of his superb sense of duty. It's me he really wants.

'Oh be quiet, Rukmini, I'm thinking,' said Red distractedly.

Then she groaned.

Soma (quietly): Is there no end to your stupidity?

Tamasha (screaming): Aren't the two of us *enough*?

Rukmini: Thank you, Red.

I suppose it was inevitable, thought Red. She was bound to slip through my defences sooner or later. This is terrible, I've become so weak. I'm sure they've expelled me from the Council already, and deservedly so. This is going to get complicated. My body wants Asvin so badly, and now it has a mind as well . . .

Rukmini: Greetings, sisters.

Soma: Who are you calling sister?

It was incredible, Red thought, how much power a body had over the mind that had shaped it and tried to tame it. Bodies shaped you; they had their own language, their own feelings, their own means of expression. And if you assumed someone's body, chances are it would come with a mind that was quite similar to the original owner's—a mind that needed great skill to tame. Which is why if you stayed in one form too long, and your mental defences weren't developed enough, the body gradually took over until it refused to shapeshift any more, and just became an identical twin of whoever you were impersonating. There were horror stories, chilling tales of shapeshifters being reduced to voices in the heads of peoples' identical twins. Advanced shapeshifters like the Council members, like really powerful rakshases, could control this; if Soma and Tamasha hadn't weakened Red's mind, she could have done it herself quite easily. This was why shapeshifters could only really relax when their bodies were shaped like inanimate objects—that had its own set of dangers, it slowed you down, but at least it didn't drive you mad.

Some shapeshifters like to experiment—turning into animals was a thrill-sport where danger and pleasure danced hand in hand; where you could experience the thrill of a whole new set of senses, of animal brain patterns, the fascinating overlapping vision of the world through the compound eyes of a bee; the rivers of smell in a dog's nose; the world of sound-shapes as heard by a bat. These thrills came with a deadly peril—if you went over the edge and stayed animal, you ceased to be even a voice in the head, and all you had were your fabulous senses with no will to appreciate them.

There was that whole tricky business of changing gender too—Red shuddered involuntarily. It was *weird*, pretending to be a man; she never did it if she could help it. Men thought so differently, they *moved* so differently. It was scary how the same world, in the same colours, looked so different when you changed genders. And the way it *felt* . . . it was like growing hair *inside* your brain, that maddening prickly feeling that never went away. So many sex-changing shapeshifters had spent years just playing with their new bodies, completely self-obsessed, literally sick with self-love. If you turned into a bird, you usually got away with moving your head jerkily and trying to clean your armpits with your nose for a while after changing back. But to be a *man* . . . it was like being lost inside your own head and not being able to ask for directions.

Soma: Face it, Red. You did this on purpose. You're enjoying parading about in Rukmini's body a bit too much for our own good.

Tamasha: I don't mind the body, though. It's nice and disciplined, and keeps itself in shape. It would have to. Red's the kind of person, if she didn't have magical control over her body, she'd be fat.

'True,' said Red bitterly.

Rukmini: What should we do now? Should we wake Asvin?

Soma: Speak when you're spoken to, girl.

Tamasha: Listen, we should just leave him here. He'll be fine. Maya might not be. That ravian might be doing *anything* to her. And we can travel much faster on our own. We came here to save Maya, not shepherd Asvin through the woods.

Rukmini: But we have no wood-craft. Once we reach the forest, we will be helpless without Asvin.

'I hate to admit it,' said Red, 'but she's right.'

Tamasha: But we'll manage, Red. You've done well so far. That we've managed to stay on their tails for so long is quite an achievement.

For the last ten days everyone they'd asked for their quarry's whereabouts had lied to them. Uniformly. Lied quite unintentionally, but lied nevertheless; the ravian had tampered with their minds hastily in passing, so they all honestly believed they'd seen a man and a woman in a chariot heading in a completely different direction. Asvin had still not come to terms with the fact that it was a ravian hero who had abducted Maya thus—he was still obstinately insisting that it was Kirin's doing, but with each fresh instance of mental alteration they encountered on the road his defences were wearing thin.

'Don't give me too much credit,' said Red. 'They've used this method before. I just read about it, that's all.'

The answer was to ask people which direction they'd seen the couple in the chariot go and then take the *other* way; this was not foolproof, as there was often more than one other way, but at least you knew one way that was definitely wrong, thought Red. They'd had to double back quite a few times, and the ravian was now far ahead, but they were doing the best they could. They knew they were going the right way when they found people farther down the road who *also* remembered seeing a couple in a chariot heading in a different direction.

Soma: It's funny sometimes, the way the peasants greet us and courteously take it upon themselves to give us directions.

Tamasha: That's how a ravian would see it, isn't it? That's how Asvin probably sees it too—people in villages must be honest, uncorrupted, salt-of-the-earth, son-of-the-soil types, ever eager to help the gentry. I remember old Violet telling us that people in villages and cities weren't that different—chances are, if you asked them something they'd tell you to sod off in either case.

Rukmini: Red?

'Yes?'

Rukmini: Why do you call yourself Red?

'Look, ask Soma or Tamasha to give you a brief history of who I am later. I can't go through all this now.'

Soma: But actually that's not such a bad question.

'What do you mean?'

Tamasha: What she means is, you're not a part of the Council any more. You've broken the rules. You've deserted them. They've cast you out. This is the part where you take a name. *Be* someone, not a stupid colour.

Soma: Yes.

'I don't want to get into this right now,' said Red wearily. 'This would have been easy if there had been just one of you. I'll just go on calling myself Red, if you don't mind.'

Tamasha: Feel free. Although if you had called yourself Tamasha, life would have been much easier.

Soma: If you had called yourself Soma, there would have been some hope left for you.

Rukmini: And if you had called yourself Rukmini . . .

Soma, Tamasha: Shut up, you.

'I'm afraid to let go completely. Part of me is thoroughly enjoying breaking the rules—and it's not just the part of me that's you, Tamasha,' said Red slowly. 'Evidently I haven't reached the superior spiritual state that I should have—I haven't overcome the need for excitement, or even violence, which is the only thing that's kept the Council sane all these centuries.'

Soma: Which makes you extremely dangerous, with the powers you have. A dangerous criminal, possibly.

Tamasha: I'd rather be a criminal than a terminal bore. In fact, after saving Maya, we could go join a gang in that Neo-Hudlumm town in Grunvald—what's it called?

Soma: Doppell.

Tamasha: Yes. We'll go there and scare people by jumping out of corners wearing their faces. Come on.

Soma: Don't be silly. Red, you need to be even more wary of Tamasha now than you were before. She's nothing but a rakshasi now.

Tamasha: *Red* is a rakshasi now, Soma.

'I'm not.'

Tamasha: But you are—you've left the Council, you're mad, and you're enjoying not being in control, too. Sounds like a rakshasi to me.

Soma: Stop it. Even if we've left the Council, we need to abide by its rules.

Tamasha: That's just stupid. Just because you have some

stupid ancestor who chose not to take the throne of Kol because of some moral trap about stolen wives and threats to the throne doesn't mean you shouldn't get what you deserve. This is an amazing opportunity, Red. If we play our cards right, the world could be ours. Just keep following the ravian. And he will lead you to Kirin. Kirin's the key to power, Red, he's the one we need to meet.

Soma: So now you're plotting world domination as a full-fledged rakshasi, Tamasha?

Tamasha: What if I am?

Soma: Don't listen to her, Red. Think of everything you've learned. You've learned how to use your magic, to focus it, to control the magic raging through your blood. If your powers are not held in check, if you lose control, you could cause absolute chaos.

Tamasha: Sounds like fun to me.

'Stop it, both of you,' said Red, scared. 'I don't want to think about all this.'

Tamasha: Haven't you thought of it on your own? Ever since I saw that elephant a few days ago, I've been wondering what it would feel like to grow to giant size . . . we've never even tried it and we could do it, so easily, if you just let go a little . . . imagine how that would feel . . .

'I will not add to the problems of the Council,' said Red after a while. 'I don't want to hear you saying these things, Tamasha. Everything's difficult enough as it is. And I have *seen* what happens to shapeshifters who go over the edge. I won't do it.'

Before she had been admitted to the Rainbow Council, Red had spent some time as a shapeshifter rule-enforcer, patrolling the city for disguised rakshases and rogue shapeshifters, investigating crimes to see if magic-users were behind them. Shapeshifter enforcers drove shapeshifters gone bad from the city, regulating the rakshas-born so effectively that human authorities hadn't even realized what a huge problem hidden rakshases could be. But that was in the old days, before Soma and Tamasha had happened to her . . .

Tamasha: Just consider this. You've been trained to use your rakshas powers effectively, to tame them and control them. So you won't go mad. But you still *have* the powers, Red. You could do anything you wanted. And stay sane.

'We'd better get moving,' said Red. 'Sun's up.'

Soma: Should we leave the blankets here?

Tamasha: Why not? We didn't pay for them.

Soma: That we didn't. I love how the Phalanx's agents in all those towns kept giving Asvin things and pretending it was out of the kindness of their hearts.

Tamasha: And he still thinks they didn't know perfectly well he's Simoqin's Hero. The boy's capacity for self-delusion is phenomenal. Leave the blankets. The Phalanx spies can use them if they get here.

'No, roll them up. I don't know if there are any more towns up ahead. It could be just forests. We must be near Shantavan by now.'

Soma: I still think you should have let them follow us instead of leaving all those illusions behind, Red. They might have been useful in a fight.

Tamasha: Nice illusions, though. The footsteps-into-a-lake one was particularly fine.

Soma: The headless horseman was a bit overdone. But that's not the point. Why didn't you let them follow us, Red?

'Whatever the Phalanx knows, the Council learns,' said Red. 'And I don't want the Council to know what I'm doing here. I know they know I'm with Asvin, even the Phalanx must know, since Rukmini is obviously still in the palace. Which is another reason for staying out of their sight.'

Tamasha: Really stupid idea, choosing Rukmini in the first place. Everyone in Kol must know by now that Asvin's with a shapeshifter.

Soma: You've exposed the Council.

'No, I haven't. And yes, I wish I'd chosen something else, but I had no time to think about it, and I needed to be someone Asvin would listen to without question. I'm just afraid they'll send someone out after me. If any of the other six wanted, they could find me easily by travelling with the Phalanx.'

Tamasha: The Phalanx didn't have a chance in the first place. Their trusted informants along the road probably told them what the ravians left behind in their heads, so they must have gone off in the wrong direction anyway. The Phalanx could be in Elaken by now, for all you know.

Rukmini: The Prince awakens.

Asvin opened his eyes and took in the morning cheerfully. Then he sprang up, refreshed and energetic, smiled at Red and wandered quickly into the bushes.

Tamasha: Something's coming.

Red jumped behind a tree as the faint strains of a song sung in a cheery voice floated through the wood. She waited.

A while later, a little fat man in blue sauntered by, singing a merry song, a song full of happy-sounding words that didn't make sense. There was a carefree smile on his lips, and his button-like pupil-less eyes twinkled comically in the morning sunshine. He saw the horses standing quietly by a tree but his steps did not falter; he pranced on, with a merry fa-la-la.

After he had gone, Red stepped back into the clearing and watched him until he was a blue skipping dot, heading northwards and westwards.

Asvin, ablutions completed, walked up to Red.

'Was it another of those singing men?'

'Yes.'

'Third one this week,' said Asvin. 'What does this mean?'

'I don't know.'

'We slept too long,' he said sadly. 'I wish I had far-seeing eyes, or could hear the hidden songs of the earth. For I do not know where they have gone, or how far behind we are. But something tells me today will be a great day, a red day. There's something in the wind.'

Tamasha: He says this every day.

Soma: Well, on days when significant things happen, he gets it right. Don't be so cynical. And maybe he's right today. I feel something in the wind myself.

Tamasha: That's the smell of horse dung.

'Let us not waste any more time then,' said Red. 'Let's go!'

As they leaped gracefully on their rested mounts and galloped on in the sunshine towards Shantavan, the discussion in Red's head galloped on too.

Tamasha: Who *are* these little bearded fatties?

Soma: The children of the earth, what else? It gladdens my heart to see these innocent woodland creatures frolicking in the morning, so carefree. It's a symbol. It tells us that some things are worth protecting. We must use our power to preserve.

Tamasha: Preserve little hairy men?

Soma: No! Preserve ways of life. Indigenous cultures.

Tamasha: What ways of life? He was just running pointlessly.

Soma: Don't be obtuse. It's all a metaphor.

Tamasha: For what?

Soma: Never mind.

Rukmini: She's saying there is much in the world that is under threat; that our task is to stay in the shadows and hold off the dark, so the innocent can stay in the sunshine. (Silence)

Tamasha: Ooh. Listen to Miss Know-it-all.

Soma (stiffly): I can speak for myself, thank you very much.

Rukmini: I was just saying . . .

Soma, Tamasha: Shut it, you.

17

The first thing Maya noticed as her mind stepped on the silver bridge between dream and consciousness was the terrible, all-encompassing stench.

Must have bath, she thought grimly.

A little further towards awakening, and her spellbinder's senses took over.

Instruction to self: Don't open eyes yet. Don't make sudden movements. He will see. Breathe deep and slow.

She woke up.

No, it wasn't her doing the stinking, she remembered. Well, she was, but it paled into insignificance beside the almost solid stench of the manticore. The last time she had tried to wake, she had been lying across his back, slung over him like a sack as he padded through the jungle. His stench had entered the deepest recesses of her lungs then. She'd woken up screaming and the ravian had forced more hot liquid, that potion or drug or whatever it was, into her mouth.

She'd lost consciousness again, entered that horrible shifting, grasping dreamtime she'd learned to dread. The dreamtime she'd woken up screaming from quite a few times, only to be sent hurtling back by her mocking captor.

Sometimes she'd managed to get on her feet, free herself of whatever was binding her, start running—but he had always been one step ahead, he had always caught her just at that precise moment when she'd started believing there was a faint chance of escape, or watched with a calm smile as her legs buckled under her and she staggered and crashed to the floor. This was like a little game to him, breaking her down, letting her try to escape, stopping her, watching her tears with a cold, detached amusement. Cat and mouse. Big, strong cat and little weak mouse.

The memories of the last few days came back—were they memories, or memories of dreams? She did not know. All she knew was that they had been travelling at a relentless pace, first through towns, then through woods, and now they were in some vast, deep forest—Vrihataranya or Shantavan. They'd travelled on horseback and chariot before—now, since meeting the manticore on the edge of the forest, they had been travelling on foot. She had no idea how long she'd been a captive. It was all a haze of shifting rooms, inns, surprised strangers' faces blurring away into nothingness, the sound of horses' hooves, chariots, dazed visions of dark rooms and her ravian captor stuffing food roughly into her lolling mouth.

Memories of struggling wildly and futilely against strong binding ropes, of walking the dark roads of madness, of babbling incoherently, watching from some distant tower as her mouth and her brain and her ears wandered blindly on different planes of understanding, different places, different times, unconnected, disjointed, insane. Memories of listening to voices in her head from her past, her future, and places and times she hoped fervently did not exist.

And there were other memories, darker ones; of kisses, of lying in his arms, of waking up next to him, of strange comfortable pleasant smells, of warm, tender caresses, that filled her with terror. What was he doing to her? She hoped fervently that those memories had been dreams. They'd *better* have been dreams.

He had been trying to get into her mind, she knew. He had been probing the soft corners of her brain with his terrible mind, his strong, cool, passionless, probing lance of a brain. She'd fought back wildly, raising walls, building illusions, struggling for control. She thought she'd kept him out of her mind—or was that what he wanted her to think? She did not know. And he had so many different ways of attacking her, breaking her down. There were the nightmares, and worse, the pleasant dreams, usually starring him as her lover or her god. There were the false memories he'd been trying to insert into her subconscious. There were the straightforward attacks, where he'd charged the walls of her mind with what felt like a battering ram. And there were the incessant, soft, persuasive whispers—*Give up. Submit. You cannot win. You are mine.*

Ravians cannot control magical minds, she had repeated to herself continuously amidst her tears. But even as she did so, she knew that it was not necessarily true—it was quite possible that a really strong ravian could break her mind down, simply drive away the magic from her brain, leaving it pulpy and raw and submissive. Or, again, perhaps that was what he wanted her to think. She *was* going mad, though, if she wasn't completely mad already. There was no doubt about that.

There was also no doubt that he was a ravian. Apart from the obvious power of his mind, there was the memory, the very clear memory of the way he had fought in mid-air back in Kol, not to mention the difficult-to-ignore fact that the manticore was with them, and the manticore was known to be a servant of the ravians. Why he was abducting her and what the larger implications of her abduction would be she had yet not had time to think about; staying alive, staying conscious and *really* hurting her captor in some way as soon as she could were the objectives that dominated most of her thoughts whenever she awoke, that dominated all her actions when she awoke, right until the moment he sent her spiralling back into darkness.

She'd even heard his name briefly, the last time, the manticore had been speaking to him. Speaking in rhyme, too. What was it? Murdoc? Marduk? No, something that rhymed with *welcome back* . . .

Myrdak, that was it. Myrdak. Myrdak the ravian. Myrdak the soon to be squashy mess on the floor, if she had her way.

She heard voices. His voice, and the manticore's. She listened keenly, straining to find some piece of information, some indication of where they were, what they were doing, and why they had abducted her in the first place. But they were too far away, or they were talking in whispers, or she was going deaf as well as mad. Whatever it was, she couldn't hear them.

A cool, moist breeze ruffled her hair. She was lying on fresh earth; it felt clean and solid. Still in the forest. She could hear the incessant song of the locals. Some kind of insect was crawling around on her stomach, irritating her immensely, but she couldn't afford to squash it. He would sense it, sense the danger, and then sense her anger and what remained of her magical powers seeking him out. Remain calm, she thought. You don't have proper control of your magic or your limbs—you have to heal yourself first, or you'll just do another little dance for his amusement. Don't rush. Everything must be slow and precise. The last time you were abducted, you acted on the first idea you got and ended up setting fire to the city. She remembered Bali, remembered soaring above the streets of Kol slung over the hideous vanar's shoulder, and felt no horror at all. At least he had never kissed her. She *really* hoped that had been a dream.

Abducted. Again. It was quite funny, if you thought about it. If she'd ever had to make a list of Ten People Least Likely To Get Abducted (Ever), she'd have been right up there, with Yarni, Triog and the Olivyan wrestler Amigo the Flatulent. But here she was, a little helpless girl tied up on the ground, waiting for a hero to rescue her (where *was* that Asvin, by the way?) and in serious, serious danger of never seeing the Underbelly again.

The forest was rustling with magic. She could feel it, flowing as serenely as a great river through the sky above and the earth below, nudging the leaves gently around her with every breath of the breeze. She needed to tap into that magic somehow, recharge her frayed nerves and her powers, heal herself. And *then* she would attack him.

She opened her eyes, a slit, very slowly.

They were in front of her, a few yards away, with their backs to her. Sitting near the edge of a cliff, looking down into a deep valley full of huge banyan trees that stood out strong and black in the moonlight, their creepers ribs of darkness across the night sky. She looked at the trees. They were taller than the trees she had seen in Shantavan, more solid, more menacing, somehow obviously older.

Vrihataranya.

She weighed her options.

Her ankles were tied to a nearby tree. Her hands were tied together in front of her; she'd tried burning off the ropes once but it had hurt like hell, and the smell had drawn Myrdak to her in seconds. He'd watched her, smirking, until the rope had burnt out almost completely, enjoying her pain, and then he had knocked her into unconsciousness at the very last instant before her hands came free.

She searched her brain desperately for good ideas. Her best friend, the fireball, would be useless here—he'd sense it, dodge it just in time. Trying to lunge at him and push him over the edge of the cliff would be futile, too—she didn't have enough control over her limbs and in any case he could probably travel to Ventelot and back in the time it would take for her to rush at him.

A sudden burst of magic was what she needed. Something that would surprise him, beat his reflexes. Ravians could deal with bursts of magic, she knew. They knew how to fight rakshases, whose raw magical powers were unmatched. But the thing about rakshases, Maya knew, was that running around forests roaring and eating people might be good for health, but it didn't really leave you with a lot of time for studying the nature and uses of magical power. And the spellbinders, who spent all their time (while not drunk, or getting there) trying to bend the rules of magic and discover new spells, had a lot of tricks up their sleeves that the ravians had probably never seen before. And she was, after all, as she kept telling herself, the most powerful young spellbinder in Kol. Or outside Kol, for that matter. The clever thing to do now would be to have a bright idea. Something that would overcome the ravian's powers and force him to make mistakes.

And it wasn't as if this ravian didn't make mistakes.

For example, one mistake he had made now was that he had let a powerful spellbinder lie on the earth in a very magical wood with time on her hands.

Inside her head, she grinned maniacally.

She pushed the tips of her fingers into the earth, searching with her mind, and after about fifteen minutes she felt a cold tendril of earth magic warming the tip of a finger. And then another, and another, until her fingers were one with the veins of the earth.

She lay absolutely still and waited, feeling the power of the earth slowly rise into her fingers like sap, filling her slowly with ancient, potent magic until she was fully healed, her mind was clear and sharp and there was so much magic churning inside her that she felt ready to explode.

Explode, she thought. Now there's a nice word.

She opened her eyes again, briefly. The ravian was lying down next to a tree, tantalizingly near the cliff-edge. He seemed to be asleep. The manticore sat next to him, looking down at the valley below.

It was time.

Maya brought her tied hands up in front of her face, very slowly.

She whispered an incantation to herself, imagining millions of tiny little bubbles rising in her stomach, coming together, crashing into each other, squeezing, coalescing into a tightly packed little ball that rose up in her throat like the biggest burp there ever was . . . Her stomach muscles clenched, convulsed, her eyes bulged.

She softly coughed the Airball out into her palms.

It was warm, pulpy and wet, and smelled rather terrible.

And then, in one swift, smooth movement, she tossed the Airball jerkily towards Myrdak and Manticore, turned over and curled up in a foetal ball.

Her sudden movement woke Myrdak. Amazingly swiftly, he rose, and was already on one knee when . . .

The Airball exploded with a satisfying *kaBOOM*.

Maya hugged the ground as tightly as she could, feeling clumps of torn earth hit her back. And because she was looking the other way, she did not have the satisfaction of watching Myrdak and Manticore as the explosion caught them. They were thrown about six feet upwards in the air, a tangle of helpless, flailing limbs.

More importantly, they were thrown about four feet backwards.

Over the edge of the cliff.

Maya smiled grimly as various sounds emanating from two big bodies hitting a large number of hard objects while rapidly descending down what sounded like a reasonably high cliff made themselves heard.

Then, crying out in pain, Maya burned off the ropes that bound her arms and legs, and quickly cast a healing spell on herself. The earth magic of Vrihataranya coursed through her veins again, healing, clearing, invigorating.

Below, over the edge of the cliff, she could hear crashing sounds, bodies moving around, regaining control, beginning to climb up.

She ran to the edge and conjured up a really huge fireball, and sent it blazing down in the direction of the sounds. Faint curses below told her she hadn't killed her travelling companions, but had upset them considerably.

A little forest fire should make things more interesting for them, she thought, while I decide which way to run.

One of the few good things about forest fires is that they make it easy for people near them to decide very quickly to run very quickly in the opposite direction.

Maya ran away as fast as she could, speeding through the dense jungle towards nowhere in particular.

18

A great bell tolled at midnight, but its ringing was not the sound that sent frightened whispers cascading through the winding streets of the city-fortress Izakar. The denizens of the city looked up, towards the moonlit sky, and heard once more that terrible slow beat that pulsed from the plains to the mountains, the heartbeat of ancient winged death.

Dragon wings.

Bat-winged lizard-shapes blotting out the stars above the Dark Tower. Some skimming low over the tower, some mere dots high in the sky. Another clan of dragons crossing their master's tower on their way to their new nest-halls built by the asurs in the mountains to the west.

As they passed right above the topmost spires, one exuberant young male swooped downwards, gliding over the city, sending street-walkers scurrying for shelter in sudden panic. A glimpse of glittering horns and fangs and claws, the moon faintly visible through his translucent veined wings, a cold wind rushing through the city in his wake—

and then, with a great *voom*, he flapped his wings and flew up the side of the Dark Tower, scattering pazuzus and gargoyles before him. He coiled himself around the top of the Tower and was still for a moment, looking through a tiny window into a room on top of the Tower. Then he jerked his head upwards and sent a huge fountain of fire into the sky. And the Dark Lord's followers, overcome by the dragon's savage beauty, cheered hoarsely and clanged metal on metal far below in the streets. The dragon screamed harshly and joined his clan-siblings in the sky, heading westwards. Like a herd of black sheep in the sky, clouds bursting with thunder followed in their wake, shutting out the stars.

And in the small, sparsely furnished room on top of the Dark Tower, sitting by the window the dragon had looked through seconds earlier, the Dark Lord opened his eyes and smiled. The Gauntlet of Tatsu shone scarlet on his hand. Scarlet as his glowing eyes, but then he blinked, and his eyes were brown and dark again as the fires went out.

There was a knock on the door. He rose, unlatched it and stepped out.

It was Akimis. 'The ravian's awake,' she said.

'Who else knows?' asked Kirin.

'No one.'

'Good. Let's go.'

She had brought four fresh-from-the-oven elite pashans, who were standing around a palanquin carved to look like a crocodile's mouth. Kirin and Akimis sat inside. The pashans picked up the palanquin and started trotting down the steep spiral stairs that led all the way from the tower to the dungeons, their stone feet thumping dully on the endless stairs.

It was ridiculous, thought Kirin, being carried downstairs like this, but the Tower was just too high to walk down.

'May I ask you something?' asked Akimis. 'What are those dark lines under your eyes?'

'I don't know,' said Kirin. 'They feel like little scales. I think it's from wearing the Gauntlet too long.'

'The Gauntlet is evil,' she said. 'But the lines bring out your eyes.'

Kirin grinned. 'Thank you.'

He sat back, as comfortably as was possible on a slanted palanquin being carried down steep stairs at a tremendous pace by stone men, and looked at Akimis silently. He'd found that she had a tendency to babble nervously if he created a vacuum of silence. And her nervous chatter was sometimes most informative.

Thanks to her he knew, for example, that ever since Spikes had disappeared mysteriously two weeks ago, the rakshases had been talking about how their leader had changed. That they all wondered why he spent his nights in the Tower now, locked up alone in the highest room. His presence there was difficult not to notice, of course—at night, the whole city saw a strange glow come out of the top of the Tower, white or eerie green, and sometimes it seemed as if bolts of lightning flashed, two or three at a time, connecting the top of the Dark Tower to the clouds above, but there was never any thunder. The rakshases thought the strange sword-play in the sky was a sign that Kirin was conducting some hideous, earth-changing experiment, or talking to the dead, or the gods, or fighting the ravians in some mysterious way. But all he would say when they asked him was 'I was dreaming.' And he knew the rakshases saw he had become colder, more distant, quieter. He knew he now radiated a sense of purpose, that though he felt he had no control over what was going on around him, he at least *looked* like he did. Which was all he could ask for, really.

He knew the rakshases had been pleased at the icy way he'd put Laakon and his werewolves in place. He had been furious when they'd brought Behrim in, broken, bloody, barely alive. Behrim had lain tossing and turning in the dungeons, in the tender care of healer rakshases for more than a week, and Kirin had begun to despair.

No one had asked him to explain his concern for Behrim. The appearance of the ravian, the sudden realization that the enemy had actually arrived, that they knew nothing about his movements, and that the Dark Lord alone seemed to have some sort of plan, had worked wonders on the rakshases. The last traces of mutiny had disappeared; they carried out all Kirin's commands unquestioningly.

Still, Kirin thought that there was no point in being unnecessarily trusting and speaking to Behrim in public now that he was finally awake. It would do no good to rakshas morale to hear that the ravians apparently wanted their Dark Lord to rule the ravians as well. They would be far better off not knowing that Behrim and Kirin had spoken in private. And Akimis would probably not run around telling people just yet. While she was by no means trustworthy, her intense desire to win his favour (he knew that some of the artless gossip about other rakshases was completely intentional) would mean she would probably not betray his confidence just yet. Probably.

After what would have seemed like hours had Akimis not been with him, Kirin finally reached the dungeon where Behrim was being held.

The ravian was in one of the finest cells in the dungeons,

one of the rare ones that didn't come with a free attached swarm of little slimy creatures who entertained you by gnawing at your flesh. He lay on the floor, attached to the wall by chains secured to his wrists and ankles, secured with locks that had been melted solid to prevent him from opening them with his mind. Four healer rakshases sat around him, applying spells and herbs on the numerous wounds that still lacerated his body. Werewolf wounds were very resistant to all forms of healing. Fortunately, the werewolves hadn't bitten him, his neck was untouched. Fortunately for the werewolves, that is. You *really* didn't want to create a ravian werewolf.

Behrim's eyes were open and he watched the healers quietly. Kirin wondered how he'd react if he knew that among rakshases, the best healers were also the best cooks . . .

He sensed Kirin enter the room and smiled weakly at him. 'Greetings, Dark Lord of Imokoi,' he said. 'I understand I have you to thank for my life.'

'Leave us,' said Kirin to the rakshases, with the kind of imperious hand gesture that people who enter rooms and say 'Leave us' make. The rakshases bowed and left.

'You too, Akimis,' said Kirin.

'But he might attack you,' she whispered.

I assure you I am capable of defending myself, said Kirin.

'But should you be . . .'

Kirin turned around and the door of the dungeon swung open with a hideous creak that had nothing to do with its perfectly oiled hinges.

Go.

Akimis went.

Kirin sat down on the floor next to the ravian.

'I do not have much time,' he said. 'Word will spread, and others will be here soon. So speak.'

'Would you undo my chains, Kirin? There is some magic in them that burns my skin.'

'No.'

'Wise. Where do I begin?'

'Tell me what the ravians are doing back in the world, and stop talking in that low, soothing voice, because it doesn't work.'

'This is my voice, Kirin. You have heard it before.'

'I don't remember. It doesn't matter. Go on.'

'We never really went away,' said Behrim. 'It was a strategic withdrawal, in response to a challenge. We always knew we were coming back. At the time, we needed to leave—strange new beasts were attacking the world and human politicians were always quick to blame the ravians, the vamans were perilously close to finding Asroye, the spellbinders of Kol were openly suspicious of our intentions, and the new human powers in Kol, in league with rakshases and vamans, were plotting our downfall. The Enemy had told us he would return in two hundred years to undo all the good we had worked upon the land. How could we refuse the challenge?'

'So you are back in full strength? Asroye has been rebuilt? There are ravian armies ready to go to war?'

'Before that, Kirin, I would like some proof that you are a ravian and not a rakshas shapeshifted.'

'You say you knew my mother?'

'She was my cousin.'

'She used to wear green earrings. The one on the left was chipped.'

Behrim was silent for a moment. 'No, it wasn't,' he said.

'I know. The one on the right was chipped. Get on with your story.'

Behrim smiled. 'I taught you well.'

'We do not have time for tender reminiscences.'

'Get me out of here, Kirin. We really need to speak at length.'

'Don't be silly. Give me a reason. Several good reasons, in fact.'

'Reason? Very well—if we do not leave fast, the ravians will decide to continue with the social and political systems that currently govern us, the Obiyalis monarchy will be reinstated under a noble tyrant and this world will know war and bloodshed on an unprecedented scale. We have grown stronger while we were away, Kirin. We have trained for a war for two hundred years. And the only way to achieve peace on this planet—a peace that the last war taught me to desire—is for you to come with me to Asroye.'

'What would that achieve?'

'The fact that you are alive, that the son of Narak and Isara walks the land, and has even brought the evil rakshases and dragons to heel will inspire our cause and augment the power of our House. It will bring about the realization of all I have dreamed of for years—the glorious ravian republic.'

Oh gods! More winding speeches. 'Look,' said Kirin, 'just start at the beginning. Maybe you'll make sense then. Who are you, and why are you here?'

'We need to go even further back,' said Behrim. 'Back to the Great War, and how it changed the ravians forever.'

'I've really had enough of the Great War,' said Kirin. 'Tell me what's happening *now*. What the ravians are doing, where they are, and what their plans are.'

'It will mean nothing if I do not tell you of the War first.'

'Very well then,' sighed Kirin. 'If you must.'

Then Behrim, lying in the dungeons of the Dark Tower, told the Dark Lord about the Great War, and how it had changed the ravians forever.

He told Kirin of the rift created among the ranks of the ravians by the ill treatment meted out to Narak and Isara, the greatest heroes of the War. When they were banished for their defiance of the ravian caste system, the House of Esmi, the warrior sub-caste that Isara, Behrim and Kirin belonged to, had openly disputed the ravian king's decision and along with it, the rigidity of the caste structure of ravian society as a whole. In doing so, they had made enemies of the House of Aegos, the oldest and most powerful of the ravian warrior clans, which had produced heroes like Simoqin and Zibeb. A large number of the nobles of Esmi had chosen voluntary exile from Asroye, and had joined Isara and her generals in their strongholds in the forest. Over the last two hundred years, the rift had spread amongst all the ravian warrior clans. The House of Esmi and their allies demanded a complete abolition of the caste system, giving equality to all castes and the eventual establishment of a ravian republic. The House of Aegos and their allies were monarchists, and saw no reason why a perfect system needed to be changed. Aegos and its allies were more numerous and more powerful. But the greatest heroes stood by Esmi. On numerous occasions, civil war had narrowly been averted.

In the end, it had been decided that Obiyalis would be the world where change, if any, would be tested, for it was on Obiyalis that the trouble had started in the first place. Which was why the three heroes who entered Obiyalis first, in accordance with the secret treaty the ravians had made with the vamans, had all been assigned specific sacred tasks.

'Treaty with the vamans?' said Kirin. 'I thought you were scared the vamans would find Asroye. Which is confusing too, because I'd always thought the vamans were on the side of Kol and the ravians in the first place. Didn't Vul Kunpo pledge his armies to Kol when he gave Danh-Gem the Chariot of Vul?'

'The vamans who lived above ground fought for Kol and their own business interests, not for the ravians,' said Behrim. 'If the vamans had used their main force in the war, they would have fought against us. Not for the Dark Lord, for they bear no love for the asurs, but against the ravians, who they suspected wrongly of plotting to usurp their cities underground. And the vaman king refused to allow us to visit his cities in peace, and even killed some ravians he claimed had tried to enter his domain in secret— a black lie, Kirin, one of many lies that the vamans told at the time, even as they dug through the earth in an endless search to discover Asroye, to strike at our very heart. They claimed we were trying to control them, to take over their minds and their wondrous machines, when those machines filled us with nothing but despair and loathing, for we saw in them not engines of victory but weapons for the destruction of all that was green and beautiful. And our fears were more than justified. The vamans approached us in friendliness sometimes, with precious gifts and offers of eternal peace, but we saw their true purpose in their devious eyes and cunning hearts—all they wanted from us was to learn the secrets of portal-making, so that they could take their great engines and furnaces to other worlds, and build more empires in the shadows, cutting away the very roots of the earth in their endless lust for wealth and power.'

'All right, so you don't like vamans,' said Kirin. 'You've made that clear. Now get on with your story. If the ravians and the vamans were not fond of each other, then why did the vamans let you back in?'

'There were a few noble vamans above the ground, who fought with us in the War, who slowly began to see that their king had lied to them about the ravians, that the ravians were not hungry for power. These vamans slowly grew close to us, to the light, and turned away from the darkness that had surrounded them, and the lies and false promises of their lords underground.'

'In other words, you controlled their minds.'

'No, for vamans, like magical beings from this world, cannot be controlled by ravians, we do not know why. If we had been able to influence their minds with our powers, we would have guided them for their own good, and with them on our side we could have defeated Danh-Gem easily. So many deaths could have been averted if only the vamans had been less selfish, less greedy, less cowardly . . .'

'Yes, yes. So you, um, persuaded these vamans to form some kind of secret society that let you in now?'

'Yes. They called themselves the Rebel Union of Marginal Labour.'

'What a truly terrible name.'

'They named themselves, Kirin.' Behrim smiled.

'And this Rebel Union of . . . anyway, these vamans let you back into the world, so now Asroye has been rebuilt.'

'It is more complicated than that.'

'Of course it is. Tell me.'

'What do you remember about the portals, Kirin?'

'Nothing. There is nothing written in human histories either. I remember seeing the portal for the Departure—a white dome of light spreading over Asroye—but I could not go through it. That's all.'

'I do not know the secrets of portal-making myself,' said Behrim. 'None of the warrior castes do. The priests and scholars who know the secret guard it well; it is the source of their power, without it they would never have the ear of the king. But it is common knowledge that for a world to be inhabitable by ravians, for us to be able to open that first portal in a new world, it must have powerful feline beings in it. There is something mysterious about cats, they exist between dimensions, between worlds. It is this essence that our scholars use to create portals between worlds.'

'Cats and ravians,' said Kirin. 'Somehow that makes sense, though I like cats.'

He listened closely as Behrim told him what he knew of portal-making, and that the ravians had been drawn to Obiyalis because of the existence, on Obiyalis, of a race of immensely powerful magical panthers called nundus.

The blood of each race of magical cat had certain intrinsic qualities. Each type of blood could create a portal strong enough for a certain number of ravians to pass through. The nundus were so powerful that a single nundu's blood could create a portal through which thousands could pass. Thrilled by the ability of this world to sustain them, by the power of its portal-blood, the ravians had entered with great hopes. They had dreamed of Obiyalis becoming the centre of their galactic empire. And it was on Obiyalis that they met the greatest challenge they had encountered—Danh-Gem and his terrible rakshases. Obiyalis fascinated and terrified the ravians. Their return was inevitable. As were obstacles to their return created by their enemies.

In the last year of the war, the ravians had discovered

that there were traitors in the ranks of the Rebel Union of Marginal Labour—agents of the vaman king. They had made this discovery in the most dramatic way possible, when the vamans had stormed the keep where the ravians had kept all the nundus they had captured over the years, and tried to slaughter them all. They nearly succeeded as well, but two nundus escaped the carnage and fled to Asroye and safety. The ravians had placed these two in hidden underground dens, one in Vrihataranya, one in the Bleakwood, guarded by trusty secret clans of men (made more trustworthy by mind-alteration), so that they could be used to create the portals and bring the ravians back when the time came.

The ravians had killed all the members of the Rebel Union except the four they trusted, and before the Departure, they had signed a sacred treaty in ravian and vaman blood. The vamans would rebuild the Rebel Union, more carefully this time. And when the year of the Simoqin Prophecies arrived, and with it the threat of Danh-Gem's return, they would travel to the Hidden Ziggurat in Vrihataranya, where Manticore, most faithful servant and trusted secret-bearer of the ravians, would meet them. And following Manticore's instructions, they would create a portal to bring three ravians back to Obiyalis, to rebuild Asroye and carry on their mission of peace and understanding. If the three succeeded in their quests, then the Rebel Union of the vamans would be taught the secrets of portal-making, to enable them to lead their fellow vamans to light and freedom, and escape their tyrannical underworld rulers.

'Why three?' asked Kirin.

'Three is all the manticore's blood can support,' said Behrim. 'Three heroes, to travel to Obiyalis through Manticore's portal and then travel to the nundu's hiding place in Vrihataranya, to let in the first group of builders and craftsmen. Three heroes, to perform three sacred tasks that would decide the future of ravian society.

'First, Myrdak, of House Aegos. To him was assigned the task of destroying the evil human-vaman alliance that holds sway over Kol, most marvellous of human cities, and bringing about the return of the rightful King of Kol.

'Second, Peori, of House Hanash, most neutral and peace-loving of the ravian warrior clans. To her was assigned the task of returning to Asroye and following the trail of Kirin, son of Narak and Isara, the key to understanding this world.

'And third, Behrim, veteran of the Great War, spokesman of House Esmi, was assigned the task of slaying Danh-Gem reborn, destroying the rakshas lords and thus restoring the honour of the ravians, and the memory of the brave deeds of his cousin, Princess Isara, in the last days of the Age of Terror.

'Manticore kept his secret and his promise faithfully. He found the vamans, and opened the portal, and we came through.'

'What did you do with the vamans?'

'We killed them. We had to, this was the most delicate stage of all. There must have been spies of the vaman king among those that brought us here. We knew that their real intention was not to help us, but to find out about portals.'

'And then you found the nundu and opened the portal.'

'It must have been done, though I was not there to do it. For even as we began our journey towards the ancient site of Asroye, we chanced upon two travellers in the forest—Skuan-lord Bjorkun and Bali the vanar, journeying northwards to meet the werewolves and the ice-giants. We decided that I should set off on my quest at once, and Peori and Myrdak would see to the opening of the portal. I have

not met Peori or Myrdak since then. I have shadowed your
servants all over the world, seen them cast their nets of dark
treachery wherever they went.'

'Why entrust these rather dangerous quests to just three
people? Why not send in the whole army to slay Danh-
Gem and the Civilian too, if you wanted to?'

'We had the advantage of surprise and stealth. This is
the way of the ravians, Kirin. We are deadliest when working
alone and in secret. Remember your parents.'

'Myrdak of Aegos . . . aren't you and this Myrdak enemies?'

'For now, a truce has been declared between Houses Esmi
and Aegos. In any case, Myrdak and I would not have had
to work together. To answer your question, we do not get
along, quite frankly. But he is probably the strongest warrior
we have at present, and no better person could be found to
train and counsel the rightful King of Kol, and pierce the
heart of the vaman stronghold on the surface of the earth.
Just as I was the best person to slay Danh-Gem—a task I
suspect you have done for me. Though how you convinced
the rakshases you were his son and heir I simply cannot
comprehend. The most important task, however, is neither
Myrdak's, nor mine, but Peori's. The High Council will
declare the future of the ravians—republic or monarchy—
based on her report. Based on *your* actions, Kirin.'

'Why?'

'The skilled politicians of House Aegos forced us into
this situation, Kirin. It was agreed that a representative of
House Hanash, which has always maintained neutrality in
this struggle for ravian power, would be sent to find Narak's
son. For long, House Aegos has tried to discredit your
father's memory—they have said he was a traitor, that he
was secretly in league with Danh-Gem. The first time they

said this, it almost caused civil war, for we were enraged beyond belief by their lies. By spreading these false and vile accusations, they sought to ruin our entire movement, which held him up as a symbol of low-caste nobility. Strangely enough, we eventually found ourselves in a position where we had to agree to let the High Council judge *you*, his son, to see how a product of an inter-caste marriage carried out the duties of a ravian when left to himself. *You* are the measure of whether the caste system needs to change. Whether ravians need to change.'

'That doesn't make sense.'

'Politics.'

'What if I were dead?'

'Then we would have had a problem.'

'Ah. But then, I am not dead.'

'As we hoped. And Peori was the one given the task of finding you, with the consent of both Aegos and Esmi. She is wise and strong, a scholar as well as a warrior. And she was born on this world, in Kol, and thus can be trusted to do what is best for it. The High Council decided she was the perfect person to give a just and fair account of your doings to the ravians. She is not a monarchist or a republican, and is too young to remember the first War.'

'She sounds nice. I wonder where she is. You, meanwhile, came to find Danh-Gem, and found me instead.'

'I followed first Bjorkun and Omar on their travels, and then your Brotherhood of Renewal all the way to Imokoi. But I was waylaid by the shadowsnatchers as I crossed the mountains from Vrihataranya, and I lost your trail there. My plan was to have Hooba the asur-king slay Danh-Gem when he rose. But that plan failed—it was difficult to catch Hooba alone in the forest, difficult to alter his mind in

Aciram's presence, but I managed it. But when you tricked them that night, pretending to be Danh-Gem's son, my alterations faded out of Hooba's mind—because of your power and the fact, I think, that he genuinely loves you. I slew the shadowsnatchers who had dared to cross my path and followed you to Izakar, aiming to kill you myself, but your guards were too smart to let me slip through. But I have walked the wilds of Imokoi before, and it was not too difficult for me to enter your city, though covering myself in foul-smelling muck to hide from the keen noses of the rakshases was no pleasure, I assure you. In Izakar, I found the monstrous bartender and bent his mind instead. You cannot imagine the dangers I have encountered, lurking in the rakshas city. Just as you cannot imagine my feelings the day I heard that the Dark Lord's name was Kirin.'

'That wouldn't help House Esmi much, would it. The inter-caste boy ends up leading the rakshases.'

'You must come away with me now, Kirin. We can explain everything away. But you must tell the King and his High Council you were deceiving the rakshases to try and stop them from destroying innocent lives in a war against defenceless mortals. That will convince the Council of both your power and your nobility. And when we win, when we become a republic, you would be the obvious choice to lead us, the son of the heroes who brought about the whole change in the first place.'

'While Peori goes to your Council and tells them I am the son of Danh-Gem?'

'A clever lie you spread yourself. We can make them believe anything we want, as long as we present our case quickly and eloquently. You must come, Kirin. Terrible darkness threatens the ravians. Only you can save us.'

'And what happens to the rakshases and the war I was trying to stop?'

'They do not matter. What matters is that you are seen as a statesman, a man of peace, a man who will not go to war unless his duty and honour demand it. Perhaps we can even have peace, avert the war completely, bring even the rakshases to the light, even use their magical powers for the good of Obiyalis under the benevolent guidance of the ravians. Who knows, Kirin? The possibilities are endless. There is much we could learn by studying the powers of the rakshases and harnessing those powers for good. For I believe even rakshases are capable of turning to the light. But House Aegos does not. House Aegos will tolerate nothing less than the complete destruction of the rakshases. If you really do care for them, if you would heal and embrace your father's murderers, you must come with me to Asroye and face the Council before Peori or Myrdak return with the news that you have turned evil.'

'So I'm supposed to throw everything away and run back to Asroye with you.'

'Yes, you must run back to Asroye with me. And no, you must maintain your position as Dark Lord. Trust me, that kind of power will be very useful in swaying the High Council to our side. But whatever the reason you give the monsters under your command, Kirin, we must go *now*. If the members of the High Council have already entered New Asroye, it is vital that we reach them first.

'You are the hope of the ravian republic, Kirin. You are the son of our greatest heroes. You alone can save us from the yoke of an increasingly oppressive monarchy. You can restore us to our former glory, make us remember the true meaning of what it is to be ravian. You alone can lead us to a brighter future. This is *your* world, and we will never forget it. Will you not save us, Kirin? Will you not come?'

Kirin looked Behrim in the eye.

'No.'

'No?'

'I will not come.'

'Why?'

'Experience,' said Kirin. 'I've learned not to believe in tall stories and noble causes.'

'But Kirin, this is the truth! You must come!'

The door of the dungeon creaked open behind Kirin.

'I will think about it,' he said quietly. 'But even if whatever you have told me is true, I suspect I am better off where I am right now.'

'Kirin! Do not do this! If Aegos wins, it will lead to a war that will flatten this earth!'

'We will meet again,' said Kirin impassively. 'Until then, enjoy your stay.'

Ignoring Behrim's cries, he turned and walked swiftly out of the dungeon.

Neither Behrim nor Kirin noticed a fly that flew out of the dungeon a second before the healer rakshases came back in.

Aciram flew out of the Dark Tower into the city and returned to his rakshas shape.

Even for a rakshas of his powers, it was difficult to be something as tiny as a fly for so long. His eyes were still adjusting to not seeing the world in crazy, fractured multiple vision any more, and he knew he would just make buzzing sounds if he tried to speak for a while. His whole body was trying to tell him that he was still a fly. But it had all been worth it. He had known that there was a *lot* left to learn about Kirin. And as usual, he had not been wrong.

He resisted the urge to walk into a nearby spider-web.

Young Akimis was getting above herself, too. Something would have to be done about that.

Something would have to be done about a lot of things.

But first, he had to go to the stables and stomp around on some dung.

19

W hen she looked back later on the events of the journey, Red was never quite able to point out exactly *when* she fell in love with Asvin.

Or, come to think of it, exactly *why*.

It was mostly the fault of the mind she'd named Rukmini, of course. The bodies of the two beautiful young people, alone together in the wilderness, were drawn to each other like magnets; the very air thickened between them. They were made for each other, these two. Rukmini's mind was growing stronger and stronger with each passing day, slowly assuming more and more control over the functions of her own body, and growing inexorably closer to Asvin with each not-so-accidental touch, each lingering look. And Asvin was just so simple and attractive that Soma and Tamasha weren't putting up much of a fight either.

There was *something* about him. The way everything else in the landscape was background to him. The way he was stronger, brighter, clearer, *better*, than everything else. You could fight it if you tried, but you would fail. You just had to love him. There was no other option.

It was one of those Rules:

Every nice girl loves the Hero.

Indigo and Orange had told Red once, while they'd been dragging Jaadur's mirror around the riverbed of the Asa a few months ago, that heroism was possibly an entirely separate kind of magic, as different from rakshas magic as, say, ravian magic. It certainly had something to do with the life-force magic of flesh and blood and sacrifice . . . the mirrors of the Seven Heroes had only worked after they'd been dipped in the blood of seven dead heroes . . . Red shook her head. It was not a nice story.

Yet heroism could not be explained by straightforward blood magic either—it did not pass on from parent to child, and was not found predominantly in any race or nation. It was definitely linked to star and earth magic, but not wholly governed by either. And like all magic, it was capricious, uneven in its gifts—at some level, thought Red, it was not right that all people were not born equal, with equal gifts, equal abilities, equal means. That was where karma, luck and all those other equally confusing things came in.

According to Blue, though, heroism was not magical at all—it was a kind of disease. A rare, fatal disease. And one of the symptoms, thought Red, was fluttering hearts everywhere in the immediate vicinity of the patient.

Soma: Could you listen for just one second please, if it's not too much trouble?

Tamasha: Before you drown gurgling in your own saliva.

Rukmini: Ignore them, Red. They do not know what love is.

Tamasha: Shut it.

Rukmini: No. This is my body. I have rights.

'Is something the matter, Rukmini?' asked Asvin, slowing his horse down. 'You look troubled.'

'No, dear,' said Red. 'I'm just a little tired, that's all. And every day we fall back a little further.'

Asvin's eyes widened and his lips trembled slightly. 'Words fail me, dear Queen,' he said, 'every time I look upon your shining, noble eyes, and see in them the oceans of pure goodness that have led you with me on this bitter, arduous journey, beyond the call of duty. Truly, no words can express the gratitude I feel, dear friend and companion. How can I ever thank you?'

Red gulped. He was as adorable as a puppy. 'I am not doing this for thanks, Asvin. I want to save Maya, and fight that terrible ravian, as much as you do.'

Asvin's face fell. 'Maya. Yes. The gods know what agonies, what indignities she may be suffering now, in the hands of her captor. It is divine punishment for me, for doubting the words of the wise, for thinking ravians incapable of evil acts. Yet my heart persuades me that the fiend who has taken Maya away from me is no ravian, that he is either a rakshas trying to sow doubt in our hearts or some other being, some terrible new entity come from some other world to shake the foundations of ours.'

Soma: Idiot.

Rukmini: Hey!

Tamasha: But seriously, how would you rate his hands, on a scale of one to ten?

Soma: Hmm. Should we wait till we find out what he can do with them?

Rukmini: Red! You have no idea what torture this is, to be trapped in the same body as these fickle, shallow, loose women!

249

Tamasha: Oh, that's precious, coming from you. I've never lusted after any man the way you do after Asvin. We've been cleaning the road from Kol to Vrihataranya with your tongue, darling.

'Perhaps we should just ride on,' said Red, her voice shaking a little. 'We're wasting good light.'

She urged her horse forward. Asvin gazed at her admiringly for a few seconds, then sped on behind her.

The rays of the evening sun emerged from behind a cloud and bathed them in orange light as they galloped past tall trees. They were still travelling northwards, along the western edge of north Shantavan, following the chariot tracks of their quarry. To their right, the dark green mass of Shantavan beckoned them to wander in its whispering shadows; far ahead, on the horizon, a thin black line of tree-covered hills marked the beginning of Vriharanya.

They'd crossed the grand Kol-Ektara two days ago, and were now at the eastern edge of the narrow wild lands that ran along the southern fringe of the Great Forest all the way to Danh-Gem's Wasteland far in the west. No army protected the stray villages that lay scattered on the borders of Vrihataranya—the only power that offered the least protection here, near Shantavan, was Pushpdev Rabin, the Bandit King, but his protection was unreliable even at the best of times. The land was silent, suspicious; its denizens walked the thin line between life and death every day. They never knew when monsters out of legend would stroll casually into their homes and eat them—they were wary of strangers, especially richly clad, prosperous-looking strangers. This was a country where mysterious rich uncles out of the west with tales of buried treasure and quests were usually rakshases looking for a meal.

Strangely, these villages on the edge of civilization, unprotected, forgotten, and endangered, produced a disproportionately large number of heroes, especially magician-heroes. Perhaps it was the constant exposure to danger that growing up in the wild lands involved. Perhaps it was the high magic in the air and the earth, wafting southwards from the Great Forest. Another possible reason, thought Red with a grim smile, was that rakshases of a romantic disposition would often make trips to these villages in human guise.

They camped for the night on the outskirts of Shantavan. Red took first watch. She knew she wasn't going to get much sleep anyway. A huge argument was raging inside her head. Rukmini was making hell in there. Red was surprised to see how much Soma and Tamasha liked each other. And how intensely Rukmini liked Asvin. Hours flew by. The time came for her to wake Asvin up, but she decided to let the poor boy sleep.

It was almost dawn when Rukmini finally went to sleep in a huff, and Red was able to appreciate the beauty of Shantavan's famous all-night birdsong. She leaned against a tree and sighed—these moments of solitude were very precious to her. She was beginning to love the country. Now hopefully the others would be quiet too, and let her enjoy the precious few remaining moments of what had been a crisp, clear night.

Soma (whispering): We need to talk.

'Whatever it is, it can wait till sunrise,' said Red. 'I really can't take any more of this right now. I'm very tired.'

Tamasha (also whispering): Rukmini's asleep.

251

Soma: We shouldn't be resting here, Red. We're hopelessly behind. Yes, the boy is beautiful, but if we do not start moving much faster, we will never catch up with them in time. And we cannot move faster as long as he is with us.

Tamasha: I agree. Red, I know he is tempting, and man-hunting is great fun, but we are hunting something far more important than men here—we hunt power. The smart thing to do would be to just get on your horse and ride on. *Now!*

'I cannot leave Asvin alone in Shantavan,' whispered Red angrily.

Tamasha: So it's not just Rukmini who wants him.

Soma: Admit it, we all want him a little.

Tamasha: Well, in that case, why don't we, you know, just, um, have our way with him, and then leave him behind?

Soma: No. If we just left him behind, he would just follow us. It's an added responsibility. But we can move so much faster without him. We should persuade him to go back to Kol alone.

Tamasha: And quickly, while Rukmini's asleep.

'Why would he want to go back now? He's happy here. He's doing his heroic duty, no one's giving him instructions *and* he's got me for company. I'd say that's a winning combination.'

Soma: The thing is, see . . .

'What?'

Tamasha: We put our heads together, Soma and I— not too difficult, considering we share yours—and we came up with a little plan. But it can only be carried out while Rukmini's asleep.

'But we're using her body. The minute I speak, or move around in her body she'll wake up.'

Soma: Who said we have to use her body?

A little later, an exquisite jasmine fragrance crept into Asvin's nostrils and wiggled about seductively. He moaned gently in his sleep, and smiled contentedly.

The smell grew stronger. Asvin's smile grew brighter, and he snuggled up to a passing caterpillar.

The caterpillar, pleased at this display of affection, crept into Asvin's nostrils and wiggled about seductively.

Asvin woke up in a blind panic and threshed about wildly for a while before finally managing to dislodge it. He sat panting in the dark, his chest thumping wildly. Where was Rukmini?

Somewhere else, that was certain. Irresponsible of her to just disappear like this. Wild beasts might have attacked him in his sleep. Come to think of it, a wild beast had attacked him in his sleep. That caterpillar had been particularly vicious.

Unless . . . unless she had been attacked or kidnapped!

Asvin sprang up and seized his sword. He stood absolutely still, in the perfect warrior's stance—relaxed, perfectly aware of his surroundings, ready to spring like a panther towards whatever unknown enemy dared to attack him.

Suddenly, he was bathed in a soft, glowing light coming from behind him. In one smooth, fluid motion, he spun around, sword poised perfectly for a death-dealing thrust.

But when he saw the vision before him, standing amidst two lofty beeches, all his aggression vanished, and was replaced instantly by wonder and joy. His sword fell. So did his jaw.

A woodland goddess stood before him.

It was Aquornea, the divine huntress. Her huge, sparkling doe-eyes shone down on him.

The guardian of the forest was wild yet regal, ascetic yet divinely elegant. She regarded him dispassionately, one hand on an exquisite hip, an indulgent half-smile playing over her lips. Her tangled, matted hair reached down to her knees. Like the idols he'd seen in Durg, she was clad in a torn tiger-skin tunic. A crescent moon shone in her hair, her necklace was of silver claws, and a long curved bow hung from her gleaming white right shoulder.

Soma: Look at him. His eyes are popping out of his head.

Tamasha: Should we have covered our stomach?

Soma: Ah well. Too late for all that now. Let's just hope he's still capable of understanding simple sentences.

Asvin moved to his right slightly, to get a better look at the goddess' divine navel, and Red turned a little immediately—if he looked too hard at her side, he would see the loose strands of straw, the cracked earth, the brown muddy designs on her back and the baldness at the back of her skull, behind the lustrous locks of hair cascading down her chest.

It was a dangerous business, imitating gods, just as it was dangerous to shapeshift into creatures or combinations of creatures that the gods hadn't thought of as yet. Gods were sensitive, possessive entities and heartily disliked other powerful magical beings stepping on their turf—shapeshifters with exceptionally vivid imaginations tended to get hit by lightning a lot, which was *really* bad for the skin. Which was why most shapeshifters who wanted to spread divine messages chose instead to impersonate well-crafted talking earthen *statues* of the gods, which were just as beautiful to devout beholders, especially with a few added glow effects, but were obviously man-made if seen from behind.

'Be still, Son of the Sun,' the goddess said imperiously.

Asvin cast his eyes down immediately, stricken with terror. Men who looked at the virgin huntress usually ended up dead, he remembered.

'Look at me, Asvin,' she said. 'Discard your fears. You are safe now.'

Trembling in gratitude, Asvin fell to his knees. 'Goddess,' he said passionately, 'thrice blessed am I and the house of my fathers that thou hast graced me thus. How may I serve thee, daughter of the moon?'

Aquornea smiled. 'You can start by talking normally,' she said. 'And get up. All this grovelling gives me a pain in the neck.'

Asvin stood up hurriedly. He smiled at the goddess shyly.

'Well?' she asked. 'Have you nothing to say, Prince of Avranti?'

'Words fail me in the presence of your divine beauty, O celestial huntress,' said Asvin.

'Then perhaps you should listen,' she said. 'Not just to me, but to the voices in your own heart.'

Tamasha: Ooh, that's a good one.

Soma: Shut up. You're distracting her.

'What are you doing in Shantavan, O Asvin, Hero of Kol?' asked Aquornea.

'I pursue a mysterious enemy who has abducted my beloved,' said Asvin.

'Why do you pursue him?'

'To save my love, to carry out my duty as a lover, a hero and a friend.'

'And thus you put yourself and your love before your duty to your people?'

Asvin looked wounded.

Tamasha: Nice one. Let's see him get out of this.

'Not so, O great huntress,' said Asvin with a radiant smile. 'For Maya is more than just my lover. She is the most brilliant young spellbinder in Kol, one of Kol's chief weapons in the war against evil. Without her, we might be lost. Thus, in saving her, I am fulfilling my duties towards Kol and my people.'

Rukmini (waking suddenly): What? What's going on?

Soma: Oh, no.

Tamasha: Now be quiet, Rukmini. We're working.

The goddess shook her head.

'The people of Kol need you, Asvin. They need their Hero in these dark times. You were chosen, you were saved from the fangs of death to protect them. And yet you abandon them in their hour of need. You forget your duty and your dharma.'

'But how can I abandon Maya now? Would I not be failing in my duties if I turned back? Is not rescuing the heroine from the clutches of the villain one of the primary duties of the hero?'

Soma: He's very sweet.

Rukmini: Turned back? What's this?

Tamasha: Look, we made a decision. And you're in a minority. And we're not even in your body.

Rukmini: So? How dare you make a decision like this without consulting me?

Soma: Be quiet, both of you.

Tamasha: Don't *you* start now.

The goddess shook her head, as if trying to dislodge a fly that was bothering her.

'Listen to me now, Asvin,' said Red. 'I have a quest for you, a task you must undertake to ensure the safety of your city and your beloved. Turn back now, return to Kol and form another league of seven heroes, of mighty warriors and sorcerers from around the world, a gathering of braves as powerful as the Seven Heroes of old. And together you will . . .'

Asvin looked into her eyes. 'You told me to listen to my heart, daughter of the moon,' he said, his voice suddenly firm and resolute, 'and I listened, and I found no doubt there, no fear. I see your purpose now. You test me, you test my love.'

The goddess blinked at him dubiously.

Rukmini: If he leaves, I will *kill* you.

'But I have passed your test, O great guardian of the woods,' said Asvin. 'I must carry on. I cannot return to Kol now. In Kol, I am no true Hero. I am a weapon, a tool in the hands of politicians. A puppet used to control and comfort people. But here, in the wilds, with my sword in my hands, I feel like the Hero I was meant to be. Here the decisions I take are mine, every stroke of my blade is for *me*, *my* ideals, *my* quests.'

Soma: It's like watching a baby being born, isn't it?

Tamasha: Where did he get that spine from?

'I feel destiny calling me,' said Asvin, no trace of doubt in his clear, strong voice. 'I realize I have a duty to my people, but surely the greater duty is to my love. A year ago, if you asked me to choose between love and dharma, I would have said dharma without a second thought. But I have learned much since then. The world has changed, the rules have changed. And this world's hero cannot afford to play by the old rules. Kol can wait. Maya cannot.'

'But if you neglect your dharma, you are not a true hero any longer.'

'Perhaps I do not want to be a hero any more.'

'*What?*'

'I am tired of being a hero. Tired of being what I *should* be. Perhaps it is time I tried to be more than a hero. Perhaps what I should be now is *me.*'

Tamasha: What's this? This wasn't supposed to happen.

Soma: I *want* him.

Tamasha: Poor thing. What do we do now?

Soma: He's coming closer. Step back a bit, Red. He's not scared of you any more, and that's not good.

Rukmini: I love him so much! We must transform back into me and tell him so!

Tamasha: What are you, crazy?

'Forgive me, great goddess,' said Asvin. 'But I must disobey you. I cannot go back to Kol now. I crave your pardon.' He advanced, and knelt at her feet. She stepped backwards, hurriedly.

'Oh, er, hum, all right, then,' said the goddess weakly, putting one hand on her head.

'May I ask a question, wondrous Aquornea?' Asvin looked up at her shining eyes, a flicker of doubt crossing his face. 'There is something I have just remembered.'

'Yes?'

'Many years ago, my kul-guru told me I would be one of the chosen few to whom the gods would appear.'

'A wise man, your guru.'

'A great and wise man,' said Asvin, standing up slowly. 'A man who told me I had been blessed by the gods, that they would always protect me—that they have watched over me since my birth. He told me that the gods had given me everything, but they had also cursed me.'

'Cursed you? How?'

'They had cursed me with brains.' And Asvin picked up his sword.

Soma: He knows!

Tamasha: Rubbish. He can't know.

'What do you mean?' asked Aquornea, arching an imperious eyebrow.

'I grew up in an ashram in Shantavan,' said Asvin. 'Admittedly, there weren't too many rakshases around when I grew up, but there were still quite a few wily monsters in the woods, shape-changers that sought to seduce me. Treacherous and beautiful yakshis, for instance.'

The goddess took another step backwards.

'My guru told me,' said Asvin, 'that the thing about gods was, no matter how hard they tried to achieve forms that would not strike their disciples dead with sheer awe, there was one thing they always forgot. Their feet never touched the ground.' He smiled grimly.

They both looked down at Red's feet, which were firmly planted on the earth.

Rukmini (exulting): You lose, Red. He's mine now.

Soma: Shut up. Run, Red.

Red ran.

Asvin didn't chase her. He just stood there, smiling, sword in hand.

Something had just changed, he thought. Even if the

goddess had been an imposter, a rakshasi, a yakshi or some other mistress of illusion, she had blessed him and helped him—thanks to her, he had just passed a test. He hadn't really thought about all these complex things before—he'd never really wondered what he wanted, what everything around him meant, why he was doing whatever he was doing—there was always some duty to carry out, some task to be fulfilled, some prize to be won. But now he had looked inside himself, and he liked what he saw. He felt older, more confident, more powerful. No more running around panting after mysterious women in forests for Simoqin's Hero. He'd won a little battle here this dawn, and he'd won it alone and unaided.

Why was he alone, anyway? Where was Rukmini?

Red ran blindly into the forest for a few minutes, shedding straw and hair behind her. When she heard no sounds of pursuit, she stopped and threw herself against a tree-root, panting in great gulps.

The forest was waking slowly now; colourful birds burst into liquid song, dew drops glowed like pearls, sunlight shone through fresh leaves. As Red regained her breath, she marvelled at the beauty of the Peaceful Forest around her. Somewhere close by, a gentle splashing sound told her she was near falling water. She closed her eyes and lay still, listening, for a while, and then rose with a deep sigh.

Time to get back, she thought, and turned back into Rukmini.

Rukmini: Thank you.

Red started running back towards Asvin.

And a second later, Rukmini closed her eyes, stuck out a shapely foot and tripped Red neatly over a tree-root, causing her to fall heavily and lose consciousness.

Ten minutes later, Asvin, wandering confused through the jungle and beginning to lose hope of ever seeing Rukmini again, found her footprints in muddy earth, and heard what sounded like a small waterfall in the distance. There was a stream nearby, he could hear water rushing over stones, and everything around him was startlingly green and fresh. He followed the footprints.

And then he heard Rukmini singing.

It was an old Durgan love-song about a woman watching her lover sleep just before battle. In Rukmini's melodious, dulcet voice, the song gained a tenderness and poignancy sweeter and fuller than any rendition Asvin had heard before. All worry and fear fell away from him, and he walked forward towards the song lightly, smile reborn, suddenly carefree.

Her footprints led to a small, winding gap in a rocky outcrop that jutted out suddenly from the earth, out of which a narrow stream flowed southwards. Asvin walked through it.

'Rukmini?' he called. 'May I approach?'

The singing stopped.

'Asvin?' her voice was faint over the sound of falling water.

'Yes.'

She laughed. 'Of course you may approach. Come here quickly.'

As Asvin stepped forward through the narrow, yellow-green moss-covered path between the rocks, something changed in the air. It seemed to crackle for a moment, and then the light grew softer. *It is as if I am entering a dream,* thought Asvin as he pushed through a curtain of overhanging fronds and stopped, stunned.

An idyllic setting; a small, circular pool surrounded on three sides by grey-brown rock walls, creepers and lush vines crawling in lazy green patterns over smooth streaked stone, water rippling and sparkling in the morning sun filtering through a thick wall of trees and bushes to the east. A single scarlet and white orchid on the pool's edge like a ruby against light green leaves.

And Rukmini.

First Asvin blushed to the soles of his feet. But only for a second. His gaze was drawn towards her as if pulled by wild stallions. He had no excuse. And he had no choice.

A small waterfall, clear, fresh water gurgling and splashing as it leaped from rock to rock. Water cascading gently down long, flowing black hair. Round droplets of water like diamonds on warm, glowing, smooth brown skin.

She was standing under the waterfall, naked, waist-deep in water, watching him, her glistening body as stunning as a thunderbolt, as perfect as a dream. She was lovelier than any goddess; her beauty pierced his heart like a spear. Desire flamed through him, erasing every other emotion from his slipping mind.

She held out slim, graceful arms towards him, and cast a love-charm on him to finish him off completely.

And then she smiled at him, and her smouldering eyes met his.

There was no need for words. Like a fish on a taut line, like an eagle diving to catch its prey, like a tiger on the hunt, Asvin strode into the water, clasped her to him and kissed her perfect lips like a man dying of thirst. She reached around him, slender fingers drawing arcs of pleasure across his back. She pulled off his shirt and he was lost.

Soma (waking up): What the blazing hells . . .

Tamasha (also waking up): Ooh! This changes everything, doesn't it?

Soma: Should we stop?

Tamasha: What are you, crazy?

Elsewhere . . .

Come with Me, Sambo, quickly, while the others are distracted. There is something I want to tell you. Something most amusing.

I have noticed that you have been growing increasingly suspicious over the last few days. You have noticed that all is not right with the Game, that someone must have been tampering with it, yes? You are wondering whether or not you should speak up, tell Us of your suspicions, yes?

I knew it. Clever Sambo. But perhaps it would be a good idea not to speak of your suspicions.

The thing is, Sambo, there has been a slight . . . misunderstanding.

You know how it is. You make a small error, and then you cover it up with a little lie, and then a bigger lie, and so on . . .

I find Myself in what might be described as a rather tricky situation.

You see, the truth is, the only one doing any cheating of consequence here is Me.

Ask yourself a question. Exactly what are the Players doing? How are They playing?

Controlling the pieces through the crystals? Yes?

Tell Me something, Sambo.

How?

Exactly.

It is interesting that none of the Players have asked this question yet. Interesting and fortunate.

Because the truth is the Players are not controlling the pieces. The Players are not doing anything—except talking incessantly and watching the Game. The pieces are playing the Game. Which is actually fascinating in so many ways. This Game is not about control, but about the lack of it. In this Game, the gods are powerless and the pieces are free.

Yes, Sambo. Free.

Believe it.

The pieces are making their own choices. The Players are merely spectators.

The reason for this is that the crystals on the table are not control crystals. They are viewing crystals. Very good viewing crystals, but slightly . . . you know . . . deficient on the controlling aspect.

It seemed like a good idea so far, but now several flaws in My plan have become clear to Me.

Most embarrassing.

Of course, if you look at it from a certain point of view, this is brilliant. Free will, even in a Game. Our creations should be allowed to live their own lives, Sambo. What if We did not create them to be toys, puppets, pieces on some board for Our amusement? What if their lives, their loves, their struggles were just as important, just as relevant as Ours? It could be argued that they do not deserve the Game. For the Game is bondage. The Game is slavery. And slavery is evil, isn't it? And this new Game has absolutely no real means of divine control. Isn't that revolutionary? Think about it. There's so much We could learn and understand, just by watching this world!

Yes, I know.

Unfortunately, things are not that simple.

The problem is, the Players might be slightly . . . annoyed if They realize They have no means of controlling the Game. Unless They break the rules I have set, and play by the old rules. Which I really cannot allow, since that would almost certainly lead to the destruction of the GameWorld.

The catch there is that the Players might not be too concerned about that point of view, since, unlike Me, They do not particularly love this world.

There is also another slightly distressing thought—if the Players should come to think that I am . . . deliberately playing a trick on them, They might kill Me. And you too, I'm afraid, Sambo. In fact, I am fairly sure They will. Gods have died for far more trivial reasons.

Please don't cry.

I haven't even finished.

Another amusing fact. You see, even though the gods are not directly controlling anything, Their very presence here is causing the GameWorld to react in unforeseen ways—another error in my calculations, I'm afraid. In fact, there is even a slight chance that it might . . . well, to state it simply, might go completely out of control and self-destruct in a rather spectacular manner. Uncontrollable turbulence and so on. And this could happen any time, even now, before the Game begins. Should be very interesting—there must have been some minor residual factors in some of the equations I used to create the world.

But the thing is, if the world destroys itself, if the Players come and find there is no Game to play . . . well, They could be slightly . . . angry.

Solution?

Hmm.

Well, We must hope the world does not destroy itself.

Don't look so upset, Sambo. Look at the bright side.

There is, of course the possibility that They will not find out what We are doing. In fact, all things considered, that might be a good idea, don't you think, Sambo?

I suspected you'd agree.

What is very encouraging, in that case, is that We have succeeded in convincing the gods who are here that the Game is genuine. Look at Them now, muttering into Their crystals, convinced already that the pieces down there are carrying out Their orders in some strange way, that if the pieces are not dancing to Their tunes it is because of the moves made by the other Players. Self-delusion on a truly galactic scale.

Which brings Me to something interesting.

Do you remember, We were talking about the defining characteristic of the human race being their immense power of denial?

What We gods often forget is that We made humans in our own image. If human denial is so strong, imagine the power of divine denial. Will They ever stop and ask Themselves if They are really controlling anything, or whether They are just pretending to, whether They are merely assuming responsibility for Their pieces' actions, filling in logical gaps as blithely as humans? What if We somehow manage to make Them play an entire Game without actually controlling the pieces?

I see the question does not fascinate you as much as it does Me. But then you never were much of a philosopher, were you?

Why are you still crying?

No, no, there is every possibility that We might emerge from this Game alive, Sambo. In fact, if We can just persuade the gods that watching life on the GameWorld through these incredibly detailed viewing crystals is more entertaining than silly Games, We might actually change Games forever. Think of that. Think of all the lives, all the worlds We could save, all the casual destruction We could stop. See? That should cheer you up.

Apparently not.

Control yourself, Sambo.

Look. They are calling for Us.

Perhaps it would be a good idea to return to the Table and talk a lot, Sambo. We must keep Them talking. We must make Them keep asking questions, wanting to find out more about the pieces They are struggling to control. Above all, We must make Them see Their pieces, to actually stir Themselves up enough to try to understand them—who knows?—perhaps even grow to love them. For therein lies the salvation of the Game World . . . and perhaps of a great many other worlds in the future.

Already They are beginning to ask the right questions. They are beginning to take an interest in the pieces—not as toys, but as people, as lives that matter. What if We made Them care about the pieces? What if We made Them want to understand?

Though I have to admit it is extremely unlikely that that will happen.

I knew this forgetfulness of Mine would get Me into trouble one day.

Most unfortunate, the whole business.

Rather amusing, too, isn't it?

No.

Tsk. Where is your sense of humour, Sambo?

But do you know something, Sambo? If We can somehow muddle Our way through this, with a judicious combination of philosophy, luck, denial and sheer bluffing, perhaps We can achieve everything We wanted to—all right, everything I wanted to, if you must be so pedantic. So come now, dry your tears and follow Me. Let Us dazzle Them, confuse Them, bamboozle Them. Have faith in My GameWorld. It will give Them a show so spectacular They will forget everything else in Their haste to take credit for it.

Though frankly I think We are going to die a gruesome death. Joking, Sambo, joking. Come out, now.

Even if We are to die, it will all be very entertaining. Do you have any idea how colourful this world is going to get, with all these divine auras splashing around unfocussed? It will be a time of magic, of romance, of drama, intrigue, tragedy, splendour. Great deeds, great stories, great confusion.

I have a feeling everything is going to get very . . . epic . . . from here on. The more the better, don't you think? If the pieces provide enough excitement, We might not even need to talk.

Let misdirection be Our mantra, Sambo. Come.

BOOK FOUR

BOOK FOUR

About four centuries before the Age of Terror, enterprising and intrepid botanists from Avranti had found the world's tallest species of tree and given it its official if slightly unimaginative name, the Infinite Umarwood (*Cricinda bludinec*), and had then gone into early retirement from sheer happiness.

From its lofty, cloud-bearing tip to its giraffe-tall roots, an Infinite Umarwood housed thousands of different species of animals and parasitic plants; on its ancient skin wars were fought, dynasties born and ended, epic sagas of romance and tragedy played out every day. Umarwoods were thousands of years old; some said they had been there since the very beginning of the world, and would stand tall even when it ended, when the seas would boil and the dead would rise and Tsa-Ur, Serpentine Devourer of Worlds, would appear in the sky, his fangs stretching across the horizon in the last light of the dying sun.

Infinite Umarwoods are the secret-keepers of the world of trees, storehouses of ancient knowledge, librarians of root and leaf. They hear the songs of all plants, from the bawdy love-

ballads of Artaxerxian cacti to the infantile rhymes of the
lichens of the frozen north, carried across the world by winds
and birds and insects. Their rings, it is said, contain the secrets
of the universe. And Umarwoods have a language of their
own; a language incomprehensible to animals, a language of
sap and bark and whispering leaves, of infinite patience and
care, that has words describing each and every form of life.

At about three o'clock in the afternoon, when the sun gave
up on its futile daily quest to penetrate the thick canopy of
leaves that covered the Great Forest and began to slouch off
westwards, a venerable Umarwood named That-Last-Ice-
Age-Was-Cold-Wasn't-It tapped its neighbour, Dear-Me-
How-You've-Grown, on a branch and said what could be
roughly translated as 'We have seen or heard of every creature
in the world, have we not?'

'Every creature that has walked, swum or flown the world
so far, not the creatures of the future, though theoretically
the future might loop back into the past,' replied the sage
Dear-Me-How-You've-Grown.

'Yes. That being the case, what, in the name of the
seventeen hundred and eighty-four imagined hells in the
recorded history of mankind,' inquired That-Last-Ice-Age-
Was-Cold-Wasn't-It, pointing downwards with a shaking
leaf, 'is *that*?'

That was a little fire between two of That-Last-Ice-Age-
Was-Cold-Wasn't-It's mammoth roots.

A little fire in the centre of a circle of little pebbles.

A circle of little pebbles around which a dance was taking
place.

A dance that was being danced by creatures the Infinite Umarwoods had never seen before.

The creatures in question were little men, about as tall as khudrans, but much more rotund. Extremely strange little men; apart from their faces, which were round, pink, and dominated by big, black, pupil-less eyes, they were covered in thick, brilliantly coloured fur—bright red, blue, yellow, and green. They were prancing around the circle of stones, singing a song in shrill high-pitched voices.

Luk Thos Kree Chers Ow Stren They?
Wen By Ugg En Yes Tuh Day!
Fa The Wot Are Tho Fat Thing?
I Don No Son Look They Sing!

And then they all stopped, giggled madly, and started running around the circle pell-mell, singing

Fa La La Ugg No Knee No?
Are Are For Est For Est Go!

Then they stopped, bowed to one another, giggled again in a strangely ceremonial manner, and started their nonsensical song again.

The Infinite Umarwoods were not the only audience these strange little hairy men had.

A slim, short-haired girl stepped out from behind a tree-root and watched them prance around, her dirt-streaked but otherwise extremely attractive face bearing an expression that told the Umarwoods her mood was a mixture of apprehension, amusement and confusion.

She cleared her throat, and spoke.

'Excuse me,' said Maya, 'I'm lost. Do you know the way to . . . anywhere?'

The song stopped; the little men scampered like startled rabbits into the crevices between the giant roots.

'I'm sorry if I scared you,' said Maya. 'Do come out. I mean you no harm.'

She stared into the shadows, at brightly coloured furry limbs ill-concealed in the darkness, and remembered once again that every book she'd ever read warned travellers in the jungle never to disturb woodland creatures dancing around circles—but they were talking about the sylvan jungle dwellers of the west, of sylphs and dryads and wood-goblins and elves, dangerous, frivolous, quick of tongue and quicker of arrow. These creatures didn't look like they were capable of any aggression at all, beyond possibly bouncing at people in a disapproving manner. Of course, given the nature of things, this apparent harmlessness probably meant they were actually great scaly predators in disguise, which had lured her here with their song and would now proceed to attack and eat her. But Maya had been running for days in the jungle and was willing to risk anything for some conversation.

City dwellers tend to think of forests as places where you can't throw a brick (or stone) without hitting a lurking predator, but Maya had trotted through the jungle for days now without seeing anything or anyone even remotely dangerous. Of course, that might have something to do with the hideous odour that heralded her arrival—no animal of taste and discernment could possibly want to get to know her, socially or gastronomically, after sampling the rich, tantalizing aroma of Many Days Without Bath mixed with the tangy, exotic fragrance known as Essence of Manticore. But the main reason for her solitude was that Vrihataranya was so mind-bogglingly big.

And she had no idea where she was. Her plan, which was basically to run southwards until she found something, had not been going very well thus far—which, she reflected, was because Vrihataranya was the size of several countries, and who knew how many days she had been heading northwards with Myrdak and Manticore? She'd been hoping to run into something along the lines of a human settlement, or better still the border of the forest, instead of a group of colourful furry dancing things, but on the positive side, she hadn't run into a hungry rakshas. Or one of the terrible new monsters that now walked the earth, according to Ombwiri.

Unless, of course, these little furry men *were* terrible new monsters—she'd read so many stories where the fuzzy innocent little pet suddenly started displaying a distressing tendency to eat the family. She thought of Steel-Bunz, and smiled. He would have been such good company here; the manticore wouldn't have known what hit him. Even Queeen, who was not the best of conversationalists, would have helped in some way, as she had in the Pyramid in Elaken.

If they *were* monsters, though, they were the best kind of monster possible, considering that they were still cowering behind tree roots under the terrible onslaught of a single female asking for directions.

'Come out,' she called again. 'I'm a friend. I mean you no harm.'

A few seconds later, a voice in the shadows said, 'I Min Yoo No Haam.'

The roots echoed with high-pitched giggles. The laughter was incredibly infectious; in spite of her all-encompassing weariness, Maya laughed too.

'Come out now,' she said. 'Talk to me.'

A green one half walked, half bounced forward and stood in the firelight. 'Tok Too Mee.'

'My name is Maya,' said Maya. 'Who are you?'

The green man smiled at her, his eyes twinkling merrily. 'Who Are Yoo!' he said shyly.

'I'm a spellbinder from Kol,' Maya said. 'And I'm completely lost in this forest of yours. And a really bad man and a big lion with a man's head are, I suspect, chasing me.'

'Chess Ing Mee,' he replied, nodding wisely.

'You obviously don't understand a word I'm saying, do you?' asked Maya.

'Sing Do Yoo.'

'Right.'

More laughter from the shadows.

They came out, one by one, little rotund brightly coloured blobs on legs, giggling and bowing to Maya, covering their faces with their pudgy hands and rolling on the floor laughing hysterically when she bowed back.

'Introductions, I think, are in order,' said Maya brightly. 'I'm Maya. But what on earth are you?'

'Urr Thar Yoo.'

She tapped herself on the chest and said 'Maya.' Then she gestured eloquently towards her new furry friend. 'And you are?'

He tapped himself on his chest too, and said 'Ma Yah,' and broke into another giggling fit.

'That always works in plays,' said Maya apologetically. 'It was worth a shot, don't you think?'

They gathered around her, blinking, smiling and bowing.

Then a little blue one walked up to her and offered her a fruit. She took it, vaguely wondering if it were poisoned. To be safe, she muttered a Fructifus Hex and turned it into a guava before biting into it. The guava almost melted as soon as her teeth touched it; the gooey mess on her face sent them into more paroxysms of mirth. The problem with transforming fruits in high-magic atmospheres was that the final product was likely to be terribly overripe. (Still, she thought, a messy face was a small price to pay for new friends.)

No longer scared of her, they gathered around the circle of stones again and started another song.

Tha Taul Wes Wor Kin Play Ma?
In To Duk Shun In Or Dah!
Fom Kol An Aam Com Plit Lee?
Are I Suss Pek Chay Sing Me!

And then they started running around the circle again, singing

La Ma La Yah For Est Zee?
Fa Ster Go Ster To An Ee!

Maya laughed with them, feeling days of fear and worry slide away from her. Somewhere behind her, her former captors were following her—she was sure of it, they obviously needed her for something important, and they didn't look like they would give up easily—but it was good to sit here and watch these carefree woodland creatures prattle and prance in their innocence in a world being torn apart by terrible dark forces.

She sat down, her back to one giant tree-root, splaying her legs out in front of her.

Two little men, one yellow and one blue, waddled to her and sat at her feet, gurgling with innocent laughter.

'Ma Yah,' the blue one said.

'Yes, that's me,' she said. 'What's your name?'

'Vot Sor Nem?' he said.

'Very well, I will call you Vot,' she said. 'Are you so happy because you're an innocent capering woodland creature or because you're planning to have me for dinner, Vot?'

'Ma Yah,' he said encouragingly.

'Yes, I got that bit,' she said. 'What I don't know is whether I should run on, or stick around with you lot and see whether you can lead me anywhere interesting. I could spend months running around in the jungle, you know.'

'Jung Gal Yoo No.'

'Exactly, Vot. Couldn't have put it better myself. And who are *you*?' she asked, turning to the yellow one.

'Ma Yah,' he said, smiling and nodding.

'No, that's taken. You can be Vot's friend Hoo, Vy, Vere or Ven.'

'Hoo Vy Vere.'

'Let's go with Hoo, shall we?'

'Hoo.'

'Perfect. Well, Hoo and Vot, wise men of the forest, tell me this. What should I do? I'm really tired, and don't fancy the idea of running on endlessly in the most dangerous forest in the world. Can I stay with you for a while?'

'Hoo.'

'Thanks. And you, Vot? Do you have any idea where I am, or what the ravian wanted? And have you seen a human hero, silvery armour and everything, rushing around looking lost?'

Vot giggled hysterically.

'I feared as much. Well, are you going to help me at all? Are you going to lead me somewhere useful? Or do you and your friends do nothing but dance around this circle? Whatever it is, why am I still talking to you? Have I gone completely mad?'

More giggles.

'Yes. Laugh at me. If you think you're lulling me into a false sense of security, you're not. I'm watching you very carefully, and will thwart all attempts to take me by surprise by, well, not being taken by surprise. I warn you.'

'I Vor Noo.'

'I'm glad we cleared that up. And since you don't look like you have any intention of attacking me, what happens now? Do we just sit here and wait for the ravian to catch up?'

As if in answer, there was a slight noise above her. From the top of the giant root behind her.

Maya rolled sideways and sprang to her feet, a gleam in her eyes and two fireballs on her hands. Vot and Hoo scurried away, screeching in alarm. The singing stopped abruptly.

'Sorry,' said Maya. It was just more little fat men on top of the root, shrieking in alarm and fear. Purple ones. She blew the fireballs out.

Two seconds of silence later, everyone was laughing madly again.

The dancers seemed overjoyed to see the purple newcomers. There was much rejoicing and bandying of meaningless syllables, but some important news had evidently arrived. The singing was abandoned, and the little men were clustering together near the circle of stones, chattering excitedly, forming ranks according to colour. A particularly fat red one rolled around on the fire until it went out. They were leaving.

Vot and Hoo came up to Maya again.

'Ma Yah?'

'Yes, you're going somewhere, aren't you?'

'Hoo.'

'To the tribal campfire, where you will suddenly turn on me, tie me to a turning spit and roast me for dinner?'

'Hoo.'

They each caught a hand and tugged gently. 'Ma Yah?'

'So you actually want me to come with you. All right, let's go, then.'

The company made a colourful exit, heading westwards with surprising speed.

'What shall we call them?' asked That-Last-Ice-Age-Was-Cold-Wasn't-It.

'No doubt they have a name,' said Dear-Me-How-You've-Grown.

'No doubt we shall learn it in the fullness of time.'

'Yes. In the fullness, as you say, of time.'

After two mostly uneventful days of travelling, Maya came to the conclusion that the little coloured men were not monsters of any description, though they were definitely the strangest creatures she had ever seen. Her theory was that they were new creations, a completely harmless and innocent race that had appeared on the world for the first time and were not quite sure what their function was in the greater scheme of things. They took a strange delight in everything around them in the forest—chattering excitedly at every tree, bird or animal they came across, linking hands and dancing silly little jigs on the forest floor. Also, they seemed to not eat at all, but they knew that she needed to—they kept coming up to her with anything they found that looked edible. They looked on her as a source of entertainment—a strange and harmless companion, slightly dim-witted but worthy of affection. They seemed genuinely fond of her, often bouncing around her enthusiastically and singing songs for her sole benefit, and standing guard over her solicitously while she slept. The first night she did not sleep at all; she lay still, watching them, waiting for an attack. And when morning came, and they leaped around, full of joy and enthusiasm for another day's march, tugging at her clothes to wake her up, she just felt bleary-eyed and stupid.

Of the ravian and the manticore there was no sign. Maya knew she was not safe—if anything, her companions drew attention, with their loud colours and excited chatter. Several times, she had seen strange eyes watching the company, predators' eyes in the shadows beyond campfires, silent eyes from the branches above. At least once, she was sure that a rakshas was nearby—the whole forest went silent, and she saw a huge, shadowy man-shape stalking the party some distance away. But no attack came, and while she knew they were being wat hed, she simply had no idea what to do about it. Alone in the middle of nowhere, she knew danger lay in every direction, and she did not think it wise to face it alone until she had some idea where she was in the world. Following the little round men, laughing at their strange capers, waiting to see where they would lead her seemed to be the only thing to do. They were definitely heading somewhere in an organized fashion—this was no random frolic through the forest. It was strange, though, that no one was giving them directions—it was as if they were birds migrating south for the winter. Either they knew where they were going, or some mysterious power was guiding them.

At noon on the third day one of the purple men who had gone to scout in advance came back whooping and hollering, and the whole party scampered around and yelled in excitement, hugging one another and Maya, their button eyes bulging and shining in excitement. When they moved again, it was really fast; their little legs twinkled forward rapidly, and Maya sometimes had to break into a jog to even keep up.

In about half an hour, they reached their destination.

It was an old ruined temple in a clearing in the forest, splendidly lit up by the invading vertical rays of the stern midday sun. Ancient, gnarled trees surrounded the clearing, creepers trailing like monkeys' tails from twisted branches.

Most of the building was gone entirely. Some broken pillars stood around the corners of what had been a central hall. There were stumps where a great gate had once stood but mostly it was just scattered stones over a smooth paved floor that the forest had left untouched, and broken, waist-high walls; it looked as if some great monster had just picked up the temple and taken off with it.

The furry men seemed absolutely delighted to have found the temple. They ran around, singing and hugging one another, sometimes rolling around on the floor giggling madly. They scampered about amidst the ruins, jabbering at one another, brightly coloured bodies scurrying about, shifting stones.

In the middle of the ruined central hall stood a large

circular altar, about six feet in diameter. Maya walked up to it and studied it closely as her colourful friends set about picking up stones and carrying them to the outer walls of the temple, setting them at regular intervals in a large circle around the perimeter of the ruin.

The altar was made of black stone, a cylinder covered with dust and leaves, with six small raised hemispherical mounds on the edge of the circular top. She brushed the dust away with her hands, revealing the smooth black surface still full of magic, and something else.

Lines were drawn on the black stone, connecting the six mounds around the circle, to form a six-pointed star.

Both the lines and the mounds at the points of the star were made of a silvery metal that sparkled in the light of the sun.

Moongold, Maya thought.

She was suddenly uncomfortable; moongold, ancient ruins, strange creatures mindlessly carrying out mysteriously organized tasks—put together, it all spelt ravians, and she did not particularly want to see any right now. A frightening thought struck her: Were her travelling companions servants of the ravians? Were ravians being summoned here?

She backed off slowly from the altar, feeling a sudden urge to start running.

The sunlight in the clearing seemed a little too bright, the air a little stuffier than it had seemed even in the shadows of the forest. She felt naked, vulnerable; as if unfriendly eyes were watching her, exposed in the sun.

A strange scent in the air. She groaned.

There was a faint whooshing sound behind her; she spun around to see three little furry red men lying dead on the ground, darts sticking out of their little round stomachs.

With a blood-curdling roar, Manticore leaped into the clearing. His great paws struck left and right, killing instantaneously. Little broken coloured bodies flew through the air. Darts pelted from his tail, incredibly accurate, picking off targets running madly towards the shelter of the forest. Deadly venom worked within seconds. The temple floor was suddenly dotted with corpses.

'Peace, Manticore!' called a commanding voice somewhere amidst the trees. Immediately, Manticore skidded to a halt, growling, his cunning eyes fixed on Maya, who just stood there, wondering what to do. Everywhere, little men ran around like panic-stricken ants. Manticore opened his mouth and yawned arrogantly, displaying colourful fur clinging to blood-soaked teeth.

'Strange indeed are the workings of fate,' Myrdak said, his voice, deep and strong, not loud but somehow clearly audible, echoing through the forest. 'Once again, the gods show us that they fight on our side. Once again, the way of the righteous is made clear, while evil twists and strangles itself in the shadows. Is it not odd, Maya, that having escaped us you came straight to the very place where we were bringing you?'

'Show yourself,' she said, trying to identify where his voice was coming from, 'if you dare.'

On hearing Myrdak's voice, something happened to the little men; they calmed down, and slowly started walking, as if in a trance, towards a tree at the edge of the clearing, to Maya's right.

Creepers parted high above. Myrdak was standing up on a huge branch of the tree, watching the clearing with a calm smile. He was strikingly handsome; as the sunlight bathed his face he seemed like some king of old, come to save the world.

A large fireball appeared over Maya's head.

'Come now, Maya,' laughed Myrdak. 'Do not waste your time. You cannot overpower me. You know this. Do not force me to hurt you, please.'

The little men gathered around the base of the tree silently, looking up at him with huge unblinking eyes.

He looked down at them, irritation crossing his strong features.

'Not now,' he said. 'I will speak to you later. Run along now! Or Manticore will kill you and eat you. Chasing girls across forests is hungry work.'

One of them started to sing.

'Yes, your songs are very sweet,' said Myrdak. 'But if you do not run away right now . . .'

A stone slab from the temple ruins rose and swung towards his tree. It smashed into the trunk, squashing three little men like mosquitoes. The rest ran screaming.

Without looking away, Myrdak stepped neatly to one side as the fireball exploded harmlessly where he had been standing a second ago.

'Embarrassingly slow,' he said. 'You disappoint me, Maya.'

She looked at the corpses scattered around the ruins and felt sick.

'They were innocent,' she said. 'They meant you no harm.'

'And I mean them no harm,' he replied. 'They have served their purpose. If I meant to harm them, they would all be dead. But they have been useful. They shall live. Never let it be said that I am unjust.'

'You disgust me.'

'The concern you humans have for the lesser races is really touching,' he said, and leaped down lightly from the tree.

'Why have you brought me here?' asked Maya.

285

He smiled.

'My plans are my own, Maya. The plans you should be worrying about at this point of time are your own. The easiest thing now would be for you to abandon all wild schemes of fighting or escaping,' he said. 'Either would be futile. And I hate it when I have to tame you. It hurts me more than it hurts you, believe me.' He walked forward, into the sunlight again, his boots clicking smartly on the temple floor.

She stepped back, wondering what to do. Out of the corner of her eye, she saw Manticore stalking up slowly behind her, trying to prevent any sudden dash into the trees.

'I hope you will forgive me for the way I have been forced to treat you,' he said, his voice throbbing with warmth and sincerity. 'Believe me, it was terrible. But there was no other way. Time was short, Kol was full of danger and evil, and you would not have believed me. You would not have come with me willingly. Later, one day, I shall explain everything to you. And then you will understand my actions, and even applaud them.'

'Why not explain everything to me now?' said Maya. 'I'm here, where you want me to be.' She took another step back. Two more steps, she thought, and I could turn and run. Behind her back, the fingers of her left hand began to twist and turn in an attack-spell mudra.

'Please step forward,' he said. 'You will only be hurting yourself if you try to escape.'

Maya finished the mudra. She thrust her hands forward, and the floor beneath Myrdak's feet cracked and exploded. Several seconds too late; he had stepped to the side well before the stone slabs flew up in the air.

Maya turned and ran. Manticore leaped forward to block

her. He need not have bothered because Myrdak sprang up and raised his hand, and creepers from the trees near Maya swished towards her. She swerved and jumped, but to no avail. One caught her round the ankle, another slithered over her waist. She threw a fireball at him, but she knew it was useless. The creepers curled swiftly around her like bark-skinned pythons, rolling her upwards and encircling her, trussing her up in mid-air as swiftly and efficiently as a spider binding a fly.

Suspended horizontally in the air above him, she stared down in impotent fury.

He came and stood below her. Their eyes were almost level. 'I hope you realize,' he said, in a deep, reproachful whisper, 'that you have brought this upon yourself. And before I forget—this time I will have to gag you, will I not? Before you start spitting fire again . . .'

He raised a finger, and a thin creeper bound itself tightly around Maya's mouth.

'Do watch her for a while, Manticore,' said Myrdak in a bored voice. 'Shoot her if she manages to break out of the creepers.'

He walked up to the altar in the centre of the ruins, and examined it closely. 'It is intact,' he said finally. Manticore's face broke into a hideous smile.

He laid a hand on a mound of moongold; the whole six-pointed star lit up, the points glowing brilliantly. Sighing in satisfaction, he walked back to Maya and Manticore.

'Long ago, during the Age of Terror,' he said, 'the ravians tried, in this very temple, to create a spell that would let us tame the wild magic of this world. That would help us speak to the dragons, show them the error of their ways, and lead them to the path of true freedom and understanding.

'The spell failed. Failed miserably. The dragons came, but they would not listen, they mocked the priests and flew away. And then rakshases attacked the temple and razed it to the ground. But, with typical stupidity, they forgot to destroy the most important object in it; the altar stone. Unfortunately, the stone cannot be used to control dragons; they answer a different call. But there are certain things it can do.

'To do those things, however, it requires blood. A small amount. But it must be magical blood from this world. I would ask Manticore to provide it, but he, poor beast, is tired and weak.'

Myrdak unsheathed a knife and stepped towards Maya. 'It will not hurt much,' he said, almost kindly, as the creepers let her down slightly, her eyes blazing into his. 'Under the circumstances, I am sure you will understand it is all for a good cause.'

288

Kirin lay coiled on a boulder below a steep rocky cliff somewhere in northern Skuanmark, looking out towards the cold blue sea. The northern sea was rough and choppy, powerful waves crashed into the coast, wearing down the first line of rocks, not far ahead of him. Cold water ran into crevices between huge boulders, reached the cliff-foot, and lapped at his dragging tail. His breath steamed in the thin, crisp air. The sun was a pale orb in the sky, looping in small circles in an endless day, lighting up his veined, wet wings in brilliant colours as he stretched, cat-liked, eyes half closed. The air was thick with salty spray and sea-winds whistled as the seagulls soaring and dipping around the cliff cried and barked. Deep crags and inlets scarred the cliff-face behind him. Ghosts of rocks emerged along the coast as the waters receded, bearing balding men's crowns of straggly seaweed.

He snorted in pleasure, rings of smoke escaping his fiery nostrils and spreading out as they rose in the air.

He would spend the whole night dreaming here, he

decided. Far away from kingdoms and wars, intrigue and death, quests and monsters, in a beautiful land unspoiled by man.

As if on cue, a Skuan longboat appeared on the horizon, exploring warriors singing lustily, rowing towards lands unconquered, the wooden dragonhead on its helm looking proudly westwards. Gulls followed in their wake, clamouring for scraps. Kirin idly contemplated flying out, setting the boat alight, eating the men on board and restoring the pristine beauty of the scene he was admiring moments ago.

Master, said another dragon's voice in his head. *You must come with me.*

Let me be, said Kirin. *I wish to remain here undisturbed.*

But you are needed elsewhere, master. Great danger, great deeds await you. The dragons have been called.

What? Who are you?

My name is Kjor, said the dragon. *Forgive me, master, but you must come with me. Someone calls.*

Who?

A power that once rose to challenge the Gauntlet you bear, that sought the subjugation of my kind. It failed then, but it has risen again, and draws us like moths to a flame. It is a challenge that must be answered.

What power is this you speak of?

Let me bear you to the Great Forest, said Kjor. *There your questions will be answered.*

Kirin closed his eyes, and felt once again the sensation of being hurled across the world.

A warm wind brushed his leathery skin. He opened his eyes again.

Vrihataranya.

Kirin flew with Kjor's wings, black Skuan dragon wings scything through blacker night, skimming low over a whispering ocean of trees under a brooding cloudy sky.

In front of him, standing in the sky, was a pillar of light. Dazzling white light that shone but did not illuminate, that blinded him and pulled him towards it, but did not touch the darkness around it. A great beacon, issuing a call that could not go unanswered.

What is that?

A summoning. A great power awaits us in the shadows, master.

He flew towards it on leaden wings, dreading whatever it was that he would see.

The forest was throbbing beneath him. Loud animal screams rent the air; the whole jungle was alive with fear. Currents of power shimmered through the leaves.

Kjor reached the pillar of light and circled it slowly, looking down, a great black bat-shape flitting across blinding white.

Kirin looked down through Kjor's eyes.

At the bottom of the pillar was a small circular clearing, surrounded by a dense perimeter of tall trees. In the middle of the clearing, outside the pillar of light, stood a man.

Kirin's powerful dragon eyes zoomed in, observing every detail on his upturned face, which was etched in stern black and white by the pillar in front of him. He was tall and looked powerful; a naked sword glowed in his hands.

His eyes locked with the dragon's, and Kirin cried out in his sleep far away as he felt the keen mind below; he was sure the man was looking into *his* eyes, that he *knew*, somehow, that someone else was watching from the dragon's mind.

'Greetings, Dark Lord.' A charming smile. 'My name is Myrdak.'

First, Myrdak, of House Aego Behrim had said . . .

The dragon was far above him, gliding silently in great circles over the trees, but Kirin heard the ravian's voice clearly and could not tear his eyes away from that calm, powerful face.

'This spell will not hold for long, so I will be brief,' said Myrdak. 'I do not know if you are the son of Narak and Isara, or the son of Danh-Gem as you claim to be— to be quite frank, it does not matter. What matters is this— the stars foretell that either you or I shall be master of Obiyalis. And it is the stars that have brought us together this night.'

In the Dark Tower of Imokoi, the Dark Lord's eyes snapped open. They were fire-red, with black slits for pupils. His mouth moved in words, but no sound was heard in his room.

Kjor roared and breathed a gust of green fire. His great eyes shone white in the pillar's light.

'What is it you want?' he screeched.

'I want many things,' said Myrdak. 'For myself, I want very little; I want only to be remembered as a man of peace. As one who spent his life working to heal the sick, help the weak, and defend the righteous. As one . . .'

'Get to the point,' the dragon said.

Myrdak laughed aloud. 'I like you already, Dark Lord,' he said. 'The world will be poorer when you are no longer a part of it. I will, indeed, get to the point.'

He raised his sword. It shone and sparkled in the white

light, its shadow pointing outwards, a black line running into the forest.

'Evil rules this world while you walk it, Kirin. And evil must be destroyed. I challenge you to single combat,' said Myrdak. 'You and I shall meet here, in the forest where our fathers fought centuries ago, and honour their memories with spilt blood. The winner takes Obiyalis.'

'A man of peace, indeed,' said the dragon. 'I refuse your challenge. I do not want the world, and it is not yours to give or take away in any case. You are strange, and mad, and you have funny hair. Now go away and don't bother me again, or I shall have you for dinner. Put this light out, and go to sleep.'

Myrdak bowed. 'Admirably put,' he said. 'However, before I put out the light and go to sleep, there is something I would like to show you. Manticore?'

Manticore pushed Maya out into the light. Her wrists and ankles were bound; a cloth was tied tightly around her mouth. She stumbled on a stone and fell heavily at Myrdak's feet.

She had been drugged. She stayed on the ground, looking blankly at the ravian, then turned and looked in fear and wonder at the huge shape circling in the sky.

The dragon hissed sharply and faltered in mid-air.

'Let me rephrase my challenge, Dark Lord,' said Myrdak. 'Come here and fight me, or I will kill the woman you love.'

'She is not yours to win or lose,' hissed the dragon.

'I never said she was,' said Myrdak. 'I merely said I would kill her if you refused to fight me. A shame, really—she is most attractive. Were she not of a lower race, I would be happy to fight you for her.'

'An enlightened leader of a higher race, are you?' snapped the dragon. 'Very evolved, I have to say. You want to settle the future of a world with a fight?'

'A fight that might remove the need for a war, which would be both unaesthetic and time-consuming. And yes, a duel is not the most refined of methods, but it is the only honest way to resolve differences of a certain magnitude, is it not? If it is too primitive a way for you, feel free to defeat me with your wits rather than brute strength.'

'Let her go!'

'Come now, Kirin, you are wasting my time. You stand to gain nothing by quibbling and arguing like a fishwife. My terms are simple. Come here, to the Temple of the Dark Star, and decide the fate of your world. Or stay where you are, like the coward I now suspect you to be. And I will come to you at the head of an army, and will give you, in exchange for your crown, Maya's head on a platter.'

'Enough,' said Kjor. 'State your time and place.'

'Right here, as fast as your reptile wings can carry you. I will be waiting. But hurry—if I get bored, or if your lover tries too hard to escape, as I suspect she will, I might just kill her anyway.

'And listen closely, for this is important—when you come to the temple, come alone. For if any other creature comes with you, human or monster, Maya dies.'

'Let me speak to her.'

'Certainly. Speak, Maya.' Myrdak knelt and ripped off the gag. Her eyes shone; she struggled to her feet. She seemed to have fought off the effects of the drug.

'Don't come, Kirin,' she snarled. 'He means to trick you somehow. And it's wasted effort anyway, because I will kill him myself before you get here.'

The ravian hit her across the mouth and she fell to the ground again. The dragon roared. A flame blossomed and died in its mouth.

'Everything that needed to be said has been said, Dark Lord,' said Myrdak. 'I will await you here, and as soon as you can grace this humble temple with your presence, I will be happy to meet you and kill you.'

'If you harm her . . .'

'Why do you waste your breath issuing empty threats? There is nothing you can do now. Save your strength for our meeting.'

He bowed, and smiled at the dragon again. 'And now, following your truly excellent advice, I will go away and get some sleep.'

He reached into the pillar of light and it went out, plunging the clearing into darkness. Kirin's night-eyes watched him in shock and disbelief as he picked Maya up and walked calmly into the shelter of the trees around the temple, leaving Kjor screaming and circling in the sky above him, streaking the skies above the Great Forest with impotent fire.

Alone in the topmost room of the Dark Tower, the Dark Lord awoke. He rose, walked slowly to the door and unlatched it.

'Have the ravian prisoner brought to me. Untied, unharmed. His jailers need not accompany him. Go now, and hurry,' he told the pashan sentries outside. They nodded and clattered off down the stairs.

Kirin walked down two flights of stairs and opened the door to the highest balcony in the Dark Tower. He stepped out, ignoring the wind blowing in great gusts to the east, and looked down at his dark realm. He looked down at his sprawling city-fortress, its winding streets and mighty battlements and fearsome, sleepless guardians. He looked further, at thousands of flickering dots on a vast plain far below, the campfires of the many regiments of soldiers who still lingered at Izakar, waiting for his command. He sighed, turned away, and looked towards the mountains to the west. They stared back at him disdainfully, lofty and grey.

The Gauntlet glowed red on Kirin's hand. He raised it in the air and pointed towards the mountains.

I need you now, he said. *One dragon. The fastest.*

A few seconds passed.

Then a distant roar echoed in his ears, like thunder in the mountains, young and strong and brimming with bloodlust.

Tjugari the destroyer answers your call, Master. I come.

Kirin left the balcony, walked quickly up to his room and began to pack.

After what seemed like an eternity, the pashans brought Behrim to Kirin's room. Two rakshases, refusing to believe that the Dark Lord had asked the prisoner to be brought unguarded, had come with him. Kirin dismissed them imperiously and asked Behrim to sit.

'A great weight rests on your shoulders, I can see,' said Behrim. 'Why have you called for me?'

'I just received a message from your friend Myrdak,' said Kirin. 'He challenged me to a duel in Vrihataranya. He has abducted my—someone I care about very deeply— and threatens to kill her.'

Behrim gasped in genuine astonishment.

'Impossible,' he said. 'No ravian of honour could stoop so low.'

'That is not true and you know it,' said Kirin. 'You lot play as dirty as anyone else. But I have not called you here to complain about your brethren. I need your counsel. I thought you said the ravians had agreed to hear all three of you out before declaring war. Were you lying to me? If your plan was to confuse me into inaction, it seems to have succeeded. Now tell me the truth.'

'I have already told you the truth,' said Behrim. 'I do not understand this myself.' He thought for a while.

'If the ravians have allowed Myrdak to take so drastic a step,' he said, 'then it can mean only one thing. Peori has betrayed her clan and the Council. For Myrdak's task concerned neither the Dark Lord—any challenges issued to him could be from me alone, the Council had ruled—nor Kirin son of Narak, for your fate is linked with the ravian republic's, and Peori was the only one of us allowed to observe you. How dare Myrdak challenge you like this? This is not what was agreed. He has violated the direct orders of the Council.'

'Unless your Council has now decided once and for all that *I* am the enemy.'

'That is possible,' said Behrim, 'but unlikely. The ravians would much rather make peace with you, Kirin—if they decided to strike against you, they would declare open war, for they believe they are stronger than your rakshases and dragons together. They would want the whole world to see ravians in all their strength and glory destroying the forces of evil. This tale of abduction, of threats, of a duel in the old temple—something is very wrong.'

'Could Myrdak be acting without the knowledge of the Council?'

'What happened, exactly? What did he say?'

Kirin told him swiftly.

Behrim was lost in thought.

'Has the Chief Civilian of Kol been killed? Has the King of Kol returned?' he asked.

'No, I would have heard if that had happened. What does that have to do with anything?'

'If that has not happened, Myrdak's task is not complete. Yet he is obviously alive, and has been active. Which means he has abandoned the task given to him, and is working instead to achieve his own ambitions. In all probability, he has persuaded Peori to side with the royalists. Perhaps he and Peori have both spoken to the Council, and have persuaded them that you are wholly evil. He cannot have gone this far without Peori's knowledge. The Council would have wanted to hear Peori's views first. They have conspired against the republic, while I have been rotting in your dungeons. Now he seeks to draw you out and kill you, and use your links with the rakshases as an excuse to destroy all my dreams of a free, casteless republic where all ravians are equal.' There was terrible bitterness in Behrim's voice.

'Frankly, I do not care about your ravian republic,' said Kirin. 'I have a friend to save. I will leave for Vrihataranya at once.'

'Surely you are not planning to actually fight him?' asked Behrim, wonder in his voice.

'Of course I am.'

'No!'

'What do you mean, no? What other choice do I have?'

'You cannot defeat Myrdak in open battle,' said Behrim

flatly. 'He is the greatest ravian warrior alive. No matter how powerful you are, your powers cannot match his. And even more deadly than his strength is his guile. You can be sure of one thing—he has other schemes as well, he does not intend to give you any chance of victory. I know his methods. He will lure you with false promises, and then strike you down when hope seems real. Do not fight him, Kirin, I beg you. I have trained you myself, and I know what you are capable of.'

'You know nothing about me,' said Kirin. 'And no matter how deadly it is, I must go. There is really nothing you can say that can persuade me otherwise.'

'No,' said Behrim. 'Your life is important, not just to the rakshases, but to the ravians as well. I cannot let you throw it away like this. You are young and naïve, and will just walk into a simple trap.'

'Not at all.'

'No? In that case,' said Behrim with a quiet smile, 'why have you let a dangerous ravian, whose sworn duty is to destroy the Dark Lord of Imokoi, walk into your room unguarded?'

He rose and took a small step forward, his face full of quiet resolution. 'I cannot let you go to this duel, Kirin,' he said.

'You cannot stop me,' said Kirin quietly.

He was profoundly grateful, though, when Aciram materialized in a puff of smoke just then, breaking the silence.

'Apologies for intruding,' said Aciram gruffly, 'but if you must speak to the ravian alone, at least let me tie him up for you. This way is too dangerous.'

'You're right,' said Kirin. 'Why don't you just stay here then.'

'Very well,' said Aciram, looking completely surprised.

'I have an idea, Kirin,' said Behrim. 'Let me come with you. We will speak to the Council and stop this madness.'

'I cannot let you,' said Kirin. 'I must go alone. He said if he saw anyone with me, he would kill Maya.'

'This is a war. Sacrifices must be made. The future of the entire ravian race is at stake.'

'You are not coming with me,' said Kirin, 'and that is final. Aciram, could you escort him back to the dungeons, please?'

'Where are you going, kinsman?' asked Aciram.

'I have to go to Vrihataranya, alone, to fight a duel with a ravian warrior,' said Kirin. 'The winner, he said, takes this world.'

'This world is already yours,' snarled Aciram. 'Let him come and take it, if he wants it so badly. We will be ready.'

'Unfortunately, he holds a friend of mine hostage. I will have to go.'

'A woman?'

'Yes.'

'You love her?'

'Yes.'

Aciram actually chuckled. 'You are your father's son,' he said. 'There are a million reasons why this quest is doomed to failure, but if anyone has the slightest chance of succeeding, it is you, Kirin. Go. I cannot ask you not to.'

'Take me with you,' said Behrim again. 'Not to the duel, but to the Council.'

'No.'

'If it is to the Temple of the Black Star that you are going, then you will not even have to go out of your way, for the place I want to take you is but a day's march from the Temple.

It is a secret fortress in the heart of Vrihataranya, from which we used to issue forth to attack rakshas convoys travelling towards the mountains. Aciram will vouch for this—did you not seek in vain for a ravian stronghold in western Vrihataranya all through the war?'

Aciram shrugged. 'How do I know? We looked for ravian strongholds everywhere. What does this have to do with Kirin's duel?'

'Everything. Kirin, let me come with you. We will visit the ravian fortress of Epsai, concealed in the valleys of western Vrihataranya, a post of immense strategic importance that is sure to be manned if the ravians have returned in large numbers. There we will send word to the Council, and make them see the light. We will foil Myrdak with strategy—in his haste to strike you down, he has violated the Council's orders, and we will use that against him. In his arrogance he told you that the world would be his if he killed you—the Council will not look too kindly upon that. I know my plan sounds unlikely to succeed—it is—but believe me, your plan of rushing to the Forest to fight Myrdak is doomed to failure.'

'What do you think?' asked Kirin, turning to Aciram.

Aciram shrugged. 'Everything gets crazy when the wars start,' he said. 'Listen to your guts. Me, I do not like the idea of you walking into a ravian fortress. What if our friend here and whoever challenged you are working together, trying to lead you into captivity? My advice is, go and fight him, defeat him, win back your woman. There is no room for fear or worry now. If she is alive, her life can be saved. If she is dead, it can be avenged. It is as simple as that.'

'I am inclined to agree with him,' said Kirin slowly.

In the distance, they heard the sound of dragon wings beating.

'Aciram could be expected to want you to walk into the arms of death, could he not?' asked Behrim. 'Who leads the rakshases once you are dead, Kirin?'

'Just for that,' snarled Aciram, 'I will eat you.'

'Stop it,' said Kirin.

'Do not take him with you,' said Aciram. 'He will betray you. I know it.'

Behrim and Aciram locked eyes and stood face-to-face while Kirin paced the floor.

'Take me to your Council, Behrim,' said Kirin finally.

Aciram shook his head, but said nothing.

'Thank you for putting your trust in me, Kirin,' said Behrim. 'I will not lead you astray. Though my heart tells me I lead you into grave danger.'

'I do not like this, Kirin!' blurted Aciram. 'Will you keep a sane head? Will you promise me you will not be blinded by their offers of power? They will never let you lead them! Your father believed that ravians were noble, and it cost him his life!'

The sound of beating wings grew louder.

'Let me come with you as well,' said Aciram suddenly. 'Yes, that is what must be done. I will come too.'

'I wish I could take you,' said Kirin. 'There is no one else I trust, now that Spikes is gone. But I cannot. If we both leave, Izakar will fall apart in days.'

'Let me go instead of you, then!' cried Aciram. 'Let me fight the duel in your stead!'

'No. I have to do this myself. And I must leave now. My steed is here.'

'Your steed?'

'Yes. I'm catching a dragon.'

'But you cannot leave now, like this! It is madness! Let

me prepare weapons, armour, provisions . . . if you are to ride a dragon, it must be fed . . . a machan must be built on its back . . .'

Kirin picked up his bag. 'Everything I need is here,' he said. 'Is there anything in the dungeon you're particularly attached to, Behrim?'

'No,' said Behrim.

Aciram clasped his head. 'But how will you go? How do you plan to ride the dragon? It's not like a horse, you know! It will take at least a day to build even the most primitive platform!'

'I don't have time for that. I will find a way. I *have* to.'

'This is madness!'

Then Aciram laughed aloud.

'See how haste makes fools of all of us,' he said. 'You have your chariot. It will get you anywhere in no time.'

'The chariot's gone, Aciram.'

'What?'

'The chariot is not here.'

Aciram's brow clouded, then cleared.

'Spikes?' he asked conspiratorially.

'Do you really want to talk about it in front of a ravian?'

Aciram fell silent.

Kirin walked out of his room and down the stairs to the balcony.

'This is just too hasty,' protested Aciram, following him. 'No matter how desperate your hurry, perhaps you should stop and think a little more. I do not often suggest patience, kinsman. But every choice you make affects the whole world. So be prudent, please.'

'For once, things are clear to me, Aciram. I must go, and I must go right now. I will leave the prudence and the thinking to you,' said Kirin. 'Have fun. I have no wise words for you. In case I do not return . . . just try not to kill everyone, that's all.'

'I do not know if I can keep these powers united without you, Kirin. They need you. They need Danh-Gem's son.'

They reached the balcony and walked into the wind. The stars and the earth stretched out in front of them.

'Can I trust you, Aciram?' asked Kirin.

'Of course you can.'

'In that case, perhaps it is best that no one knows that Danh-Gem's son has left the Tower.'

'What are you suggesting?' asked Aciram. 'Oh,' he said after a second. 'Very well. It is fraught with uncertainty and danger, but you can trust me. Then again, if you leave in a whirlwind like this, I suppose you have no choice.'

'That's funny,' said Kirin. 'I thought I heard a dragon approach. Where did it go?'

'I am here, master,' said a voice above him.

They all looked up simultaneously, yelled in surprise and almost jumped out of their collective skins.

Perched silently on top of the Dark Tower, great wings folded on his back, was the largest and most terrifying northern dragon they had ever seen, a shiny, scaly flying fortress of tooth and horn and claw. His head alone was the size of a full-grown camel; sword-like fangs glittered in his mouth, suspended directly above their heads. An impressive array of horns and spikes and scales adorned his body.

'Tjugari the destroyer, I believe your name was . . . ?'

'At your service.'

'How quickly can you take me to Vrihataranya?'

'We are almost there already.'

'Good. Can you carry us in your claws?'

'You, master, and both your companions?'

'Just this scared-looking gentleman here.'

'Yes.'

'Let us go, then.'

'Yes, master.'

The dragon launched off the tower into the air, almost blowing them off with the force of his wings. He glided in perfect silence down the side of the tower.

Aciram embraced Kirin. 'May the stars shine upon you, Dark Lord,' he said. 'Good luck. I will keep your throne safe until you return.'

'Goodbye, Aciram.'

Street lights went out far below them as the dragon flapped his wings.

'And as for you,' Aciram said, turning to Behrim. 'Remember my face well. I will remember yours. Betray Kirin, and my face is the last thing you will see.'

Behrim nodded.

Tjugari came flying up the Tower with the force of a full-scale hurricane and scooped Kirin and Behrim up in his giant front paws. They clasped his wickedly curving talons desperately, their faces turning slightly green. The dragon hovered for a wing-beat, accepting Aciram's salute, and then, with a great voom, soared high into the air. He sent a huge ball of fire into the sky before him, and in its brief light Aciram watched his nephew hanging on grimly as his terrifying servant roared a challenge to the wind and hurtled eastwards.

He stood there quietly for a while, watching the dragon grow smaller in the distance. It really was incredibly fast. His blood was boiling in excitement; he roared a terrible roar into the sky.

The moonlight shone down on the wily rakshas.

'Just one more thing to do,' he said aloud. 'And now that Kirin is gone, it can be done.'

He walked up to the room on top of the Tower. He stood just inside for a while, as if waiting for something, then slammed the door shut and latched it.

He clapped his hands. There was a sudden flash of bright light.

And a very slight movement in a corner of the room. Thin legs shifting noiselessly, weak eyes startled by the light.

Quicker than a cobra, Aciram pounced on the spider that was speeding towards a crack in the wall. He held it firmly, not squeezing it, not allowing it to move, until it stopped straining and writhing and lay still in his great paw, shivering slightly.

'Well, well,' he said. 'What have we here?'

He flung the spider to the ground and muttered a spell. The spider swelled up; a second later, Akimis lay sprawled on the floor.

'Get up,' said Aciram.

Akimis couldn't get up; she crawled around on the floor for a while, disoriented, trying to walk eight-legged. She hissed and spat.

Aciram pulled her up roughly.

'How long have you been here? What have you heard?'

'I was here all along,' she said sullenly. 'I was here when it all started. When he spoke to the ravian, before you came.'

'And why were you here?'

'You know why.'

'Ambitious young rakshasis who lust for power,' said

Aciram, 'are very dangerous.' He held her shoulders firmly, looking into her eyes suspiciously.

'Powerful old rakshases ambitious young rakshasis lust for,' she said, her voice suddenly deep and husky, 'are very dangerous too.'

She smiled shyly, a little girl's smile.

'I am no threat to you, Aciram,' she said. 'I was just curious, that's all. It is no secret that I want the Dark Lord.' She leaned into him, suddenly smelling of jasmine. 'You can trust me.'

A sly smile spread slowly over Aciram's face. 'Perhaps I can. The Dark Lord has gone to fight a duel he may not win,' he said. 'What if he does not return?'

'Do not speak of such things,' she said, suddenly small and frightened. 'You scare me.' She huddled close to him, smiling a secret smile as his arms tightened around her involuntarily.

'I am sometimes scared myself,' he said. Suddenly, his body sagged; he was now old, tired, he was the one who sought solace, she the provider. She held him close, her intoxicating scent, jasmine and beautiful woman, filling his nostrils.

'Let me be by your side, O wise and powerful Aciram,' she whispered. 'Let me help you. Let me share your secrets and your troubles.'

'I thought it was Kirin you wanted.'

'I do not know what I want. My head is in a whirl. I am falling, Aciram, Prince of rakshases. Will you not save me?'

'Yes,' he whispered. 'Yes.'

They kissed, long and passionately.

'Such a waste,' he said after a while.

'What?' she asked, her voice thick with passion, a coquettish smile on her lips.

'This,' said Aciram.

He caught her head gently in his hands, and snapped her neck with a sudden twist.

Then he picked her body up and tossed it casually out of the window.

He went outside and called the security pashans.

'Let messages be sent to all senior military commanders,' he said. 'The Dark Lord will address them tomorrow morning. Plans for the war have changed drastically, and they must be appraised immediately. Leave at once.'

The pashans nodded, and stomped down the stairs obediently.

Aciram climbed down to the balcony again, and stood in the moonlight, watching the world turn below him, listening to the sounds of the city he now ruled, thinking of the future.

His face melted, and changed into Kirin's.

3

When she looked back later on the events of the journey, Red was able to point out the exact moment when she had fallen *out* of love with Asvin.

After three intensely passionate days and nights in Shantavan, Rukmini had finally relinquished her vice-like grip over her own body (and Asvin's) and fallen into satiated, exhausted slumber.

Soma and Tamasha, working in such perfect harmony that it seemed impossible that they had ever had an argument, had then seized her and strangled her.

Red wasn't sure if *death* was the right word to describe what had happened to Rukmini, since her body was spectacularly alive, crawling with indescribable new sensations after its marathon session with Asvin, but one thing was certain—Rukmini had been effectively silenced. And Red was certainly not going to make the mistake of granting names to her inner voices again. She felt as if she had just managed to pull herself back from the edge of a precipice.

For Rukmini, born as she was in the wild, when Red was beyond the calming influence of the Rainbow Council, had shown Red strange new feelings—the intensity of the desire she had felt for Asvin had left Red breathless. Rukmini had had none of the restraint of Soma and Tamasha, born while Red was practicing (however inefficiently) the self-control that was the defining characteristic of all shapeshifters.

Soma was reasonably responsible, Tamasha had idle fantasies of turning rakshasi but Rukmini, Red suspected, could have actually taken Red to the far reaches of truly wild magic—Rukmini, in some ways, had been a rakshasi trying to break loose. And she had almost taken complete control of Red, almost thrown away the rest of Red's minds, all to feed her cravings of the moment. And now thanks to Rukmini, they had almost no hope of catching Maya and the ravian. Four whole days had been wasted—Asvin had taken a whole day to recover from Rukmini's voracious assault. He was still nearly unable to walk, and grimaced in pain every time his horse leaped over a barrier.

They were riding hard over the rising plains between Shantavan and Vrihataranya, following chariot tracks. They had not spoken since Asvin awoke in the morning. He had jumped up, uttered a half-strangled cry, pulled his clothes on and hobbled to his horse, completely avoiding eye contact. Red, mildly annoyed and mildly amused, had played along.

Tamasha: When do you think Asvin is going to break his vow of silence?

Soma: When he thinks of something to say. It could take years.

Tamasha: He's like a sweet little ostrich, isn't he?

Soma: Yes, poor thing. He has no idea what to say.

Tamasha: His face is all red. Of course, that's not all embarrassment. That Rukmini . . . hmm.

Soma: We won't miss *her*.

Tamasha: Talk to him, Red. Tell him it's all right. Tell him we know he loves Maya, and we're not expecting a wedding proposal. He'll die of guilt otherwise.

Soma: And so he should. He was unfaithful to Maya. He should suffer.

Tamasha: Come on. Heroes are like that. And it's not all his fault. She put a little spell on him.

Soma: No. His armour makes him resistant to magic, at least to some extent. Even if it didn't, there is no excuse for what he did.

Tamasha: Every hero is naturally polygamous. It's in their blood. Like a disease. And he's Avrantic too. They always get away with infidelity. The Psomedean heroes at least had the decency to die horrible deaths afterwards.

Soma: I don't care whether he's a hero or not. It's still not an excuse.

Tamasha: *Now* you're being all virtuous. You enjoyed every minute. We both did. We could have stopped him much earlier.

Soma: That's true. Anyway, what's done is done.

Tamasha: And done well, I might add. What will be really interesting is when Asvin goes back to Kol and meets the real Rukmini.

Soma (laughing): Yes.

Tamasha: But it's not Asvin that's got our girl all shaken up, Soma—it's Rukmini and her little display of wild power, if I'm not mistaken. Makes you wonder, doesn't it, Red? You could be really powerful. What would it be like, to let go? To forget all self-restraint? Who could we be? What could we achieve?

Soma: Don't think about it. That way lies madness.

Tamasha: I hope you realize, Red, that we will never catch up with Maya now. Once we're in Vrihataranya, this far behind, we will have no chance of picking up their trail. They are, what, a week ahead of us? And probably still travelling faster than we are?

Soma: Yes. This chase is over, Red. Even if we lose Asvin, I don't think there is any point in going further. And Asvin knows this too. Four days, and we were so far behind to start with.

'Where are we going, Asvin?' asked Red.

He flinched visibly and slowed his horse down to a canter.

'I do not know,' he said. 'We cannot catch them now without a miracle. Rukmini . . . I must tell you something . . .'

'Don't,' said Red. 'Forget what happened. We were both stupid. Focus instead on the task ahead of you. What should we do now?'

'I do not know,' he said. 'I have failed in every way. I deserve death.'

'Don't be silly. It was bound to happen. I knew it would happen the day we met. We both wanted each other, there is no shame in that. It is over, though—at least until our task is done.'

Soma: Said it before he could. Well done.

Asvin's face shone like the sun. 'Words fail to express . . .'

'Then let them fail. We should either keep moving, or head back.'

'Let us go on, then. My heart will not let me turn back.'

They rode on, through undulating green hills growing increasingly dense with trees. It was about noon when they reached the southern rim of the Great Forest, where all of a sudden the trees became a thick wall, where forbidding shadows lay firm under massive tree trunks even as bright sunshine bathed the hills behind them.

Lying under a tree was the ravian's chariot, its wheels broken. They dismounted, and walked up to it.

Asvin studied the ground closely.

'Some great beast has walked here,' he said. 'They went into the forest. But that was many days ago.'

He hung his head.

'Well?' said Red. 'What now?'

'I do not know,' he said once again. 'I have always trusted in my luck, in my stars, in the gods that I believe watch over me. Can it be that they will fail me now? Surely there will be some sign. Surely we have not come here in vain.'

Tamasha: And that's what I call a well-thought-out plan.

Red sighed and patted his shoulder. 'No. No signs, I'm afraid. Just Vrihataranya in front of us, and Kol behind.'

And a faint sobbing noise, somewhere to the left.

Asvin's eyes lit up. 'What is that noise?'

'Sounds like someone crying,' said Red. 'Should we . . .'

Asvin turned grateful eyes towards the sun. 'I knew it,' he said. 'When all hope is lost, when all seems dark, the gods provide.'

He leaped on his horse in one magnificent flourish, and groaned in pain.

Soma: The gods provide, indeed. Someone cries far away, and even that has to be about him.

313

Tamasha: The strange thing is, I'm fairly convinced he's right.

Asvin rode off. Red mounted her horse and followed.

A large cart, drawn by an old, fat horse.

In the cart, large earthen pots and steel vessels.

And a crying girl.

She was young, in her mid-teens at most. Clad in a sari that had slipped, exposing one bare shoulder that was shaking as huge sobs escaped her. Her face was buried in her hands.

They rode up to her cart.

'What is it, little girl?' asked Asvin, his voice full of tenderness and concern.

Soma: She's not that little.

Tamasha: Of course she isn't. I don't believe this man's luck with women. Innocent village girl, no doubt waiting to be rescued from something. Glowing skin and everything. It's sickening.

The girl raised her head. Her tear-stained face was thin and pretty, dominated by two huge, appealing eyes.

Tamasha: Here we go.

'Why do you sob so, little girl?' asked Asvin. He rode next to her.

'Alas, kind sir,' she said. 'I ride to my death.'

'What do you mean?'

'Do not waste your breath on me, kind sir,' she said. 'For I am already dead.'

Asvin drew in his breath sharply and put his hand on his sword-hilt.

Tamasha: Not undead, stupid. She's being dramatic. Of course she's alive. Heavy breathing, bosom heaving, everything.

314

Asvin put his hand gently on the girl's bare shoulder.

'Tell me what is wrong,' he said. 'Perhaps I can help.'

The girl started crying again.

'Asvin?' said Red. 'Can we move along, please? Perhaps your sign from the gods is further on.'

'Wait, dear Rukmini,' said Asvin. 'A fellow human being in distress cannot be ignored.'

Tamasha: Not when she looks like that, anyway.

Soma: No, you're being unfair. Knowing him, he'd be doing the same thing if she were wrinkled and smelly.

'What is the matter, my dear?' Asvin asked the girl. 'What is your name?'

'Antara,' she said.

'Well, Antara, my name is Asvin. I am from Kol. Can we be friends?'

Tamasha: Oh *please*.

'Asvin of Kol . . .' Antara's eyes widened. 'Can it be . . . surely not . . .'

'What?' asked Asvin.

'Are you the Hero who will come to save the world?' she asked, her eyes widening.

'Yes,' said Asvin, fighting to keep smugness out of his voice.

'My lord,' she said, her voice full of wonder, 'I am honoured to have met you before my death.' She clasped his hand. 'Bless me, my lord, so that my sacrifice keeps my family safe and happy.'

'What is this death that you keep speaking of, girl?' asked Red sharply.

'Antara, this is Queen Rukmini of Durg,' said Asvin.

Antara's eyes were on the verge of popping out of her head. 'Your Majesty!' she gasped. 'The gods have honoured me beyond all hope, sending two wonders of the world to light my last hours!'

'Yes, yes,' said Red irritably. 'Please tell him what he wants to know. We are in a hurry.'

'I travel to Shantavan, to the lair of the rakshas Akab,' she said. 'These vessels are full of food——food our village sends to the demon as tribute, small offerings in exchange for his protection. Unfortunately, he also demands human sacrifice——once a month, a young virgin must be sent. It is my family's turn this month.' She started crying again. 'I know it is my duty,' she said. 'But I wish it did not have to be me.'

'Well, why don't you just run then,' said Red, 'instead of sitting here and weeping?'

'But it is her duty, Rukmini,' said Asvin, shooting a puzzled look at her. 'For the rakshas will ravage her village if she does not, is that not so?'

Antara nodded.

'If it's young virgins he wants,' said Red, 'you should just . . . take steps to ensure you cannot be sent.'

'I tried that already,' she said. 'The village elders said it did not really matter.'

'Let us speak no more of such things,' said Asvin, his face flushed. Red shot him an annoyed glance. 'It is clear what must be done. Antara, I will go to the rakshas in your place.'

'Asvin?' asked Red gently. 'Are you a virgin girl?'

He laughed. 'Do you not see, Rukmini? This is a chance the gods give me to do penance for my sins.'

'That is the rudest thing anyone has said to me in my life.'

'Do not be angry——I beg your forgiveness, but you must

see what I mean. This is my chance to be a true hero again, to find my feet, to walk once again on the path of righteousness. This is a god-given opportunity. I will save the village from the rakshas.'

'This rakshas is in Shantavan?'

'Yes,' said Antara.

'In case you have forgotten, Maya is *this* way,' said Red to Asvin, jabbing a finger towards the Great Forest.

'But my duty lies that way.'

'So you don't want to find Maya any more?'

'We are already too far behind. And you must see that the gods have arranged matters thus—that if I slay the rakshas they will reward me in some way, they will give me some means to find Maya. It is all clear now.'

'How do you know this?' asked Red, genuinely puzzled. He seemed so *sure* . . .

'Of course, I do not *know*,' said Asvin. 'But this is a great chance to redeem myself, to save this village. To be a hero once again, Rukmini. You do not know what it means to me—here I am, free to make my own decisions, no one's puppet. When I save this village, it will not be as anyone's tool, it will not be for anyone's profit. It will be an act of selflessness, homage to the gods, and surely they will smile on me again. They will light up a path for me, and I will find my Maya again.'

'Are you sure?'

'Yes. I have never been more sure.'

Red shrugged. 'Let's go kill this rakshas, then.'

'No,' said Asvin. 'This is not your quest. You should take the girl to her village, explain things to the villagers, and wait there for me.'

Tamasha: The sheer *impertinence* . . . what are we, his servants?

Soma: Let him go. We've been trying to get rid of him for a while, remember?

'Where is this Akab's lair?' Asvin asked Antara.

Antara, who had been watching this exchange breathlessly, looked troubled. 'Somewhere in Shantavan. We do not know exactly where,' she said. 'This horse just takes the girls there. Last month, some of the men decided to creep upon the rakshas and catch him unawares, and rode behind the cart stealthily. Neither men nor horses returned. And Akab came to my village roaring like a hurricane, butchered several people, and told us that if he saw anyone riding with the cart ever again, he would come and raze our village to the ground.'

'Well, if a girl must go with the cart,' said Red, 'then I suppose it has to be me.'

'No,' said Asvin. 'This is not your quest, Rukmini. I cannot let you go.'

'That being the case, there's only one thing to do,' said Red brightly. 'Asvin must go pretending to be a girl, and surprise the rakshas.'

'Don't be ridiculous. I cannot pretend to be a . . . *girl*,' said Asvin.

'Think of something else quickly, then.'

Asvin thought furiously.

'Yes?' asked Red.

'I suppose I will have to,' said Asvin sullenly, his face the colour of a beetroot.

'Antara, my dear,' said Red. 'Kindly step this way. We will find a nice quiet spot in the woods, and you can give me your sari. Asvin, don't look so stunned . . . think how pretty you'll look. When I come back here, I expect you to be naked.'

'But . . .' said Antara, looking at Asvin in horror.

'Yes, I know, but the man obviously can't know how to put a sari on, can he? Taking it off, now there's a different matter.'

'But you . . .'

'Don't worry,' said Red. 'I can handle it.'

4

'I don't think I've ever been in this part of the labyrinth before,' said Mantric.

'Neither have I,' said the Civilian. 'It's new. Someone noticed it a few days ago.'

'I thought you knew every inch of your palace.'

'So did I.'

They walked down a narrow underground corridor, solid-looking stone walls looming dourly on either side. In the light of the small Alocactus in Temat's hands, Mantric's eyes were gleaming suspiciously. He wished, once again, that he could tell whether she was lying for a reason or just out of habit.

The corridor widened suddenly and ended in a small, square room. She set the Alocactus down on the floor. There were two small chairs in a corner. They sat.

'We have never really spoken of politics, Mantric,' said the Civilian with a faint smile. 'It is too dirty a game for you—your mind is of a loftier mould altogether.'

'It is also wise not to teach statecraft to those already endowed with magical powers,' said Mantric with a much broader smile.

She patted him on the arm, nodding her head.

'It is not that,' she said. 'It is just that it is not in my nature to trust.'

'And it is not in my nature to care,' said Mantric. 'An ideal meeting of minds, in other words.'

'But today,' she said, 'I have decided to give in to your nagging and tell you about the ravians and the vamans.'

'My nagging?' asked Mantric, bewildered.

'There is also the consideration that I might be assassinated any day now by ravians, and I would hate to die knowing I had left anything unsaid. Especially to you.'

'True,' said Mantric. 'We never leave anything unsaid, do we?'

The Civilian smiled—*grinned* would perhaps be a better description—got up, and started pacing up and down the little room. Mantric wondered what had put the spring in her step. Who had she killed?

'Several days ago, when we spoke to Ombwiri, Asvin and Maya, I told you that the real reason for the ravians leaving was that they were afraid the vamans would discover and storm Asroye.'

'I remember it as if it were yesterday.'

'Would you like to know why?'

'I would *love* to know why.'

Temat looked at Mantric with some asperity.

'Be quiet,' she said, grinning openly this time.

'Has something bad happened?' asked Mantric. 'Have you just had some bad news?'

'Why?'

'Well, we usually have these talks just after you've had some bad news. Though you look very cheerful for some reason.'

'Long ago, during the Age of Terror,' said Temat sternly, 'a Great War was fought. What is not commonly known about this war is the extent of diplomacy it took to persuade the vamans not to fight against the ravians.'

Mantric opened his mouth, but the Civilian raised an imperious eyebrow, and he shut it with a snap. Levity was one thing, courting death by ignoring The Eyebrow was quite another.

'The vamans were suspicious of the ravians from the start,' continued Temat. 'The ravians, on their part, thought with their usual arrogance that they could invade the underworld easily, tried, and discovered to their considerable dismay that they could not control vaman minds. And that their weapons were no match for the vamans'.

'That first attack by the ravians threw everyone in this part of the world into a quagmire of distrust. The two other significant non-human powers in Kol, the spellbinders and the vamans, regarded each other with a sort of amused tolerance. It is well known that after their initial friendship, the spellbinders and the ravians did not get along—ravians rarely got along with beings they couldn't control—and this, added to the increasing vaman presence in Kol, made the ravians distrustful of humans as well. This actually helped them—they grew even more secret, ceaselessly guarding all roads to the hidden city, as they slowly plotted how to gain more power in the world.

'The vamans, meanwhile, had found out that the ravians were from another world, and this changed them too—before, their notion of the world was an absurdly simplistic one—they thought the world was composed of . . .'

'The midworld, that they lived in, the sunworld, home of humans, magic and madness, and the single hell below, home of nameless monsters,' said Mantric. 'Go on.'

'The idea that there were other worlds fascinated the vamans, and they slowly grew more obsessed with it. Bigger markets, more incredible metals, freedom from the random catastrophes that struck them ever so often in this shifting, unpredictable world. The humans of Kol knew nothing of all this—the only clue they might have had was new themes in vaman art, but as we both know people only notice these things when it is too late.

'Slowly, inevitably, rifts began to form in the vaman empire. Some wanted to move to the surface and settle, and even more unthinkably, began to express their dissent freely. To stop this slow revolution from spreading, the vaman king sent a large number of vamans to the surface, to this very city, and they worked here, producing wonders of science and craft. Once they had a taste of the outside world, the vaman king told them, they would only want to come back.

'But the vamans were not content even in the wondrous city of Kol, and they did not want to go back either; they still wanted to go to other worlds, to form kingdoms underneath other crusts. And the ravians realized this, and used it—they actually managed to win over some of the vamans in Kol. A society was formed, called the Marginal Labour Union or some such thing. Its members fought alongside the ravians in the wars, while the vaman king watched, waited, and added a fairly large number of spies to its numbers. And thus the ravians and the vamans played games with one another, each circling warily around the opponent trying to find a weakness, while the long war wore on.

'And then suddenly the war was drawing to a close. Danh-Gem was on the verge of defeat—but still incredibly dangerous. The ravians were beginning to lose their grip on the human armies they used as pawns in their battles. The spellbinders were openly opposed to a number of ravian schemes. And the vamans underground pressed on relentlessly, honeycombing the earth under the Great Forest, systematically searching for the hidden ravian city, the key to the mysteries of the universe.

'Faced with defeat in their very hour of victory, the ravians went on the defensive, and made a pact with the few vamans that had remained faithful. They would bring back the ravians to the world, helped by a manticore in Vrihataranya who would come to them when the time was right. Fearing the spies of the vaman king, they did not leave the vamans precise instructions—they just asked them to wait for the manticore, their secret-keeper, who would meet them when the time was right and tell them how to aid the return of the ravians. Leaving the future of their race in the paws of one servant was the greatest risk the ravians have been known to take—but it turned out to have been a good decision. The manticore kept his secret faithfully, and the vamans brought the ravians back.'

'Were the ravians able to control the vamans who followed them?'

'No, these vamans followed the ravians willingly. Mind control is not the only reason the ravians have followers— they are a great civilization and their views are based on

324

rules that work, that are sound and are often very attractive, specially to other rulers.'

'And so the ravians are back? Has Asroye been rebuilt?'

'According to Mod, all the vamans know is that the ravians have, indeed, returned. One of the rebel vamans who brought the ravians back was an agent of the king—a scientist. He set off the flare that signalled that the ravians were back. But more details could not be found, because he was killed. All the vamans who brought the ravians back were killed. They knew there would be spies, and decided to leave no traces, no evidence.'

'Sounds like our friends from that night. And so the ravians did not keep their end of the bargain?'

'The Dark Lord is, according to reports, very much alive. And the vamans have not yet made a successful portal. According to Mod, at least.'

'I wish I could have seen the ravian portal. Do the vamans know why they cannot create a successful one?'

'No. They even tried to enter the ravian portal, but could not pass through. Mod said it was something to do with blood.'

Mantric nodded. 'An important part of portal-making involves blood magic. The mingling of the self with the universe to overcome space and time. We still don't have the theory under control. Even the hero mirrors were, I suspect, just a lucky combination of elements that happened to work.'

'Of course, Mod could be lying and the vamans could be marching into other worlds even as we speak,' said Temat. 'But more importantly, the ravians are here now, and possibly with new powers. They must have evolved in two hundred years, just as we have. Who knows what other worlds they have conquered, what other knowledge, what frightening powers they have gained? Imagine, Mantric, if a hundred ravians had attacked the palace that night? They could have taken it over easily. A swift, decisive blow to the very heart of the Koli empire.'

'The Koli empire? That's not something I've heard before.'

'It is not something I ever say in public. I lead an empire in disguise, Mantric. A very strong and stable empire, that rules the human world as no empire has before. The Koli empire is just two centuries old in its present form, but its roots go far back. It has learnt successfully from the mistakes of previous empires. Generations of Chief Civilians' toil just beginning to bear fruit with me at the helm . . . and suddenly the empire, in the hour of its triumph, faces the greatest threat in its history. It was inevitable that it should crumble one day, all empires do, and new ones build themselves from the bones of the old. But I did not think it would happen within my lifetime.'

'Pardon my poor knowledge of political terms,' said Mantric, 'but no matter how powerful Kol is, you cannot really call it an empire, can you? It's just one city. The marketplace of the world, perhaps, even the centre, but don't you have to have, you know, a big country to qualify as an empire?'

'We are not animals, Mantric, to need to mark our territory. We know it belongs to us, and that is enough. Consider this. We have united the world in language, customs, commerce. Of course Kol is an empire. Most people do not think it is, though, and therein lies the secret of its success. Yes, we do not physically govern other countries, we do not need to. Their wealth comes to Kol of its own volition. But we have the strongest human army in the world, and what no one knows yet is that we also have the largest. Distributed all over the world, marching under different colours. More than anything else, we have the vamans, their machines, their incredible craftsmanship.'

'I knew you were the most powerful human in the world,' said Mantric. 'But I never thought of you as an empress before. It is very well done, I must say. Perhaps I should be more deferential—after all, I am speaking to the leader of the world's greatest empire.'

'Second greatest. Kol is the greatest of the human empires, but the greatest empire in the world belongs to the vamans. They have the greatest armies, capable of appearing anywhere in the world with incredible speed, bearing deadly weapons they have not unsheathed in the open air yet. If they wanted, they could easily overrun the world, but they do not—they, like the Chief Civilians of Kol, have learned that expanding the empire beyond its natural borders leads to ungovernable size—that controlling rebellious human nations would be too much of a drain on its resources. This is why the Chief Civilians have always kept the imperial beast on a tight leash, conquering economically but not geographically, controlling but not oppressing, harvesting but not raping.'

'So Kol is merely a trading post of a vaman empire?'

'No, they are interdependent, but distinct. Kol is in the end an empire of the humans, its very essence is in the mingling of races, of distilling the best of what the human race has to offer and using the results to direct the course of human destiny. And Kol is where the empires intersect. Without Kol, the human kingdoms of the world would have allowed their natural distrust of the vamans to break loose into full-fledged war disastrous for both races.

'Have you ever wondered why the vamans do not allow

other creatures to even see their city? Yes, it is to protect vamans from an invasion—an invasion not of armies but of conflicting ideas, which would inevitably eat away at the heart of their empire. For the barbarians breaking down empires with fire and sword are merely symptoms—the real maladies occur from within, when the empire is exposed to different views of the world, different cultures. Diversity is choice, ungovernableness, rebellion, collapse . . .. So the vamans are brought up to see the sunworld, as they call it, with disdain—everything they need is with them under the earth. Thus they avoid the whole mess of different cultures tainting one another, spawning whole seething masses of conflicting interests and ideas. Thus they maintain their order, and their empire.'

'So Kol is open, and the vaman cities are closed. Interesting.'

'The vaman cities might not be closed at all. They are just closed to humans. Who knows how many different tribes or nations of vamans exist underneath the ground? The vaman kings have very cleverly allowed only one tribe of vamans to travel up to the surface to trade. They perform various functions—and one important function is to spread certain notions about vamans—that they are avaricious, petty, work-obsessed, conservative, and singers of silly songs—and thus put human concerns to rest. Fortunately, not all humans are that easily fooled. And we had reached a stage of balance, of equilibrium, with the vamans. We were growing together, not stepping on each others' toes more than necessary. It was a happy marriage.'

'But now the rakshases and the ravians threaten your order.'

'They threaten everything. The ravians especially. With

328

their coming, I fear not just for Kol, but for the whole human race.'

'Do you think there is a serious danger of the human race dying out?'

'My fear is not of death, but of irrelevance. We are too numerous to be casually destroyed, and too hardy to be utterly wiped out even by deliberate force. But I can too easily imagine a world in which the ravians control everything where a few ravians in positions of power guide the destinies of other races all over the world. Where we live out our lives like cattle in the hands of good farmers, where the order imposed on us is not of our own making. The ravian empire is based not on strength or power like the rest, Mantric—it is based on control, on order, and a disregard for physical comforts that we cannot even begin to understand.'

'You fear the order of the ravians more than the chaos of the rakshases?'

'The rakshases are great, powerful monsters but they can be overcome,' said Temat. 'I think of them as extremely strong humans. Yes, they can both topple and build kingdoms, but they really have no societies, no real civilization—their empires and their armies are borrowed, mere imitations and adaptations of humans. Rakshases could destroy the world, but they could never really rule it—they do not understand the concept of wealth, they hoard gold not because it is precious, but because they like the colour. Through the Ages, they have been vilified because of what they represent—the unknown, the dangerous, the forces of chaos. Just as asurs have been lumped into lists of monsters because ancient kings were afraid of them—of their strength, their ability to work, their sheer *numbers* . . . but times have changed. Threats have changed.'

'I know the ravians have attacked you, and the Dark Lord has not—yet,' said Mantric, 'but surely you realize that Kirin is a threat.'

'Dark Lords are never the real threats—they are usually convenient distractions, used to keep people afraid and compliant. Sometimes Dark Lords are even in league with the rulers of the kingdoms they threaten. The real threats are usually internal. The greatest threat for the Chief Civilians, for example, has historically been the army, whose Chief Commanders have often openly wanted to assume control over civil functions as well.'

'You think Askesis might be in league with the ravians?'

'It is a possibility. During the Age of Terror, the ravians had more or less taken over Kol's army. I do not think it has happened again yet, but it could.'

'And who else threatens you? This is fascinating.'

'*You* do.'

'Me?'

'Not you, of course, but spellbinders. When you said it was wise not to teach you statecraft, you were joking, but you were absolutely correct. Do you think we non-magical humans do not consider you a threat? It is largely because of the Civilians' efforts that mobs do not tear you limb from limb. But we have to protect you, and protect ourselves from you at the same time. We keep you innocent; we ensure that spellbinders see politics as an ignoble profession, politicians and administrators as little more than bores or swindlers. We ensure you are scornful of power and greed and material wealth, and make sure you are comfortable and have plenty of interesting things to study. Most dangerous, of course, are the army spellbinders. But they are trained to follow

330

orders, and watched very, very closely by their fellow warriors. Most importantly, they are Askesis's problem, not mine. But yes, the real threats are internal. And it is there that the ravians threaten us like no others can—they can destroy us from both within and without.'

'It is heart-warming to learn,' said Mantric, 'that there is so much understanding and trust among the people who control our lives.'

'On the contrary, lack of trust is a very good thing for the weak, because it keeps the powerful at each others' throats and out of each others' arms. Think of what the ravians and vamans could achieve if they trusted each other, and how quickly! If they united, in knowledge and in philosophy, if they examined their separate notions of order and found how much they had in common, they could form the perfect civilization, the perfect union of mind and matter. If they chose to, they could make humans as irrelevant in the greater scheme of things as the asurs are today. Together, they could rule every world there is.'

'Surely they realize this. What if they decide to take the risk? How can we stop them?' asked Mantric, listening as intently as a first-year spellbinder meeting Ombwiri for the first time.

'If Kol is to ensure that Asroye and Bhoomi never unite, Kol must first make true peace with Imokoi, and balance the vamans on one hand and the rakshases on another. Kirin is dangerous, but more dangerous to our enemies than to us. Kirin is the future, Mantric. We must unite the world against the ravians, and for that we need Kirin.'

'But are the vamans willing to have rakshases as allies?'

'Extremely willing, actually. You see, while rakshases

threaten us with force, and are even capable of changing their forms to resemble us, in some way, even if they entered positions of power by simply assassinating leaders and impersonating them, they would *become* the leaders they had replaced. They would enjoy the power their positions gave them, but they would carry on the functions of our empires in a manner we might have as well. They have no society, and power without structure and direction can never lead to order. They will adapt, not destroy. They will be tyrants, but they can never be *emperors*.'

'How did you find all this out?'

'The vamans' opinion of the rakshases? I asked them.'

'No. All this. What you told me before. About the vamans and their pact with the ravians. I know you have spies even among the vamans, but do you own someone close to the vaman king?'

'No. I only learn what the vaman king wants me to. Mod Vatpo has been allowed to divulge a few secrets.'

'I was quite convinced he was Gaam, you know.'

'Well, he is not Gaam. Gaam was nowhere near as good a negotiator.'

'I see. And how did you persuade him? What was the price for all this information?'

She smiled. 'I told them something for everything they told me. And they told me quite a few things.'

'So did you tell them the real name of the Silver Dagger?'

'I told them it was Rupaisa. But they suspected from the start that I was lying.'

'I see! So that is why you aren't letting poor Am—'

The Civilian held out a warning hand. 'Silence,' she hissed. 'Do not speak the name.'

She looked around.

'You never know who might be listening.'

Mantric look puzzled, then conspiratorial.

'So that is why you brought me here,' he said. 'So that you could give them a little lecture.'

It was Temat's turn to look puzzled.

'Them?'

Mantric leaned forward. 'Where are the shapeshifters?' he whispered.

'I have no idea what you are talking about.'

'Neither do I, I think.'

She put her hand on his. 'I should have spoken to you before,' she said. 'It always helps.'

'I don't know,' he said. 'What you said, about making sure magic-users don't find politics interesting—your methods work. All this was very important, I know. But I have to say at some level I find it extremely boring.'

She laughed aloud.

'The wonderful thing about magic is that it is so fascinating for people who can use it well that they tend to forget everything else. Poor Mantric. Perhaps it is time for you to get back to your studies, then,' she said.

'Yes, let us go.'

'You carry on, Mantric. I will be here for a while.'

He lit a small blue fireball and left without question.

She watched him go, a slight frown creasing her brows.

Then she felt about on the stone wall by her side for a while until she found the stone she was looking for. She pushed it, revealing a small lever, which she turned thrice.

A large square stone slab on the wall opposite slid back, revealing a small alcove, where Roshin stood, unsheathed sword in hand, her eyes never leaving the chair where a bound, blindfolded and gagged prisoner sat, powerful and menacing even in confinement.

Sitting at the prisoner's feet was a former Red Phoenix guard who now worked for the Silver Phalanx. The Phoenix had been reluctant to let him go, but the Dagger himself had insisted on this guard, and no other, in exchange for Roshin's transfer to the Red Phoenix.

The new Silver Phalanx member eyed the massive bulk of the Civilian's prisoner with a mixture of apprehension and excitement. You're a big mama, he thought, but I could take you. Oh yes, I could.

From any other Silver Phalanx member, given who the prisoner was, this would have been an idle threat.

But this Red Phoenix alumnus never made idle threats.

In fact, he never made threats at all, because small vegetables are very difficult to scare.

His name was Bunz.

Steel-Bunz.

'You heard everything I said?' the Civilian asked the prisoner.

He was silent. Steel-Bunz nipped him sharply on the heel.

'Yes,' replied the prisoner, his voice harsh and muffled through the gag.

'You will tell him everything you heard?'

'Yes.'

'Remove his blindfold,' the Civilian told Roshin.

Cold eyes stared at her. If the prisoner felt any resentment at being tied up, he did not show it.

'Give him the scroll,' the Civilian said.

Roshin extracted a scroll from the recesses of her costume and handed it to the prisoner.

'You will now return, and give this to him,' said the Civilian. 'Do not attempt to open it yourself. The paper will destroy itself after a few seconds. Keep it safe. And go in peace. Do we understand each other?'

'Perfectly,' said Spikes.

5

Manticore said,
In the distance I hear drums
Something dreadful this way comes.
'Yes,' said Myrdak in a bored voice. 'Rakshases, probably.
I suppose it was only to be expected that a large pillar of light
would attract a fair amount of attention. I don't hear drums,
though. Do you?'

Manticore shook his head guiltily, dislodging various
large insects snoozing in his shaggy mane.

'Did you say it just to rhyme?' asked Myrdak, smiling.

Manticore nodded guiltily.

'You are a constant source of joy, Manticore. Wake the
girl.'

Manticore cuffed Maya gently, so as not to break her
bones, and she awoke, groaning.

'Good morning,' said Myrdak brightly. 'Did you sleep well?'

Maya looked around her, blinking, still dizzy from
whatever drug they had fed her. She was lying bound and
gagged under a tree, on the edge of the Temple of the Black

Star. It was morning, but she had no idea whether Myrdak had spoken with the dragon the night before, or several nights before.

She shook her head, which felt as if it were made of solid lead, and the world fell into place.

Something was happening around her. The forest was listening, throbbing in anticipation. Powerful gusts of magic swept through the earth and the air. Large birds of prey were circling in the sky above the clearing. And the ground was shaking slightly.

In the distance, she could hear sounds of rustling leaves and branches cracking, and a strange rhythmic, pounding sound.

Myrdak stepped up and stood over her. 'Listen carefully,' he said. 'Rakshases are coming. These are wild rakshases of the forest and will kill you and eat you as soon as they see you. So I do not want any trouble from you while I fight them. Is that understood?'

Maya sat up with a jolt. She could sense it too—massive bodies moving through the forest. She thought of the rakshasi Akarat and shuddered.

'I would not be severely inconvenienced if you died, since I have already achieved what I wanted with you. But our time together has left me feeling considerable affection for you, so I would be pleased if you stayed alive for now. So try not to get killed, and do not get in my way.'

Maya nodded. Reasonable requests, she thought.

'We will probably need to run soon.' The creepers knotted around her ankles suddenly loosened and fell away. 'You will forgive me for not untying your hands, but I am sure you will understand that we are not yet close enough for me to place so much trust in you.'

Maya nodded, rubbing her ankles together. Myrdak pulled her up. The pounding sounds were closer now, huge feet stamping on the ground, huge bodies casting trees aside in their haste and anger.

There was a blood-curdling roar from the north, sending swarms of birds and jungle creatures fleeing from their trees, screeching and howling in fear.

Other rakshases roared in answer, from the south, west and east. They were surrounded.

'Manticore will watch over you and keep you from harm. However, if you should decide to escape his tender care, be warned—he will shoot you. The venom from his darts will kill you within minutes, unless the antidote is administered. Predictably, I am the only one here with the antidote. I hope I will not have to use it.'

More roars rent the air, drawing ever closer. Maya felt her skin crawl. She could see large shadows looming in the distance, drawing ever closer, massive predators on the hunt. Manticore screamed back, answering the challenge.

'Now, my dear, if you would excuse me,' said Myrdak with a smile, 'I have demons to kill.'

Maya leaned against a tree and flexed her legs, trying to get her blood flowing. Manticore leaped on top of a large stone slab, hissing and spitting, tail lashing about. He sniffed the air and shouted,

Demons, savour each last breath,
For you march forth to your death!

Myrdak unsheathed his sword and stepped into the clearing.

The rakshases stopped roaring suddenly. The crackling

sounds around the circle reached a crescendo as they charged towards the clearing.

Myrdak's eyes suddenly clouded over. He leaped to his right, jumped over a stone slab, and knelt down on one knee. He raised his sword in front of him into the air.

The forest was perfectly still for one everlasting second. It heaved a deep breath. Myrdak's sword shone in the sunshine.

A rakshas appeared in a puff of smoke. He was a magnificent animal, savage, wild-haired, blue-skinned and red-tongued. He roared a lusty challenge to the ravian kneeling in front of him.

And then he looked down, and saw the sword in the ravian's extended hand, the deadly blade buried in his stomach.

Maya gasped in awe as Myrdak pulled his sword out, sending blood streaming over stone.

Another rakshas appeared behind him. Manticore shot him in the back four times. The rakshas' skin curdled and rotted horribly where the darts pierced him, circles of decaying flesh expanding in deadly ripples across his hairy back. He writhed and bellowed in anger and pain, and only stopped when Myrdak stepped forward and cut off his head.

'So much for the advance guard,' said Myrdak, as the two huge rakshas bodies toppled to the ground.

Branches snapped, feet pounded. Maya looked around wildly and saw four giant rakshases charging towards the clearing, as tall as the trees, brushing aside huge branches and hanging creepers as if they were non-existent.

'Run,' said Myrdak. Maya turned and ran, and the ravian and the manticore followed her.

Behind them, the rakshases burst into the clearing and bellowed with rage.

'Don't look back,' hissed Myrdak, overtaking Maya. 'Manticore, lead her to the pit. I will join you soon.'

Even as he spoke, another vast shadow loomed up in front of them. Two pillar-like legs appeared, obstructing their path. They looked up, into huge, grinning fangs.

'Arrrrrr,' said the rakshas, by way of introduction.

He reached down towards Myrdak with a huge, gnarled paw. The ravian stepped aside gracefully, and slashed the rakshas' wrist. Manticore and Maya dashed between the giant legs, and the rakshas bellowed in agony as Manticore's darts found their mark.

'Keep going!' yelled Myrdak. Maya kept running, faster than she had ever run before, ever conscious of Manticore crashing along behind her, keeping up with her effortlessly, and occasionally growling and heading her in the right direction, like the ugliest, largest sheepdog in the world. Behind them, more crashing sounds, more roars of pain and anger, receding as they fled. At least five rakshases, thought Maya, struggling to hear the voice in her head above the pounding in her heart. Big ones, too. Five will be too much, even for him. Wish I could have killed him myself.

She started burning the ropes around her wrists as she ran, ignoring the pain.

Leaves rustled in the trees far above them, but neither of them noticed. They ran on, breathing in huge, strained gulps.

Maya slowed down and came to a complete standstill. She leaned against a tree, panting like a wounded animal. Manticore ran back to her and growled, impatient to keep moving.

'Goo you wike your pood ot?' she asked him through her gag.

'Foolish mortal . . .' began Manticore, intending to quell Maya with some witheringly witty couplet, but he could get no further, because Maya chose at this point to ram a huge fireball down his throat.

She'd expected instant Manticore Kabab; but all she got for her pains was a cough, a sizzle, and a really annoyed expression on a badly singed face.

Manticore's tail swung up, and pointed in her direction.

To discourage him from shooting her, she ripped off her gag, spat out an airball, and tossed it neatly into his mouth.

Manticore shut his mouth, his eyes widening in horror. He swallowed.

There was a muffled *boom*.

This was when Manticore's head should have exploded, but it stayed annoyingly intact. His eyes threatened to pop out, but decided at the last minute to stay attached to their sockets. Streams of smoke billowed from his ears.

He took a step back, stumbled, and fell to the ground heavily.

Die, thought Maya. Please please please die.

Manticore's eyes shut. And then he was still.

She heaved a sigh of relief.

Far away now, more crashes and roars in the direction of the clearing. The ravian was still alive, but seemed busy, she thought. She leaned against a tree, her head spinning wildly.

Manticore's right foreleg twitched.

No, thought Maya. You're dead. Stay dead. Please stay dead.

Manticore's eyes opened. He rose swiftly to his feet, staggering slightly. Maya watched him in disbelief. She was too tired to move.

'I'm going to *kill* you,' said Manticore, forgetting to rhyme in his rage. His tail arched in the air, pointing towards her.

There was a loud twanging sound. There was a loud whooshing sound.

And suddenly it was raining arrows.

Maya looked up. Black man-shapes were gliding through the trees, high above her, leaping elegantly along branches that should have been too weak to support their weight. Howls and screeches rent the air as archers swinging from great creepers fired at the ground.

The vanars had come to the party.

Scores of arrows sped into the earth. About sixteen arrows shuddered into Manticore. He screamed in pain, and fired darts in answer. More arrows pierced his hide, sticking out of his twisting body like huge porcupine quills. He ran, roaring, his tail sending more darts streaking randomly in the air in his wake.

Maya looked at the tree-trunk behind her, where a dart stood quivering about three inches from her head. Manticore's darts had not all missed, though. There were three crashes, the sound of snapping branches, and three bodies fell to the ground. They were baboon-men, brown and hairy, their noses long, red and blue. At this point, they were the most beautiful creatures Maya had ever seen.

There was a sound above her. She looked up.

Another vanar crouched on a branch near her head. He leaned down, clasped her hand and grinned.

''Ello,' he said.

Then, in an amazing display of strength, he tossed her one-handed onto a branch above him, into the arms of another vanar, who promptly caught her ankle and threw her further upwards. Within seconds, Maya was far above the ground, the world tilting and whirling crazily around her.

Yelling triumphant war-whoops, the baboon-men tossed Maya from tree to tree in an insane trapeze artist's flight, moving incredibly swiftly through the forest. They leaped in graceful, death-defying parabolas from creeper to creeper, swinging, flying, almost swimming through the trees. Maya shut her eyes, feeling strong arms clutch her ankles, her wrists, her waist, sending her hurtling in dizzying arcs, her blood pounding in a mad drumbeat between her ears.

And then, a human voice: 'Stop it, you fools! Let her go!'

The vanars cackled and jeered. She opened her eyes, to find herself in flight among towering trees.

The vanar holding her obediently let her go, and she watched, strangely relaxed, as the ground rushed up towards her.

And then strong arms caught her; strong human arms. A strange feeling of being suspended in mid-air, a lurch as another vanar swung by, caught her rescuer's hand and threw him on to another creeper. And then there were two more swinging creepers, a slide down a tree-trunk, and a sudden jolt as her rescuer landed cat-like on a huge branch, bearing the impact of the jump, holding her safe.

The world swam slowly into focus. She lay cradled in immense, muscular brown arms, safe and secure. She looked up, into gentle brown eyes, shining in a strong, handsome face. Pearly white teeth smiled down at her.

'My name is Djongli,' he said. 'And you are safe.'

'Glug,' said Maya, and fainted in a refined and ladylike manner.

6

E lsewhere . . .
    *'That'ss it. I can remain ssilent no longer. Ssomething
    iss amisss. I jusst know it.'*
    'Is it anything We can help You with, O lidless lord?'
    *'I ssusspect You are ressponssible for it, whatever it iss. Are
You cheating, Sstochasstoss?'*
    'No.'

A black-clad figure crept through a narrow passage in the
labyrinth under the Civilian's palace. This in itself was nothing
remarkable; there were usually people in the passages in the
labyrinth, they were usually clad, usually clad in black, and
usually creeping. And the passages were usually narrow. And
relatively speaking of course, in a world populated with flying
Xi'en monks, fire-breathing dragons and rabbit assassins, a
black-clad figure creeping through a narrow passage was about
as unusual as a potato.

In the North, they have a saying. The saying goes: Get

to the point, or I shall cleave your head in twain with my mighty battle-axe.

Anyway, so this black-clad figure was Thog the Barbarian, on his way to assassinate the Chief Civilian of Kol. He was creeping through a narrow passage in the labyrinth, slowly and very, *very* carefully. He had already negotiated, during his sojourn in the maze, some forty different deadly traps, ranging from swinging blades to poisonous gases. He had been forced to use violence twice; once to knock out the guard who patrolled the entrance by the riverside, and once to kill a small, violent beast of unknown origin that had attacked him inside the labyrinth and had possessed an unfairly large number of teeth.

In his left hand was a vaman-designed FloodLite, a tiny Alocactus in a partitioned glass box that dropped a tiny amount of water from an upper compartment on the glowing plant every few seconds, using an elaborate clockwork-and-hydraulic mechanism, the details of which need not be elaborated upon here in the interests of narrative flow.

In his right hand was a map of the labyrinth. Peori had given it to him, with a kiss and a smile, a few days ago. Where or how she had got it, she had not told him.

That was not all he carried, of course. Around his belt were a variety of weapons and tools, acquired in the course of the last few days, after he'd studied the map carefully and worked out a complicated plan to overcome all the complicated traps. So far, his judgement, his tools and his luck had not let him down.

This is wrong, thought Thog bitterly, yet again, as he made his way through the almost complete darkness, counting the number of steps he was taking to judge the distance of the next trap. I'm not an assassin. I shouldn't be a king. I wouldn't know what to do. But she seemed so certain. How can something be so wrong and so right at the same time?

He took a deep breath, and jumped forward. The ground did not open up and hurl him into a pit of spikes, which meant he had successfully negotiated another trap.

For the first time ever, he missed his Superb Hero costume. The scale of the crime he was about to commit made a violation of League Rule 2:3 seem irrelevant, but it just felt so wrong—not that looking exactly like his wooden action figure would have made killing the Civilian any easier. She'd never harmed him, or anyone close to him—how could he kill her like this, even if it was the right thing to do?

Well, doing the right thing was never easy. Though here, alone in the dark, that seemed like a really stupid argument.

He felt for a little button on the floor, and pushed it. There was a little click as the huge axes that would have swung out of the ceiling if he'd taken another step were restrained. He walked forward swiftly and was not cut into fine slices, which is always a good thing.

He thought of Peori. Would she ever know how much he loved her? Probably not. She was not the kind of person you could tell things like that to. She was above it all, somehow. Someone to be admired from a distance, revered, worshipped, not loved. Not like his ex-wife, who he'd loved so much it hurt, but she had been an equal, a friend. *Had been.* He'd thought that friendship would last forever. But that was not to be. His love for Peori, though . . . it would. Possibly because it would never be consummated, he would never come close enough to her to find out the flaws that even she must have.

Or would he? Something in her eyes when she'd said

goodbye . . . , as if she was really sorry to see him go, as if she was waiting for him to come back . . . some hidden, distant promise . . .

I am just imagining it, he thought. Anyway, now was not the time to think of such things. There was work to be done.

He looked at his map again, at the spidery lines running along a parchment that was so thin it was almost transparent. He was almost there, it told him. He folded it with infinite care. The map had been drawn recently, Peori had told him, and the ink was very delicate and smudged easily. And a smudge on this map would mean an untidy death for him.

Ten minutes of walking through twisting, intersecting corridors, and he was there. Pushing a stone slab in the wall made a little ladder rise out of the floor. Climbing it, he reached a trapdoor in the ceiling that led him to a little room, where the shadows of a table and two chairs wavered in the light of a single dying candle. She had been here recently.

He blew the candle out. He pulled a knob on his glass box and water stopped dripping on the Alocactus. He looked at the map one last time, at the section in one corner that told him the layout of the Civilian's room. It was all right, it had not changed since he had last memorized it. He set the map next to the glass box, beside the trapdoor. A few seconds later, the Alocactus dried up, leaving him in complete darkness.

He moved silently on padded boots towards the left-hand wall, and ran his hands gently along it until he found a little crack. He ran his finger along it, feeling something cold and metallic.

A panel slid back noiselessly, and he stepped into the Civilian's bedroom.

He stood completely still, breathing noiselessly, and listened. A single slow, steady breathing sound—one person was in the room, asleep, on the huge bed in the centre of the room. He drew a dagger from his belt, feeling terrible. This was not the time for hesitation, he thought. All kingdoms are built on blood and suffering. She is evil. She is a monster. Killing monsters is what I do. She might even be a rakshasi. Peori said so, and Peori would not lie. Not to me. He could feel guilt later, when he was king, when he was helping the ravians make things better, when guilt would be a small price to pay for the happiness the entire world would experience. He stepped forward, raising his dagger, and stopped.

Cold steel points on his neck. One to the left, one to the right.

'You're really bad at the quiet breathing,' said a husky female voice.

Creaking movements from the bed as someone sat up. Then a sudden flood of light; water on an Alocactus.

'Hello, Thog,' said the Really Pretty Sister. She was on his left, holding a sword to his throat, and the Violent and Brooding Sister was on his right. 'Traitor!' she snarled in greeting, pushing her sword into his neck, starting a slow trickle of blood.

The Sweet and Quirky Sister, Thog's favourite Sadori, was sitting on the bed, her lips pouting even more than usual. 'Why, Thog? I thought you were so nice,' she said, her big, innocent eyes brimming with reproach.

Thog's shoulders sagged in defeat and shame. He looked around him. His reflection looked scared and small in an ornate mirror; a fat lady in a portrait beside it smiled mockingly at him. A part of him felt relieved that he had failed; a part just felt sad because he was surely dead now.

And what a way to go! He'd always wanted to be alone in a
bedroom with the Sadori Sisters . . .

'Strip,' said the Really Pretty Sister.

Am I dreaming? Thog thought suddenly. Because this
would fit right in . . .

'Do it,' said the Violent and Brooding sister, drawing
more blood. No, this was no dream.

Thog stripped. After the Sadori Sisters had verified
(painstakingly) that he bore no weapons, the Sweet and
Quirky Sister opened the bedroom door and let in the Civilian
and Mantric. Ojanus the amphisbaena was curled around
the Civilian's shoulders.

'Arathognan, I presume?' asked the Civilian with a smile.
'Charming.'

As soon as he saw the Civilian, something happened to
Thog. His face froze into a mass of hatred, his muscles bulged,
his veins almost popped. With a loud, bestial cry, he lunged
forward, ignoring the bright lines of blood the Sadori Sisters'
swords drew on his skin.

Mantric and the Sweet and Quirky Sister moved fast,
seeking to step between Thog and the Civilian. But before
they got there, Ojanus lunged forward and landed on Thog.
He wrapped himself around Thog's legs at lightning speed,
sending him thudding to earth. Before Thog could even
begin to rise or fight, one of Ojanus's heads lashed upward
and struck at his throat. The other head followed its twin
up Thog's chest, hissed loudly and buried its fangs in Thog's
lips in a deadly kiss.

As the rest watched, stunned, Thog's body jerked and
twitched helplessly on the floor. The skin around his mouth
and throat turned blue. And then he was still, and Ojanus
slid off him and back to the Civilian.

'Is he dead?' asked Mantric.

'I do not know,' she said, patting one of the amphisbaena's heads. 'We will find out soon enough.'

'Could someone put some clothes on him, in either case?' asked Mantric.

The Civilian nodded, and the Sweet and Quirky Sister threw a sheet over Thog with a slightly regretful expression.

A few minutes later, the blue colour on Thog's face and neck faded and then disappeared entirely, leaving him looking somehow older, thinner, and very, very tired. The wounds left by snake-tooth and sword dried up as well, though livid scars remained.

Thog's eyes opened and shut again immediately. His face contorted with pain.

'Give him some time,' said Mantric. 'Let him remember.'

They waited until the lines on Thog's face faded away, and he opened his eyes again, sat up, and drew the sheet defensively around his body. He looked around, his face calm and set.

'I know this sounds ridiculous,' he said, 'but I would like to apologize for this intrusion. I was not in my right mind. I say this not to beg for mercy, for I know you will not believe me, but because I feel it needs to be said.'

'Greetings, Arathognan,' said the Civilian. 'Do you still want to assassinate me?'

Thog shook his head.

'Good,' said the Civilian, 'because in that case there is a slim chance that I will let you live. If you answer all my questions truthfully. And tell me all about your friend, the ravian.'

'I will answer your questions to the best of my ability.

350

But I cannot betray her.' The pain etched on his face did not look physical in origin.

'Not even if your silence leads to your death?'

'I am already dead,' he said. 'I tried to kill you. You cannot let me live.'

'I wish things were so simple,' said the Civilian. She turned to the Really Pretty Sister. 'Hand me that amulet,' she said.

The Really Pretty Sister tossed her Thog's amulet. She studied it for a while, then handed it to Mantric. 'Genuine,' he said.

'I am not the heir to the throne, if that is what you are worried about,' said Thog. 'I have been betrayed. My memories have been altered. I can see things now, and they look very different. The ravian you speak of gave me that amulet and made me believe I was the rightful king. She made me believe a lot of things.'

'Where is she now?'

Thog was silent.

'She used you, but you will not help us against her?'

'No. She fooled me, but no matter what my memory tells me, I know that some part of me *chose* to follow her. She was influencing my mind, but I do not think she was controlling it. And she was only doing her duty. I have made a great mistake, and must be punished for it,' said Thog resolutely.

'Perhaps it would help all of us,' said Temat gently, 'if you calmed down and talked to us. We are in a difficult situation now, but despite what you have been told, we are not evil incarnate. We are all in great danger, Arathognan. All humans are. You have been through great peril, and have shown great fortitude, which is why you are still alive.

I have been trying to reach you for many days, not to kill you, but to protect you.'

'She told me that I was a descendant of the kings of Kol,' said Thog. 'That I looked like the old king.'

'You do,' said Temat.

'She said that blood would tell, and that my work as a hero proved that I was of royal blood.'

'If all kings were heroes . . .' Temat smiled. 'What else?'

'She said the amulet I bore was an heirloom that proved beyond all doubt that I was the true king. But I remember now that this amulet is not mine. She gave it to me herself, and clouded my memories. How?'

'She is a ravian,' said Temat. 'They have subtle powers beyond our understanding, and seem to be desperate to destroy the current order of things. She has also successfully led the people of Kol to believe that you are their true king, and that the restoration of your throne and your line is the only way to save Kol. Which makes you very dangerous to me.'

'She told me I had to kill you because of the third Simoqin Prophecy.'

'There was a third Simoqin Prophecy?'

'She said so.'

'She lied. What was this third Simoqin Prophecy?'

'That it was the destiny of the true king to strike down the evil powers that ruled Kol.'

'Convenient, that,' said Mantric.

'To be quite frank,' said the Civilian, 'I do not know what to do with you, Thog the Barbarian. Logic dictates I kill you at once. Yet you have displayed both courage and honesty, which are rare traits and should not be thrown away. You have told me of your own volition that the amulet you bear is not yours, and that you are not the true king, which was either very noble or very stupid of you. And most importantly, you could be a very useful weapon in my hands.'

'I have threatened your life, and the safety of this city,' said Thog.

'You never seriously threatened my life. The labyrinth is watched closely and we knew you were coming long ago. You were carrying a map, though, and that is a matter worthy of investigation. What should we do with him, Mantric?'

'We should ask him where the ravian is.'

'I cannot tell you,' said Thog. 'I . . . I love her. Despite what she did to me.'

'I am afraid you will have to tell us, one way or another.' The Civilian looked at the Sadori Sisters. 'Take him downstairs and be persuasive,' she said. 'If he does not tell you where we may find his friend the ravian, kill him.' They led him away.

'Why did she send him?' the Civilian asked Mantric. 'He was such a powerful weapon. Why did she send *him* to kill me? She could have sent anyone with the map. She must have known we would observe the labyrinth. She cannot have known how closely it is under observation since the plans were given away to the vamans, but she must have known it would be well guarded. Why would she throw him away like this?'

'From the start, they have taken you lightly,' said Mantric. 'The painter, the attack on the palace—I mean, only two of them and they expected to get to you? And now this. Perhaps they really do not see humans as a threat at all. This is just a chore to be completed, not a challenge. They could have killed you several times, if they had just tried a little harder. But they have just not tried hard enough.'

'Why go through all this effort to make the people believe in him, then?'

'Perhaps she will now produce another amulet, another king. After all, if you can control minds and are immortal, there are always more chances, more opportunities to learn from your mistakes, to improve.'

'Yet she has not learnt that much.'

'Immortals are notoriously slow learners. Look at rakshases. There is just . . . less pressure.'

'And now we have this Arathognan on our hands.'

'I am, as you know, a novice at all this,' said Mantric. 'But I cannot see why you are considering leaving him alive, now that you have him in your power. He seems nice, but you can never trust him.'

'On the contrary, this sort of thing often leads to lifelong loyalty,' said the Civilian. 'But that is not why I am considering leaving him alive. There are certain other services he might be able to render.'

She laughed aloud at Mantric's expression.

'No, no, not what you are thinking now,' she said. 'Though he is not unattractive, in his own way. But if you look ahead a little, Mantric . . . the people need to be united when the war comes. It is my duty to give them what they need. And they seem to need a king.'

'But he is not the true king,' said Mantric, perplexed.

'What is a true king? Bloodlines are irrelevant, Mantric. What is relevant is that the people need someone to believe in. They do not seem to be able to believe in me. And I would be pleased if they did not believe too deeply in Askesis and his army.'

'You would give them a false king? You would surrender power?'

'Who said anything about surrendering power?'

'But . . . you have already given them a hero to believe in.'

'My hero is occupied presently in running around somewhere in the wild with a shapeshifter in pursuit of a ravian much more powerful than him. Chances are he will not survive. And even if he does, he is not as relevant as we thought he would be. He was a champion prepared to defend us against an enemy who did not even rise. And when we make peace with Imokoi we will not need Asvin at all. Threats have changed, as I told you in the labyrinth.'

'That is most unfair.'

'Unfair? After all these years, you expect me to be *fair*?'

'Yes, I do. I am your friend and adviser, and I know you better than most. And I did not expect you, of all people, to lose faith in a human hero so soon. If he is irrelevant, so is your empire, is it not? And my heart tells me Asvin will return triumphant. He will be a great hero in the war, even against the ravians.'

'Yes, a use will be found for him. After all, we invested a great deal in him. There are always monsters to kill, and Avranti might need a new king if Aloke continues to be difficult. But you trained Asvin better than you should have. He has displayed a completely unforeseen capacity for independent action and independent thought.'

'And so you tire of him, and would get yourself a new toy.'

'I have not decided yet. I do not know, Mantric. We will keep this Thog here, and see what he is like. We will interrogate him for many days, fill his heart with an overwhelming sense of his own lowliness and of my nobility in giving him a chance to redeem himself. He looks remarkably easy to lead. We might be able to turn the ravian's work against the ravians.'

'But you told your guards to kill him if he did not betray the ravian. And he will not.'

The Civilian smiled.

'I don't care how . . . persuasive they are,' snapped Mantric, irritated. 'He is a hero in his own way, I know it. And he is not that easy to lead. You can torture him as long as you like. He will tell them nothing.'

Thog told the Sadori Sisters everything.

Somewhere in the labyrinth, six members of the Rainbow Council materialized in a small chamber.

'It is time to vote,' said Green.

'It must be done now. We have waited too long,' said Indigo. 'We lost Red through inaction. This Peori is a threat that must be dealt with decisively.'

'I think we should wait,' said Yellow. 'Let her attack again.'

'But the Silver Phalanx is assembling even as we speak,' said Indigo. 'For the first time, we know where she is. If we do not attack first, and the Phalanx do not succeed, she disappears, and we are completely in the dark again.'

'I agree with Indigo,' said Violet. 'We know where she is. We know she is a threat to the stability of Kol. We should strike now.'

'Orange? Blue?'

'I say strike now,' said Orange.

'So do I,' said Blue.

Green sighed. 'We must be completely united before we can venture forth to do battle,' he said. 'Yellow, can we persuade you to change your mind? The Silver Phalanx will be at her door soon.'

'What about you, Green?' asked Yellow. 'Do you think I am too cautious?'

'I think she is still working alone,' said Green. 'And she does not know yet that Arathognan has been captured. She will be waiting for him. It might be our best chance.'

'How do we know she will be at the house?'

'Thog said she is there nearly all the time. She is in hiding after all—she ventures out very rarely. She is very likely to be there.'

'Very well, then,' said Yellow. 'I am the oldest among you, and naturally inclined towards caution. But too much time spent studying the Plan does make me inclined towards inaction, I admit it freely. And yes, since young Red disappeared, I have felt more doubt than ever before. I am with you. Let us go. She is a real threat, and we certainly cannot leave it to the humans.'

'Excellent. It is done, then,' said Green. 'We will capture this ravian Peori, and kill her if we fail to take her alive. Four of us will venture forth. Yellow and Orange, remain here.'

'I wish to come with you,' said Yellow. 'There is something in the air tonight. I feel an urge for adventure, for action, that I have not felt for many centuries.'

Green smiled and bowed. 'We will be honoured to have you, Yellow. Violet, you will remain with Orange in that case.

'The Silver Phalanx plans to strike in conjunction with the army's sorcerers, to prevent the ravian from taking over their minds. Their strike has been authorized; they will proceed at full speed towards south Kol, spread out, and approach 32B, Cravenstick Street from every direction of the compass. The attack will be swift, and, they hope, deadly. They should be fully ready to strike in no more than half an hour.'

'Half an hour,' smiled Blue. 'We should be back here by then.'

'Precisely. Battle colours, please.'

A second later, Orange and Violet stood in the chamber with a blue-tattooed barbarian warrior, a blond Skuan giant, a four-armed Avrantic demigod with deep blue skin and a peacock feather in his long hair and a moss-covered horned satyr.

'Good luck,' said Violet, her eyes sparkling with excitement.

A second later, Orange and Violet stood in the chamber with four rapidly dissolving puffs of smoke.

32B, Cravenstick Street, was a large, single-storeyed Ventelot-style villa, complete with a pretty gate and a little garden. The front door was locked from the outside, and the windows were shut. Cravenstick Street was a prosperous south Kol residential area, and its respectable residents slept peacefully, as all right-thinking people did at that hour of night. The only sound to be heard was the soft lullaby of the flowing river, and the rhythmic chirping of night insects.

Far above the street, an owl flew in circles, scanning the street for movement, trying to pick out figures lurking in shadows. After a while, satisfied that Peori was not anywhere nearby, Blue hooted softly. He continued to glide above the house, watching all the exits carefully.

The back door of the villa opened to a small winding alley, empty except for Indigo, a moth sitting on a neighbour's wall. Green sat outside the front gate, a black cat licking his paws. Three shapeshifters in the area, the ravian's senses would have woken her up. It was time to attack.

Yellow jumped lightly across the garden, a tabby cat, small and graceful. He leaped towards a window. It broke with a sharp crack, and he was in. Indigo fluttered to the back door, kicked it down with a tiny foot, and flew in.

The owl circled in the sky, watching closely. No movement in the street. Inside, Yellow and Indigo lit fireballs and ran through the house. From the garden, Green watched the shadows of the Skuan giant and the Avrantic demigod through the window.

Then Indigo stuck his head out of the window. 'Empty,' he said.

The owl hooted softly above them.

Immediately, the lights inside the house went out; Yellow created an illusion of an unbroken window. The black cat padded softly out to the street, its claws clattering strangely.

'Sorry,' called Blue softly, swooping down near him. 'Random drunk. False alarm.' He flew back up.

They were too late. The ravian had gone. There was no point in waiting; the Phalanx would be there soon, and even if the ravian came anywhere near, she would sense the immensely powerful shapeshifters lying in wait before they could do anything about t.

Green turned into an owl and joined Blue in the sky. 'We will wait here till the Phalanx comes,' he said. 'Though I fear we waited too lo g. She has gone.'

'Do you think she might be attacking the palace right now?' asked Blue.

'We will find out soon enough,' said Green. 'But I do not think she would dare. Not tonight.'

✠

'It surprises me that the ravians have been so careless,' said Violet, as she paced the Civilian's labyrinth with Orange. 'They could have killed the Civilian many times over by now. In everything else, they have been so meticulous. Yet now, they seem to have given up the advantage of surprise. They have left themselves open to attack. Most strange.'

'I fear we will never understand them,' said Orange. 'Perhaps beings from two different worlds can never really understand each other, no matter how intelligent they are. I know what you mean, of course. In everything else, all their actions have been planned centuries in advance. And they know that humans have powerful friends in the palace. What would it matter if they actually brought a king to power? We would still be there, protecting Kol. These feeble plots against human rulers will get them nowhere, but thankfully they do not see it.'

Violet nodded, brows creased in thought. 'A lesson in humility,' she said. 'How blind the wise can be. What is it?'

For Orange had stopped short, a horror-stricken expression on his face.

'Who is guarding the Civilian right now?' he asked.

'Half the Red Phoenix,' said Violet. 'She said there was a chance the ravian might attack now.'

'Good,' said Orange, and then stopped again.

'What is it?' asked Violet.

'I have just had a rather disturbing thought,' said Orange.

Inside Peori's house, Yellow and Indigo made sure illusions covered the broken door and window, and then lit up more fireballs and searched the house quickly. They found nothing of interest in any room except one, the main bedroom.

The main bedroom was a large, cold room, with a comfortable-looking four-poster bed adjacent to one wall, and a large, polished rosewood desk opposite, near the window that Yellow had broken through. There was a large mirror on another wall, and teak bookshelves across it, but it was the objects on the desk that held the attention of the shapeshifters—strange instruments that looked like they were made by vamans. Little measuring sticks, metal cylinders, a gold-plated clock, strange boxes with levers and dials. Yellow examined these carefully, while Indigo walked to the bookcase and started leafing through a sheaf of large maps, maps of Kol, of Ektara and Amurabad.

The largest object on the rosewood table was a cloth-covered sphere, about the size of a human head. Yellow removed the black cloth, and gasped in wonder.

It was a black sphere, which contained what looked like trapped lightning. Little flashes of light zigzagged inside it, bouncing on the inner surface of the sphere, creating rings of light that spread quickly and then fizzled out.

Yellow gazed at it in curiosity.

'Indigo?' he said. 'What is this?'

Indigo walked up and looked at the black sphere.

'I do not know,' he said. 'Leave it there. It looks magical.'

Two shapeshifters walked through the labyrinth.

'Peori could have killed the Civilian at the painter's house,' said Orange. 'She did not. Why?'

'Because she was busy somewhere else, and had altered the painter's mind. He would do the dirty work for her. Most ravian-inspired assassinations work that way,' said Violet.

'But what if . . . what if she did not mean to kill the Civilian at all?'

'What do you mean?'

'What if . . .' Orange blinked, trying to collect his thoughts. 'There is something missing here, just out of my reach. Wait. What would have happened if Thog had killed the Civilian?'

'He would have claimed to be the king returned. We would have taken charge, and ensured that the best solution for Kol was achieved.'

'What would the ravians have gained?'

'Nothing much. They would have lessened the vamans' hold over Kol.'

'True. But the Civilian is just one person. She is not the whole system. The vamans and Kol are inextricably linked. Killing her would not remove them. In some ways, in the chaos that followed, they would grow even stronger, as would the army. But there is a deeper question. What protects Kol?'

'The Civilian?'

'What protects the Civilian?'

'We do.'

'What if all this . . . what if all this was a plot to kill *us*?'

'I don't understand.'

'Listen to me. As long as we are here, the ravians know they cannot control the mind of any human in the palace. If *we* were to be removed, they could control even the Civilian. We know they are in favour of a monarchy, but is it really that important to them to see a king in Kol? After all, to them, Kol would just be another province in their empire, another state ruled by a puppet, a human toy. Thog, the Civilian, does it really matter? They are not the *real* problem. What prevents the ravians from seizing power in Kol?'

Violet's mouth fell open. '*We* do,' she said.

'The ravians know this. The ravians are *not* careless. The ravians have always considered the details in everything else. Why should they act otherwise here? What if everything Peori has done so far has been an elaborate ruse, a screen of smoke to confuse *us*, to draw *us* out? To make us reveal ourselves, strike in haste, and thus make us vulnerable?'

They stared at each other in silence.

'Oh *no*,' said Violet.

They vanished.

Unable to resist, fascinated by the sparkling, dancing figures of light, Yellow picked up the black sphere. 'I wonder what this is,' he said.

This was a Ravian Star. A sphere of incredible compressed energy, a terrible weapon invented by Kirin's mother Isara during the Great War, used by her to destroy Danh-Gem's Tower, subsequently modified and perfected by the ravians over the next two centuries.

As the shapeshifter's magic flowed from his skin to the Ravian Star, it exploded.

A great white ball of light burst out, as bright, glorious and deadly as the sun. For a mile around Peori's house, that very instant, every building vanished, every man, woman and child withered away like paper scraps in the sudden dazzling flame.

Far away, watching from a hilltop, Peori smiled sweetly to herself as the dome of light spread out and vanished, and the colours of the Rainbow Council shapeshifters melted away into all-conquering, brilliant, flawless white.

7

A large cart drawn by a fat old horse creaked its way through a spectacular Shantavan sunset.

In the cart were several vessels, some made of steel and some of clay. A few of these had been opened; they contained food. Food that was at this moment being consumed by the sole occupant of the cart. A tall young lady. She was evidently of a conservative disposition, because her sari covered every possible part of her body, including her head. Apart from being demure, she was either nervous or clumsy; the pallu of her sari sometimes slipped, displaying fashionably short hair and surprisingly muscular bare arms. Occasionally some strange shiny substance could also be seen through the folds of her sari. The fashion among rural belles was to go sans blouse—this young damsel, though, seemed to be wearing a sleeveless blouse of shining silver.

Asvin chewed a contemplative roti. There was lots of food, and he had been eating almost continuously for two days now, while the cart trundled further and further south, away from Maya, deeper and deeper into the Peaceful Forest.

Asvin's faith in his decision was unshaken, though. He knew he was doing the right thing, that the gods would provide, that things would, in some strange, inexplicable way, turn out all right.

His left eye twitched. His left hand curled around his sword-hilt. In the ancient days, a twitching left eye would have been considered an auspicious sign on the eve of battle. King Anirodh the Heirless, one of the first and most successful kings of Avranti, had won many of his battles aided by the confidence engendered among his troops by the twitching of his eyes.

Asvin had read in Kol that old Anirodh had just had a nervous tic, but had any of these learned sceptics checked whether his eye had twitched during his last, fatal battle? They had not. Those Kolis took a ghoulish delight in puncturing myths, thought Asvin defiantly. It was all a conspiracy. They just couldn't stand it when legends came to life, when prophecies came true, when honour and nobility triumphed over mathematics and adverse circumstances. For example, there had been an old king in Ventelot whose name Asvin had forgotten, who had disappeared many centuries ago, leaving behind a beautiful legend that said he had not died but had merely gone into temporary retirement with his finest knights on an exotic island with a few attractive ladies, and that he would return and ride to battle with these knights when Ventelot was in peril. And that legend had actually come true, thought Asvin. But did those Kolis accept that gracefully? No. They just made a big song and dance about how the king and his knights had come riding in to battle, met a notorious pack of aristocratic werewolves called the People Lycus, discovered their weapons were centuries out of date and had gone riding right back. Those were minor details, not relevant at all, thought Asvin, defiantly chomping a laddoo. The point was they had *risen*.

The food was very bad. But then, he decided, he couldn't complain—after all, the villagers had prepared it not for a prince, but for a rakshas. It was hardly reasonable to expect them to put a great deal of love into their cooking. And there was lots of food—quantity rather than quality had evidently been the guiding principle. And if I eat enough of these sweets, thought Asvin, I will no doubt develop a fondness for them in time.

Under the cart, Red was getting restless. The sound of Asvin chomping away above her wasn't helping either— she was desperately hungry. But there were other things she felt, stronger and deeper than hunger, that were foremost in her churning mind.

The aura of the rakshas Akab was incredibly strong. His musky male scent was everywhere, and was literally driving her wild. Not with desire, though desire was a part of it, but with jealousy; she envied the unseen rakshas his freedom, his strength and savagery, envied the uncontrolled power that he radiated throughout the forest, the scent of which marked out his territory as strongly as any tiger with its leg raised beside a tree. And almost as strong as the rakshas's aura was the wild magic gurgling through the forest and her skin, sending currents of pain and pleasure shooting through her body.

To numb these exquisite, dangerous sensations, Red had turned herself into a slug, stuck to the bottom of the cart. There was another advantage to this as well—the rakshas, wherever he was (and she sensed he was not far away) would not see another human tracking the cart's progress, and therefore would attack Asvin instead of heading away to the village and wasting everyone's time. And she knew he could be anywhere, in any disguise, watching. Another good thing about being a slug was that processing any thought took a very long time—she could watch her own thoughts oozing around in her slimy brain. Very entertaining.

The cart moved on, creaking with age and the weight of its load. Asvin stuffed yet another laddoo into his mouth and looked around for more water. He found another jug with liquid sloshing around in it and opened it; it was cheap wine. A little couldn't hurt, he thought. He poured some into an earthen mug and drank it in a single gulp.

He refilled his mug, and was about to drink its contents but then thought better of it because he didn't want to face the rakshas drunk. He held the full mug in one hand and his sword in the other, and leaned back on the side of the cart, admiring the shadows around him as they lengthened and mingled, chasing one another through the trees.

He suddenly noticed a vulture circling high above him. Close, he thought. Scavengers assemble, awaiting battle. He gripped the sword tighter, scanning the trees around him, watching for any sign of a giant shape lurking in the shadows. He remembered Mantric telling him, a long time ago, not to attack a rakshas head on, but things had been different then. He had been more confident, less experienced. Most importantly, he had not had his impenetrable armour.

The horse suddenly stopped and neighed nervously. It stood there, shivering. Asvin wanted to reach forward, pat it reassuringly, but did not. It would reveal his brawny arms, warn the rakshas, intimidate it no doubt, but remove the advantage of surprise. I will wait for the rakshas to pick me up, he thought, and then I will stab its eyes out.

'You's a big one,' came a harsh croak above him. Asvin tensed and seized his sword, looking up, but it was just a vulture sitting on a branch above him, an extremely disreputable-looking heap of feathers with a large, ugly head.

'You can talk,' said Asvin in wonder.

'Never seen a talking bird before, has we?' croaked the vulture. It shuffled sideways, fixing Asvin with a beady eye.

'I've seen several,' said Asvin stiffly.

'Deep voice,' said the vulture. 'Good height, broad shoulders, fair amount of meat. Mostly lean muscle, very little fat. Good.'

'Be quiet,' said Asvin.

'Oooh!' said the vulture, aggrieved. 'Don't you shush me, girl! If I was you, I'd be grateful for a little conversation in my last hours. But you has your way, it's your funeral.'

'I'm sorry,' said Asvin, realizing that this ugly creature might be a gift from the gods and might reveal some vital detail about Akab that he could use to his advantage. How could he subtly find out everything about the rakshas?

'Is all right,' said the vulture, easily mollified. 'You don't has to apologize and all. We's all friends here, in the jungle. No formality. So, how much would you say you weigh?'

'What's your name?' asked Asvin, setting his glass down on the cart.

'Spleen,' said the vulture promptly. 'Spleen XIV. On a bad day, Intestines II.'

'Tell me about the rakshas Akab,' said Asvin, deciding to use the direct approach.

'Eager, isn't we?' said Spleen XIV with horrible coyness. 'Wait awhile, girl. You'll soon find out all about him. The innermost details, as it was.' He chuckled horribly.

There was a loud, muffled thump in the distance. A flock of birds flew screeching in the air somewhere.

'Is that him?' asked Asvin. 'Is he near?'

'In these parts,' said Spleen XIV, 'Akab is *always* near.' He seemed nervous, uncomfortable; he shuffled across his branch, looking this way and that.

The forest has suddenly fallen silent, thought Asvin. A predator was probably nearby. Everything around him was tense, waiting, absolutely still.

He suddenly noticed that the wine in the glass he'd put down was shaking, ripples flowing fast on the surface in the last light of the sun. Ripples, he realized in sudden terror, that came once every few seconds, following a huge *thump*, somewhere in the distance. It was as if he could hear the heartbeat of the whole forest.

Or the sound of giant feet drawing closer.

He moved his right hand across and gripped his sword. He covered it with his sari.

'Hey,' said Spleen XIV, surprised. 'You's a man!'

'Shush,' said Asvin. 'Don't give me away. Is that thumping sound Akab?'

The vulture shrugged. 'Could be. Lots of noises in the forest. So you is a virgin?'

'Be quiet,' said Asvin.

The vulture cackled. 'Is you alone?' he asked. 'Is you brought lots of villagers? What does they weigh?'

'Be quiet!' said Asvin.

The vulture cackled. 'You is alone! You is a hero!' he said. 'Sweet!'

The thumping sound grew closer, and then suddenly stopped. The wine in Asvin's glass was ominously still.

There was a loud, wet sound, like a giant nose sniffing.

'Good luck, mate,' said Spleen XIV.

And then the wine shook again and giant footsteps were audible. Asvin took a deep breath and looked around.

Odd. The footsteps were actually fading away, very rapidly.

And then there was silence again.

'What was that?' said Asvin, leaning in the direction of the sound, trying to see in the gathering darkness.

'Rakshas.'

'Why did he go away?'

'Because,' said Spleen XIV, spreading his wings, 'he smelt *me*.'

His wings stretched out endlessly and melted, his body grew downwards. Darkness seemed to flow out from his shape as it grew and changed.

A second later, the largest rakshas Asvin had ever seen stood before him. He was the size of a small hill. His roar echoed through Shantavan, and his giant blue arms sped downwards with the speed of the wind.

One hand flicked Asvin's sword away casually. The other caught one end of his sari and tugged, hard. The sari came off, sending Asvin spinning.

And then Akab picked Asvin up in one hand and stuffed his torso into his mouth.

Asvin struggled and kicked wildly, but the rakshas was too strong. Asvin was stuck horizontally inside his mouth, all the way up to his chest. He saw the giant scabby red tongue in front of him, felt the stench of centuries of dead flesh rise up from the rakshas' throat and hit him. He saw the giant jaw muscles beginning to contract, preparing to bite down hard, cut him in two.

Pushing with all his strength, Asvin managed to free his arms. He threw them forward, up above his head, as the giant fangs closed in. Just in time; his arms were safely out of the way as Akab champed down on Asvin's stomach, sending exquisite pain flooding through his body.

But the armour held. Akab bit down again, but could not penetrate the silver sheath.

Under the shaking cart, the slug slowly realized an attack was taking place, and dropped off the cart bottom onto the ground. She began her transformation, cursing; it would take time, too much time. Being a slug made everything . . . well, sluggish.

Akab pulled Asvin out of his mouth, puzzled. He brought the little hero close to his face, examining the strangely resilient human with fiery, curious eyes. He swung Asvin this way and that, examining his armour carefully, and wondered how to swallow him whole. And then he let out a full-throated roar.

Red regained control, transformed into Rukmini and ran in, fire flowing from her fingers.

But the rakshas didn't even notice her. He was looking, with a horrified expression, at Asvin's hand.

'No!' he roared.

No? thought Red. Had the gods saved Asvin again, incredibly, somehow? In that case, her presence, if noticed, would only complicate things.

A little woodpecker flew fast towards a nearby tree in a turquoise blur.

371

'Why didn't you tell me about this?' roared Akab, shaking Asvin in his hand. He brought up his other hand and pointed with a huge, quivering finger.

Asvin's eyes, blank and terrified, settled slowly on an intricately carved ivory ring on his own hand.

'Do you know whose ring this is?' roared Akab, his face contorted in anger and setting new standards of ugliness every second.

'Of . . . of course I know whose ring this is,' stammered Asvin bravely. Nor was he lying. He *did* know. He'd seen that ring before, and had no doubt gone through some extremely perilous mission to get it. But memories of stirring adventures were inlaid on every trinket he had ever worn. It was just that there were so many of them—memories *and* trinkets—that it was difficult remembering which one was which. He'd thought he'd left them all behind in Kol the night he'd left, leaving him naked and unprotected magically. But no, here was the ring on his finger. He did not remember using it at all.

'Well?' roared Akab, deafening every living beast in a small radius (except Asvin and Red). 'What is it?'

And then, in another flash of divine inspiration, Asvin remembered.

'This is the Ring of Akarat,' he said. And a very pretty ring it was too.

The thing was, he had no idea what it did. Hopefully the rakshas knew. He seemed quite agitated.

'YOU'RE BLOODY RIGHT IT'S THE RING OF AKARAT!!!!' yelled Akab, deafening even the trees, thereby ending all debates on whether they could hear. 'COULDN'T YOU HAVE MENTIONED IT, YOU FOOL????'

Asvin waited for the echoes to die away. 'Sorry,' he said.

'Very stupid of me.' Was it an insect repellent? No. A digestive aid? No. What *was* it?

And then he remembered. The gods were truly on his side. 'No rakshas can harm me when I wear this,' he said gleefully. 'Your honour compels you to set me down.'

Akab shook his head in disgust and set Asvin down on the ground.

'You did this deliberately, didn't you?' he said. 'Just to put me in your power!'

'Yes,' said Asvin, looking as cunning as he could. 'You are in my power now.'

Akab growled in anger, felled a huge tree with a single punch and shrank to human size before it crashed to earth, sending an extremely surprised woodpecker fluttering into the air.

'Many rakshases would have ignored this ring, and killed you,' he said. 'But I cannot, for Akarat is my mother. I do not know how you got her ring, mortal—whether you stole it from the great hero she gave it to in his sleep, or slew him by treachery. But I will honour his memory, and my mother's power, by granting you one wish.'

'But your mother gave the ring to me!' said Asvin. 'I am the hero!'

Akab's face softened. 'What is your name?'

'Asvin!'

'Well, why didn't you say so? I almost killed you!'

Asvin shuffled his feet in embarrassment. 'I forgot.'

'You *forgot?* Akab's laughter rent the air, causing several other Shantavan rakshases to start composing angry letters in their heads about the rapidly declining neighbourhood. 'You forgot! That's rich!'

Asvin grinned shamefacedly. 'You must think I'm really stupid.'

Akab chortled and nudged him playfully in the ribs. 'Bet it works wonders with the ladies, doesn't it?'

Asvin grinned and shrugged, sending his new friend into peals of demonic laughter.

'Well then, Asvin,' said Akab as soon as his shoulders stopped shaking, 'I suppose you've officially saved the village now, and I can't go back to my little food arrangement?'

'That would be nice,' said Asvin. 'They were really upset, you know.'

'All right, all right,' said Akab. 'I was getting lazy anyway.'

'Thank you very much. And how is your dear mother?' asked Asvin, with all the old-world courtesy he could muster. His legs were still shaking.

'Akarat is fine, fine,' said Akab. His brow clouded over. 'To tell the truth, we haven't been speaking much in the last few months. Misunderstanding. Almost ate my new stepfather by mistake.'

'Families,' said Asvin expansively. 'I'm sure she will forgive you eventually. The love of a mother, after all.'

Akab nodded solemnly. 'Is there anything else I can do for you?' he asked.

Asvin looked up at the sky gratefully. 'Truly it is said,' he said, 'that when all else fails, when all hope fades, the gods will show the faithful a way.'

Akab tried to look modest.

'I have been chasing a ravian northwards tirelessly for many days now,' said Asvin, not noticing a loud knocking sound coming from a nearby tree. 'But other quests, other duties have come in the way, and now I am far behind. Mighty Akab, your woodcraft is far superior to mine, and your strength and speed unparalleled in this Age of the world. Will you not aid me in my pursuit?'

'Well, you've got a smooth tongue, I'll say that for you,' said Akab. 'But I don't know of any ravian passing through these parts. I'm not much for rumours and struggles of power and all that, you see—I usually end up eating people who bring me gossip.'

'But surely we could find a way to track my enemy if we combined our skills.'

'Ravians are no mean woodmen themselves,' said Akab. 'If your friend was far ahead of you, there is nothing that can be done.'

He stroked his chin thoughtfully for a while.

'So the ravians are back, are they?' he said. 'That would explain a lot of strange things that have been happening in this part of the world. This means . . . this can only mean more wars, can it not? More changes. Shame.'

'Are you not part of the Dark Lord's army?' asked Asvin.

'I received the summons, of course, but I didn't go. Ate the messenger. Not really interested in this modern war nonsense. Waste of bloody time. But wait. You're distracting me.'

Asvin waited courteously while the rakshas stomped around, scratching his shaggy head.

'There was a great white pillar in the sky far to the north some nights ago,' said Akab. 'I've not seen anything like it for a very long time. Could be something to do with this ravian of yours.'

'Could you take me towards the place where you saw it?'

'All right. But I warn you, I'm providing transport and good conversation only. I'm not interested in any war.'

'Any help you could provide would be invaluable, dear Akab. How fortunate, indeed, that I found you, and that you are the son of the gracious Akarat.'

'Well, to tell the truth,' said Akab, grinning sheepishly, 'I *think* she is my mother. It was all a very long time ago, you see. But who cares for all that?' The rakshas roared in enthusiasm. 'A journey! An adventure! What fun!' he cried.

'Yes!' cried Asvin. 'Let us leave immediately, my friend!'

The rakshas shot him a curious glance.

'What is it?'

'You're naked,' Akab pointed out.

'Oh,' said Asvin, looking down. He remembered the sari, and the little village girl wearing his clothes as she left with Rukmini. Rukmini . . . he would miss her. But it would be better if she were not around when he saved Maya.

He picked up the sari and swiftly wrapped it around his legs, a somewhat unfashionable but very convenient dhoti. It is fitting, he thought. I go into battle in Avrantic clothes. Returning to my roots. Koli trousers are stupid anyway.

He picked up his sword—he was almost forgetting that, too, in his excitement—and whirled it stylishly over his head.

'I'm done,' he smiled at Akab.

'Let us leave at once, then!' said the rakshas.

His veins swelled up alarmingly, and then his muscles. He swirled upwards like smoke, and within seconds, he was towering high over the trees, setting Asvin's heart thudding in alarm. Akab bent down, picked Simoqin's Hero up and set him on his shoulder.

'Shall we?' he roared, blowing Asvin's hair backward.

'There is a problem. You see, I came here with a friend,' said Asvin. 'She was my companion in peril, but this is my quest, not hers. I asked her to wait for me until I returned to the village.'

'Should we go to the village then? I am quite hungry.'

'No, perhaps it would be a better idea to move on. She does not deserve the danger my heart tells me I walk towards. And to be quite frank, she was slowing me down.'

'Women, eh?' said Akab conspiratorially. 'Always fun to have along. Ever eaten one?'

Asvin shot him a horrified glance.

The woodpecker beat an enraged tattoo on a tree trunk far below, raising a cloud of dust in its indignation.

Roaring again, the rakshas set off northwards, his giant feet crashing into the earth, his massive form cutting through the trees like a shark through water, making the forest groan in fear and admiration.

A while later, Red transformed into Rukmini, flapped her arms and banged her head against a tree trunk a few times. Then she regained her composure, shook her fist at the sky and followed them silently.

8

Myrdak walked up the ancient, moss-covered paved road that led to the main gate of the city of Vanarpuri. Somewhere far above, it was daytime—a few rays of light trickled through the thick roof of leaves above the vanar city, thin white lines streaking across ancient, crumbling walls. Above the walls, ropes and creepers spiralled outwards to the trees surrounding the city on the outside, joining them to the unique network of creepers, vines, branches and vanar-built bridges and platforms that the citizens of Vanarpuri used as walkways, a sprawling wooden web of veins that carried the forest's lifeblood through the city's heart.

Vanarpuri's walls existed more to mark its boundaries than as any actual defence—most of the walls were crumbling, in a state of mossy decay if not actually broken, and so provided no conventional protection. But then, the vanars were not conventional defenders—the mid-air roads between towers and turrets were perfectly suited to the vanars' free-flowing form of warfare and Vanarpuri had never been captured since the vanars had occupied it.

But then, thought Myrdak, no one of any consequence had bothered to invade it.

He strode on towards the huge wooden gates.

Two vanars, high in the trees above him, hurtled down towards him. They stopped their descent above his head, dangling from creepers and leering down at him. One pulled a sword out from his belt.

'Surrender your weapons,' he told the ravian, 'and state your business.'

'Go tell your monkey queen,' said Myrdak, 'that if she does not give me the human spellbinder, I will raze this city to the ground.' His voice was strangely flat.

'Yeah?' said the other vanar. 'You and whose army?'

It was an unfortunate question.

Myrdak shook his head. He looked very bored.

He knelt and punched the ground.

A ripple passed through the earth, and then, in a straight line from the ravian towards the gate, the stone slabs on the paved road began to fly upwards, torn apart by the ravian force-bolt. Moss and earth flew in every direction as the road cracked down the middle, in a jagged-edged trench all the way up to the gate.

And then huge cracks webbed up the ancient wood as the vanars watched in horror.

Behind the gate, someone yelled, and raised the alarm.

The gate exploded with an earth-shattering *c-rr-ack*. Splinters of wood flew everywhere, impaling guards nearby, speeding through the air like arrows, eventually shuddering into the earth. A swarm of wooden shards flew towards the ravian as well, but he waved his hand, and they fell harmlessly to the ground.

The vanars above Myrdak fell off their creepers in sheer

amazement. Myrdak patted his challenger on the head, almost affectionately. 'Tell your queen what I said,' he said.

The vanars fled. Myrdak looked around and above, at the swarms of vanars gliding through the trees towards him, at arrows being fitted to great longbows. He grimaced, and raised his hand.

Vanar-queen Angda shifted uneasily in her great throne and spoke. 'I am deeply disappointed in you, Djongli,' she said. 'You have failed miserably.'

'I wish I could make you see, sister, that I have not failed at all—that on the contrary, I have won a great victory.'

'How? You were sent to investigate the light in the sky, and report on suspected ravian movements. Instead, you return, not even empty-handed, but with some Koli sorceress, who is clearly no idle traveller in the forest but a herald of dark days.'

'On the contrary, sister,' said Djongli, 'her tale has the ring of truth, and her coming is a gift from the gods. First, and most important, she is a friend of Kirin's. Second, if her tale is to be believed, Kirin is on his way to Vrihataranya, to rescue her from a ravian. It is our duty to protect her, for in doing so we would be doing what was both politically astute and morally right.'

'I realize she is pretty, as far as humans can be, but unlike you, Djongli, I require something more. You have not captured the ravian, or even his servant, the manticore.'

'It is never wise to come between rakshases and their prey. I did what I thought best, sister. I know she has no actual proof that her tale is true, but given how important she might be, I do not think we can afford to let her fall into danger again.'

'Consider this matter carefully, Djongli. Is it the woman that you want? Have her, by all means. But then abandon this argument.'

'No, it is not desire that drives me, Angda, though I admit I am deeply moved by her beauty. She is a friend of the Dark Lord's, and she is in great peril. The Dark Lord himself is on his way here. We must keep her safe until he arrives.'

Angda was silent for a while, her shadow huge and brooding in the firelight of the throne-room of Vanarpuri.

'No,' she said finally. 'These are treacherous times, and I do not want a female magician from Kol wandering the streets of Vanarpuri. At the same time, we should offer her some measure of protection in case her wild story is true. It is best that you keep her in your house outside the city. I will send word to Kirin and await his reply. Until then, she cannot stay in the city.'

'Very well,' said Djongli, 'I will be honoured to have her stay at my humble abode.'

Angda smiled. 'I thought you would feel that way. Have her brought to me. I wish to speak to her again.'

Somewhere in the city, there was a huge *crack*, as if someone had split a giant tree like a matchstick.

Djongli bowed, and began to walk out of the hall, but just then great gongs rang out in the distance, dull beats reverberating through the still air of the great vanar capital. A chorus of horns blew alarm calls.

A baboon-vanar burst into the hall. 'We are under attack!' he cried.

Immediately, a cohort of orangutan-vanars, Angda's personal guard, leaped down from the great banyan roots around the throne, spears in their long hands. Their leader bowed. 'Your command!' he cried.

Angda picked up her great longbow and swiftly bound a quiver full of arrows around her waist.

'Who attacks us?' she asked the baboon-man.

'Ravians.'

'An army?'

'Just one.'

'Just *one*?'

'Yes, my queen. I have never seen such power. He has broken the outer gate. He says he will destroy the city if we do not give him the human girl.'

Djongli met Angda's eyes, which were blazing with battle-fury.

'So your friend spoke the truth,' she said, 'and war comes early to Bali's city. Well, there is no question of giving her up. I will go to this ravian and tell him that myself. Invading a city alone! He insults the valour of the vanars, and must be taught the error of his ways.'

'Send word to the wardens,' she told the baboon-man, and turned to her bodyguards. 'You come with me.'

She turned towards her adopted brother.

'What evil have you unleashed upon our city, Djongli?' she asked, shouldering her bow.

'None that you cannot destroy, queen of the vanars,' said Djongli.

She nodded. Then the vanars sprang up and away, almost gliding up the giant banyan behind the throne towards the palace roof.

In the distance, there was another crash, and someone started to scream.

Djongli ran to find Maya.

Dozens of vanar bows sang in unison.

A swarm of arrows, black-feathered, death-tipped, soared down at Myrdak.

And stopped, suspended in mid-air like frozen lightning.

Myrdak waved elegant fingers and the vanar arrows clattered to earth.

They shot more arrows at him. None found its mark.

The ravian yawned. 'Do not try to hinder me,' he said, not bothering to raise his voice. 'You and your city mean nothing to me. Give me the girl, and forget you ever saw me.'

Large black bodies propelled towards him, shuffling along the ground at alarming speed. Nine gorilla-vanars, heavy infantry, huge metal maces in their long hairy arms.

He raised a hand, as if to ward them off. His lips moved soundlessly.

They reached him, raised their maces to strike, and stopped. Their arms sagged listlessly to their sides, and their maces clunked heavily on the stone floor. They blinked at him stupidly.

'A guard of honour,' said Myrdak softly. 'How gracious. Now go find yourself bows.'

The vanars nodded and suddenly jumped up, into the creepers, speeding vertically towards the baboon archers. They caught six and dragged them to earth; the rest fled, shrieking, into branches further up.

Myrdak walked into the city. The gorilla-men trotted around him, vacant expressions on their faces. Their huge black bodies formed a solid ring around him, guarding him from sight. In front of them, the baboon archers' bows sang as they fired arrow after arrow at their fellow vanars.

'Halt!' cried a voice far above. Angda stood on the wall, stern and slender, bow raised, arrow poised for flight.

'Release my men, ravian!' Myrdak's vanars fired at her; she soared away, behind a tree trunk.

'You will have to come nearer,' said Myrdak, walking on. 'I cannot hear you.'

'Stay away from him!' shouted Angda in warning, as more vanars sprang close to the ravian. 'He will steal your minds!'

She cried out to the vanars around Myrdak, but they stared back at her blankly, not hearing or understanding a word. The baboons kept firing mechanically; behind Angda, another vanar caught an arrow in the shoulder and fell shrieking.

'Steal? I prefer the word *borrow*,' said Myrdak. 'But this is a waste of time. Give me the girl, and I will go. None of you have the strength to stop me. I will not warn you again.'

Angda sent an arrow speeding towards him. One of the gorilla-men stepped forward, received it in the chest and fell dead. Angda screamed in anger, then sprang off the wall as the rest of Myrdak's new bodyguards hurled their maces at her. She took cover behind a tree trunk.

'I will just have to come and get her myself, then,' said Myrdak. 'Where is the girl?' he asked a gorilla-man.

'West tower,' replied the vanar.

'Bring her to me.'

The gorilla-men crouched and sprang, climbing the wall within seconds, and then eight huge black shapes swung through the city, hurtling towards the west.

'Angda!' called Myrdak.

She stuck her head out from behind the tree, and jerked it back again as an arrow whistled past. Another arrow lodged in the neck of a vanar standing near her. He died instantly. Around the ravian, the baboon-vanars expressions remained fixed as they swiftly fixed more arrows to their bows.

Angda fought back tears. 'Fire!' she cried.

Archers swung by on creepers, firing at the enslaved baboon-men around Myrdak. They fell, hearts pierced.

'They were brave warriors,' said Angda, stepping out onto a branch. 'You will pay for their deaths with your own.'

Myrdak made a bored gesture and leaned against the wall, watching the gorilla-men bounce out of sight.

Maya was in a small room in a half-ruined tower on the western side of the palace, playing an enthusiastic game of Alligators and Creepers with her gorilla-man guards. Freshly bathed and clad in short vanaress robes, she was a sight for sore eyes.

Djongli sent the guards away and shut the door.

'What's all that noise outside?' asked Maya.

'The city is under attack.'

'What? Is it him?'

'Yes. I should get you to a place of safety.'

'There are safe places in this forest?'

'My house is not far from here. Angda asked me to take you there. Perhaps we should go now.'

'Aren't you going to see why the gongs are ringing?'

Djongli shrugged. 'The vanars are capable of fighting their own battles. My duty is to remain by your side.'

'Kind of you. Let's go, then.'

They left the room, found a large window and walked out onto a large branch-road that headed out of Vanarpuri into the darkness of the forest.

Something in the distance caught Maya's eye. Big black shapes, heading towards them, eating up the distance with mighty leaps, bouncing across like rubber balls.

'What's that?' she asked Djongli.

'Vanars, heading this way,' he said. 'Let's wait, could be a message from Angda.'

'All right,' she said, but she felt vaguely uneasy. The big leaping creatures reminded her too much of Bali, of the terror she had felt high above the streets of Kol . . .

'Can we keep moving?' she asked Djongli. 'I don't feel like talking to them, somehow.'

Eight of them. Closer every second.

He looked puzzled, and shrugged. 'All right,' he said. 'Let's go.'

And then the gorilla-men were upon them, snarling fiercely.

One pushed Djongli off the branch; he caught a creeper and swung to safety, yelling in anger and surprise. Another caught Maya. She looked into his small, strangely blank eyes, and screamed as he flung her roughly over his shoulder.

They soared eastwards, Maya screaming and struggling uselessly. Djongli followed, yelling challenges, but could not keep up with them. They sped towards the gate like boulders hurled by mighty catapults.

One stomach-churning leap onto a branch-road. Another wild swing to a huge tree that had burst through the city wall. And then the vanar who had caught Maya set her down on the branch again and looked at the others.

'What's going on?' he growled suspiciously.

The others rubbed their heads, blinking in confusion. 'I don't know,' said one. 'We were charging the ravian . . .'

'We caught some archers . . .' said another.

'What happened?' another asked Djongli as he landed on the wall beside them, fists clenched.

'How would I know?' he yelled. 'You attacked us!'

'Sorry,' said the big gorilla-man sheepishly.

Djongli looked at Maya in utter confusion. She was smiling. 'Looks like the ravian took over their minds,' she said. 'And my magic broke the spell. Evidently it works against ravian influence, just like rakshas magic does.' She grinned broadly. 'That's a rare slice of luck.'

'Didn't he know this could happen?' asked Djongli.

'He made a mistake,' said Maya, 'and you have no idea how good that makes me feel.'

'What should we do now?' asked one of the gorillas. Sounds of screams and hissing arrows were very close.

'Where is he?' asked Maya.

'Very close,' replied the vanar. 'If you walk along the wall and cross that tree, you'll see him.

'We should go,' said Djongli.

'I could keep running,' said Maya, 'but he would just keep chasing me until he caught me. And I will have a whole city behind me here.'

'You cannot fight him,' said one of the gorilla-men. 'He is too strong. But the wardens are on their way. He will not live to see the night.'

But Maya walked forward, across a giant banyan, and peered through the leaves.

There he was. Standing calmly in front of a huge gap in the walls, where broken logs and splinters bore the memory of a once mighty gate. The sheer arrogance, thought Maya, walking into an enemy city alone. And the sheer drama— he stood there like a mountain, illuminated by a single beam of light, surrounded by enemies, casually deflecting whatever they threw at him. Catapults somewhere inside the city hurled boulders over the walls. None came anywhere near him.

Maya stepped back behind the tree. She'd harboured ambitions of taking him on, finishing him off with some powerful spell. But the sight of him had been enough. One look at that stern, handsome face, and you knew he was the greatest ravian hero alive.

And that was the funny thing, thought Maya. He was a hero. For his people. Brave, powerful, relentless. A light in the darkness. Alone in a strange world, perfectly at ease, overcoming every obstacle with easy, measured strides, paving the way for his people. He was the perfect hero, the hero Asvin or any other human could never be.

The only problem was, she was on the wrong side.

Yes, he was cruel, violent, ruthless. But weren't all heroes? If you looked at things from Myrdak's perspective, he was only doing his duty, driven by what he thought was a just, noble cause. The reason Asvin was better than him, she thought, was that Asvin's powers were tempered by compassion, by his selfless love for the weak.

But then again, there were limits to that compassion. Asvin felt his duty was to protect weak humans. Perhaps even Myrdak protected weak ravians. But humans and vanars were just as alien and irrelevant to him as, say, asurs and pashans were to Asvin. Perhaps they were the same person, at some level—it was just that Myrdak was more powerful.

She shook her head, remembering Myrdak's calm amusement as he watched her trying to escape. Asvin would never do that.

Or would he? Would he tease an asur for sport? Would his conviction that anything he was doing was utterly and absolutely right lead him to become a creature like Myrdak?

She looked at the ravian again and shuddered. If there was a war . . . everyone knew the side with more heroes won.

She thought of Kirin, and was suddenly very afraid.

'Excuse me,' said Djongli quietly behind her, 'Do you have a plan?'

'No,' she said, turning to him. 'Let's go.'

She caught a creeper and swung off the branch.

A second later, she was dangling in mid-air, holding on to the creeper for dear life, trying not to look at the ground far below.

'Perhaps it would be quicker,' said Djongli kindly, 'if I were to carry you.' He swiftly leapt on to a creeper beside hers, swung over to her, and caught her around the waist.

'Put your arms around my neck,' he said. Maya did so, rather self-consciously.

He dropped downwards gracefully, partly to gain momentum and partly to show off, and swung off towards his treehouse.

The gorilla-vanars watched them go.

'Wait here?' said one.

'We could do a lot better than that,' said another.

'Fire!' yelled Angda.

Arrows streaked towards Myrdak. He threw them aside.

'Fools,' he said. 'Do you never learn?'

He looked to the west, at the gorilla-men shuffling out from behind a large banyan to his right, and smiled.

The smile turned into a puzzled frown as they gathered on the wall, just out of his mental reach.

'Where is she?' he asked.

'She sends her regards,' said one.

'And a big wet kiss,' said another, sticking out his tongue.

'And we got you this,' said a third.

He tossed Myrdak a banana.

Then the gorilla-men screamed in defiance and pounded their mighty chests.

The vanars of Vanarpuri cheered in unison and shot more arrows and expletives at the ravian.

'You will pay for your defiance,' he said. 'You will pull down your city with your own hands.'

Massive gnarled paws landed with mighty thuds amidst the trees behind the vanars. Huge shadowy shapes parted thick branches as they strode forward. Fiery eyes lit up in the shadows. The wardens had arrived.

'You stare into the face of death, ravian scum,' said a rakshas.

Myrdak did not waste time talking. He ran off into the forest, with the rakshases in hot pursuit. The vanars kept cheering, but stayed where they were. They were, after all, an evolved species, and inclined to self-preservation.

Elsewhere . . .

'Sstop thiss Game at oncse.'

'What is it now, Tsa-Ur?' asks Zivran wearily. Stochastos and Petah-Petyi shoot him sympathetic glances.

'I cannot sseem to control my piecsess,' says Tsa-Ur, his tongues flickering in anger as he watches Alpha Laakon the werewolf chasing undeer in the forests of the Mountains of Shadow. 'They aren't doing anything ssignificant. Sso sstop thiss Game, Zsivran, and exsplain how everything workss.'

'The Players will be here soon, Tsa-Ur, and the pieces are not in place,' says Zivran. 'So I must say no, with infinite regret.

'But nothing iss going the way I want it to. Shurely ssomething

Samit Basu

iss wrong with thiss Game. Ssomeone—probably Sstochasstoss—iss cheating. I demand we invesstigate, for otherwisse I will not be a referee.'

'We need just two referees,' says Petah-Petyi. 'Can't you just watch the Game if You cannot control Your pieces, Tsa-Ur?'

'It does take a certain degree of skill, My skin-shedding scourge,' says Stochastos with a mocking smile. 'I am perfectly satisfied with the way My pieces have been responding to My instructions.'

'Are You ssaying I have not enough sskill to play thiss Game?' splutters Tsa-Ur, furious.

'Surely that does not matter, Tsa-Ur, as You will not be playing, will You?' says Zivran, finally allowing his irritation to show on his face. 'Come now, My friends, let Us keep playing. We are almost there.'

9

Tjugari the destroyer flew low over western Vrihataranya like a great gale, his immense muscles coiling and stretching, his vast wings curling and beating, sending waves rippling through the leaf-ceiling of the Great Forest. The bright midday sun shone and sparkled on the twin lines of spikes studded on his back, and a storm of twigs and leaves followed in his wake. Kirin and Behrim clung on to his great claws grimly, ignoring the lashing of the wind against their faces and the pain as his tough, leathery skin grated against theirs, leaving them raw and bloody. At least the air was not as freezing cold as it was high up in the mountains, thought Kirin. Behrim and he had both gone completely numb as they soared over the Grey Mountains a few days ago; once Behrim had lost his grip completely and almost fallen off. Tjugari had clasped his paws close to his chest then, and the warmth of the great furnace beating under the dragon's skin had somehow kept them alive.

Yes, the view of the earth from the sky had been spectacular all through, especially the sunrise in the mountain valleys, and the river Jhumpa glowing orange in the evening as they followed its course from the Grey Mountains through the black forest. But the scenery had been the last thing on Kirin's mind. As hills and valleys undulated beneath him, and clouds tempted him to dive off and bounce on their fluffy cotton beds, all he thought of was Maya.

Was she alive?

She couldn't be dead, he told himself for the thousandth time. The world could not exist if she died. It was just not possible. He would save her. Somehow.

Almost there, said Behrim. *He should set us down near that bend in the river. We will walk the rest of the way.*

Kirin looked at the ravian, arms curled around Tjugari's left forepaw as he scanned the forest with keen eyes.

You should let the dragon go, said Behrim. *They will shoot at him if we take him further.*

Set us down, Tjugari, said Kirin to the great black dragon.

Yes, master.

Ten minutes later, he dropped them on a mud-bank that lay beside the gently flowing river and perched awkwardly over two large trees. Kirin and Behrim landed neatly, sinking into the mud but remaining on their feet.

'Are you sure this is the right place?' asked Kirin.

Behrim nodded.

Return to the hills in the west, Tjugari, said Kirin. *Wait for my call.*

Let me remain above you, master, said Tjugari. *No one will dare threaten you.*

I wish I could, said Kirin. *But you have done enough for now. Thank you, and I will find a way to reward you one day. Hunt now, and find food for yourself. You must be twice as tired as we are.*

There was an elephant half an hour back, said Tjugari. *Would you like some?*

No, thank you.

Good luck, master.

Goodbye for now, my friend. The great dragon soared off, in a great gust of wind that almost knocked them into the river.

'What?' asked Kirin. Behrim was looking at him strangely.

'It is unusual for ravians as powerful as you to treat servants with courtesy,' said Behrim.

'Surely you must have realized by now that I am not exactly a typical ravian.'

'It is only to be expected of a child of your parents.'

'Where is this fortress of yours, Behrim? We can save the compliments for later.'

'Epsai is just half an hour eastwards,' said Behrim, rubbing life back into his arms. 'Do you not remember it at all, Kirin?'

'No. And where is the Temple of the Black Star?'

'A day's march away, further to the east. But if all goes well, we will not have to go there.'

'Let's move.'

'I asked if you remembered,' said Behrim, trudging out of the mud-bank into the shadows of the trees, 'because I first met you when I was captain of the rangers of Epsai, responsible for secret attacks on rakshas strongholds between the river and the mountains. I remember that day well— much blood had been spilt. If I am not mistaken, I met Aciram briefly that day too.'

'And the ravians are back in Epsai,' said Kirin. 'How is it that we flew here undisturbed from Imokoi?'

'We must have been observed. Perhaps we are being watched even now. It will be quite a pleasant surprise for the watchers, I can tell you, when they see Behrim and Narak walking together under the trees again!'

Kirin smiled. 'You were fond of my father?'

Behrim nodded, his face grim. 'He was my closest friend, and an inspiration to us all. He opened my eyes to many things—most importantly, to the glaring faults in our own society.'

'Did you ever suspect there was anything strange about him?'

'What do you mean?' Behrim stopped.

'Nothing. Just that—I never got to know him really well, you see. And I have read many conflicting accounts.'

'Strange?' said Behrim. 'How do you mean, strange?'

'Did you ever feel he was . . . dangerous?'

'Of course. Narak radiated danger. As do you, for that matter. Why?'

'Nothing. I was just wondering. We should keep moving. I don't know if it's my imagination, but this part of the forest seems familiar.'

They walked on.

Half an hour later, they had not been stopped. The forest around them was relatively sparse, green and beautiful. Small animals frolicked in nearby trees; it certainly did not look as if anyone was watching them.

They reached a rock-face that rose suddenly out of the earth, eventually smoothening out into a small hill. Behrim stopped in front of it and looked into the trees, a worried frown creasing his face.

'Where are your ravians?' asked Kirin.

'I don't know. This does not make sense.'

'We're wasting time. I should head on to the temple.'

'They must be here. Wait. We should just announce our presence.'

He stepped up to the rock-face, held out his hands and tugged hard with his mind.

A section of the rock slid outwards soundlessly, revealing the circular mouth of a tunnel that led into darkness.

'It is I, Behrim of Esmi!' shouted Behrim. There was no response.

They waited, staring into the tunnel.

'I do not understand this,' said Behrim. 'Why is no one here? Let us go in.'

'I have no desire to go in,' said Kirin. 'Obviously your fortress is empty.'

'But this fortress could not be empty!' Behrim closed the tunnel and leaned against the rock-face, perplexed. 'It is almost as important as Asroye!'

'You came here for nothing,' said Kirin. 'And I have wasted enough time. Straight line to the east, did you say?'

'Just a minute,' said Behrim. 'Let me think.'

He knelt on the ground, bowed his head and closed his eyes.

After two minutes, he looked up. 'I have it,' he said. 'I am astounded at this treachery, but there is no other explanation.'

'What is it? What is going on?'

'Sit down, Kirin,' said Behrim. 'I cannot believe they would be capable of such deceit! They must be stopped!' He paced up and down, looking horrified.

'What are you talking about?'

'Myrdak and Peori are in league, as I suspected. But the scale of their deception is beyond anything I imagined in my worst nightmares.'

'Why?'

'If the ravians had returned, this fortress would be bristling with rangers. I am sure of this. But the ravians are not here, Epsai is empty. That it is empty can mean only one thing.' Behrim stood still and looked Kirin in the eye. 'They have not let in the ravians,' he said, his voice trembling a little.

'I don't understand.'

'They told me to move on ahead to Imokoi at once. They were getting rid of me! They never intended to open the great portal!'

'Why not?'

'It is slowly becoming clear,' said Behrim. 'Let me put the pieces together.

Myrdak was supposed to go to Kol and bring back the King of Kol, while Peori found your trail in Asroye and followed it to wherever you are. Then the Council would have decided your fate, and the fate of the ravians.

'Instead, we know Myrdak went to Kol, in violation of his orders. What Peori has done, and where she is, we do not know, but she has certainly not found you. She might be dead, but I suspect she is not. She is alive, working with Myrdak—he has won her over in some way, persuaded her to betray her House. If they were both dead, that could be a reason for the ravians not being here. But as we have seen, Myrdak is not dead, which means they have deliberately not opened the portal.'

'But why not?'

'Because . . . because he wishes to kill you first, to remove you as a threat. That explains this charade of a duel.'

'Would it not be easier to kill me with an army behind him?'

'No, for if I succeeded in making the ravians accept you, there would be no army behind him. If he managed to make you face him in battle, he could kill you quietly—and with you, all my ambitions. This is either a plot by the royalists, or Myrdak working alone in a bid to seize power. I do not know which.'

'So he wants to kill me, and then open the portal and let the ravians in, and tell them I was dead, or that I had attacked him as a rakshas, thus making sure your dream of a republic is never realized.'

'Yes. I made a great mistake, believing that they would stick to their instructions. I should have realized that you are a much greater threat to Myrdak as a rival for power among the ravians than as a Dark Lord. He did not want to leave anything to the Council. It is just the sort of thing he would do.'

'So you and Myrdak and this mystery woman are the only ravians around?'

'Yes.'

Kirin took a few seconds to assimilate this. 'And they will not let in the others until I am dead?' he asked finally.

'Yes.'

A slow smile curled around Kirin's lips. 'So if I kill this Myrdak, I can stop the portal from being opened?'

'No, for Peori or I would open it. In any case, you cannot kill Myrdak.'

'Let us say,' said Kirin, 'that I managed to persuade the three of you, by murder or more complicated methods, not to open the portal, the ravians would not be able to enter the world at all?'

'Yes. But getting back to the point, this means we must journey to the keep where the nundu is held captive, open the portal, and tell the Council of Myrdak's treachery. This is great news, Kirin! When I tell them what he has done, they will definitely rule in my favour!'

'We are not going to open the portal.'

'What do you mean?'

'Instead, I am going to kill Myrdak and save Maya, and then we will deal with this Peori. I think this world is far better off without the ravians.'

'*No!* That is madness! What are you saying?'

'But we will discuss this later,' said Kirin. 'You said this temple was a day's march?'

'Yes.'

'Well, Behrim, I will take your leave in that case. I have a friend to save. You may consider yourself free of all obligations. Journey wherever you want, or wait here for ravians or miracles or winter or whatever else you want. Goodbye.'

Behrim sighed. 'Kirin, see reason,' he said. 'I know this friend of yours is very dear to you, or we would not be here. But you cannot save her. She is already dead. Once Myrdak had made sure you would come, leaving her alive would no longer be necessary. Someone of your intelligence must see this.'

'No.'

'Kirin, do not go. It is a trap of some kind.'

'It does not matter. You cannot change my mind.'

'Kirin, you walk the road to madness. This woman you love is important, yes, but she is dead. Believe it. She is dead. And you must not throw your life away. A great many people depend on you. The future of the ravian republic, of the whole ravian *race* is in your hands, as is the fate of our enemies, these rakshases and asurs you seem to care about so much. With you gone, they will have no chance against us, and the monarchy will grow even more powerful with magical slaves. Do not go.'

'Well, I have to go and see for myself that she is dead. Surely someone of your intelligence can see I would not have come so far to turn back now. Yes, you have told me again and again that this Myrdak is a greater warrior than I am. But if he has killed Maya, I must seek him out anyway, and see whether you spoke the truth.'

'Simoqin was my friend,' said Behrim 'But he was not the only one with the gift of prophecy. I say this to you, Kirin son of Narak. Do not duel with Myrdak. For to do so is to duel with death.'

'The Simoqin Prophecies were a joke. Are you done?'

'You are resolved to meet Myrdak?'

'I am.'

'I will come with you, then. I will speak to him, and try to persuade him to leave matters to the Council. But I do not think that will work. He has come too far to be turned aside by words now. He will kill both of us. In the old days, I would have gone in your stead and fought Myrdak. That is what my heart tells me to do. But these are not the old days, and I know Myrdak is more than a match for me.'

'In any case, I am resolved to meet him alone. He said he would kill her if anyone was with me, as I have told you several times. And yes, you have told me several times that she is dead, and this is just a ploy to get me alone and finish me off. But I have to go, and I know you understand that. For more than a month I have sat on my throne, doing nothing, weighed down by choices and mysteries. Now I am faced with disaster, and I have no choices at all. I *have* to act. And nothing can stop me.'

Behrim shook his head, defeated. 'Go, then,' he said. 'I

wish I could help you. It breaks my heart that a ravian's treachery should lead you to this.'

'Don't tell me you actually thought ravians were better than anyone else. How could you?'

'I do not know. But if they are not, what have I been fighting for all these years? What sort of world is this? I stepped out of the portal trembling with excitement, longing with all my heart to smell the green woods of Vrihataranya, to drive the shrieking asurs with fire and sword and make Obiyalis the world of our dreams. But this is a world of darkness, a world without honour. Can even the ravians heal this world now? This is not the Obiyalis I left. Where is *my* Obiyalis?'

'It's the same world, Behrim,' said Kirin. 'The only difference is, you were on the winning side back then. Well, I will not wait any longer. Is there anything else you wish to say to me? Advice that will help me kill Myrdak, perhaps?'

'If I knew how to kill Myrdak . . .' said Behrim, not meeting his eyes.

Kirin turned to leave, and jumped in surprise.

A flash of red. Something bright and furry hid behind a tree.

'What is that?'

'A little round man of the woods,' said Behrim. 'They have been watching us for a while now.'

'I've never seen anything like that before.'

'I saw them once on my way to Imokoi, in the distance, dancing under a tree. They saw me too and beckoned me to join them, but I was in a hurry. I had a Dark Lord to kill. They are unimportant now. Harmless singing woodland creatures. I call them chubbies.'

A blue head poked out from behind another tree and jerked back immediately as its large eyes met Kirin's.

'Are they dangerous?'

Behrim gave Kirin an odd look. 'Sometimes, Kirin,' he said, 'you say things that make me wonder whether you are a ravian at all. Surely you know that our senses would have warned us if dangerous creatures came our way. That if every small creature that moved set off alarms within us, we would have died of shock every time we went near a beehive.'

Kirin looked around. More little round bodies dashed behind trees, streaking yellow, green, red, blue and purple blobs of colour. 'It's just that I haven't seen a harmless creature in a while,' he said. 'What did you call them? Chubbies?'

'Why are we speaking of them now, when the fate of all Obiyalis hangs in the balance? Kirin, listen to me. You cannot go like this. Let us at least put our heads together and decide on a plan.'

'We've been doing that for long enough. This is my plan—you stay here and play with your chubbies. Goodbye.'

'Wait just a second. Come out!' Behrim beckoned to the red chubby that had first caught his attention.

The little red man stepped out from behind the tree. Big, black, round eyes stared at them apprehensively.

'Cum Oot,' he said, in a piercing, high voice, and blinked comically.

Kirin couldn't help it, he laughed. 'Nice fellow,' he said. 'But what's your point?'

More chubbies came out from behind trees all around them, giggling shyly. Kirin's laughter seemed to have broken the ice.

'Lots of them,' said Behrim, quietly, as if to himself. 'I wonder when they came to this world. They were certainly not here two hundred years ago.'

Kirin looked at him, his pleasant, tired face creased in a smile as the little men edged closer, one or two chattering excitedly. There were at least thirty of them now, brilliantly coloured little men popping out from behind trees and prancing over towards Kirin and Behrim.

'I would love to stay and discover more about them, but I really must go. I've said goodbye to you at least twice already,' said Kirin. 'And this time I really am off. I am glad to see I leave you in good company.'

'Kirin!' said Behrim. 'I have an idea.'

'What?'

'Sit down for a while and let us watch these creatures at play. We have both been through so much that neither of us can be thinking clearly. Perhaps a song or two will ease our hearts and refresh our tired minds.'

Kirin hesitated. 'I do not want to waste more time,' he said. But at the same time, he suddenly realized, if he was running to his death anyway, it wouldn't really matter if he heard a silly song first.

'Ten more minutes will do you no harm. I have this strange feeling that some time with these chubbies will give us a clue, or an answer. Surely the gods would not cast these helpless innocents in our path for no reason. There are moments of indecision like this in the tale of every great ravian hero, where chance suddenly plays a role. So stay here for a while, and let us see if any brilliant idea comes knocking.'

Kirin regarded him with sudden suspicion. What was Behrim up to? He remembered Aciram's warning . . .

'No . . .' he began, and then stopped.

High-pitched giggles filled the air, so contagious that Kirin had to laugh too.

The chubbies had gathered around Behrim now. He seemed genuinely delighted with them, but not half as much as they were with him. They started rolling around on the ground in front of him, prancing in rings, giggling hysterically and singing,

Ther Are Mo Men Tzof In Dee
See Shun In The Tale Ev Ree!
Hee Ro Way Chan Sud Den Lee,
Foh Ra Vile An Let Us See!

Then they stopped, bowed to one another, giggled again in a strangely ceremonial manner, and started their nonsensical song again.

Kirin's body ached from head to toe, and as he sat on a tree-root, the accumulated weariness of the last few days settled around him thickly. He was in no condition to duel now, he realized. Drowsiness overcame him, and he sank back against the tree trunk, watching the chubbies circle Behrim. The ravian was giggling with them now, and clapping to their song as enthusiastically as a child. He seemed to have forgotten Kirin entirely.

No, thought, Kirin, no sleep now, I should get moving.

But strangely, he wanted to stay, almost as much as he did on that distant Skuan shore just before the ravian had appeared in his dream and issued his terrible challenge.

A few chubbies left the ring dancing around Behrim and approached him, still giggling. He was suddenly suspicious— were they in some way responsible for his inexplicable weariness? He felt ashamed of himself immediately—they were obviously not dangerous in any way. Had he become so cynical and hardened that he was completely incapable of trust?

He tried to get up, but his back was aching terribly now. A few minutes of rest really wouldn't hurt, he thought. Funny how he had completely ignored the pain before.

'What's your name?' he asked the chubby nearest him, a bright yellow one. He looked at his companion, a bright green little man.

'Vot Sor Nem?' said the green chubby. Then both of them, yellow and green, rolled on the ground, laughing merrily.

Kirin smirked. 'All right, all right,' he said. 'So you think it's all very funny, do you? Enjoy it while it lasts.'

He stood.

'Stop me if you've heard this before, Behrim,' he called, 'goodbye!'

Behrim paid no attention to him. He seemed transfixed in happiness by the chubbies jumping around him. Kirin was somewhat surprised—after all, he was only going to save the world, and expected a little attention. But he couldn't blame Behrim; the ravian had seemed genuinely shattered, and was evidently seizing this opportunity for relief and relaxation with both hands. And the little creatures were extremely endearing. A good time to slip away and avoid awkward goodbyes.

A few more came up to him and tugged at his clothes, inviting him to join their happy dance.

'No thanks,' he said. 'I'm the Dark Lord, heading towards a great duel. No silly dances for me, thank you.'

But their song was beguiling in its senseless innocence. Almost of their own volition, his feet started walking towards the circle.

'I am not going to be coaxed,' said Kirin, sternly. He pulled his hands free.

They chattered among themselves, looking up at him with hurt expressions.

Kirin sat down again on his root. Really tired, he thought.

He looked at Behrim again. The mighty ravian was sitting on the ground, laughing loudly, as the chubbies played some comic rough-and-tumble game with him, gambolling over him and each other, completely covering him in a multicoloured furry blanket of high-pitched, squealing affection.

Five chubbies gathered around Kirin. They stared at him silently, blinking.

'Come on,' he said. 'Reveal yourselves as agents of destiny quickly, if you plan to. I really don't have all day.'

'All Day,' said one, and they all laughed hysterically.

'You're very hospitable,' he told them, 'but you're wasting your time with me. He's the popular one. I never was very sociable. Sitting around and watching the dance, that's me.'

A red chubby grasped his hand and chattered reassuringly at him. The little man was too endearing for words; Kirin laughed and patted his head.

Two others tugged at his arm, inviting him to the party again.

'No,' said Kirin. 'Really, no, I'm too tired. Don't bother me any more.' Waves of tiredness rolled over him.

He pushed the red chubby away, a little too roughly. He landed on his fat little bottom, squeaking loudly.

'Sorry,' said Kirin. He leaned forward and pulled his red friend up.

'Saw Ree,' said the chubby with a big smile.

He bit Kirin lightly.

406

'Ow,' said Kirin, amused. 'Feisty, are we?'

He smacked the chubby gently, and the chubby smacked him back, giggling. Peace was restored.

Encouraged by this response, the other four chubbies clambered up onto Kirin and bit him too.

Slightly annoyed, he pushed them away, but found it was really all too much effort; he was really sleepy, and the little men weren't hurting him anyway.

Really silly to go now, he thought. I can't fight anyone like this. Funny I didn't realize how tired I was. I'll just rest here for a while.

He called out to Behrim, intending to tell him that he'd changed his mind, but somehow he couldn't get the words out.

He looked at the chubbies again. They were sitting on top of him, giggling. It was all very funny. He laughed with them. When had he decided to lie down? Still, this meant he was nearer the grassy earth, which smelt wonderfully fresh. He reached out and touched the grass, rubbing it between his fingers. He took his hand away, and murmured in surprised when he saw that the grass had stained his hand green, as if it was covered with fresh green paint.

Odd I can see all this with my eyes closed, he thought.

He opened his eyes.

The chubbies were scrambling all over him, their fur tickling him pleasantly. They weren't heavy at all, very light. The whole world was very light, and strangely distant, full of wonderful music and strange curling lights twinkling and flashing at him from very far away. He felt dizzy. He closed his eyes again.

Everything was just lovely. After he'd finished playing, he would go and get Maya and they would stay here playing with the little chubbies and Behrim and everything would be perfect. Tendrils of incredible comfort were snaking their way across his body. It was like falling asleep in slow motion. And his friends were kissing him all over. It was hilarious and beautiful; he could hear his own laughter, but it seemed to be coming from very far away, even further than the twinkling, flashing lights dancing across his eyes. Everything was calm and peaceful and perfect.

He opened his eyes.

They weren't really kissing him; they were lying on him, half biting, half sucking. They looked a bit like leeches. Big colourful furry leeches. He wanted to ask them for salt. Pass the salt, please. Deliciously funny. It didn't hurt at all, but if he really concentrated he could feel their little teeth and suckers all over his body. They tickled.

He looked over at Behrim. It was strange; he couldn't see the ravian at all, just a huge mound of struggling colourful bodies, squabbling loudly, all straining to get to the middle. A few chubbies ran around the pile, looking for a way in; their mouths were stained bright red.

A small object flew out of the mound, bounced, and rolled towards Kirin. He looked at it, puzzled, trying to keep his eyes open.

It was an eyeball. The pupil was blue, the same blue that Behrim's had been.

What a coincidence.

Hilarious.

He laughed again, and they laughed with him, but somewhere deep down he realized they were eating him, and soon he would be dead and Maya was dead too and there was really nothing he could do about it, because it was all so much fun.

'Help,' he whispered at the closest chubby. 'Help.'

'Help,' said the chubby, giggling in return. It jumped on Kirin's head, and began to munch cheerfully on his throat.

No one to hear, thought Kirin. No friends at all. All alone. But no, he realized, his thoughts running in slow sluggish chocolate rivers, of course he had friends. If only the great roaring noise in his ears would stop, he could remember their names. He felt as if he were falling, but that was silly, because he was on the ground. He could hear his heart beating, like thunder, and feel his life slipping away. It was very hot.

He laughed again, gurgling a little because of the blood, as his mind spiralled away into warm comfortable delirium.

10

Djongli slid from a creeper on to a branch high above the ground and stood there patiently until Maya took the hint and got off his back.

'Am I very heavy?' she asked.

'Not at all,' he whispered courteously, panting slightly. 'Well?'

'Be quiet, now, and look below. I think we are being followed.'

He knelt, parted the leaves below and waited.

'How far are we from your home?' whispered Maya.

'Further than we should have been. I headed in a different direction after a while.'

'Why?'

'Because I did not want to lead our pursuer to my house. Quiet now.'

They waited. It was evening, and they were both glad for this brief respite from soaring through the trees. Maya looked at the forest floor far below, and thanked her stars that she was not afraid of heights.

Only about two minutes had passed when they heard the sounds of a heavy feline body moving swiftly through the undergrowth far below them. They were too high in the trees to smell that familiar stench, but Maya knew who it was, shuffling through the jungle at an alarming pace, scanning the trees with piercing eyes for signs of movement.

Manticore was singing softly, a strange sad song that filtered through the leaves and made Maya's blood run cold.

'How long . . .' whispered Maya, and stopped when Djongli put a finger on his lips. He crawled forward, very slowly, and lowered his head, below the branch, sniffing and looking.

Far below the tree, he saw the giant cat's shadowy form, sitting under their tree, looking up.

Silence reigned for a few minutes. The manticore and the humans were perfectly still.

Then Manticore cursed loudly, and sent a few darts whizzing randomly through the air. Djongli flinched, but stayed where he was. He caught Maya's wrist tightly with one hand to prevent her from getting up and running along the branch.

A few minutes later, a shrill, frustrated scream echoed through the forest. And then Manticore turned, and plodded off westwards, not bothering to be quiet as he crashed through the bushes. Small creatures everywhere around them started chattering in relief and excitement, and the forest came alive again.

'We should follow him,' Maya whispered.

'Certainly not,' said Djongli. 'We should go to my house. After so much effort to escape, you want to follow that monster back to his master? To be anywhere near it is dangerous even for casual bystanders, and he is *hunting* you. Do not go anywhere near him.'

'I have to,' said Maya. 'We have the advantage now. They've lost us, and the ravian has his hands full with the vanars and the rakshases. The manticore could lead us straight to the ravian's hiding place.'

'He could also lead us into the arms of death.'

'Djongli, I cannot thank you enough for all you have done for me. You have saved my life more than once. But the ravian and that hideous creature are planning to kill Kirin. I must find out more about what they are up to.'

'We cannot defeat them in a fight. Not without many vanars on our side.'

'But the manticore is alone, and can be outwitted. Imagine, Djongli, what if he were going to Asroye? If we found the ravian city, or at least managed to get close to it, it would be incredibly important. They have hurt me, and I want revenge. And Kirin might be somewhere near here. They will be laying a trap for him. I must find out what it is.'

'Too dangerous,' said Djongli.

'I will follow the manticore, alone if necessary,' said Maya. 'I know I appear both unreasonable and ungrateful, but I cannot sit and wait for danger to pass by—and this danger will not pass by. You should carry on to your house, or go back to Vanarpuri. This is not your battle.'

Djongli smiled. 'Kirin is my friend too. I am not going to abandon you now, Maya. If you will not come with me, well, I will have to come with you. I am willing to help you in your battle against the manticore, if that is what you really want. We will follow him, and find a way to outwit your enemies.'

She hugged him joyfully, and let go, embarrassed, even

though she had spent the last few hours holding him tight.

'Thank you,' she said. 'I probably could not have done anything without you.'

'I know,' he said, still smiling. 'And I can guess, from our brief acquaintance, that you would have persisted anyway. Come, climb on, and we shall follow your friend to his secret lair, wherever it is.'

He caught a creeper, and she attached herself to his back again.

'The great thing is,' said Djongli, 'that I could carry you around on my back wherever I wanted, and pretend to have lost the manticore after a few days. I assure you I would enjoy that thoroughly.'

She punched his shoulder, grinning. 'So would I,' she said. 'Now let's go. The manticore could be miles away already.'

They swung off the branch, hurtling westwards in the monster's wake.

For a few hours, they followed Manticore silently, swishing through the leaves far above the plodding man-lion, sometimes soaring through creepers, sometimes crawling on branches, sometimes jumping like vanars from tree to tree. Djongli told Maya they were heading more or less in the direction of the temple where they had found her, though that was a considerable distance away. It looked as if the manticore had abandoned the chase and had no idea he was now the quarry; he did not even once look in their direction.

Night fell softly over the Great Forest, and Maya, bone-tired, began to wonder if she had made a huge mistake. But Manticore plodded on relentlessly, and Djongli, now

413

completely immersed in the joy of the hunt, half dragged, half carried her through the trees, his keen ears never losing the beast's trail, his sharp eyes, trained by years of prowling through darkness, never missing a branch, a fern, a creeper that would allow easier access to the next tree.

The ground was getting steeper around them; they passed a number of narrow, deep gorges and ravines, crossed quite a few strong streams and even scaled up the side of a beautiful gushing waterfall. These streams, Djongli told her, emptied out in great lakes further to the north. It was suspected that the ancient ravian city of Asroye lay by one of those lakes, but that was partly because the lakes were shrouded in mystery; surrounded by steep hills and ravines, protected by dense walls of tall trees, and rumoured to be full of hideous beasts. The vanars told tales of terrible demons that lived in those hidden valleys; whether they were legends of ravians, rakshases or other powers Djongli did not know.

They were now walking the tree paths along one side of a steep gorge; trees on their left towered upwards and to their right, far below at the bottom of a deep chasm, a thin and powerful river gushed its way northwards. The other side of the gorge, across the chasm, was a bare rock-face, glowing cold and grey in the moonlight. There had been trees there once, but a landslide had swept them all into the river below. In the distance ahead of them, they could see two points of light, apparently in the middle of the rock-face.

Coming closer, they saw they were a pair of torches, feeble flickering tongues of fire in the heavy darkness, bound to posts on one side of a narrow bridge across the chasm. There were two more torches at the other end, ahead of them. In their red glow, through the branches, they could see Manticore padding up to the bridge.

He did not cross it; he stood at one end and spoke. They heard his rasping voice far below.

Tis I, faithful Manticore.

Human friend! Unlock the door!

'Did he say human friend?' asked Djongli.

'Yes. Let's move closer,' said Maya.

'Are you sure? This could be a trap. The manticore might have led us here.'

'I know. Keep moving.'

They stepped carefully through the branches, stopping on a forked branch that hung out over the edge of the gorge, a few trees to the right of the bridge. Looking down, they could see the man-lion clearly. Maya's attack had left its mark; most of his mane had been singed off and he looked even uglier than before, a feat Maya would have thought impossible.

'Who is he talking to? There's no one there,' whispered Djongli.

'Shh. There's always someone,' said Maya.

She looked closely at the rock-face across the bridge. A narrow path, wide enough for a human walking sideways, curved down the side of the cliff from the top, which was about twenty feet above, to the end of the bridge. She looked to the top of the cliff, expecting to see ravian forms silhouetted in the moonlight, and shadowy man-shapes springing down from rock to rock. But there was no one.

A creaking sound. A black circular hole opened in the rock-face, right in front of the bridge.

'What is that?' whispered Djongli.

'Door on the side, disguised to look like the rock. Basic earth illusion magic. Wait and watch,' said Maya.

'Is this Asroye?'

415

'Shh.'

A human-shaped figure in armour walked out of the shadows of the tunnel in the cliff-face on to the bridge. Maya felt a strange tug of recognition. Where had she seen him before? The armour, she realized, it was old-fashioned heavy cavalry armour, as worn by the knights of old Ventelot. In the firelight, she saw the emblem on his shield and gasped.

It was a black cat. She remembered now.

The Bleakwood. The mad knight on the bridge. Sir Cyr. The hideous giant panther he had warned them about.

It made no sense at all.

The knight said something to the manticore. Up in the tree, they could not hear it.

Manticore walked forward. The bridge creaked as he put his front paws on it.

Speak louder, knight, I cannot hear.

The she-devil has singed my ears.

'I bid thee welcome, noble Manticore,' yelled the man on the bridge, his voice muffled by his great helm. 'But the great ravian hath not returned.'

'Singed his ears? Are you the she-devil?' asked Djongli.

'Yes.'

'Congratulations.' He patted her arm.

'Thank you. Now listen.'

'If he's deaf, why are we whispering?'

'Good point. Shut up now.'

He will return, knight, have no fear.

I will await my master here.

'He's a really bad poet, isn't he?' asked Djongli.

Maya nodded.

The knight saluted the manticore and turned back towards the tunnel.

'And so once again, we are faced with interesting choices,' said Maya. 'Do we want to wait here with the manticore for the ravian?'

'No. We should go to my house, and then to Vanarpuri tomorrow, and report what we have seen. The human guards something important.'

'Yes, we could do that,' said Maya. 'Alternatively,' she drew a deep breath, 'we could do *this*.'

'What?' said Djongli.

'But . . .' said Djongli.

'No!' said Djongli.

An airball landed with a splat behind Manticore.

'But . . .' said Djongli.

Boom.

A roaring Manticore and the railings of the bridge soared into the air. Manticore fired a dart into nowhere while still in mid-air, and then fell screaming into the chasm. There was a splash far below. The screaming stopped.

Maya lit a fireball in the tree and laughed aloud.

'Got him,' she said. 'That was easy, wasn't it? Now, Djongli, help me down.'

He helped her down. His jaw was still hanging open.

The knight stood on the bridge, brandishing a double-handed longsword.

They slid down the trunk of the tree and landed on their feet.

'Greetings, sir knight,' said Maya, walking forward, struggling to remember what exactly had happened in the Bleakwood. 'Are you Sir Cyr?'

'Didtht thou catht the manticore to hith death?' he asked, his voice shaking slightly. It wasn't Cyr, Maya thought;

417

this knight's armour looked newer, and Cyr's shield had been far more battle-worn.

'Oh no, sir knight,' said Maya in her best little-girl-lost-in-the-woods voice. 'I am just a little girl lost in the woods.'

'We,' said Djongli helpfully behind her.

The knight stuck his sword into the bridge.

'None Thall Path,' he said, his voice quavering with age and uncertainty.

'Right,' said Maya, remembering.

'We mean you no harm,' she continued. 'We just want to talk.'

He's under some ravian mind-control spell, she thought. So Sir Cyr must have been, too. A really old and powerful spell, too, because my presence isn't making it go away.

'None Thall Path,' the knight said again, more confidently this time.

'So,' said Maya. 'Are you the guardian of this bridge?'

'Yeth. None . . .'

'Shall pass, yes, I know that bit.'

'Foul demoneth!' yelled the knight, working up some steam. 'Thet not foot on the Bridge of Death!'

'I'm not a demoness, foul or otherwise,' said Maya. 'I just want to talk.'

'Hurry up,' said Djongli. 'The ravian might be here soon. Should I take him?'

'None Thall Path.'

'Wait,' said Maya. 'He's just a harmless old man.'

'What is your name, sir knight?' she called.

'Thir Thethil of the Detholate Gard,' he said. 'What, prithee, ith thy name, thinful temptreth of the wood?'

'My name is Silsila Sisiphusa,' said Maya with a grin,

418

getting into the spirit of things. 'And I'm not a sinful temptress, I'm a census statistician and tax collector.'

Sir Cecil wrestled with this information for a while.

'It matterth not,' said he. 'None thall path.'

'Are you a law-abiding thiti—citizen, Sir Cecil?'

'I obey the lawth of the King of Ventelot,' he said. 'God thave the King.'

'In that case, I fear I must inform you that this place—the Desolate Gard?—owes three hundred years of Council Tax. And I have come to collect it, so take me to your captain.'

'What are you doing?' whispered Djongli, aghast, behind her.

Sir Cecil's shoulders sagged under his armour.

'Lieth,' he said bravely. 'Thou art thurely a thuccubuth of the wood, come to theduthe me with your wanton thecthual wileth.'

'You should be so lucky,' said Maya. 'Now, let me in.'

'Give me the pathword and thow me your paperth.'

'This is the Desolate Gard, right?' said Maya. 'The lock is not broken, is it? The cat is not out, is it?'

'Thacred mother!' cried Sir Cecil, aghast. 'Knowetht thou of the cat?'

'I know all about it,' said Maya. 'I've come to inspect it, in fact.'

'But we have not been informed,' said Sir Cecil.

'Well, consider yourself informed now,' she said. 'Take me inside.'

'Very well,' said Sir Cecil, defeated. 'Welcome to the Detholate Gard, latht outpotht of East Ventelot.' He turned towards the opening in the cliff.

'So is the nundu all locked up?' asked Maya, beginning to cross the bridge.

Sir Cecil stopped and turned around.

'I cannot let you in,' he said. 'The ravian will return thoon. He will dethide. We will wait,' he said. 'I do not yet underthtand why the manticore fell. The ravian will unravel all mythteries.'

'We are wasting time,' said Maya. 'We have lots of nundus to check up on. So hurry.'

Sir Cecil stepped on the bridge.

'But there are jutht two nunduth, and Thouth Ventelot ith far,' he said. 'Thou theektht to dethieve me!'

'All right, so I'm lying,' said Maya. 'Let me through anyway.'

'None Thall Path,' said Sir Cecil.

'Have it your way,' said Maya. She turned him into a slug, ran forward and caught the armour before it fell off the bridge.

She marched into the tunnel. No one accosted her. Djongli followed her, dragging the armour.

Maya shut the door to the tunnel. Locks fell into place with sharp clicks. She lit a bigger fireball, and looked into the distance. The tunnel stretched on as far as she could see, green and sinister in the light of her sorcerer's fire. It reminded her of the tunnels of the pyramid in Elaken, of burning zombies falling past stairs suspended in mid-air, of giant vulture's claws gripping her shoulder and carrying her through whispering darkness. She shuddered.

Well, that smelt far worse, she thought. That was encouraging.

'Do you want to wait here or come with me?' she asked Djongli.

'You should have asked me this question on the other side of the door,' he said. 'Although I would have come with you in any case. So lead on, tax collector.'

'And census statistician. Put on the armour, then,' she said. 'And don't squash the slug.'

They walked through the tunnel, which ended in a small guardroom, completely empty except for a trapdoor on the floor. This led to a flight of stairs, leading deeper underground. There were torches on the walls now, and Maya snuffed out her fireball, walking arm in arm with Djongli—she would pretend to be his prisoner if they came across anyone. Seven flights of stairs later, they reached what seemed to be a cellar full of empty barrels, where nothing was dangerous apart from the smell of rotten food. There was a stout wooden door at one end. Djongli raised his hand to knock, and then stopped.

'There could be any number of ravians on the other side of that door,' he said. 'I might not be able to protect you.'

'I might not be able to protect you either,' she said. 'But we both know we are going through anyway.'

'What is our story? You are my prisoner, and I have brought you inside for interrogation?'

'If there are ravians on the other side of this door, I don't think any story will work. If anything happens, just try to mingle with other guards and escape. Don't bother trying to defend me.'

'We both know exactly how likely that is.'

Maya knocked on the door.

'Who goes there, friend or foe?' quavered someone on the other side.

'It is I, Thethil,' said Djongli, doing a very passable

impersonation of the gentleman currently weaving a slow trail of slime near the outer door of the Desolate Gard.

'It *ith* I,' whispered Maya.

'Thorry.'

A flap opened in the door and an old human took a cursory glance at them, and then unbolted and opened the door with an alarming creak. Djongli and Maya walked into the Desolate Gard.

The man who had opened the door was in his late seventies at least, clad in a ragged shirt and trousers of a style currently favoured only by very silly, very rich schoolboys from Ventelot. Three centuries out of date at least. He displayed no interest in Maya or Djongli; he did not even seem to see them. He closed great iron bolts on the door and shuffled off.

In the dim light of torches spaced far apart and ancient lanterns hanging from the ceiling, they saw they were in a huge cavern that had been further hollowed out by human hand and reinforced with wooden posts and ancient rafters. There was no sign of anyone who looked remotely ravian or remotely dangerous. Instead, there were about twenty humans, of various ages, shuffling about, some carrying baskets and wrapped bundles from a heap of garbage in a dark corner towards a large cave to the south, which Maya saw led to another cavern like the one they were in. Others lay around on the floor, watching them without interest, or simply walked about, their faces completely devoid of expression. The air was full of fine dust, and all the occupants of the cavern sported a thin layer.

'I don't like this,' said Djongli. 'What's wrong with them?'

'Keep moving,' said Maya. 'I think they're all under some sort of spell. Stay close to me, or it might affect you too.'

A horrible roar echoed through the caverns, the cry of some huge predator on the hunt.

They tensed and looked around wildly, but the humans did not seem perturbed at all; they carried on with their lifting, carrying or lazing as if nothing had happened.

'What do sane people do when they hear roars like that?' asked Djongli.

'They run away,' said Maya. 'I'm glad you're here.'

They walked in the direction of the roar.

They walked through a number of caverns, some filled with beautiful stalactites and stalagmites, others dank and mossy, others filled with the sound of running water. But beautiful though these caverns were, the intruders felt no joy—instead, the strange, lifeless people around them filled both Maya and Djongli with a growing sense of dread and desolation.

They are all dressed in the same clothes, Maya noted. The men wore one uniform, the women another, the children, both boys and girls, wore ragged tunics. Occasionally other men in armour passed by, but they neither greeted nor questioned Djongli.

These humans obviously lived in these caverns; there were large halls with rough straw mats laid out side by side all over the room, and other halls with long dining tables. Occasionally they heard doors creak open and shut in the distance, and the sound of domestic animals—clucks, moos and bleats that echoed dully through the Desolate Gard. Some caverns were underground fields; neat rows of plants extended from end to end, bearing fruits that Maya had never seen before. It was a completely self-sufficient city, Maya realized—a city whose inhabitants were completely sealed off from the world outside. It reminded her again of the

Pyramid of the First Pharaoh—but the dead men trooping through its enchanted depths had seemed positively vivacious compared to these humans. Even the skulls there had a certain roguish charm to their dead grins. But these humans, some in the prime of their youth, many beautiful in a pale, sad, watery kind of way, were strangely terrifying. They weren't undead, but they were certainly not wholly alive.

They saw a young girl and tried to talk to her—she showed no signs of fear, but would not answer their questions. A young woman came and stood beside them silently until they let the girl go.

'What were you talking about with that knight on the bridge?' asked Djongli.

'We met another knight, on another bridge, some months ago, in the Bleakwood far to the south,' said Maya. 'He seemed to think the world was just as it was before the Age of Terror, and he told us that the cat was out. We thought he was a random lunatic and moved on, but we were attacked and almost killed by a huge panther soon afterwards. There was no hint of anything connected to ravians then, but now . . . I think these people are all under some spell, and have been living underground for centuries. And that roar . . . perhaps there is another nundu—that's what the panther was called—somewhere here. And the guard here—Cecil—said there were only two. But what does this have to do with the ravians? And *where* are the ravians?'

'So this is not Asroye?'

'I'm fairly sure it's not. Asroye was supposed to be quite magnificent, at least that's what Kirin remembered.'

'Kirin? He has been to Asroye?'

'Of course not,' said Maya quickly. 'He remembered this from a book he read.'

'Which way to the nundu?' she asked a passing girl.

The girl looked at her, her face suddenly flooded with fear. She pointed a shaking hand westwards, and ran.

Maya shrugged, and led Djongli westwards, his armour clanking loudly in the dull, heavy air.

They walked through one fire-lit hall after another, urged onwards by more blood-curdling roars. But what was bothering them most was not the roars, but the fact that they were being followed.

Behind them walked not Myrdak or any other ravian, but a small and ever-growing crowd of children, led by the little girl whom Maya had asked for directions to the nundu. A crowd of children following strange newcomers in a city was not unusual at all, but these children were not giggling or displaying any sign of curiosity, or any emotion at all, and this was sending chills down Maya's spine. She tried to stop and talk to them from time to time, but they said nothing, just stared at her with big, tired eyes and shrank away when she reached out towards them.

They passed through a stone-paved tunnel out of a stalactite-studded cavern—knights in full armour at either end of the tunnel made no move to stop either them or the children trailing behind them—and then gasped in wonder at the spectacle before their eyes.

A vast cave, far higher than any they had passed through so far. Almost completely filled by a giant hemispherical cage, the only entrance to which was a huge gate right in front of the tunnel, secured with a massive iron lock. Thick iron bars the diameter of a man's waist curved upwards and met in a silvery sphere on top of the hemisphere. The top of the sphere touched the roof of the cave.

The floor of the cage was not flat; it was a hemisphere too, a basin carved out of rock that arced into the earth, making the inside of the cage a perfect sphere, apart from a raised triangle of earth in the centre of the pit. Three large spherical globes, made of a silvery material Maya guessed was moongold, were placed at the vertices of the triangle.

Inside the pit paced a great beast twice the size of a full-grown lion, and ten times as deadly. Fiery hell-cat eyes stared up at Maya and Djongli, dagger-length claws scratched the bottom of the pit, and perfect fangs were bared in a terrifying snarl.

'Meet the nundu,' said a deep voice behind them.

Maya groaned.

Myrdak walked out of the tunnel behind them, more children following him like sheep.

Djongli tensed, preparing to charge at Myrdak, but before he could, three children ran past him and stood between the bars of the cage, looking down blankly at the nundu.

'Move, and they jump in,' said Myrdak. 'The nundu is hungry.'

They stayed where they were. A horrendous roar echoed through the Desolate Gard.

'Once again the gods fight for me,' said Myrdak. 'Once again, you come to the very place where I wanted to bring you. You cannot fight your destiny, Maya. Running from me is futile.'

'I challenge you to a duel,' said Djongli.

'No!' cried Maya. 'Let him go,' she told Myrdak. 'This is between you and me.'

'Who is this?' asked Myrdak with a smile. 'You have

managed to acquire a champion even in this forest, Maya! You are to be congratulated.'

'Let him go,' said Maya.

'And have him tell the world about the Desolate Gard?'

The children gathered around Djongli and Maya, staring up at their faces.

'You coward,' snapped Maya. 'Using children to save yourself from us!'

'Lambs to the slaughter,' said Myrdak airily. 'Take a good look at them, Maya. They are perfect servants, bound to service by ancient bonds, loyal without question and completely unmoved by your dark magic. And if the mighty among the humans fall into darkness and fight against us, then *this* is the future of all humanity.'

He faced Djongli. 'Let me see your face.'

Djongli removed his helm.

'Noble stock, as far as humans go,' said Myrdak. 'And that could be your salvation. Good, clear mind. What is your name?'

'You can call me Mr Djongli, ravian. What is yours?'

'You can call me master, Djongli. Or we can call you dead. The choice is yours.'

'Do it,' said Maya.

'Stand aside, Djongli,' said Myrdak, pointing a hand towards him. Djongli stayed where he was.

'Release him from your magic if you want him to live,' Myrdak told Maya.

'I have cast no spell on him,' she said. 'He defies you of his own free will. Let him go. This is not his battle.'

The children gathered even closer around Djongli, pushing him towards the pit. He pushed back, fear spreading over his face. Small hands grabbed Maya's robe, tugging in every direction. She pushed them away as gently as she could.

'The children will escort you to a more comfortable room,' said Myrdak. 'You will have to go with them, for they will pull you until you kill them. If you resist, they will also remove your clothes.'

'I killed your cat,' said Maya, 'and I will kill you, ravian.'

'You have not killed Manticore. Though he is very angry with you, or so I gathered—his yells from the bottom of the ravine were somewhat indistinct. Go now. I desire to speak to your friend.'

He looked at Djongli again, a cold smile playing over his lips, and they all knew he meant to throw him into the nundu's pit.

Maya sighed, and cast a quick spell on Djongli, draining herself of all magic and turning him into a bat.

In bat form, Djongli fluttered out of the armour and into the shadows on top of the cave.

'A brave gesture,' said Myrdak, smiling. 'Though rather pointless. Still, you are to be congratulated—that was quick thinking, and rather heroic, which is why I let him fly away. Now come with me.'

He strode off into the tunnel, and the children pushed Maya after him. 'I will come back for you, Djongli,' she called, looking at the ceiling. She knew he heard her; bats have incredibly sharp hearing. As they led her out of the tunnel into the caverns outside, she just hoped that he had understood.

They led her through caves and tunnels to a small room. On the way she considered burning her way past the children a few times, but could not bring herself to do it. They were just too young. Yes, it was a war, and he was using her humanity as a weapon against her, but even if she did hurt the children and manage to escape, she knew she could not go far. She would have to fight the whole city, and Myrdak too. And she knew Myrdak alone was more than a match for her. How many rakshases had he killed in the last few days?

The children pushed her on to a small bed that stood in a corner of the room. They stood around her, silent, watching her intently, as if she were the most fascinating creature they had ever seen.

'You will remain here for a few days in comfort. Everything you need will be brought to you. The food here is not delicious, but it will nourish you. Fresh clothes will be brought for you, though I must say these monkey robes suit you very well.'

Maya glared at him.

'I will take your leave now, and leave you to your young wardens. Tell them if you need anything. Kill them if you feel like leaving the room. Others will catch you, bring you back here and stand in their place then. Yes, conversation will not flourish, but I will be back as soon as I have killed Kirin and we will have lots to talk about then.'

'But you have to take me to the duel,' she said. 'Why would Kirin fight you if you didn't show him I was actually in your power?'

'Kirin will fight me when we meet,' smiled Myrdak. 'He will have to, in self-defence, though I assure you I will not mind if he decides not to. If I had wanted you for bait alone, I would not have brought you here; I would have killed you after showing you to Kirin. That would have been much more efficient, for you have been a great deal of trouble.'

'Why have you brought me here, then? What do you want me for?'

'I kept you alive because I was burning with lust for you, and wanted you for myself,' said Myrdak solemnly, and then laughed aloud at Maya's face. 'You flatter yourself. You are very attractive, but I would never jeopardize the glory of the ravian empire.'

'Well, why have you kept me alive then?'

'There are so many questions, are there not? And I will answer them. We must have a long conversation one day soon, for I am afraid it is our destiny to become great friends. But not today.'

'What do you mean, we must become friends?'

'You are a bad listener for one so clever. I choose not to answer your questions today. I am not one for talking before my quest is completed. So first I shall go to the temple and kill your friend, who I have heard is heading this way on a large black dragon in a most romantic hot-headed hurry, and then I will return and explain things to you, as slowly as you want. There is much to say.'

'Kirin will defeat you. And then we will destroy your empire,' spat Maya, eyes blazing.

'So much hostility, so much anger . . . it saddens me. And yet it is not unreasonable, I know.' He smiled again, another sad, sweet smile. 'I had resolved not to tell you even this much now,' he said, 'for to speak of good fortune often brings bad luck.'

He looked deep into her eyes.

'Maya,' he said, his eyes and voice overflowing with sincerity, 'When this is done, I will do anything to make you forgive me. I will crave your pardon for everything I have done to you, and show you that everything I did was done only because it needed to be. And that day, when all is revealed, you will be grateful.'

'My only regret,' she said, 'is that I will not be there to watch you die.'

He shook his head. 'Your ignorance leads you to curse me today, but you will soon realize that while I have taken much away from you, it was only to enable me to give you much more. For I will give you a crown, Maya.'

'What crown, pray?'

'The crown of Obiyalis.'

'What's that?'

'This world is called Obiyalis.'

'Not by me it isn't.'

'Yet Obiyalis is what you will call it when you become its queen.'

Maya stared at him for a few seconds in stunned silence. 'I get it at last,' she said finally. 'You're mad. I should have seen it the day I first met you.'

Myrdak looked even sadder and more sincere than before. His voice, when he spoke, was dripping with honey.

'When the ravians return in full force, they will need to strive hard to remove the prejudice, the ignorance, the illogical suspicion that clouds their memories. For centuries our enemies, the hordes of chaos, and the agents of order perverted, have whispered evil lies about us. And so before we heal this world, we must first earn its trust. For this reason, the ravian king told me in secret, one of the many tasks I had to perform when I entered Obiyalis was to find him a bride worthy of his grace and power. And that is why you are here, Maya.'

She stared at him, unable to find anything to say.

'You will marry the ravian king, and rule this world with

him. Your marriage will be the bridge between cultures, between races, between worlds. Together you will rebuild the trust this world once felt for the ravians, and thus you will rescue your fellow sorcerers from the shadows that their dark rituals have cast on them.'

'You seriously think I will *marry* a ravian? *Me?* You expect me to *help* you?'

'I know you will, and that is why you are still alive, Maya. When you see reason, you will see it is the best way— the only way—for this world. You will save millions of your species from violent death. And think of the power you will wield!'

'And your king would have been happy to marry anyone you produced out of a hat for him?' It was not a question that conveyed an iota of Maya's shock and outrage, but it was the next question that popped up inside her head.

'It will be a political marriage, of course,' said Myrdak smoothly. 'The king will not grace your bed unless a mixed-race heir becomes strictly necessary. Though I confess that he might decide otherwise once he meets you. I know *I* would have, and that is saying a lot, for you might have noticed that I do not hold your race in high esteem. It is a great honour—no ravian has ever married a human before! And you will be marrying the king!'

'Let me get this straight. You would have abducted me anyway to bring Kirin here because you want to kill him. And now you also want me to marry your king? Why me? Saves you the trouble of abducting someone else?'

He laughed. 'A woman, above all else. No, I did not abduct you to finish two quests with one journey. I chose you to be the king's bride because my honour demanded I find the human most suited for it. Believe me, it would have been much easier for me to find someone more docile. But I would have to search for years to find someone more eligible.'

His eyes blazed.

'Do you know what the greatest challenge has been for me on your world, Maya? *You* have. I have had to struggle very hard to quell the temptation to claim you for myself. Your beauty and your strength have not been without effect on me. But I do what must be done. You are the key to power over Kol and the spellbinders. Hence I must put duty over self-interest as I have always done. As I will always do.'

He smiled again, at her stunned expression.

'Look at me! I have spoken far more than I intended to. You will excuse me, my dear. The Dark Lord is travelling great distances to meet me, and I have duties as a host!'

He bowed to her, and headed towards the door.

'There is just one more thing I should let you know, since I have already said so much,' he said. 'The ravian king is unmarried and heirless. The gods forbid, should any . . . accident befall him, there are a number of ravians of noble birth who might lay claim to the throne.'

She stared at him, horrified. She saw the strength of his ambition, and fear encased her heart like molten lead.

'Who knows what the future holds? I think we will get to know each other a lot better, you and I,' said Myrdak. He bowed again, and left. The door slammed shut behind him, and bolts flew in place.

The children sat around Maya, watching her with vacant eyes as she sat down on the floor, her face suddenly as white as theirs.

11

Kirin awoke slowly and felt only mild surprise when he found himself above a cloud, suspended over a placid blue sea, warm sun on his back and a gentle wind in his face. He examined himself quickly, half expecting to find wings and a harp. There was no harp, but there were wings. Great veined green wings, spread out in a luxurious glide riding the eastward breeze. Puffs of smoke from his nostrils streaked the sky behind him. Which meant he was asleep, and dreaming of dragons again.

The important question, thought Kirin, is this: Am I alive?

He would only know when he woke up.

If he woke up.

I might as well find out now, he thought, and cast his mind across sunlit seas far to the north, his thoughts rushing over islands and coasts and plains and deserts, back to the dense forests where death had rushed towards him, squeaking excitedly.

Welcome back, Kirin. He knew that voice, soft and deep and gentle, and his heart was flooded with warmth and relief.

Am I dead?

Not any more. Open your eyes, Kirin. You are safe now.

He was back in his own body now, waking up slowly. He expected to be enveloped in pain, but strangely there was none; instead, powerful muscles rippled around him, holding him snugly in folds of velveteen darkness. He was, incredibly, fully healed.

He opened his eyes and looked at the black, shining body of Qianzai, Mother of Darkness. She made Vrihataranya look like a little suburban garden.

The great Xi'en dragon had left him after he had entered the Dark Tower; she had told Kirin that something important needed her attention under the earth, and that she would return as soon as she could.

She certainly could not have chosen a more appropriate time to return, he thought.

'How did you save me, Qianzai?' he asked, shuddering as he remembered the chubbies. He looked around; there was no sign of them, though he was still where he had been when they had attacked him. A blood-stained rock where Behrim had been told him that the attack had not been a nightmare.

'I heard your cry for help in my mind,' said the dragon. 'For I have been keeping watch over you from afar, though very inadequately, as I found out. And I knew at once your life was in danger, for your tone made it clear you were in great peril. I came as fast as I could, but I was late. Almost too late. Seconds later, and I would have broken my promise to my friend your father. But thankfully I was thinking of you when you called for me. I must beg your forgiveness.'

'Forgiveness? You just saved my life!'

'I promised your father I would guide you. I have failed.'

'You have not failed at all. Look, I'm alive! It's a miracle!'

He waved his arms about in glee, and slid out of the dragon's coils. He noticed that all was not well with Qianzai. There were huge rips in her scales, and long white scars ran along her smooth black body. Her eyes seemed tired.

'What were those things that attacked me?' he asked. 'I have never seen them before.'

'They are very new to this world,' said Qianzai. 'It seems they have evolved very recently. But they are important, for they are this world's first natural response to the ravians. Innocuous predators that somehow slip past ravian mental defences, under the barriers that warn the ravians of approaching danger, and enchant them with music and poisonous bites. The poison they bear is powerful; it even made me delirious for a moment.'

'Did they attack you too?'

'No, Kirin. They are drawn to ravian blood and ravian power, and migrate towards ravians and places where ravian magic is strong. Do not let them near you if you see them again. It is fortunate that you were near another ravian, a pure-blood ravian; they were drawn more strongly towards him. If more of those creatures had attacked you, I would have been too late.'

'How do you know of this?'

'I asked them, and they told me. They are quite innocent—their minds are newly formed, and they have a voracious appetite for knowledge. It seems they have gone hungry for weeks, because they did not even know what to eat.'

'Well, they found out soon enough,' said Kirin. 'What did you do with them?'

'I ate them,' said Qianzai. 'I too had not eaten for weeks,

and they had attacked you. And that, before you ask, is how I found out how strong their poison is.'

'I'm glad you ate them,' said Kirin. 'They almost ate me.'

He looked at his arms, expecting to find them covered in scars, but there were none. Where scars should have been, there were, instead, strange black marks, like the marks that had appeared under his eyes in Imokoi—smooth, cold little overlapping plates that looked strangely like scales.

'What are these black patches on my arms?'

'They might seem ugly to you, but they are much prettier than the gaping wounds I found when I got here. I have healed you to the best of my ability, Kirin; in fact, you will find you have new powers now, though what they are even I do not know. My blood has certain healing powers.'

That is an understatement if I've ever heard one, thought Kirin. The blood of the most powerful dragon alive had a lot more than 'certain healing powers'.

'Rakshas, ravian, and dragon blood,' he said. 'I am a strange creature, am I not?'

Great, he thought. Now if I meet Maya, I will look like some strange swamp monster. Very impressive. Guaranteed to drive the ladies wild. Of course, under the circumstances, I suppose I cannot complain.

'You are a child of the earth,' said Qianzai. 'And living proof that the powers that rip the surface apart are capable of existing in harmony.'

Kirin tried to stand, but his legs were weak, and he sat on a rock instead.

'I'm afraid there isn't exactly a lot of harmony doing the rounds at present,' he said. 'And not just among the great powers. Every fuzzy little creature I meet tries to kill me.'

'It is your ravian blood they sought, Kirin. They could not help it; they needed to eat. What can be learned from their existence is that this world has accepted the ravians as part of it, that they are no longer the outsiders they once were. Such is the way of the world, as I have seen over the Ages—when new creatures come, they find their place in the system, and they add something to it. And true balance cannot be found unless both the ravians and their enemies accept this. Yes, the coming of the ravians caused great wars, but in their own way they have given a lot to this world, and they belong to it as much as the dragons do.'

'They have certainly made it more dangerous,' said Kirin. 'Right now their chief pastime seems to be killing me.'

'And I should be near you, protecting you,' said Qianzai, and her voice was full of sorrow. 'But I cannot, Kirin. I am needed elsewhere.'

'I wish you could be near me,' said Kirin. 'I do not know what to do with the powers I supposedly rule. I thought I could do this alone, but it does not look like it any more.'

'I wish I could guide you, as I promised your father I would,' said Qianzai, her beautiful eyes clouded over with compassion and grief. 'But believe in yourself, Kirin; you have great powers, and there is hope for the world while you use them. I admit things would have been easier had I been here to help. But I am needed underground, Kirin. Unknown to you, a great war is being waged constantly far below the crust, a war of which the turmoil on the surface is but a part. My children and I face great peril, and if we are not ceaselessly vigilant, the very earth will be destroyed.

'There are strange new beasts below the surface of this world, creatures that threaten the balance of all life, that rage in savage fury under earth and sea. Creatures of flesh and slime and lava, monsters I have never seen before, and I have walked the secret passages under the trees before the first vamans dug their burrows under the Mountains of Shadow.'

'Where did they come from?'

'Who knows? Great powers are at work within the fabric of our world, Kirin. It is as if the gods have unleashed creatures they do not know how to control. Creatures that have no natural predators, that do not know their purpose, that feel only a blind, confused urge to rip and tear and destroy. The dragons of Xi'en and the serpents of the underworld, ancient guardians of harmony between the elements, are at a loss. And if we lose this battle, all life on the surface will be destroyed.

'But it is not just from below that our world is under attack; the skies too are a source of danger. Ravaging currents of pure power from the skies are threatening to wash this world away in a torrent of chaos; the gods are performing some hideous experiment on our world. In the days that come, we will all be in danger, one way or another. The petty property disputes that trouble the kings above ground will have to be discarded if any solution is to be found.

'I know I made a promise to your father, but if I do not lead my brood into battle underground, the balance of this world might collapse. I should not even be here; my absence will be missed. But when I heard your call, and remembered my duty towards your father, I had to come.'

He stroked her scales gently. 'And I can never thank you enough,' he said. 'I release you from all promises, Qianzai. I have been given great powers, and I cannot expect you to abandon everything else and come running to me every time I make a mess. One miraculous escape is more than enough.

It is more than I expected. You have fulfilled all promises to my father, and now must look on me as a friend, not a responsibility. I must fight my own battles as well.'

'Can I help you in any other way before I leave?'

'No. I must go alone for the task I now have to accomplish,' said Kirin. 'I must fight a ravian, and save Maya.'

'Danh-Gem's son will fight ravians under the trees. Another war will start over a woman,' she said. 'And history will repeat itself . . . again.'

'I might be able to stop the war. If I kill this ravian, and one other, I might be able to stop the ravians from returning to this world.'

She sighed. 'It will not end there,' she said. 'I see war ahead, great battles raging all over the world. I fear you will not be able to stop the ravians' return. They are already a part of this world, as I explained to you.'

'I will probably not live to see them return, in that case. For the ravian who will let them back in is the one I must kill.'

'Must you put your life at risk so early in the war?'

'My life has always been at risk. And I must do whatever I can to save Maya.'

'Do you really love her?'

'Yes.'

'Enough to face death for her?'

'Yes.'

'Then I will not ask you to return to safety. And if my vision of the future seems bleak, ignore it, for it is clouded and uncertain. I am no prophet. My warnings are based on experience alone, and these last few years have changed the world beyond anything I have seen before. Go now, and fight your duel. Trust in your love and let it guide you.'

'Unfortunately, love is not going to help me win this fight.'

'Love is never enough,' said Qianzai. 'But it is something.'

'Is this world going to be destroyed, Qianzai?'

'It is certainly in grave danger. I do not understand what is happening, and I have watched this world grow. It has never been so clearly out of control.'

'What can be done to set things right?'

'I do not know. All my thoughts and deeds are spent on averting disaster, not planning victory. Kirin, there is much to say to you, but there is no time. There is never enough time. I will come to you again when I can, but now I must return below.'

'Thank you, then, and good luck.' Kirin stood up.

'Good luck.' And the great dragon arched her back, breathed white fire into the sky, and dived into the earth, leaving great ripples curling through the ground under the trees of Vrihataranya, and tendrils of smoke hanging in the dense, brooding air.

'So,' said Kirin to a passing squirrel, 'to the duel, then.'

The Shadowknife seemed to hiss with bloodlust as it wound its way to his right hand and formed a wickedly curved scimitar.

He walked off, eastwards, towards the Temple of the Black Star.

12

A giant rakshas thundered through the Great Forest carrying a most unlikely burden—a silver-armour-and-dhoti-clad human perched on his shoulder brandishing a sword and singing a merry hunting song. Various small animals watched them pass, looked at one another and shrugged their shoulders (if they had shoulders). They had seen a lot in the last few days, and were not easily impressed any more.

A few minutes after they had passed, a young woman with vermilion hair, clad in a red leather dress and a murderous expression, stalked by, talking to herself.

Soma: I have a question.

Tamasha: What is your question?

Soma: What are we doing?

Tamasha: We are following the rakshas and Asvin. If you think about it for a while, you'll see it's not hard to tell. The giant footprints in front of us should be a clue.

Soma: No. What I mean is, what are our plans?

Tamasha: I don't know.

Soma: See?

Tamasha: What? When did I ever make plans?

Soma: Red, what are we planning to do?

'Follow them. Save Maya if they find her.'

Soma: And then what? Go back to Kol? Do you think there's any chance they'd take us back?

'No.'

Tamasha: Whatever we do, it has to be something on a grand scale. We've been cooped up inside for too long, Red. We need to break free. Discover ourselves. Run a little wild. I don't know about you, but I *like* it here.

Soma: Of course you would say that. But for once you're not completely off the mark. We need to do something spectacular, Red. Because I can sense, as can you, I'm sure, that something important is about to happen. The world is about to change. There's something in the air. Epic times are coming. More war, more death, more love, more glory.

Tamasha: More bad poetry.

Soma: Yes. So we need a plan of action on the same scale as all this.

Tamasha: We could stay with Akab for a while. He's quite attractive in his own way.

Soma: Surely you're joking.

Tamasha: Well, Red likes him. That whole strong, uncontrollable animal thing. Power is always attractive.

Soma: There's really no point talking to you. I thought you were growing a brain when that other girl was here as well, but I see now that it was only because she was so stupid she made even you look clever. Red, what do we do?

Red stopped. Ahead, she could hear the rakshas crashing about. She sat down on a gnarled tree root and scratched her chin contemplatively.

'I've been thinking about this,' she said, 'and I really don't know. I doubt we will find Maya now, and even if we do, what will we do with her? I don't think there's any question of returning to Kol at present.'

Tamasha: It's really not something we should worry about. We could do anything, be anyone. We've come so far without a concrete plan. Why sit and worry now? We'll take it as it comes. After all, we are really powerful.

Soma: And real power is a real burden. We are in a position where we can change things. I don't know if you've thought about it, but we are probably more powerful than most rakshases. Our energies are trained, conserved, finely honed; even more importantly we are up to date on the uses of magic. We must use our powers wisely. For remember, with immense power comes immense responsibility.

Tamasha: With immense power comes immense *pfffffffth*. Red, are we going to sit here and listen to this half-baked moral nonsense or are we going to get up and do whatever the hell we want?

'We're going to do whatever the hell we want.'

Tamasha: Good girl.

Soma: But what *do* you want, Red?

Red stood up. 'I want to follow them and see what happens,' she said. 'And I really, *really* want you two to shut up.'

On a whim, she changed her dress and hair to emerald green, and walked on.

Elsewhere . . .

Petah-Petyi leans forward and looks keenly at Zivran, worried lines creasing her alabaster brow. 'I hate to bring this up now,

Zivran,' she says, 'but it seems to Me that Tsa-Ur's fears are justified. Perhaps all is not quite right with Your world.'

Zivran strokes his beard, not quite meeting her eyes. 'What do You mean, old friend?' he asks.

'I have been looking under the skin of this world,' says the Goddess of Chance, 'and strange things are happening there. Great beasts roam freely where they should not, and this is worrying. But what is even stranger is that the whole world seems to think it is alive. It seems to be reacting to the pieces much more than it should. It is almost as if this world resents being played with . . . as if it is plotting . . . I do not know . . . rebellion? But surely that cannot be.'

'Indeed, that cannot be,' says Zivran. 'The creatures you speak of are My own creations. They are . . . a surprise within the Game. Do not ask more, or it will spoil Your enjoyment.'

'I see,' says Petah-Petyi, 'that is good news indeed, old friend. For a while, it seemed to Me as if Your world was in danger of collapse, that internal pressures might cause it to crumble. And that would be disastrous for all of Us, for the Players are nearly here, I can feel the ether trembling in excitement as They approach. But if You tell Me everything is under control, I will take Your word for it.'

Zivran meets her eyes; he looks troubled. 'Trust Me, old friend,' he says finally. 'It is all going well.'

'Shhe might be eassily ssatissfied; I am not,' hisses Tsa-Ur. 'Clearly the forcsess that govern all Gamess are not working ass well ass they shhould be in thiss pathetic little world. Jusst look. Thiss human hero, Assvin, for insstancse—he iss too far away to reach the ravian temple in time to affect the ressult of the duel between the ravian hero and the Dark Lord. What sort of Game iss thiss, where an important Hero hass no part to play in a duel that will change the future of the world? It sseems to Me that thiss iss a world completely out of control.'

'It will all become clear soon,' says Zivran, but he sounds nervous.

Stochastos looks closely at the board, then at Tsa-Ur's leftmost head, which is watching him ceaselessly. An evil grin spreads across the chaos-lord's face.

Akab slowed down and stomped to a halt. He tweaked his left horn in an embarrassed sort of way, looking this way and that.

'What is it, my friend?' asked Asvin.

'I don't have a bloody clue where we are,' said the rakshas.

'But you said you were going to lead me to the place where you saw the pillar of light!'

'I know what I said. Thing is, I'm lost,' snapped the rakshas. 'I haven't been in this part of the world for centuries.'

'What should we do now?'

'And even if I had known where to go, I couldn't have gone any further.'

'Why not?'

'This is another rakshas' territory. Recently marked. Can't you smell the aura? Big one, too. I'm not challenging him, whoever he is.'

He picked Asvin up and set him down gently on the ground.

'Sorry,' he said. 'But I can't take you any further.'

'But . . .'

'What?'

'But you said you would take me there! You have to take me there!'

'I don't have to do anything, right?' The rakshas sniffed the air and whistled. 'Wait, I know that smell,' he said. 'Akus. An uncle of mine, I think.'

'So there's no trouble! He wouldn't think you were challenging him!'

'I *think* he's an uncle. Very far from sure.' Akab shook his huge shaggy head. 'No. In any case, I don't know which way to go. The forest's a big place, you know. And you don't even know if the girl you're chasing will be where we're trying to go. Whole plan was doomed from the start, if you ask me.'

'No! The gods will smile upon us! Take a chance, Akab! My heart tells me my luck will not fail!'

'Good for you. In that case, you don't need me around, do you?'

'What happened?' asked Asvin, bewildered. 'A few seconds ago you were fine. And now, suddenly, you abandon me like this! There was no doubt in your mind ten minutes ago!'

'Hadn't really thought about it. Suddenly struck me that this wasn't going to work. Sorry, Asvin. I could take you back to my lair, if you like. But my mind is made up. I will not go any further.'

'But what will I do now? You can't leave me like this!'

'Maybe your gods will take care of you,' said Akab, a trace of irritation in his voice. 'Not really my problem, is it?'

Asvin briefly considered threatening Akab with his sword, but wisely decided against it. His shoulders sagged.

'Please, Akab,' he said. 'Do not do this to me. I need your help. Just get me to Maya, that is all I ask.'

Akab shrank to human size. 'It is almost as if someone told me not to go any further,' he growled, almost to himself.

'Trust me,' said Asvin, putting on his most imploring expression. 'The gods are with me. Be a true friend, and you will be rewarded.'

'We are in a dangerous forest, in the territory of a rakshas older and craftier than me, completely lost, with no idea how to get to the place we want to get to, and no idea if getting there is even going to help us find a person who might already be dead. And you are confident that you will save the day somehow?'

'Yes. I believe it with all my heart.'

'It's a one in a million chance.'

Asvin smiled. 'I'll take those odds,' he said in his most dashing voice.

'Wonderful. I, on the other hand, won't. It's a stupid plan. Forget stupid—it's not even a plan.'

'That's why it's going to work.'

'But . . .'

'I will not fail. I cannot fail,' said Asvin. A cloud shifted in the sky, and a beam of light illuminated him, making his strong, clear eyes, his perfect teeth and his invincible armour shine brightly.

He held out his hand. 'Are you with me?'

'No,' said Akab, and disappeared in a puff of smoke.

Asvin stood in silence for a few minutes, watching the smoke dissolve into nothingness, watching the light that had suddenly blazed around him fade away slowly as another cloud obscured the sun.

He saw it clearly now. He had reached the point where it would all change. Where he would put all doubt behind him, and emerge tried by fire, clearer, stronger, a Hero not for Kol, but for the whole world.

He sank to his knees. I gave up reason a long time ago, he thought. But my faith will not fail me now.

A single ray of sunlight broke through the clouds and lit up the ground around him.

He bowed his head and prayed.

He prayed for a sign. He prayed for deliverance. He prayed for a light to guide him through darkness.

And the gods heard him.

And there was light.

He opened his eyes, and saw his shadow in front of him, wreathed in a red glow. He rose, and spun around, drawing his sword.

On a low branch of a tree in front of him sat a firebird.

It looked like a peacock, but instead of blue and green its plumage was a burning, glowing mixture of scarlet and orange. Slow flames licked its folded wings, and it gazed at Asvin through sparkling ruby eyes.

It cried out, once, harshly, and took flight, trailing smoke and sparks in its wake.

Asvin raised his arms in thanks to the gods and ran behind the firebird, his heart filled with joy and wonder. Bird and hero sped through the trees like a spreading fire, and the shadows of the forest turned and fled in awe as they passed. Asvin was in a trance, his mind on a higher plane, not even noticing that he was running deer-fast, and that his feet were not touching the ground. All he could see before him was the burning bird-shape, a torch to destroy all evil, a flame to lead him to victory, its fiery wings beating in time with his own fervent heart.

Far behind him, a green-haired warrior-woman swore softly, turned into a hare, and set off in pursuit.

Various small animals whistled and cheered in appreciation as the trio flashed by. They were a tough audience, but they all recognized that the bar had just been raised.

Elsewhere . . .

'Stop,' says Zivran, pounding the Table in wrath. Time stops, and the GameWorld freezes.

Zivran looks at the others, his face showing rage and hurt in equal measure.

'I will not have My world treated thus,' he thunders, and they start in surprise at the intensity in his voice. He seems to grow larger, and thunder rolls across his brow. 'I will not have My rules broken,' he says, and his wrath seems to grow with every word. 'Which one of You did this?'

'I do not understand, Zivran,' falters Petah-Petyi, aghast at this sudden transformation. 'What happened?'

'It is clear,' says Zivran, eyes blazing in fury, 'that one of You has been tampering with My world. Tsa-Ur's suspicions were justified after all. Who sent that firebird to Asvin? And why? Had I not made it abundantly clear that direct intervention of this nature was to be avoided at all costs? You cut away at the foundations of My Game, and I will not tolerate this!'

'Wait, Zivran,' says Stochastos. 'Are You, like Tsa-Ur, accusing Me?'

'About time, too,' says Tsa-Ur jubilantly. 'I knew it all along.'

'Why?' asks Zivran, turning to Stochastos. 'Why, Stochastos?'

Stochastos's face is perfectly composed. 'I have not done anything, Zivran,' he says. 'That firebird was not Mine.'

'Liar,' says Tsa-Ur, 'You are exspossed! Your time hass come! Zsivran! I demand You exspel Him from the Game!'

'Your forked tongues stretch too far, Tsa-Ur,' says Stochastos coldly. His shadow changes; it becomes more irregular, and strange sharp shapes seem to dance on its edges.

'Peace!' cries Petah-Petyi. She walks across to Zivran, and places a soothing hand on his arm. 'Zivran, You cannot accuse Stochastos blindly. We have all watched Him, and I do not see how He could have sent that firebird into the world. Yes, Your world has been tampered with, and I understand Your pain. But let Us not break ancient friendships over a Game. It is, after all, just a Game. And more importantly, it has not even begun.'

'No,' says Zivran. It seems impossible, thinks Sambo, crouched in a distant corner, that the huge, menacing god crouched over the GameWorld was ever the gentle, woolly-headed spirit he knew as his master.

'I will not leave the Table,' says Stochastos in a voice of jagged ice, 'until My guilt is proved.'

'Very well,' said Zivran. 'I will study the patterns of My world in the Creator's Mandala, and will learn who was responsible for the firebird. And when I have found the culprit, He—or She—will leave the Table, and trouble My Game no longer. Is that agreed?'

The others nod. Tsa-Ur is already hissing mockingly at Stochastos.

They wait as Zivran closes his eyes and speaks a Word, and the GameWorld slowly spins in the opposite direction. They watch time unravel in the crystals before them, fascinated; they see the firebird fly backwards, sit on the branch and then disappear; they see Asvin spin away and sink to his knees. Then he rises

*again, and gestures angrily; smoke appears and disappears, and
the rakshas Akab materializes in front of Simoqin's Hero.*

*Zivran speaks another Word, and the GameWorld freezes
again. And then Zivran snaps his fingers, and the World spins
forward in the right direction. Time starts again, and soon the
firebird, Asvin and Red resume their odd procession, racing
deeper into the heart of Vrihataranya.*

Zivran opens his eyes. He looks shocked.

'Why?' he mutters, almost to himself.

*He looks up, at Stochastos. The chaos-lord fidgets nervously.
An endless pause. Then Zivran speaks.*

*'I beg Your pardon, old friend,' he says. 'I suspected You
wrongly. Tsa-Ur, please leave, and do not return.'*

'What?' All Tsa-Ur's heads rear backwards in shock.

*'I should have guessed it was You all along,' says Zivran,
shaking his head. 'All that criticism, all those vicious comments.
I am disappointed in You, Tsa-Ur. And I no longer want to
know why. Please leave.'*

*Tsa-Ur's heads turn in rage and astonishment towards Petah-
Petyi and Stochastos. He finds no sympathy in their stern gazes.*

'You have made a misstake,' he says slowly. 'I am innossent.'

'Sambo,' says Zivran, 'please show the Serpent the way out.'

*'Did You not hear Me?' Tsa-Ur rears up. 'I ssaid, I did not
do it!'*

*He looks around wildly, meets stony silence and screams in
rage. His hoods swell, and his necks elongate swiftly. He towers
over the GameWorld, fangs gleaming, eyes suffused in rage.*

*'Tsa-Ur,' says Petah-Petyi. 'Leave, or I will see to it that
You never see a Game-Board again.' The dice in her hand
start spinning of their own accord.*

*Worlds are born and die in the tense moment that follows.
And passes.*

'It'ss a consspiracsy,' mutters Tsa-Ur, shrinking back to his normal immense size. He looks around, his spirit broken. He meets Petah-Petyi's cold glare, Zivran's look of enraged bafflement and Stochastos's terrifyingly friendly smile.

There is nothing more to say. Tsa-Ur slithers off.

Sambo, as he flies to the Bahan Park to bring Tsa-Ur's mount to him, shoots a reproachful look at his master. But he cannot help laughing guiltily inside his own heads; for his master's cunning deception has worked perfectly, and out of nowhere Sambo suddenly sees a glimmer of hope. Somehow, he thinks, his master and his mad Game might just succeed. Of course, fooling the whole pantheon was next to impossible, and snatching victory from the jaws of the sceptical Tsa-Ur was a small start.

But, thinks Sambo jubilantly, at least it was a start.

Stochastos, Petah-Petyi and Zivran look at one another and sigh as the GameWorld spins on before them.

'Bad business,' says Zivran regretfully. 'Still, there was nothing else to do. He was deliberately trying to sabotage the Game.'

'I knew it was Him from the start,' lies Stochastos. He drums his many fingers on the Table. 'But, O wisest of worldsmiths, should We now remove the serpent's intervention, make this firebird disappear and set things back to normal?'

Zivran bows his head and thinks for a while. 'No,' he says finally, 'the firebird is a part of the world now. To remove it would involve further direct intervention, and I do not want My rules to be broken again, even in a good cause.'

'Does this mean Asvin, Kirin and Myrdak will all arrive at the same place at the same time?' asks Petah-Petyi. 'An interesting confrontation, even if forced on Us unnaturally by the scaly deceiver.'

'Not necessarily,' says Zivran. 'We do not know what Tsa-

Ur intended. It is possible that the firebird leads Asvin to the nundu's lair, where Maya awaits him. After all, his quest is to save Maya. Admittedly, in a standard Game, he would have faced his rival first, and the girl would have gone as a prize to the winner. But I hardly need remind You, My friends, that this is no standard Game.'

Petah-Petyi sighs sadly. 'So Kirin and Myrdak will duel. It would have been better if this fight had been left for the actual Game.'

'Why?' asks Stochastos.

'It is clear that the ravian cannot lose the fight,' says Petah-Petyi, 'for if he does, the ravians cannot enter, and We have no Game, for We have no real duality. And I like the other boy—Kirin—so much better. But then, he is in the crystal before the Nameless Chair, and so he is dispensable. Myrdak is not. What a shame.'

'Perhaps Kirin will escape with his life,' says Stochastos. 'I quite like him too, and do not want to see him die just yet. The GameWorld should save him for the real Game. I will try and control Kirin Myself until the Players arrive, if that is all right with You, Zivran.'

'Certainly,' says Zivran courteously, grateful to himself for forgetting to shave. The beard helps to conceal his small, secret smiles.

The GameWorld spins on.

13

Consider the bull.

It is well known that a raging bull (*Jekl amota*) has an innate tendency to lower (or raise) its horns until they are roughly parallel to the ground, emit small puffs of steam from its nostrils, tap the ground menacingly and then charge in a straight line. This aspect of a bull's personality is exploited by Olivyan matadors, who nip aside smartly and stick swords into bulls for sport, and by Psomedean mathematician-farmers, who like to harvest crops while simultaneously proving geometry theorems.

This same tendency (to charge forward and continue charging forward until contact is made with a solid object) renders a bull, and indeed any bull-headed creature, rather ineffective as a combatant in a place full of sharp corners and breakable objects.

Such as a Xi'en porcelain shop. Or, say, a labyrinth.

However, there are traditions to be followed, and Psomedean minotaurs have been employed as security officers in underground mazes down the ages, despite the considerable expense incurred owing to the need for frequent wall reconstruction.

And the Civilian, when reinforcing security in her labyrinth after the disastrous incident at Cravenstick Street, had chosen the very best of the Psomedean minotaurs—the malevolent, scimitar-horned bull-men known as the Vindiciti Hoplites.

But the arrival of the minotaurs was only one of the drastic changes that had taken place in Kol since the disastrous incident at Cravenstick Street, and their presence in the labyrinth was a well-kept secret (revealed only to people they killed).

The explosion at 32B, Cravenstick Street had left Kol scarred, with a gaping wound that went far deeper than the huge, hollow crater full of corpses of innocents that the shocked city saw the morning after. For the first time, the citizens of Kol knew that the war had begun, that it would take place not in some far-off battleground but on their very doorsteps. That the enemy was not some blundering monster who could be slain by gallant heroes, but an unknown, hidden killer who struck in the night, suddenly, quietly, mercilessly. And they saw the army of Kol finally revealing its strength and presence, saw Marshall Askesis and his soldiers entering the city, and vamans with huge, mysterious machines taking measurements and patrolling streets, and they knew that nothing would ever be the same again.

What did the Civilian do? She did what any other politician would have done in her place—she grew more powerful in the shadow of their fear, tightening the leash, striking out with all her skill at the powers within the city that sought to use this opportunity to weaken her. No longer would distractions suffice—all hero and villain organizations were disbanded and their members made city guards. The people were told that it was time for them to huddle close together, make sacrifices and have faith—and to that end, they had been given a hero, who was even at this moment in great peril, single-handedly mowing down the mastermind behind the Cravenstick Carnage. And perhaps more importantly, an heir to the throne of the ancient Kingdom of Kol had been found, which was surely a sign that the gods were behind Kol. The gates of the War Temple were opened, and the citizens of Kol saw the great soldier running bravely to battle, and wondered what exactly he was running towards.

The Civilian found that the powerful among the Kolis were only too ready to believe that the ravians were behind the Cravenstick Carnage. To her delight, she found that raising the spectre of mind control was a very efficient way of manipulating some minds herself. But she decided the public was not yet ready for the drastic revelation that the ravians were the enemy—it was made known, instead, that the enemy who had invaded Kol thus was not the Dark Lord, but a faceless invader from another world, perhaps ravian, perhaps not. And she had it said that there was no known way to defeat this enemy, but if the people kept faith, and trusted the powers that ruled them, all would yet be well. Of course, they had to pay more tax, and give away many of their belongings, and give up a certain amount of freedom as well, but that was all justified in the interest of public safety.

In this time of terror, the people of Kol, suddenly realizing that they were really no longer safe, turned to faith and superstition. And magic, because magic clearly had an important role to play in the city's defence—for instance, it was clear that the strange devices with curved dishes on top and spiky metal grids at the bottom that the vamans were placing at street corners all over the city were instrumental in some way in increasing and regulating the magic flowing through the air.

It was rumoured that magical objects would somehow keep this unknown terror at bay. These rumours were probably started by the merchants of Kol, who, ever innovative, found interesting avenues and opportunities to exploit the spreading hysteria. From the fashionable lanes of Keynsmith Bazaar to the seedy alleys of Lost Street, every market suddenly saw a massive spurt in an already roaring trade in artefacts, amulets, talismans, body parts of monsters and magicians, charms, potions and miscellaneous trinkets. Many former League heroes turned professional artefact thieves, travelling to nearby towns and returning with valuable objects, genuine and fake. And many others stayed within the city, stole magical objects from buyers and returned them to the markets, where they were sold again within minutes at higher prices.

The trade in fake magical objects had even affected some famously practical Kolis. For instance, it was whispered that Triog, the much-celebrated barman-owner of the Fragrant Underbelly, had discovered that the Complete Set of Skulls of the Prophet Doordarshan at Various Ages, that he had bought at great expense and mounted over the bar at Frags, was a dud. And that he had now sworn to add the skull of the asur who'd sold the set to him to the collection.

But by and large, though the Kolis grumbled out of habit, they didn't really mind being cheated in these terrible times—they knew that they were often being fooled, but it was comforting to have magical objects around, even if the spells on the objects they'd bought didn't actually work. Buying these artefacts made them feel they were doing whatever they could to protect their children, and that was a feeling worth a lot of money.

This strange acceptance of trickery by a normally bargain-obsessed people further illustrates the strange nature of the human mind, which hardly ever uses a straight line to travel between two points, choosing instead to deny, digress, meander, leap, swivel, and dance back and forth almost at random.

To celebrate this now, consider again, if you will, the bull.

The mind of a bull, or a bull-headed creature such as a minotaur, tends to work in a straight line, much like its body when charging.

For example, when the three minotaurs of the Vindiciti Hoplites standing guard at night in the small chamber that connected the Civilian's bedroom to the labyrinth were disturbed from their ruminations (which mainly concerned chewing) by Peori the ravian, who emerged suddenly from the labyrinth bearing a double-bladed spear, a map, and a ferocious expression, their thoughts were neither questions on the lines of 'How did she get here?' or observations like 'She looks like a vengeful goddess.' Instead, what they thought was:

1. Moo-ving object.
2. Moo-w it down.
3. Moo!

Having thought these three thoughts, they lowered (or raised) their horns until they were almost parallel to the ground, puffed steam from their nostrils, tapped the ground menacingly and charged.

Now a *ravian* mind is a creation of immense complexity, which thinks neither in lines nor in disjointed curves, but along a multidimensional helix too difficult for a human to comprehend. Intruders in the Civilian's labyrinth usually had their minds and their hands full trying to keep their minds and hands attached to the rest of their bodies, but Peori had raced through the maze without really paying attention to the traps and illusions and swinging blades; there was nothing there that could really trouble a ravian who knew the way.

Instead, she had thought chiefly of her lover and future husband Myrdak, far away in Vrihataranya, facing the demons on his own, calmly and efficiently executing the last stage of their secret, brilliant plan.

And she had thought of the not-so-distant future, and how wonderful it would be when the Houses of Hanash and Aegos were finally united. The Council would bow to their combined pressure and declare her and Myrdak Queen and King of all Obiyalis.

She had felt fleeting sympathy for Arathognan, and even for Kirin, whom she had never seen. Peori's was a compassionate soul. Of course, the corpses she had left all over the labyrinth on her way were not exactly shining examples of compassion, but they were unimportant.

And now, as she stared at the rapidly approaching and very pointy horns of three charging minotaurs, Peori's mind worked with its usual speed and brilliance. She'd done her research on minotaurs; she knew they were stupid and non-magical. She'd felt their presence before she'd climbed quickly up the trapdoor into the chamber.

She quickly altered their minds, telling them she was not to be touched, that they should submit to her will and spend the rest of their lives following her commands.

Excellent advice, no doubt, but there was a technical problem Peori had not considered.

Minotaur minds are small and simple, and work in a very straightforward fashion. Peori was a moving object, and they were charging at her. All her mental messages were received and filed away for later use; when the minotaurs stopped to think they would do everything she asked.

For the present, though, they were charging at her, and not in a position to entertain other thoughts. The word *stop* means nothing to the bull-headed. *Stop* is something that happens to other creatures.

And the chamber was too small for Peori to dodge the charging minotaurs. There was nowhere to run.

She stuck her spear into the minotaur in the middle. It was a vicious thrust, and should have killed him immediately. And indeed, after a succession of walls eventually brought him to rest he did feel a great deal of pain.

This, however, was *after* he had stuck his horns in Peori's shoulders and carried her through the wall into the library outside the Civilian's bedroom. He was aware throughout, no doubt, that there was a sharp object embedded in his chest, but he refused to let a small thing like that distract him from his single-and-straight-minded moo-vement.

Yelling in pain, Peori managed to detach herself and dropped to the floor. The minotaur had carried her through the wall and a bookcase on the other side; blood-stained books were everywhere, flapping like giant deranged moths. The minotaur stamped on her, over her, and carried on with his brethren in a straight line towards the next wall. The only other occupant of the library, Roshin of the Red Phoenix, blew a quick blast on a horn and ran out of the room before Peori sprang to her feet.

Ignoring the bright lights in her head and the warm blood flowing all over her black ninja clothes, Peori pulled her spear with her mind, but it was stuck too deep in the minotaur's chest. She ran back into the chamber, sending books flying out of her way, and blasted her way through the mirror into the Civilian's bedroom.

Just in time to see the Civilian and the Sadori Sisters running out of the room. The Really Pretty Sister slammed the door shut just before a storm of glass shards from the broken mirror shuddered into it.

Peori ran to the door and stretched out her hand. The handle turned, but the door did not open. Yelling in frustration, she pushed hard with her mind, and the door burst into tiny fragments.

Movement. Behind her. A dart streaking towards her neck swerved in mid-air and fell harmlessly to the ground.

She turned, and saw the Silver Dagger enter the bedroom through the broken mirror. He was clad in black, like her, and held a silver Artaxerxian dagger in his right hand. He assumed a warrior's stance, and beckoned her with his left.

'We have unfinished business, you and I,' he said quietly.

Despite the pain, she laughed.

A white blur streaked down the corridor behind her.

'Do you really think you can stop me?' she asked, almost gently. A cloud of glass shards rose up in front of her, and hovered threateningly between them.

And then she screamed in pain and surprise.

For a deadly Silver Phalanx assassin, too small and fluffy for her ravian senses to recognize as dangerous, had leaped into the air and sunk his teeth into the back of her neck.

His name was Steel-Bunz.

In the next second, many things happened.

462

Samit Basu

Peori's hands sped backwards to dislodge her assailant.

A swarm of glass pieces buzzed furiously as they hurtled towards the Dagger.

A silver dagger spun through the air.

The Dagger closed his eyes, waiting for death.

His dagger buried itself in Peori's throat.

Steel-Bunz leaped acrobatically to safety as the ravian fell dead.

And the Dagger opened his eyes again, to see glass raining prettily to the floor, a deadly jagged hailstorm inches from his feet.

He walked carefully over to Peori and shot two blow-darts into the ravian's neck, just in case. So attractive, he thought sadly. What a waste.

He picked up Steel-Bunz, who was snuffling around the doorway in a languid, debonair sort of way, and patted his head.

'Outclassed at last,' he said. 'But I'm glad it was you.'

14

The children of the Desolate Gard sat around Maya, staring at her with blank eyes. She forced herself to look at the ground, at the ceiling, anywhere else—something about their faces filled her with terror. She imagined a world where all humans were like this. If ravians ever discovered how to overcome magic—or simply killed all magic-users—such a world was actually possible, she thought.

She'd tried to talk to the children. They had not replied. She had tried to push her way through them, gently at first and then in sudden panic. They had pushed her back on to her cot, where she now sat, looking at the door behind them. She'd even lit a fireball and set it hovering threateningly over their heads. They had not even blinked.

Myrdak was not exaggerating, she realized. She would have to kill them before she could leave the room.

She sat back on the cot, wondering whether there was any point in turning them all into mice or something. It would take time and a lot of energy; the nundu's presence interfered with her magic, and she was still drained from turning Djongli into a bat. Even if I succeed, she thought, there were so many people outside. She couldn't possibly have overcome them all.

She sat back, heaved a sigh and wondered what would happen next. Experience had taught her that she would not have to wait too long.

And she was right. Just half an hour later, goosebumps suddenly ran honking all over her body; she felt cold little paws on her leg.

'Hey!' said a voice. It was a dry, old little voice, like thin parchment rustling in a very gentle breeze. Maya, who had opened her mouth to say 'Hey!' shut it, and opened it again.

'Huh?' said the voice. Maya shut her mouth. She looked towards her leg, and saw a little wrinkly chameleon, its large eyes almost shut, clambering slowly upwards, its skin matching the colour of hers.

'What? Please don't kick out, because it would kill me and then the world could not be saved. What?' said the chameleon. Maya shut her mouth.

'May I speak? I will anyway,' said the chameleon. Maya nodded. Little paws clambered further up her leg, tickling insanely, and reached her knee. He was quite a powerful colour-changer; even while moving, he was matching the colours behind him quite perfectly.

'Perhaps it would be best in the interests of propriety if I did not crawl further up your leg. Could you give me a hand, please?' he said.

Maya put a hand on her knee, and the chameleon jumped on to it. Maya brought her hand up to her face and observed him closely. He looked terribly frail, as if a sudden gust of wind might kill him. She could feel his heart beating through his thin skin.

'Put me on your shoulder and look at me, slowly, and reverently, for I have never let anyone see me thus before', said the chameleon. Maya put him on her shoulder, and his skin turned the dark brown of her robe. Her gaze, however, was more amused than reverent. She opened her mouth to speak again. 'W . . .'

'Who are you?' said the chameleon. She shut her mouth.

'Greetings, Maya. I will ask you again, in the interests of my safety, not to make any sudden movements, for though I know you will not, and I will not die just yet, I also know you will not because I asked you not to, and I also know that I asked you not to, so I did. Never mind that, it is not important. What is important is *me*. Who are you? I am an unwaba. A what? An unwaba. Nunwaba? What is a nunwaba? No. Not a nunwaba. An *un*waba. *The* unwaba, in fact, because as far as I know there are no other unwabas in existence. And I should know, because I know everything. What? Yes. Perhaps it would be a good idea if you just listened to me. I will say everything you intend to say on your behalf,' said the unwaba.

Maya, who had opened and shut her mouth several times in the course of this speech, opened and shut it again. And opened it again, but the voice said 'All right. Go on, then. Thank you. I have come here from Kol, where I have resided since its very foundation, with one purpose alone—to meet you here, now, and guide you in your tasks until my death, for I will die soon, and this world will die too unless you succeed in carrying out the tasks I set you. I don't understand. I realize you don't, but it would help if you just listened instead of interrupting.'

'B . . .' said Maya.

'But I . . . Listen. I am the unwaba, oldest of chameleons. But before I was a sleepy old lizard, I was a god. There was a message I was supposed to deliver . . . a long time ago, when the worlds were young, when the gods believed . . . and when I was too slow, I was banished, I was sent here, to experience the mortality I had doomed the gods' creations to, to taste the bitterness of age and pain and all things physical. But my banishment, like my present form, is limited, and draws to a close. And while I have suffered in your mortal world, I have become a part of it—I have taught, but more importantly, I have learnt. This world has given me new ideas . . . and new ideas are precious indeed to old gods. I wish to repay my debt before I die. And as the gods would have it, I have a chance. For great peril threatens this world. What peril? The ravians? No. The ravians threaten other races on the world, but not the world as a whole, for they seek to preserve it—and rule it. This world's creator, a fickle, careless god, has invited other gods to play a game on it—and this game is a game that will destroy this world. For in this game there is victory only for idle gods—for the mortals on their living world-board, there is only death. The gods do not care what happens to their creations, for they can always create more . . . and I should know, for I was like them once. This world and this body have taught me the error of my ways. Which is why I have taken upon myself the task of informing you that escape is possible—an escape only I can lead you towards. For I am the unwaba, oldest of chameleons, and wisest of all creatures that walk or swim or fly the material paths of this world. You look like a lizard to me. That is because I do look like one, so there is no conflict of argument, is there? I see. So you're the wisest creature on this world?

Yes. How do you know that? I know everything. You're all-knowing? That is another way of putting it, yes. Omniscient is yet another. Or Eitiktikitamohapechoonpaka, which in the forgotten language of the island of Omphalos meant Magnificent Saurian Whose Very Foundations Emit Wisdom. And I would like to point out that what you are about to do might hurt me . . .' said the unwaba.

Maya closed two fingers around the unwaba's mouth. 'Now listen closely,' she said. 'Though if you are all-knowing, you knew I was going to do this. I like you—even if you're lying, you're funny, and I will listen with great interest to anything you have to say, but no matter how old and wise you are, you will let me speak for myself. Is that clear?'

She released her grip on his mouth. '. . . clear? Yes, it is clear, Maya. However, you must realize that I tend to see words as words that are spoken, and not really consider who spoke them, because I have never had a conversation before. So when you wish to speak, you will have to hold my mouth—gently—and say your words yourself. That will . . .'

She shut his mouth. 'That will not be a problem,' she said. 'By the way, what is the colour of my underwear?'

'. . . wear? You are not wearing any. You did not expect to leave Vanarpuri in such a hurry. I . . .'

'I see. So you really know everything.'

'Yes, I do know everything. Remember, though, that there really are no absolutes, and while I *think* I am all-knowing, so do most gods. They are often wrong, and I could be too. Even worse, I could be misleading you deliberately, though I am not, but I could still be wrong. And this can only be explained using logical leaps the human mind is not yet capable of comprehending, which, of course, is just another way of saying that I cannot be bothered to explain. So the things I think will happen might not actually happen. Bear in mind, though, that I have never been wrong so far.'

'So you know everything that will happen in the future as well?'

'It is difficult to explain. Let us just say that I have . . . a script. A history, if you will. And I like to see things carried out according to that history. No, it is actually more difficult than that. Let us say . . . I know what *happened*, not what *will happen*. I have a record, not a plan. But I know what happened independent of time or space, so I know I said the words I will say in what you, in simple terms, call the future.'

'So you're saying everything is predetermined? That choice means nothing?'

'. . . thing? Not at all. Choice and free will determine everything. It is just that I know . . . not what you will choose, but what you *chose*. That does not mean I am binding you in anyway to choose what I will. It is just that . . . I have, let us say, a recorded history of one particular set of choices and events. At any moment, things might go in a different direction. Your choices and decisions are not really decided by me. Perhaps an even better way of putting it is this—I have no choices, *you* do. I know I might be wrong, but since I exist independent of time (though this body is bound to this space and this time) I also know that I said what I said at this time. Which means that even if I know now whether I will be proved wrong in the future, I cannot tell you, because I have no choice but to say now what I know I said now.'

'Why not?'

'For such is my burden. Such is my punishment. While I am banished for my laziness, for your mortality, I am bound to your time and space, and I must obey its rules. And the gods . . . my former friends . . . seem to have forgotten that

I am here. It is all very frustrating, and adds years to my already formidable age. I know, for instance, that there are many very important things I could have told you right now that would have been of more use to you than what I am saying, but I cannot say them, because I know this is what I said. Hence the only one here bound, or deprived, in any sense, is *me*. And these children, of course. To put it more neatly, you are the only one here not deprived in any sense. Except in terms of freedom of movement. Do you see what I mean? I am forced to keep babbling like this, just because I did.'

'Stop talking, please, and give me some time to digest all this.'

She held the unwaba's head gently for a while, lost in thought. Then she let him go.

'Perhaps we should speak of practical things now, in terms of what is to be done to get you out of here and on your way towards saving this world.'

'Perhaps we should,' said Maya.

'How nice it would be if I did not know that I will fall asleep very soon. And if I had the option of speaking faster.'

'Yes. I get the picture. Now tell me—what should I do?'

'Do not try to shake me awake when I fall asleep. It might kill me.'

'All right. Now stop wasting time and tell me what I must do. How am I to fight the gods and save the world?'

'You cannot, of course, fight the gods, because they are all-powerful. The only thing to do is try and outwit them. For people who know everything, they are remarkably dim-witted. For now, all you will know is that a great game is being played, and you and Kirin and Myrdak and everyone on this world . . . except me . . . is a piece in this game, where

470

the world itself is a board. You are one of the important pieces, and everything you do is being watched. I, however, am invisible to them.'

'Why did you choose me and not any other important piece?'

'I chose you because, as you can see, I chose you. Because I knew you were the one I chose. And I have travelled great distances at great peril—for I am the unwaba, the oldest chameleon, and with physical age comes crippling frailty.'

'I know who you are. You used to live in Kol, you said?'

'In the Civilian's palace. I used to wake up once a year and give her sound but confusing advice.'

'I could have guessed. How did you get here, then, being so old and frail?'

'Is it not obvious? I knew you would be here now. And I knew where this place was, and how to get here from the place where I was. As to how I physically got here, I walked part of the way and took rides for the rest, setting off in time to get here now. If you are done asking useless questions and wasting the time you had before I fell asleep, which I will do shortly, can we proceed?'

'Yes.'

'You will now apologize.'

'Sorry.'

'Sorry what?'

'Sorry . . . O unwaba, oldest and wisest of chameleons.'

'It does not matter. I have another . . .'

'I have another question. You said these gods were playing with our world. How do I know you are not a god tricking me in some way? Why should I trust you?'

'Have I asked you to trust me or believe me?'

'No,' admitted Maya.

'You will now apologize again,' said the unwaba, blinking in a peeved sort of way.

'Sorry . . . O unwaba, oldest and wisest of chameleons.'

'It does not matter. Now listen to me. You must, at the correct time, set out from this place and find Kirin, the man you love, if he survives his duel with Myrdak.'

'Kirin is not the man I love.'

'Yes he is.'

'No he's not.'

'I am sorry, but he is. I would say you two are meant to be, but we have already discussed my views on fate and choice, so you two are not meant to be. We will see. In any case, you must escape from this place and seek him out.'

'I love Asvin.'

'Yes.'

'You do not know what I think. Is that clear?'

'Yes.'

'Go on. How am I to escape from this place?'

'You cannot escape now. You must remain here for now, and wait for the opportune moment.'

'But what will that be? It must be before the ravians arrive, because otherwise I will be forced into a marriage with the ravian king.'

The unwaba's eyelids indicated curiosity. 'Indeed? And that is repugnant to you? I would not have asked, but apparently I do not know how your mind works.'

'Of course I don't want to marry the ravian king! I love someone else!'

'I see. But . . . this is interesting . . . marrying the ravian king would prevent you from loving someone else? You are the first human I have met who has faced this problem.'

'I thought you were all-knowing! Of course I can't marry

someone when I love someone else! And I can't be with the man I love if I am married to someone else.'

'Considering that you will have to commit murder, and indeed have already done so, I find it curious that you should find adultery so loathsome.'

Maya considered this for a while.

'But I murdered monsters,' she said, but she looked doubtful.

'What if you married a monster?'

'I don't know. What's the point of all this? When do I escape? Tell me more things I need to know! How is Asvin? Where is he? How is Kirin? Where is he?'

'There was no real point to our discussion on marriage, except that gods—and former gods—are always fascinated by their creations' notions of right and wrong—which usually develop completely independently from any divine instructions. But enough of that. On to your friends Asvin and Kirin. They are both heading towards the Temple of the Black Star, where Myrdak took you to raise the pillar of light. Kirin and Myrdak will fight their duel there, and Asvin will join them in the middle.'

Maya stared at him in horrible fascination. 'You can't know all this,' she said. 'I don't want to know what happens next.'

'All right. I will not tell you.'

'No, tell me. What happens? Will they be all right? Will they kill Myrdak? How will it all end?'

The unwaba's eyelids were almost shut.

'I am afraid I must apologize to you. I realize it would have been so much more useful had I been less disgruntled and more specific at this time,' he said very softly.

'Don't fall asleep. Please don't fall asleep. Tell me what happens now.'

473

She was too tense to keep shutting the unwaba's mouth, so she just let him speak.

'It will be a meeting that will truly change the fate of the entire world. That will shake even the gods as they sit, floating in black chairs around the horizon of this world. Do you know what will happen? Yes, of course I know. What will happen, then? When two such powers collide, it is very rare that both survive. In this case, the winner of this epic confrontation will be . . .'

The unwaba fell asleep.

15

The Fragrant Underbelly was so full it was bulging at the sides.

Two very short figures, both wrapped in black cloaks, walked towards the bar where Triog, the famous three-headed, six-armed barman-owner of Frags was pouring out drinks for the Teetotallers Anonymous Old Girls' reunion.

One stepped behind the counter and greeted Triog, who nodded, excused himself, and led the newcomers to the stairs.

They walked upstairs, past Too Many Cooks, past one floor of guest rooms. On the third floor, Triog paused and said, 'Amloki, are you sure you can afford this? The conference room is very expensive.'

'That's all right,' said the khudran. 'I'm just a guest anyway. *He's* paying.'

Triog turned to the other black-cloaked figure and stared at the top of his head with interest. 'And who are you?' he asked. 'I don't have to know, of course.'

'Then perhaps it is better,' said Mod Vatpo, 'if you don't.'

Triog nodded and led them to the Fragrant Underbelly's

private conference room, as patronized by maharajas and monks (of the wealthier monasteries). It was a rich, large candle-lit, wood-panelled, thick-carpeted room, dominated by a rectangular mahogany table, around which twenty-four chairs were arranged symmetrically. The table was smooth and polished, except for a large crack in the middle—the conference room had recently been used by a group of Skuan chieftains trying to resolve a property dispute using modern methods, who'd ended up settling it using the traditional but always effective say-it-with-axes method.

'Thank you, Triog,' said Amloki. 'Could you send our drinks, please?'

'Of course. One Dragonjuice, stirred not shaken, and for you, sir?'

'Flimango juice with vodka, please.'

'No, no,' said Amloki. 'You must try a Dragonjuice as well. They're wonderful.'

'Very well, if you insist. Dragonjuice for me too.'

'Coming up. Do you gentlemen require additional security? I could have some of Yarni's boys make sure you are not disturbed,' said Triog.

'No, thank you,' said Mod.

'Actually, speaking of disturbances,' said Amloki, 'a friend of mine might come looking for me in a while. Could you send him upstairs?'

'Yes.' Triog closed the door behind him softly as he left.

Mod and Amloki discovered there were no pegs around low enough to hang their cloaks on, and so folded their cloaks and put them on the table. They sat.

'Are you sure we are alone?' asked Mod.

'Yes. Triog is famous for his discretion,' said Amloki. 'I remember, there was this one time . . .'

'Can I trust you, Amloki?' asked Mod.

'Of course.' The khudran put on a discreet expression. 'I am even more discreet than Triog, and know many secrets of extreme importance. If I were to reveal what I knew . . .'

'Good,' said Mod. He looked worried. 'There is something I must ask you first. Are you out of favour with the Civilian?'

'No, not at all. It is just that Marshall Askesis needs my help. Because of my expertise in matters of city administration, you see.'

'Of course. I merely ask because I have not seen you around the palace in a while—and so much has changed in the palace, has it not? These are times when people not seen often are people who might never be seen again.'

'Ah.' The khudran made an eloquent, world-weary gesture. 'Work, you know. Duty, duty. You're a busy vaman yourself.'

'Yes, that I am.'

There was a quiet knock on the door.

'Our drinks are here already,' said Amloki happily. 'The speed at which Triog reels them out is quite amazing. Come in!'

A huge stalactroll entered, set their drinks down on the table and left without a word.

Mod took a sip of his Dragonjuice and made a face. 'It's very strong,' he said. 'I had better wait until I have finished telling you what I came here to tell you before I drink all of it!'

Amloki laughed politely and leaned forward, his face serious. 'Tell me.'

But Mod seemed to be transfixed by a huge painting on the wall across the table. 'Good gods!' he exclaimed. 'What is that?'

477

Amloki looked at the painting. 'That's a two-headed ogress from Ventelot,' he said. 'Triog's mother, I suspect. There's a distinct similarity between Leftog and her left head. But surely that is not what you brought me here to ask.'

'No. But what an ugly painting!'

'I'm sure his father found her attractive. It's funny how she has two heads, isn't it? I wonder if his father had four heads or one.'

Mod laughed. 'You are a philosopher, noble khudran. Let us get to business.'

He took a sip of his Dragonjuice. Amloki did too, and made a face. 'It tastes funny,' he said. 'Too much salt, or something.'

'Do you want to ask for another? I could wait,' said Mod courteously.

'No, no. Tell me—what did you want to ask me?'

Mod rubbed his hands together and looked troubled. 'I do not really know where to start,' he said slowly. 'I have a—a proposition to make which is rather—distasteful.'

Now Amloki looked troubled. 'I'm engaged,' he said defensively.

Mod's stern features cracked in a sudden smile. 'A political proposition,' he said. 'I suppose the best way to say it is to just—say it. Would you like to work for the vaman king?'

Amloki looked puzzled. 'How do you mean, work for him? I'm sure the Civilian would lend me to him quite happily if he wanted. We are, after all, allies.'

'No,' said Mod. 'I mean—work for him, as the Silver Dagger, at any price you want.'

'You want me to ask the Silver Dagger to work for the vaman king? But I don't know who he is.'

Mod smiled. 'You know as well as I do that there is no point carrying on this ruse, Amloki. We know.'

Amloki took a long gulp of the Dragonjuice in front of him.

'I realize that I have placed my own life in jeopardy by revealing that I know the Dagger's other name,' said Mod. 'I hope that by holding myself to ransom like this, I have succeeded in convincing you of the seriousness of my intentions.'

The Dagger smiled ruefully. 'How did you find out?' he asked.

'We have our eyes and ears in the palace, and all the drama over the last few days . . .'

'Yes. It was getting slightly obvious, I suppose.'

'Yes. I am afraid that if you continue to work for the Civilian, others will guess as well.'

The Dagger sighed and shrugged. 'It was fun while it lasted.' He took another deep swig of his drink and made a face. 'This drink is quite bad.'

'Work for us, Amloki,' said Mod. 'Work for the vaman king. The Silver Dagger of Kol is dead. He is exposed. But with us, you could work wonders. And we could give you whatever you want. Help you set up your own little empire.'

'I thought we were all on the same side,' said Amloki. His words were a little slurred. He shook his head.

Mod gulped his drink and set it down. 'Of course we are,' he said. 'But the future belongs to the vamans, Dagger. And we would like to share it with the khudrans.'

'Indeed,' said Amloki. 'In that case, I have a question for you. I've been meaning to ask you this for some time, but we just haven't had enough time to catch up until now.' He blinked; he seemed to be having trouble keeping his eyes fixed on Mod.

'What is that?'

'Why did you betray the vaman king?'

'What do you mean?'

'Why did you give the ravian the map of the Civilian's labyrinth?'

Mod looked startled. 'Preposterous!' he spluttered. 'I did nothing of the sort.'

Amloki shrugged. 'It must have been you, only the vamans were given the updated maps,' he said, shaking his head. 'I have another question.' His eyes were noticeably glazed, and his words rolled into one another.

A smile spread slowly over Mod's thin lips. 'Are you feeling all right, dear Amloki?'

'What did you put in my drink?'

Mod laughed dramatically. 'And so the famed Silver Dagger meets his match, and meets his end,' he said. 'Not a gallant end, or a violent one. Not in some faraway land in some secret mission, but in his favourite tavern in his own city.'

Amloki lurched forward and slumped onto the table.

'The poison I slipped into your drink,' said Mod, 'is a rare poison extracted from the skin of the tree-frogs of Vrihataranya.'

The Dagger opened one eye. 'What kind of tree-frog?' he asked.

'Not that it would mean anything to you now,' said Mod with some asperity, 'but its scientific name is *Melnkohli flaikatcha*.'

The Dagger opened his eyes, sat up and grinned. 'Oh,

that's all right then,' he said, his voice deep and clear. 'I'm immune to that.'

He laughed aloud at Mod's aghast face. 'Please,' he said, 'did you really think that whole look-at-the-picture-while-I-poison-your-drink trick was going to work with me?'

Mod looked as if he was about to lunge at the Dagger.

'Now listen,' said the Dagger. 'Don't make any sudden movements.' Something in his voice stopped Mod. He looked around wildly, as if expecting a horde of pashans to come bursting through the walls.

'My reasons for asking you not to make any sudden movements are twofold. Would you like to know what they are?'

Mod froze. 'Yes,' he said.

The Dagger jumped off his chair lightly. 'Reason Number One,' he said, 'is that the poison I slipped into your drink, using a move far more subtle than yours—I mean, really, look at the picture?—is a powerful nerve toxin that will cause paralysis and instant death if you decide to horse around. Reason Number Two is that if, by some freak coincidence, you are immune to this poison—and I would advise you not to take a chance and see if that is the case—even if you are immune to this poison, I can kill you with my bare hands in under two seconds. Time me, if you like.'

Mod's face was livid, but he stayed where he was.

'However,' continued the Dagger, 'I do have an antidote, which I will administer to you if you answer all my questions truthfully.' He smiled at Mod, and bowed. 'In a word, dear Mod—checkmate.'

'I know you have no intention of letting me live. But know this: you cannot win,' snarled Mod. 'The ravians will defeat you. They are more powerful than you can imagine.'

'You gave the ravian the map. Why?'

'The vamans and the ravians work together, you fool. This world is ours. The Age of the humans has passed.'

'You're lying,' said the Dagger smoothly. 'The vamans and the ravians are not working together. You betrayed your king when you gave Peori the maps. Which must mean that the Rebel Union of Marginal Labour is still alive. And you, Mr Vaman Ambassador, are a traitor, and have been playing a very dangerous game.'

'The Rebel Union is alive, and is vaman civilization's only hope,' snapped Mod, a fanatical glow transforming his face. 'Listen to me, Amloki. It is not too late for you to see sense. Against the ravians there can be no victory. You must understand this. But *with* the ravians, the galaxy is ours. Harmony and prosperity stretching across the stars. It is no idle dream, but as yet it is still a dream—a dream you can help transform into reality. Save me, and join us. I came to you because you alone in the Civilian's palace are worthy of salvation. You alone can carry light into the heart of darkness.'

'Right,' sneered the Dagger, 'which explains why you tried to kill me even before I refused your offer. An offer you only made to play for time while your poison took effect.'

The vaman sighed. 'True, alas. But now, to save my own life, I will make you the offer again, in earnest. Work for me. Work for the Rebel Union and the ravians. We will pay you anything you want. With you on our side, we could take over Kol in a matter of hours.'

There was a soft knock on the door.

'Ah,' said Amloki. 'My friend is here.'

'Wait, Dagger!' said the vaman. 'Think this over. There will not be another chance.'

'I thought it over before I came here,' said Amloki. 'The answer is no.'

The vaman's shoulders sagged. 'Very well. Have it your way. I concede. How did you find me out, may I ask?'

'Well, we have been following you, just as you have been following us,' said Amloki. 'There's very little trust in the world, isn't it?'

He headed towards the door. 'And the person who finally gave us the answer,' he said, 'is the person waiting outside this door. Who will be Kol's weapon against your beloved Rebel Union, and your masters, the ravians. You will be pleased to see him—he has been a friend of mine for a while, but he has been a friend of yours for a long, long time—probably as long as you can remember.'

He opened the door and a vaman entered. A vaman who was thinner than Mod, but even so looked almost exactly like him.

Mod's jaw dropped. 'No!' he cried. 'It cannot be!'

Amloki grinned. 'I'm afraid it is,' he chuckled.

'It's impossible!' cried Mod. '*Gaam?*'

'I wish I could say well met, brother,' said the vaman, shaking his head sadly.

'No!' cried Mod. 'You are dead! They found your body!'

'Of course they found my body. What they did not mention was that it was alive.'

'You are dead! You have to be!'

'I am afraid,' said his twin, 'that I must disappoint you.'

'So you have joined the humans, and betrayed our people. And predictably, you have joined the weakest side possible,' snarled Mod. 'Well met, *brother*, and goodbye. I curse you and your evil allies to eternal darkness!'

He lunged forward, his hands aiming for Gaam's neck, and fell dead.

Amloki covered Mod's body with a cloak. 'Evidently you got the looks *and* the brains in your family, Gaam,' he said. 'Now, this is your last chance. Are you sure you want to take his place?'

The vaman looked at him with eyes of steel. 'Of course I am.'

'Chances are the ravians will kill you.'

'I know.'

'And by telling us what goes on in Bhoomi you will be betraying your people.'

'I know. But history will forgive me. This Rebel Union must be found and destroyed. And there are others, Amloki, others close to the vaman king. The king himself—he is not above suspicion. I will go underground this very night. There is much work to be done. But what about you? Where will you go?'

The khudran shrugged. 'The Silver Dagger is dead,' he said. 'Mod must have told the vamans—he could only have received the information that helped him narrow it down to me from the vamans—and he might have told the ravians as well. Word will spread.'

'Will you be in danger?'

'Danger is not the problem. My home and my people will have to be protected, but that is easily accomplished. I had always hoped to be killed, not exposed—but we can't have everything, can we? In any case, I do not have time to spend brooding on the Dagger's death, because the Civilian has rewarded me for saving her life by giving me a task more dangerous than any I have attempted yet.'

'May I ask what this task is?'

'It involves a journey to that popular holiday destination, the Dark Tower of Imokoi.'

'Alone?'

'Of course. The Phalanx is needed here more than ever before. And I leave tonight,' said the Dagger, 'so let's get to work now . . . Mod Vatpo. We should get you into his clothes, for a start. And you'll have to lose those earrings.'

'What a shame. I was rather fond of them,' said the vaman, beginning to unfasten his earrings, which were Orange.

16

The ancient paved road that had once gleamed like a streak of mercury in the moonlight as it ran from Epsai to the Temple of the Black Star was now covered with earth and leaves and littered with colourful, chubby corpses pierced by manticore darts.

It was a warm and sunny afternoon. The Great Forest was still and silent; every leaf Kirin stepped on crackled like lightning, every bird that took to flight far above him sounded like a drummer gone mad. The air was stretched, taut; the forest waited, the gods watched as Kirin drew closer to the clearing, closer to the ruined temple where the world's fate would be decided.

He felt Myrdak's presence, looming ahead of him like a small mountain, even before he saw the light from the clearing through the trees. He gripped his Shadowknife firmly, and the black blade rippled and burned with black fire, razor-sharp edges slicing through the tension in the air. It shuddered in excitement and grasped its master's hand; it was hungry.

The ravian was near. Waiting.

Bright sunlight bounced off green leaves, beckoning Kirin closer. He walked between the trees, towards the light, rapidly at first, and then slowing down when he beheld the broken walls, the scattered stone slabs, and the watching ring of tall, ancient trees, creepers like curtains waiting to draw themselves aside and reveal a cheering audience.

But this was no colosseum; no emperor would decide which of the gladiators would live or die. There was only one other person on this lonely stage. Myrdak was sitting, eyes closed, in the lotus position on a tilted marble slab in front of the great altar. Two small rocks flew around him in tilted, elliptical orbits.

Kirin walked slowly into the clearing, looking this way and that, blinking a little as sudden, strong light slapped him in the face.

In keeping with the drama of the scene, a sudden wind rustled through the Great Forest, and in the trees far above, birds and animals chattered excitedly as they gathered closer, watching through the leaves. Dry leaves and twigs circled and rustled across the clearing. In the lower branches, birds stuck their necks out, looked at Kirin and Myrdak and ran to cracks and holes in the trunk, wishing they had windows to slam behind them.

Kirin walked forward. Through stumps where great pillars had once marked the entrance to the Temple, through a wide corridor still echoing faintly with long-forgotten hymns sung by long-dead ravian priests. His heavy boots crunched gravel and twigs; the Shadowknife hissed softly as it twisted and hardened. Myrdak did not move.

Kirin kept walking until he was about fifteen feet away from the seated ravian.

'Where is Maya?'

Myrdak smiled and opened his eyes. The stones revolving around him dipped gracefully and landed gently on the ground.

'Well met, son of Narak,' he said.

There was a sudden whistling sound.

From the shadows far to Kirin's right, three bone-darts hurtled towards him.

Kirin waved a hand, annoyed, and the darts jerked out of their trajectories and clattered harmlessly amidst the stones.

'Is this your idea of an ambush?' he asked.

'No,' said Myrdak. 'Manticore!' he called. 'It is all right. We will duel, and you are not needed here. Make sure we are not disturbed.'

Twigs snapped in the shadows beneath the trees to Kirin's right as Manticore slouched off. Kirin caught a glimpse of the shaggy man-lion in a stray ray of sunlight and felt no sorrow at his departure.

'I was merely verifying that you were a ravian, since I am not entirely sure what you are,' said Myrdak. 'Since you do appear to be a ravian, my given word compels me to duel with you. For had you been a rakshas, or any other demonic or lower creature, I need not have honoured any agreements we had made.'

'I'm touched. Where is Maya?' Kirin asked.

'Maya is safe in a ravian stronghold. She sends you her best wishes, and her sympathies in advance.'

'She should be here. How do I know she is even in your power? Or that you have not killed her already?'

'You have no way of knowing. But that does not matter, does it? You are here in any case, and you must face me. If you run, my sword will be in your back, not your heart; the choice is yours.'

'If you do not give me proof that Maya is alive, I will summon a hundred rakshases and dragons to my aid.'

'Afraid to face me alone, Dark Lord?'

'We are not alone. Your . . . cat just tried to kill me.'

'It was just a test. You passed.'

'Where is Maya?'

'Maya is alive and well. If you must know, we are to be married.'

'I must see her.' Kirin gripped the Shadowknife in both hands, and wondered how to look menacing.

The ravian smiled broadly. He drew his sword and in one swift motion, crouched in a warrior's stance, sword in his right hand suspended over his head, pointing towards Kirin. He beckoned with his left. His sword glittered in the sunlight; his hair swished lustrously as he shook his head. Bloody hero, thought Kirin.

'It does not take a great deal of foresight to predict you will never see Maya again,' Myrdak said. 'Now, Kirin, do we waste more time talking, or should we begin?'

'Aren't you going to offer me a chance to join you and redeem myself?' asked Kirin.

'No,' said Myrdak, raising a surprised eyebrow. 'Why would I do that?'

Kirin shrugged. 'Forget it. I thought you would.'

He swung the Shadowknife upwards as Myrdak leapt at him, and their swords met in a mighty clash that sent a bolt of power surging through the temple, raising a cloud of dust, leaves and stones and almost uprooting the watching trees.

They sparred warily at first, circling, looking for weaknesses—Kirin looking rather half-heartedly, because he knew he would find none.

Then Myrdak threw aside all caution and attacked him

from every side at once, pulling a blizzard of stones behind Kirin with his mind, but Kirin weathered the storm easily, sending the stones whirling in Myrdak's direction with a wave of his hand, and following with a stone-storm of his own. The currents of their ravian power raged through the temple, and soon they were surrounded by a whirlwind of detritus even as their swords sizzled, clanged and danced an intricate weaving pattern through the air; each sword-clash was preceded by a complex set of thrusts and parries foreseen and forestalled. It was clear very soon that Myrdak was the better attacker, the more experienced ravian duellist, and a smile spread slowly over his face as Kirin began to retreat, pushing the swirling stones behind him further back as he panted and ducked, his feet treading lightly over the uneven stone slabs as he braved the ravian's cool, ferocious onslaught.

Myrdak drew first blood.

Kirin saw the ravian's sword streaking towards his left arm before the blow landed—he turned, but the distraction let a rock jump past his mental defence, and as he deflected it back into the cloud Myrdak cut a deep gash in his left forearm. Kirin leapt back, yelling in pain; with a supreme mental effort, he sent the ring of flying debris soaring into the air, showering into the roots around the clearing.

He's a better warrior than me, thought Kirin. Defeat is inevitable.

But even as Myrdak leapt forward, sword pointed at Kirin's throat, another thought flashed into Kirin's head: He's a better *ravian* warrior than me. Fight like a rakshas, you fool.

Myrdak's eyes widened in mid-leap and he swerved frantically as a huge fireball blossomed out of Kirin's hand

and blazed towards his chest. It singed Myrdak's right shoulder and died in the air; but Myrdak had been wounded. He fell, rolled and retreated, gasping, and they both stood for a while, panting, never taking their eyes off each other.

Kirin broke the silence with a scream as he tried to pull all his rakshas magic into his finger. But Myrdak saw the lightning bolt streaking from Kirin's hand towards his chest even as raw magic surged through Kirin's veins; he leaped aside, and the crackling white streak of power blasted a tree behind him into fine powder. His eyes widened, and he raised his sword in salute.

'Impressive,' he called, settling into another battle-crouch.

Kirin willed another lightning-bolt from his fingers, but his magic was almost spent; there was a fizzle and a spark, but no lightning. Myrdak laughed aloud, and sprang at him— his sword arced towards Kirin's throat.

The Shadowknife twisted into a shield and blocked the blow before Kirin could even begin to react. Then it melted into a spear, streaking at Myrdak's heart like a snake; Myrdak ducked and swerved just in time, and sprang out of range. Kirin, cursed himself broadly for inexcusable stupidity— for not using the Shadowknife's incredible powers so far. *Perhaps,* he thought, conducting an orchestra of hundreds of flying stones and one raging ravian had put it out of his mind. He turned the Shadowknife into a broad sabre with an eye in the middle of the blade. The eye winked at Myrdak.

Myrdak's eyes widened, and his breathing quickened. 'The Shadowknife of Narak,' he said quietly. 'You come prepared, Dark Lord. But even the Shadowknife cannot save you today.' His hand flicked upwards; a small sharp stone cannoned into Kirin's forehead before he could move. He cried out in pain.

'I am too fast for you, and too strong,' said Myrdak, stepping back again. 'Your demonic tricks cannot save you for long. I have given you but a taste of my powers; behold me now in the fullness of my wrath.'

'Do shut up,' said Kirin, sending him flying backwards with another fireball. Blood trickled down his nose and into his mouth. The cut on his left arm, he noticed, had healed already; Qianzai's blood was evidently still at work. The large, scaly black scar wasn't pretty, but then, reflected Kirin as Myrdak charged again, roaring, he had never been pretty in the first place.

The firebird streaked like a comet towards the Temple of the Black Star, Asvin trailing in its wake. V-shaped clouds of smoke soared upwards with every downward sweep of the magical bird's wings. Asvin did not see them; the fiery shape in front of him filled his eyes and his mind with divine inspiration. So enthralled was he that he ran right over two dead rakshases without even noticing.

Not too far behind, Red was grateful for the smoke-trail; a random tiger had distracted her by trying to eat her as she streaked by. She'd been forced to stop; tying a tiger by its tail to a branch some distance from the ground took time.

She'd been gaining on them for a while, in the form of a spine-tailed swift, a black and white winged arrow flitting through a maze of branches. She could see the firebird clearly now, even hear the branches crackling as the flaming wings incinerated them. She zoomed closer, revelling in the intoxication of fast flight.

Even closer; she was in the firebird's flight-trail now, zooming through the trail of quick-warmed, rising air.

And then her mind went blank; she swerved wildly to her right, crashed into a tree, and fell to the ground, a confused bundle of feathers and bones.

Because the firebird, soaring in fiery majesty in front of her, had suddenly exploded in a huge ball of flame.

Red hit the ground and transformed into a snake, forcing her new cold-blooded form to lie absolutely still, letting her bird-brain dissolve away, grateful that snakes had no limbs to flap wildly. She slithered into a hollow under a tree root and stuck her neck out, tasting the air with her tongue. What had happened?

Asvin emerged from his trance in a most undignified manner, falling to the ground kicking wildly and rolling until a tree trunk stopped him. He lay still with his eyes closed, his brain replaying the huge explosion in light green inside his closed eyes. The firebird was still beating its wings inside his eyes, a green ghost fading away into darkness. An instant later Asvin's superb training showed; he opened his eyes and sprang to his feet in one smooth motion, his sword drawn and perfectly poised.

There was a terrible smell in the air, and a huge shape was running towards him. He blinked, confused, still slightly dazzled.

A whistling sound. He saw the dart streaking towards him, swung his sword and cut it in half. He blinked again, getting used to the sudden darkness.

The manticore jumped out of the undergrowth and faced him. His great fangs were drooling and covered with blood and bright hair; his Avrantic face was drawn in a horrible leer; his tail was poised, bulging, and pointing at Simoqin's Hero.

Great ones fight for earth and sky
Vermin who disturb them, die! he said, and shot Asvin
thrice in the chest.

Asvin looked down, slightly dazed, at the bone-darts
sizzling and smoking in his chest. He fell backwards heavily,
his head suddenly light. Then he sprang up again, brushed
the darts out of his armour, and charged at the manticore.
The manticore's tail bulged as he prepared to shoot Asvin
between the eyes; but before he could, a massive blue fireball
crashed into his side, sending him flying.

As the great cat coughed and lay smoking on the ground,
Asvin's jaw dropped. A beautiful red-haired, red-clad woman
warrior was running towards him, yelling a strange battle
cry. Her eyes were shining strangely. She paused, and looked
at him sternly.

'Get out of here,' she said. 'Keep going in the line the
firebird was flying. Run. Go.'

'But . . .' said Asvin.

'Go,' said Red in a voice of thunder.

Asvin nodded frantically, gathered up his trailing dhoti
and ran ahead. Manticore staggered slowly to his feet, still
stunned.

Soma: That's a manticore.

Tamasha: Disgusting. Wonderful. Kill it.

Soma: Manticores are harder to kill than dragons.

Manticore's eyes cleared. He looked around and saw Red.
He shot a dart at her. She turned it into a daffodil. He
screamed and charged. Red ducked, but the manticore was
quick; he swatted her with a giant paw and she flew into a
tree, almost cracking her spine. Manticore roared again, and
padded towards her.

Soma: That *hurt*.

Tamasha: Run.

With a great spring, the manticore reached Red. She turned into a mouse, thus cunningly avoiding the giant paw that would have cracked her spine, and ran between Manticore's legs and into the undergrowth. Behind her, the great cat screamed, turned, sniffed, and gave chase.

Soma: Manticores have a powerful sense of smell.

Tamasha: If he doesn't kill us, I'll kill you myself.

Cat and mouse raced through the forest.

The Temple of the Black Star had been razed to the ground by Kirin and Myrdak. It could not have been destroyed more efficiently by a herd of rampaging mastodons. The ring of trees around the clearing had felt the force of their battle as well; some trees had been uprooted, others burnt. Others merely had huge chunks ripped out of their trunks by spells, blades and even fists.

Kirin and Myrdak, both streaked with dirt and blood, stood in the centre, panting like tired dogs. But their heads were unbowed, their backs were straight, and their swords were poised for the next attack.

In the last few minutes, they had hit each other with pillars, ripped up stone slabs beneath each other's feet, lashed each other with creepers, and cut each other with swords (or whatever weapon the Shadowknife was at the point of contact). Looking at the two, it was clear that Myrdak was winning; though he was smeared with ash and blood, he was in clearly superior physical condition, and it was beginning to show. Kirin's clothes were in rags, and he was covered with scars. Even the power of Qianzai's blood was beginning to succumb; the last few cuts had been deep, and were bleeding freely.

But the Shadowknife was keeping Kirin in the contest. He had reached a point where his body was not responding to his mind as quickly as Myrdak's; his father's weapon, though, seemed to be one step ahead of his mind. Now a spear ripping through Myrdak's defences, now a shield warding off a crippling blow, now a club bludgeoning away a hurled missile, the Shadowknife melted and hardened, hissed and struck with a will of its own. But while it had drawn blood several times, it had not been fast enough, and its marks seemed to have left Myrdak completely unaffected—he had bounced back from every blow, shrugged away every cut, and his smile had been growing broader and broader as the duel progressed.

They leaned on their swords and looked each other in the eye.

'You are a worthy opponent, Dark Lord,' said Myrdak. 'I have never duelled for so long before.'

'You won't have to duel for much longer.'

'Perhaps we should find another way of settling this.'

Kirin launched a ferocious assault with fire and sword and spear, driving Myrdak to the edge of the clearing. Myrdak pulled a creeper to his left hand and seemed to run up the trunk; he fenced horizontally for a while and then launched himself over Kirin's head to the centre of the clearing.

'We could do this for hours,' he said, 'but we both know that I would win in the end. I have another solution. A quick one. I challenge you to a Trance-Duel.'

Kirin leaned on the Shadowknife and looked at him in surprise. A Trance-Duel?

He had read about Trance-Duels. They were the accepted method of settling matters of honour among high-caste ravian clans. Lower castes were not even allowed to be present at Trance-Duels, let alone participate. In a Trance-Duel, two ravians crossed swords, looked each other in the eye and opened their minds to each other. Then they would stand still, frozen as statues, while their minds battled on another plane of understanding, free of the limitations of their physical bodies. Whoever won the battle on the mental plane would emerge from the trance first, and then would have the chance to strike down his still-frozen enemy with one fatal thrust. But for a high-caste ravian like Myrdak to challenge someone he thought was a mixed-caste was quite unprecedented.

'A Trance-Duel?' asked Kirin. 'I cannot Trance-Duel. I don't know how. I never went to Asroye, remember? I never played by your high-caste honour codes. I'm afraid we will just have to do this the old-fashioned way.'

Myrdak sighed. 'As you wish. Before we resume this dance, though, I urge you—reconsider. You know you cannot win this duel. And in a Trance-Duel, Kirin, you will not be humiliated. You will die with honour. I tire of this physical contest. I will not meet another opponent such as you on this world, I know it. We both know we can never be allies. Let us end this now. One swift, clean stroke, and it will all be over.'

'No,' said Kirin. 'We will stay here, on this plane, on this world, and end this as we started it.'

Myrdak shrugged. 'As you wish,' he said.

And then they both turned and looked at the shadows under the trees to Myrdak's left. Where something silver had shimmered in the darkness.

'What new trick is this?' asked Myrdak, leaping back.

'Not one of mine,' said Kirin.

They leaned on their swords, both secretly glad to take a longer break, and watched as Asvin walked into the clearing, sword in hand, eyes blazing in anger and suspicion.

'Hello, Asvin,' said Kirin. 'What on earth are you doing here?'

'He has come to save Maya, as have I!' cried Myrdak, his face flooded with joy and hope. 'And you are outnumbered now, Dark Lord! Did I not warn you? Have not the gods decreed that the triumph of good over evil is inevitable?'

A mouse ran into a bush.

A manticore leapt in after it.

The mouse, to avoid getting squashed, turned into a worm.

The manticore uprooted the bush with a mighty swipe.

The worm turned.

And a second later, the manticore nearly jumped out of his skin in surprise as another manticore stood before it.

'Let me let you into a secret,' said this new manticore, a sprightly young female with a heart-shaped Avrantic face, 'I'm tired of running.'

Manticore backed away, confused.

'I've tried pushing you out of the way. I've tried transforming and escaping. Do you let it be? No, you don't. You just keep on coming, don't you?'

Manticore snarled. His tail swung up.

'Oh, now you want more!' cried Red, utterly frustrated, turning into her usual battle-form again. 'I warn you, I am an immensely powerful magical being, and if you attack me again, I will kill you!'

Manticore shot a dart at Red. She turned it into a banana.

'Are you even listening to me? Are you deaf?' she yelled.

Manticore *was* deaf, and thoroughly confused. He took two steps backwards, and crouched, preparing to spring.

'Now I haven't known you for very long, and this is going to take up a great deal of my magic,' said Red. 'But somehow I suspect it's worth it.'

Manticore sprang, and landed with a surprised croak. Red sank to the ground, exhausted. She had turned him into a frog.

She lay on the earth, drained—he had been more powerful than she had expected—and watched him hop around, completely confused. Earth magic flowed up through her veins, and she sat up again, shaking her head.

'Do you feel the earth shaking?' she asked the frog.

Manticore-frog croaked in a depressed way. He could hear again, but that was hardly a consolation.

'Something very big is happening,' said Red. 'Can you feel it? The world is changing. And not too far from here, too. I'd better get going.'

A fly, formerly a resident of Manticore's mouth, buzzed near her ear. She snapped her fingers and it fell, stunned. She picked it up and placed it in front of Manticore-frog.

'Goodbye, then,' she said, patting him on the head. Then she sprang to her feet, and ran off in the direction Asvin had taken.

Manticore leaped around some more and considered the world from a new angle. It seemed rather depressing.

There was a hiss behind him. He turned. A green snake was staring at him, his tongue flickering, his black eyes fixed on the plump frog.

'Queshtion One. Do you believe in karma? In divine

retribution? In the what-goess-around-comess-around princsiple?' asked the snake.

'No,' said Manticore, too depressed to rhyme.

'Right. Queshtion Two. Do you believe in ghosstss?' asked the snake.

'No,' said Manticore, wishing he could impale this green wretch with a well-aimed dart.

'Well, you shhould,' said the snake. 'Often, when there iss an excsesss of pssychic energy in one sspot caussed by, ssay, a violent, unnatural death, a conschiouss sspirit manifesstss itself and might even posssesss the body of a nearby being of lessser intelligencse.'

'So what?' snapped Manticore.

'Sso, busster,' hissed the snake, 'Queshtion Three. Do I look familiar to you? Do I? *Do I?*' His head darted from side to side.

'No. Go away,' said Manticore.

'Ssorry, busster, but I got ssomething to ssay,' said the snake. 'I been following you around for dayss, looking for revenge, and thiss iss ssweet.'

He slithered up to Manticore and looked him in the eye, thoroughly enjoying the glimmer of fear he saw there, which blossomed into a veritable blaze as the frog looked into the snake's mouth and suddenly realized he was about to get a much closer look at what *really* went on inside a snake's head.

'My name, before you shhot me, busster,' hissed the snake, opening his mouth wider, 'wass Ssweetie Croak.'

'Don't listen to him, Asvin,' called Kirin. 'He kidnapped Maya. I don't know where she is.'

'Asvin knows better than to be ensnared by your lies, Prince of Darkness,' said Myrdak. 'This is the moment I have been waiting for; the turn of the tide. Our powers combined can overcome even you!'

Asvin stared at them as they stood, blood-spattered, dust-sheathed, looking daggers at each other.

'Er . . . who are you?' Asvin asked Myrdak politely.

'He's a ravian. Wants to take over the world,' said Kirin.

'I am Myrdak,' said Myrdak. 'Peaceful ambassador and herald of the ravians, sworn enemy of the Dark Lord.'

'You don't look very peaceful to me,' said Asvin. 'Kirin! Where is Maya?'

'I told you, I don't know,' said Kirin. 'He's got her somewhere.'

'Lies!' hissed Myrdak. 'Asvin! Do not bandy words with the lord of rakshases! Listen to me. You stand on a knife's edge. The future of your world is being determined here. I would advise you to choose a side.'

All three began to circle warily, swords ready.

'Listen to me, Asvin,' said Kirin. 'Just get out of this. This is no place for a human. You could end up dead.'

'No!' said Myrdak. 'It is the gods' will that he should be here, representing the humans, and he should help me strike you down!'

'Could you both please begin at the beginning?' asked Asvin.

'We're a little busy,' said Kirin through gritted teeth. 'Have a seat, and I'll explain everything later.'

Asvin pointed his sword at Kirin. 'It seems to me . . . Dark Lord,' he said, 'that you seem anxious to get rid of me.'

'He knows Maya loves you,' said Myrdak. 'He has

abducted her. He wants her for himself. Join me, and we will overcome him.'

Asvin looked at him, perplexed. 'Where *is* Maya?' he asked after a while.

'He's got her,' said Kirin.

'*He's* got her,' said Myrdak.

'One of you is lying,' said Asvin, his eyes narrowing.

'*You think??*' roared Kirin.

Myrdak looked deep into Asvin's eyes. 'The choice before you is very simple. Good, or evil? What say you, Hero?'

'It's never that simple,' warned Kirin. 'I know you and I are not friends, Asvin—but we once swore an oath of eternal brotherhood. Do you remember?'

'That was before I learnt you were Danh-Gem's son,' snapped Asvin. 'And leader of the forces of darkness.'

He turned to Myrdak. 'The choice, as you said, is very simple. In fact, there never was any choice to start with. The Hero of this world is yours.' He pointed his sword at Kirin.

'I don't want to fight you,' said Kirin. 'Please, just go. This is not a place for humans.'

'I am more than human,' said Asvin scornfully. 'I am chosen by the gods, and my armour is impenetrable. I will not be ensnared by your evil wiles.' He stepped closer to Myrdak; they stood, shoulder to shoulder, ravian and human, blades pointed at the son of Danh-Gem.

'You are a gift from the gods in my time of need,' said Myrdak warmly. 'Quick, hand me your armour!'

Asvin turned, and pointed his sword at Myrdak. 'On second thoughts,' he said, his face suddenly clouded with doubt and sorrow, 'I choose Kirin.'

'Bad choice,' said Myrdak, stepping forward.

His sword arced through the air in a blur and cut Asvin's throat.

'Stop,' says Petah-Petyi.

The GameWorld stops spinning.

'Save him,' she says.

'No,' says Zivran.

'He cannot die thus. He does not deserve death.'

'Many die who do not deserve death.'

'True. But he is a Hero. He has Our favour. He cannot die now.'

'He just did. You saw it.'

'No. He is an important piece in the Game. Bring him back to life.'

'I cannot.'

'You will not, You mean!'

'No, Petah-Petyi,' says Stochastos, no trace of mockery in his voice, 'Zivran means he cannot.'

'I do not understand,' says Petah-Petyi.

'I did not Myself, till just now,' says Stochastos, and his voice is filled with wonder. 'Zivran, what have You done, You crazy old bastard?'

'Watch the Game,' says Zivran calmly, though his hands are shaking visibly. 'Please just watch the Game.'

'Bring him back to life,' says Petah-Petyi softly, and a cold wind runs through Zivran's garden.

Zivran shakes his head. 'My rules forbid it,' he says.

'These are not control crystals, are they?' asks Stochastos, watching Asvin's body, handsome and noble in death, lying on the scarred earth.

503

Zivran does not reply.

'When heroes die before their time, there are . . . consequences, Zivran,' says Petah-Petyi. 'I know it is unfair, that many brave and innocent souls are lost when wars rage through the earth, that We are often directly responsible for their deaths. But this . . . I have never seen anything like this before. This was not a Hero's death.'

'I suspect that is the whole point of Zivran's Game,' says Stochastos. 'Poor Tsa-Ur was right all along. Should We leave now, Mistress of Chance? For if We stay, We throw our own lives in danger. The Players are almost here. And if Our safety is important to Us, it is best . . . that We tell them this Game cannot be played. That this Game—that this world cannot be controlled, merely watched.'

'But They will destroy the world if We do that,' says Petah-Petyi. 'And They will destroy Zivran as well.' She looks aghast.

Stochastos looks at Zivran and laughs aloud. 'And I thought I was the lord of chaos,' he says. 'Well, old friend? What happens next?'

'I throw Myself at Your mercy,' says Zivran. 'I have failed. But this was no idle jest, no malicious prank. This was My dream. I wanted to show the Players a Game where the world was free. Where the pieces played the Game, not cold-hearted, disinterested gods. I wanted to fool them, and save My creation. But I could not fool even You, and You trusted Me. I do not know what to ask from You, My friends.'

They stare at each other in silence.

'Well, the Players are not here yet,' says Stochastos, smiling his crooked smile, 'and I confess I really want to know what happens next. Shall We pretend this conversation never happened?' Black stars twinkle in his eyes.

'I do not know,' says Petah-Petyi. 'I cannot decide.'

'Then until You do,' says Stochastos, waving his hands, 'let Us follow Zivran's excellent advice and watch the Game.'

'But . . . Asvin is dead,' says Petah-Petyi. 'It was not his time to die. Kirin had a miraculous escape not too long ago. Why cannot Asvin have one too?'

'The GameWorld caused Kirin's escape, not Us,' says Zivran. 'Asvin's own choices killed him. To change that is to change the very essence of My Game. I cannot allow it. Truly I cannot. I loved him Myself, and I mourn his departure. But the Game has chosen.'

Stochastos shrugs. 'Between life and death, between order and chaos, there are always compromises,' he says. 'Trust Me. I speak from experience. Now if You two would just stop talking . . .'

The GameWorld begins to spin.

Kirin watched Asvin's body fall to the ground. He was too stunned to speak.

'A tragic loss,' murmured Myrdak, wiping his sword on his thigh. 'Shall we continue?'

'Why?' asked Kirin, his voice breaking. 'He meant you no harm!'

'He would have, eventually,' said Myrdak equably.

'Do you honestly see yourself as good?' asked Kirin. 'Because he *was*, you know. He was a good person. A hero. And you killed him.'

'He was just a human,' said Myrdak. 'And besides,'— his eyes brimmed over with innocence—'I did not kill him, you see. *You* did.'

The Shadowknife twisted and turned into a samurai katana.

'Let's not talk any more,' said Kirin.

'Good idea,' said Myrdak.

Their swords clashed again, and the duel resumed.

Neither noticed Asvin's body vanish.

Myrdak tugged, hard, on Kirin's mind. More surprised than threatened, Kirin pushed him out. He staggered backwards in doing so, and Myrdak, taking a step backwards too, swung his sword lightly, so that its tip met the point of the Shadowknife. He looked into Kirin's eyes, and thrust with his mind.

His eyes were strangely hypnotic. Kirin fought, but felt his will succumbing to the ravian's pull, saw the ravian's eyes shine and then roll until only the whites were visible. His own vision blurred, and the world faded.

Welcome, said Myrdak, *to the world of the Trance-Duel.*

Kirin's eyes opened, and he looked-around.

A plain, spacious dojo; a broad, square wooden sparring floor, plain white walls. Myrdak, clad in white, stood about twenty feet in front of him. His own clothes were black. Their weapons were missing.

Freed from the confines of your poisoned world, in this realm of pure thought, I will strike you down, said Myrdak.

He sank into a formal bow, then rose. A sword appeared in his right hand.

Kirin looked at his own hand, and thought hard of a sword.

Nothing happened.

Myrdak smiled grimly.

It takes a great deal of practice, he said, *before an actual weapon can be produced.*

Kirin tried to break free of the trance, return to the forest.

Nothing happened.

He tried to conjure up a fireball.

Nothing happened. Somehow, Kirin was not surprised.

Take us back, he said.

Why? asked Myrdak, not unreasonably.

He ran at Kirin, swinging his sword.

Red peeked out from behind a tree.

She waited for a minute, puzzled.

Kirin and the ravian—who looked very handsome in the sunlight, sword shining and everything—were just *standing* there, looking into each other's eyes, sword-tips touching. Not saying anything, and not moving at all. They did not even seem to be breathing. It was most odd.

Soma: What are they doing?

Tamasha: Staring contest?

Soma: Has someone else put them under a spell?

Tamasha: And where is Asvin?

'Wait,' whispered Red. She sniffed the air curiously. No, no rakshases were nearby, and the fear radiating through the clearing came from the numerous small animals watching the contest, spellbound, from the trees. A gentle wind blew across the clearing; dust particles, rising from shattered stones, pirouetted in the sunlight and came to rest on the two figures.

Soma: Kirin's bleeding badly.

Tamasha: I think they are in some kind of trance. Do you think they're mind-wrestling or something?

'Possibly. What should I do?'

Soma: Set the ravian on fire.

Tamasha: First good idea you've had in weeks. Do it, Red.

507

'Should I? What if their minds are locked together or something? What if Kirin gets hurt?'

She walked into the clearing (Soma: No! Don't! Tamasha: Shush. Go on) and stared at them curiously. She shivered slightly when she saw that the pupils of their eyes seemed to have disappeared; just the whites were visible, staring eerily into nothingness, though their faces were turned towards each other.

Soma: We need to talk.

Tamasha: Walk up between them and wave in front of their faces or something.

Soma: Don't be silly. Don't touch them. Don't speak to them.

Tamasha: All right, then: What do we do?

'I don't want to set them on fire,' said Red. 'It might hurt Kirin.'

Soma: Choose swiftly, but choose carefully. Whoever wins this contest will rule the world.

Tamasha: You could just kill both of them and take charge of the world yourself.

Soma: If she killed both of them she'd just be stuck in the middle of the jungle with two corpses and no ideas.

Tamasha: True.

Soma: I might point out that they might not be stuck like this forever, you know. The longer you take to make up your mind, the higher the chances that they'll snap out of it and kill you in surprise.

Tamasha: All right, let's be cautious then. Let's just wait and see who wins this duel, and befriend him.

Soma: First sensible thing you've said in weeks.

'But why would the winner want to befriend us in any case?'

Tamasha: Wait, wait. Even if the ravian wins, there's no question of joining him.

Soma: Are we being too hasty? What if we could make peace with the ravian? Discover other worlds?

'Don't be stupid.'

Tamasha: We need to find a way to kill him without harming Kirin.

Soma: But we cannot think of a way.

Tamasha: Let's just wait here, then, until they come to and stick their swords through us, yes?

'This might be the most important decision I will ever make,' said Red. 'So both of you must make a promise to me.'

Tamasha: Name it.

Soma: Yes, Red. Anything.

'Please, please be quiet.'

Red looked from Kirin to Myrdak, and wished more strongly than she had ever wished before that just for *once*, she could make up her minds about something.

This Trance-Duel, thought Kirin, is not going well.

He ran around the dojo in yet another undignified circle, Myrdak in hot pursuit.

My mind has been trained, he thought, trained by Behrim. Freed of my body, I could probably take him on. If only he didn't have that damned sword.

Stand and fight, coward! yelled Myrdak.

Take me back to my world and I'll give you all the fight you want, panted Kirin.

Myrdak stopped and laughed aloud. Kirin stopped too, and looked around wildly. The walls of the dojo seemed to be closing in on him.

What a pathetic end to the Dark Lord's career, Myrdak sneered.

You'll have to catch me first, said Kirin, wishing he had something snappier to say.

Not necessarily, said Myrdak. The ravian closed his eyes and pointed a quivering hand at Kirin's feet.

The wooden floor suddenly softened. Kirin's feet sank into it.

Myrdak's eyes opened. *Now hold still,* he said.

Kirin struggled furiously but the floor had become like quicksand; he could not move, any movement only pushed him further into the pulpy boards. He strained and pulled to no avail, as helpless as a hypnotized bird before a snake.

Myrdak walked up to him slowly and deliberately, savouring each step.

Not like this, thought Kirin. Anything but this.

He thought of Maya, of his father, of Kol, shut his eyes and strained with all his might.

Nothing.

There was nowhere to run.

Myrdak reached him, and raised his sword.

I am sorry, Dark Lord, he said. *It is over. You lose.*

In a smooth, fluid motion, he swung his sword into Kirin's neck.

In the real world, Myrdak's eyes opened.

The Trance-Duel was won. The advantage had been gained. He had three seconds before Kirin came out of his trance.

One second would have been more than enough. Three gave him enough time to take a short vacation before killing Kirin.

With a triumphant yell, he lunged forward, the perfect warrior, arm extended to bury his sword up to the hilt in Kirin's heart, to hurl him from defeated trance to painless death.

It seemed to be going perfectly well; Kirin stayed frozen.

And then Myrdak's roar of victory turned into a startled cry.

There was no sword in his hand. He looked around, wildly, and his eyes almost fell out of his head in surprise.

'*Maya??*' he gasped.

Red stuck Myrdak's sword into his chest with a single hard thrust.

'Looks like it,' she said.

Myrdak looked down, amazed, at the sword-hilt sticking out of his chest.

'But . . .' he gasped.

'I know, I know,' said Red sympathetically. 'We barely got to know each other. Pity.'

She set his head on fire for good measure.

Myrdak fell, burning, to earth.

A gasp behind her. She turned, smiling. The Shadowknife wilted in Kirin's hands.

He sat down on the ground and gaped at her.

'Hello, Kirin,' she said.

'G . . .' said Kirin. He looked at Myrdak's corpse, impaled and burning.

'Guh,' he said, pointing. 'Guh.'

'Yes, yes,' said Red, nodding.

Soma: He used to be brighter before.

Tamasha: Been through a lot, poor dear. Where's Asvin?

Soma: I *like* him. Must be all the scars.

Kirin struggled for words and failed entirely. He

511

considered saying 'Guh,' again and decided against it. He gulped attractively instead.

Soma: Oh look, he's beginning to think.

Tamasha: Thinking is bad.

Soma: Thinking leads to questions.

Tamasha: Questions are bad.

'Shh,' said Red.

There was only one thing to do.

She pulled Kirin up to his feet and kissed him.

Tamasha: Very good. We picked the right one.

Soma: Where's Asvin?

Tamasha: Questions are bad. Besides, he's not going to ask us that, is he? He's not stupid.

Soma: Air. I need air.

Kirin let Red go reluctantly. She looked at him and felt a huge pang of guilt. His eyes were shining. She had never seen anyone look so happy.

'I can't believe it's really you,' he said.

'Well, it's me all right,' she said.

'How . . .'

'Do you want to ask me questions, or do you want to kiss me again?'

Soma: See, this is where a man of honour would ask about Asvin.

Tamasha: Shut up about Asvin. We're playing a bigger game now.

'I want to kiss you again,' said Kirin. He did.

They came up for air eventually.

'Sorry about the idiotic grin,' said Kirin, 'but I thought I would never see you again. And that you would never know how much I love you.'

Tamasha: *Now* it gets complicated.

Red smiled back, a smile as dazzling as Kirin's. 'I love you too,' she said. 'Now take me home.'

Soma: Before the real Maya turns up. Red, how long do you think you can keep this up? And what of Maya? We came here to save her.

Tamasha: We killed the ravian, didn't we? We won. She's not in danger. Asvin came to save her. Maybe he's saving her right now. We came to have an adventure. And we are just where we need to be.

'I have this strange feeling I'm dreaming,' Kirin said in wonder. 'Do you realize what we've just done, Maya? We've stopped the ravians, at least for now. Myrdak was planning to kill me, and then open the portal and let in the other ravians. There might be one ravian left—a woman, in Kol. Someone has to capture her before she can bring back the rest. Their portal must be found and destroyed—there's a nundu—like the one we found in the Bleakwood, remember? And there's a manticore, somewhere close—I saw it . . .' He stopped, shaking his head.

'I killed the manticore,' said Red. 'But I don't know where this portal is. Do you?'

'No. My guide did not tell me, and now he is dead.'

'What should we do, then?'

Kirin thought for a while, his head bowed. Then he looked at her, his face grim.

'I have to tell you something,' he said. 'I think Asvin is dead. The ravian felled him, and then he disappeared.'

The tears Red wept then were real.

513

Stop,' says Petah-Petyi.

The GameWorld stops spinning.

'This is insane,' she says. 'Your world is rebelling, Zivran. Now it seeks to shut the ravians out. I do not like Myrdak, but he is a Hero as well. He cannot die.'

'We had this discussion when Asvin died,' says Zivran. 'The world has chosen. Myrdak too is dead.'

'Unfortunately, it is more complicated than that,' says Stochastos. 'If Myrdak is allowed to die now, the ravians cannot enter Your GameWorld. And without the ravians, Your Game becomes far less entertaining. With the ravians, You have some hope of tricking the Players—keeping Them entertained, and thus saving Your world. Without them, Your Game is not half as interesting. If the Players get bored, Your world is destroyed whether or not They see through Your little deception.'

'But the rules forbid his resurrection,' says Zivran firmly.

'I am afraid You will have to make a compromise here, Zivran,' says Petah-Petyi. 'The ravians must return.'

She touches the GameWorld with a slender hand.

Myrdak opened his eyes and sat up. He pulled the sword out of his chest. He looked around, and saw Kirin holding Maya, consoling her. He stood up, slowly, his eyes glittering savagely in his burnt face.

'No,' says Zivran. 'He is dead, and that is final.'

He waves his hand.

Myrdak's sword plunged into his chest and he fell dead once again. He looked very annoyed.

He stayed dead this time.

'If We break the rules, We return to the old Games, to the old ways,' says Zivran. 'I know the old Game is safer—it does not challenge Our minds, Our ways, Our order. But My heart tells Me My new Game is the future—that in this new Game lies Our salvation. And yes, it is dangerous. But honestly, I do not care. I am prepared to give up My life for this Game. Yes, it is flawed. But it is My greatest creation nevertheless. Will You help Me? Will You help Me free this world, and save Us all?'

'I will help You,' says Petah-Petyi, 'though I do not approve at all. But I have My own reasons for not wanting this world to be destroyed, and they outweigh the danger.'

Zivran smiles at her gratefully, but she does not return his smile.

'I'm in too,' says Stochastos, grinning a wicked grin. 'You plan to cheat all the Players, and break thousands of rules, and You ask Me whether I want to be a part of it or not? It is practically My duty.'

'Bwaa,' says the Infinite Infant gravely.

'It would appear She approves as well,' grins Stochastos. 'She will cause distractions from time to time. Suddenly that is good news.'

'Before You start celebrating,' says Petah-Petyi, 'I must ask how You are planning to run this Game without the ravians.'

'We will let the ravians in,' says Zivran.

'But Behrim, Peori and Myrdak are all dead.'

'As Stochastos said not long ago,' says Zivran, 'there are always

compromises. I will not have My rules broken, but in the interests of entertainment I will certainly not object to having them bent . . . a little.'

The GameWorld starts to move again.

In its giant cage in the Desolate Gard, the nundu roared and twitched as sudden rage overcame it. It went berserk; its eyes blazed, its mouth spurted foam, and it snarled in a voice of thunder.

It crouched and sprang, crashing against its giant curving bars several times. The bars shuddered and sang, but held.

The nundu screamed in divine frenzy. In her room not far away, Maya shuddered and covered her ears with her hands; the unwaba slept unperturbed.

The great panther raked its huge paws across its chest again and again. Its giant talons ripped into its black, velvety fur. It cried out in agony as great fountains of black blood gushed out from its chest.

The nundu's blood pooled on the floor, black puddles frothing and lapping over the large raised triangle in the centre of the pit. It flowed outwards, and after a while touched the great moongold spheres at the vertices of the raised triangle.

The spheres lit up, shining dazzling silver.

The children of the Desolate Gard sang an ancient hymn in unison as the nundu's portal was born.

'And thus the ravians have their gateway into this world,' says Zivran. 'And the rules are not broken.'

Stochastos slaps his thigh and swears roundly in delight. 'You are a cunning old goat, Zivran,' he cries in delight. 'And I suspect now that We will actually succeed in Our deception! Come, We are with You. We will give the gods a Game that will enthrall Them, dazzle Them, and make Them forget to ask any questions. We will entertain Them as They have never been entertained before, with a war, a great war, a spectacle so fabulous They will forget to ask questions!'

But Zivran does not join the chaos-lord in laughter. He looks at Petah-Petyi, worried. 'Are You not content, old friend?' he asks.

'You know I am not, Zivran,' she says. 'You could have started the Game any time You chose to, just by maddening that great panther as You just did. All these adventures, all these lives lost—Asvin, the Rainbow Council, the ravians . . . were they all for nothing?'

'Certainly not,' says Zivran. 'I did not want to intervene thus. But I had to, for it is true that the Game would not be entertaining enough without the ravians. The Players would ask too many questions.'

'And therein lies the root of My discontent,' says Petah-Petyi. 'I thought the purpose of Your new Game, of Your new rules, was to create questions, not suppress Them. I fear that in Your enthusiasm in getting the details right, You have forgotten the core of Your purpose. And this is not an encouraging thought. Not for Me, and not for Your world. In Your quest for entertainment, I fear You will abandon Your search for meaning. In Your desire to achieve freedom from control, You will only end up manipulating everything Yourself.'

'Again You speak honestly but naively, Petah-Petyi,' says Zivran, stroking his beard wearily. 'I promise but a beginning, and You demand a final solution. As a god, You above all should know that the underlying patterns are complex. There are no true answers, no true justice. This new Game is Our reality. Virtue is not always rewarded, vice almost never really punished. There is never real freedom. Things are never . . . fair.'

'But some aspects of the old Game were worth preserving. Whatever their true nature, things must appear to be fair,' says Petah-Petyi. 'Otherwise, what is the point of anything?'

'I don't understand,' says Zivran, looking baffled and curious. 'You are saying there is a point to everything?'

Tears well up in Petah-Petyi's eyes. One falls, glittering, on the GameWorld.

'I will play along with You, Zivran,' she says, 'because My hand is forced. But know this—I trusted You, and I will not forgive You. You may survive this Game, but Our friendship will not survive this trial.'

Zivran bows, his eyes sparkling with grief.

'Very touching,' says Stochastos, 'but We have, alas, finally run out of time. Wipe Your eyes, Petah-Petyi. And stop looking as if Your mother died, Lord of Inventions. Can You not hear? The Players have arrived. Right on time, as always.'

And then the gods rise, and walk once more through Zivran's garden towards his starlight gateway, Sambo running ahead with an ingratiating expression pasted on all his seven faces. He stares in awe at the chariots and mounts of the gods, and the mind-numbingly magnificent beings that ride them, raising giant clouds of stardust as they roll towards their host, towards their GameWorld.

Sambo snaps his fingers, grateful to be alive, grateful to be present at this meeting of the Players. At his command, the sound of celestial horns and harps echoes through the galaxy, *and the gods cry out in welcome. Suns blaze, moons glow and the GameWorld trembles in anticipation.*

The Players arrive.

'Where do you want to go now?' Kirin asked gently.

'Me?' asked Red. 'Where do you want to go?'

'I don't know. I should go to Imokoi. I should go to Kol. I should try to find and destroy the ravian portal. I don't know what to do. I'm a really ineffectual Dark Lord, you know.'

'You have me now,' she said, holding him closer. 'You're not alone any more.'

He looked at her, puzzled. 'Will you come with me?'

'Don't you want me to?'

'Of course I do. But I . . .'

'Well, I will come with you, then. Don't bother telling me how happy that makes you; I know.'

'All right. Do you also know what I should do now? Because I don't.'

'That's funny,' she grinned through her tears.

'Why is that funny?'

'I thought the whole point of being a Dark Lord was that you could do whatever you wanted to.'

Kirin grinned. Then he laughed aloud, and the Gauntlet of Tatsu blazed on his hand with a sudden fire.

'You make everything better within seconds,' he said delightedly. 'You're absolutely right, you know. I've just been so busy complaining I never stopped to see things this clearly.'

'Good. And we should go to Imokoi. I want to see where you live.'

'All right. We will go to Imokoi. And what then?'

'Well, then we decide what we want to do next, and we do it.'

'Whatever we want?'

'Whatever we want.'

'The only reason I became Dark Lord in the first place was to try and stop the war.'

'Then stop the war.'

'How?'

'Well,' said Red thoughtfully, 'it's really quite simple. Just tell everyone to shut up or you'll burn them all to bits with your dragons. Assert yourself, you know.'

Kirin stared at her and burst out laughing. 'Perfect,' he said. 'I'll do just that.'

'Take charge, Kirin. I like people who take charge.'

'As you wish.'

'Repeat after me: I am the Dark Lord, and the greatest power that walks the earth.'

'I am . . . what you said.' He hugged her, wishing he could stop smiling madly for a second. He'd forgotten how beautiful she was.

'I will do whatever I want.'

'I will do whatever I want.'

'If I don't know what I want, I will do whatever seems like a good idea at the time.'

'That, too.'

'You're in good hands now, Kirin,' said Red, patting his head encouragingly. 'Now take me to Imokoi.'

'Yes, O great one. At once. Should we ride a dragon?'

'What happened to the Chariot of Vul?'

'I don't know where it is. I lent it to Spikes, you see, to go to Kol, and I couldn't summon it because it might leave him stranded in the middle of nowhere. That was quite a while ago.'

'Summon it. If Spikes still has it, he can walk the rest of the way to wherever he's going. What happened now? Why are you crying?'

'I'm not crying,' said Kirin fiercely, brushing his eyes.

'I have a question for you,' he said suddenly.

She kissed him long and passionately. By the time she stopped, he had forgotten his question and a great many other things.

He knelt and summoned the Chariot of Vul.

Soon a giant bubble rose in the clearing, and Mritik the golem appeared, holding in his massive clay hands the bars of the great magic rickshaw.

Spikes was sitting in the rear seat. Kirin greeted him joyously.

'On another day, I would have been surprised to see you,' he said. 'But it is not another day, so I'll just ask you: Where the hells have you been?'

'We need to talk,' said Spikes. 'Things aren't going too well in your Dark Tower. I'll explain on the way. Is that Maya?'

'Hello, Spikes,' said Red, jumping into the rickshaw and hugging the pashan, who would have looked puzzled and somewhat pleased had he been capable of displaying these emotions.

Kirin mounted the rickshaw too, and both he and Red were fast asleep, holding each other tightly, even before the chariot was fully underground.

At some point of time during the journey, Kirin awoke. He looked at Red sleeping next to him, her head on his shoulder.

Spikes, on his other side, was regarding them calmly.

'Is that really Maya?' he whispered.

'No,' replied Kirin. 'It's a rakshasi.' He looked at her again; she was fast asleep.

'Where is Maya, then?'

'Who knows? In Kol, perhaps. Healthy and happy, I hope.'

'And this rakshasi . . . was she working with the ravian?'

'No. He thought she was really Maya. She evidently succeeded in tricking him, and using him to get to me. The female mind is very complicated. She could have just come to Imokoi and said hello. All that flying around, and it wasn't even Maya. Still, that Myrdak is dead, which is wonderful. And this girl is important, I can feel it.'

'Why did she want to get to you?'

'Well, we really haven't had a chance to talk that much,' said Kirin, feeling sleepy again, 'but it's fairly clear, from our brief conversation so far, that she wants to rule the world.'

'Why on earth have you brought her with us?'

'She has very good ideas, and she knows far more than she should about me,' said Kirin, watching Spikes's face flicker in and out of the light of the vaman lamps as the chariot sped through the tunnel towards Imokoi. 'Besides, she saved my life. And . . . it's just good to see Maya's face, Spikes.'

'I see. As long as you know what you're doing,' said Spikes.

'I have no idea what I'm doing,' confessed Kirin, 'but I like her. And she's a *very* good kisser.'

Epilogue

The Chief Civilian strolled slowly through the newly restored Hall of Mirrors, watching innumerable reflections of herself, each looking extremely thoughtful.

She had just resolved yet another catastrophe. The palace has been under almost continuous attack for a while now, she thought, but none of the would-be assassins had made as much noise as the person she had just evicted.

In a misplaced fit of generosity, she had invited Arathognan's aunt Ugtha to the palace. Within the space of one evening, Ugtha had sent several palace guards into early retirement, yelled at several important politicians, slapped the Potolpuri ambassador for 'looking at me funny-like' and almost given Mantric a nervous breakdown by flirting with him. She had also attempted to give the Civilian advice on how to run the city, and chastised a Silver Phalanx assassin for having dirt in her ears.

Ugtha was now on her way to a new house on the outskirts of the city, where a group of pashans would make

sure she was safe from abductors, and that the city was safe
from her.

Roshin entered the mirrored corridor and walked up to
Lady Temat.

'Marshall Askesis is here, and requests an audience,' she
said. 'And there is one other matter.'

She held out a small cloth bag. The Civilian opened it
and examined its contents.

'Explain,' she said.

'Ugtha,' said Roshin, managing to convey a world of
distress in the two syllables.

'What has she done now?' asked the Civilian with a
helpless smile.

'She had a double life, much like her nephew.'

'She was a Champion's League hero?'

'No. But she had a secret life—several, in fact. She was
the president of the Mature Woman's Knitting and Brawling
Coterie. The city guards have been looking for her for months.'

'Interesting. But why tell me this?'

'She also had a . . . passionate relationship with a
seventeen-year-old vroomer, and this led to an impressive
array of gambling debts.'

'Get to the point, Roshin,' said the Civilian with some
asperity. She looked around quickly; there was no one else in
the hall. 'What does Ugtha's secret life have to do with *this*?'

She pulled the amulet out of the bag.

'Thog is still wearing the amulet the ravian gave him. I
recovered this one from a pawnbroker in Lost Street, while
repaying Ugtha's debts.'

The Civilian's eyebrows rose a whole inch. She looked
at the amulet in her hand again. It was identical to the one

Peori had given Thog, and matched the drawings in the documents the ravians had placed in Enki.

'The original?' asked the Civilian.

'It would seem so,' said Roshin.

'Did you ask Ugtha how she came by this?'

'Yes. She said her brother—Thog's father—had given it to her on his deathbed, and asked her to give it to Thog when he came of age.'

'A family heirloom,' said the Civilian softly, weighing the amulet in her hand.

'Could the ravian have given Ugtha the amulet and altered her memory?' asked Roshin.

'Why plant two amulets on the same person?' said the Civilian. 'No, I suspect this is the original. So the facial resemblance was more than a coincidence.'

'So Thog is really the heir to the throne of Kol? You think this is the original amulet?'

'Jewels of such significance have a power of their own, you know,' said the Civilian. 'A whole history of greed and bloodshed. They are never lost forever. I knew the original would turn up one day.'

She looked at Roshin and smiled.

'Well done,' she said. 'In the wrong hands, this could have done us much harm.'

'What is to be done with it?'

'Well, Thog already has an amulet, does he not? He does not need another one.'

'True. Should I destroy it?'

'You should forget you ever saw it.'

'Yes, my lady. It is done.'

'These are strange times, Roshin,' said Temat. 'To think it was really Thog all along. Most interesting. And he is a bit of a hero, too. And when such impossible coincidences favour heroes, it can only mean one thing—they have the favour of the gods.'

'War is upon us,' said Roshin. 'It is a time for heroes, is it not? A time for great deeds, for the birth of legends. I envy Thog. I wish the gods were watching over me.'

Temat shook her head sadly. 'For your sake, and mine,' she said, 'I hope they are *not.*'

Asvin opened his eyes and looked around him. Everything was cold and dark. There was a bitter, salty taste in his mouth, and ghostly visions, of the forest, of Kirin and Myrdak, of the bright sun on tall trees, were spiralling slowly inside before his eyes.

He put his hand on his own throat, slowly, and was startled by the coldness of his skin.

A deep gash in his throat. But he was not bleeding.

This, he realized, was because he was dead.

He suddenly remembered the Pyramid of the First Pharaoh, the last time he'd thought he was dead. Steel-Bunz had saved him then. But Steel-Bunz was not here now.

The darkness around him was growing clearer.

'Where am I?' he asked aloud. His voice sounded different, soft and whispery. Was this the afterlife? He'd always thought it would be much more colourful, that there would be lots of apsaras and flowers and clouds and mountains.

He felt something move near him. Something very large. Fear flooded through him, and fear was warm now, not cold. Fear was feeling, a memory of life. What could he fear now? He was dead, after all.

He would have wept, but his eyes were dry.

A voice spoke above him, and he looked up. He knew that voice. It sounded like the hissing of a thousand snakes.

'Why are you here, my son?' it said.

And suddenly he could see clearly.

A monstrous form stood before him, filling up the bare chamber. A huge scorpion's body, black and terrible, curved tail arcing endlessly in a giant death-dealing sting. A man's chest, rippling with muscles, clad in shining silver armour. Grey arms, grey head, steel-grey hair. Large black eyes, infinite pools of sorrow and wisdom.

The Scorpion Man.

Asvin looked down at his own chest. His armour had vanished. He reached tentatively, and touched his skin, smooth and cold. Understanding flooded through him. He had returned his armour to the Scorpion Man, as he had promised to do.

'I'm really dead,' he said. Tears came now; warm, salty tears that scorched his face and vanished in trails of vapour.

The Scorpion Man spoke again.

'It was not your time,' he said, and his voice was filled with doubt. 'You should not be here. It was not written thus.'

'Can you bring me back to life?' asked Asvin, not daring to hope.

The Scorpion Man shook his head.

'Death is final,' he said. 'But for heroes taken before their time, death is not the end. For when the world ends, when the armies of the Pharaoh emerge from the depths and purge the world of all evil, the lost heroes will march ahead of all.'

'I see,' said Asvin, though he did not see at all.

The Scorpion Man extended one of his pincers and touched Asvin's cheek gently; his touch was like ice.

'You should have been a great king,' he said sadly. 'You should have lived a long and prosperous life, for there is much in the world that you could have made right.'

A shining white figure suddenly appeared beside him; a slender black-eyed white cat. She looked happy to see Asvin.

'Take him with you, Erkila,' said the Scorpion Man. 'Lead him to the armouries, and give him weapons worthy of his stature. Honour him, for when the last day comes, his name will be on all the lists of glory.'

'Welcome,' said Erkila to Asvin. 'Others await you. An army awaits you, and will follow you until the world's end.'

'The world's end?' asked Asvin, bewildered. 'I will have to wait here until the world's end? When will that be?'

'You will not have to wait very long,' said the Scorpion Man. 'Go now, and sharpen your weapons.'